THE LAFAYETTE CIRCLE

S.W. O'Connell

Lanyard Press
Leesburg, Virginia

The Lafayette Circle

Lanyard Press
Leesburg, Virginia

First edition January 2024

ISBN Number: 978-1-7376636-9-0

Cover art by Jennifer Gibson
www.JenniferGibson.ca

Lafayette Art by Bryon Line

Printed in the United States of America

Other Books by S.W. O'Connell

The Patriot Spy

~

The Cavalier Spy

~

The Winter Spy

~

Envoy of the Lord

~

The North Spy

S.W. O'Connell's books are available for kindle and in print at Amazon, Barnes and Noble, and others

For my brother Dermot

"May the friends of America rejoice! May her enemies be humbled and her censors silenced at the news of her noble exertions in continuance of those principles which have placed her so high in the annals of history and among the nations of the earth."

— Marquis de Lafayette

Prologue

CIA Headquarters, Navy Hill, Foggy Bottom, Washington, DC, September 1st, 1954

Jake Tolbert rolled his eyes as he yanked open another dust-caked box. Since getting his job as a staff historian for the nation's new intelligence agency, the Central Intelligence Agency historian, Doctor Raymond Canavan, buried him in Room SB-311, essentially a cramped archive storage room below the basement.

"To analyze today and predict tomorrow, we must first understand the past," Canavan said. "All successful intelligence is grounded on what came before, so nothing is more important to this agency than its knowledge of history."

His task was equal to the musty locale — sift through crates of old files gathered from legacy intelligence organs formerly scattered across the federal government.

His mouth twisted in a grimace. "Crap, another Blue Goose to examine." Blue Goose was the derisive term used for musty old files from obscure agencies long gone. "When will this freaking end?" He knew the answer, of course, when he quit.

This box seemed different — older than most. The label was faded black ink in a script Tolbert had never seen. The package came from the basement of an old Navy archive building in the Washington Navy Yard. The labeling was unusual:

File LC /Chancery/ 1827

A recent Fordham College graduate with a B.A. in history, Tolbert knew a chancery was the administrative seat of a Roman Catholic bishop. He carefully opened the file, which was several inches thick, and carefully removed the papers one by one.

His eyes widened with surprise as he went through the contents, which included what looked like an after-action report with over a score of newspaper articles spanning 1824 and 1825. Yet everything he had read or was told indicated American intelligence died with the Treaty of Ghent ending the War of 1812 and was only revived somewhat during the Civil War. *Even the war with Mexico was conducted in an intelligence vacuum.* Or so he was led to believe.

Tolbert had his head in the files for hours that stretched to days. When he finally closed the last of the folders, he made notes summarizing what he had learned. And what he had learned gave him the makings of a headache, for the Chancery file produced more questions than answers.

Chapter 1

Madrid, January 1823

Thud! The carriage door slammed shut, and the driver's stiff leather whip cracked across the backs of the gray Andalusians. Powerful legs began pounding up the frozen road, heavy shod hooves scattering diamond-like crystals everywhere. The leading passenger huddled in the back seat, his heavy cloak wrapping him like a sausage skin.

Across from him sat a heavy-set man in the uniform of a colonel of the Royal Carabiniers. His cloak was thrown open, revealing a score of medals, earned and otherwise. His gloved hand held a large envelope.

The passenger glanced through the frosted glass window at the mounted escort. Steam blew from their mouths and their horses' nostrils. "Our escort is cold. Are six of your carabiniers sufficient?"

The carriage picked up speed but swayed side to side as hooves and wheels skimmed patches of ice on the King's Highway. The stately homes and buildings of Madrid's outskirts now surrounded them.

"Too many would slow us down. If the driver can keep this pace, your meeting with King Ferdinand should go as scheduled," said the colonel as the carriage rocked from the measured strains of the horses. "I am sure he is anxious to meet with such a great representative of the people."

Their grim laughter filled the cabin.

General Rafael del Riego y Florez was a legendary champion of the people of Spain who, as a lieutenant colonel, managed to topple the country's moribund government. He planned to transition Spain from a caretaker junta to a more modern democracy.

The other passenger's eyes narrowed. "Anxious, yes. Eager and willing, no."

"Perhaps he'll reconsider when he reads *your* plan, General." The colonel waved the envelope. "After all, it does more than reorganize Spain's provinces. It cements them with a democratic form of government. What absolute monarch would not embrace such a plan?"

More laughter and heads nodding.

"I think you are a dreamer, Colonel. But he will be persuaded. There is a banknote along with the agreement. Drawn on the Bank of England, which makes it better than gold. Fighting the rebels at home and abroad has reduced King Ferdinand to little more than a beggar in fine clothes."

The carriage began to slow, and the driver hollered a warning.

"What did he say?" asked the colonel.

"I think he said there's a dead burro on the road."

"A dead burro? Probably froze in this cold. Very well. The escort will move it, general."

***

The lieutenant in charge of the carabiniers raised his hand, and the troopers slowed to a halt. "Move the burro!"

The *crack* of a distant rifle stirred the cold morning air, and the driver tumbled from his perch and hit the ice-crusted road with a *crunch*. The carabiniers drew their pistols and fired toward the puff of smoke from the sniper's rifle. One reached for the driving lines to lead the draft horses out of the line of fire. A figure in a black cape stepped out of one of the buildings and emptied one of his pistols into him. He then spun and shot down a second carabinier.

A small figure scurried up to the coach and tossed a *hissing* package under it before another of the carabiniers cut him down with a heavy saber.

The lieutenant heard a *sizzling* beneath the floorboards. His eyes widened in dread acknowledgment that he had lived his last day. Before he could speak or move, a blast lifted the carriage off the ground and broke it in two. Iron fittings, shards of wood, and chunks of flesh and bone flew in all directions.

The lieutenant went down with his horse. His leg throbbed. Shards of metal protruded from his boot, which oozed blood.

The distant rifle erupted again. Another carabinier slumped in his saddle. His horse squealed in terror before bolting up the road.

The lieutenant struggled to his feet and drew his saber. Around him, the blood-soaked pieces of the colonel and their charge lay scattered across the glistening pavers.

***

Palacio Real de Madrid

King Ferdinand reviewed the papers spread before him. His finger slid along the map's boundaries, and he seemed to calculate the extent of each domain that would now be a province rather than royal property. He straightened to his full height. His deep-set eyes bore in on the man standing before him. "You have planned wisely, General Riego. Although I will no longer rule these domains, I will be satisfied that Spain will be stronger for it."

"You shall reign like an English monarch, Your Excellency."

10

Ferdinand managed a wry smile. "But you will lead them, General Rafael del Riego y Florez." The monarch sat at the table and slowly signed the papers that would transform his land while destroying his dynasty.

When he finished, a servant in fine livery approached with a tray of champagne and poured each a goblet. As the servant swept off, Florez raised his glass in a toast. "To Your Majesty, King Ferdinand of Spain."

"To a democratic Spain, may she prosper as such," replied the king before downing his champagne like it was bile.

Florez felt sorry for the man but not the monarch or monarchy. *The world is changing.*

The king pulled out his watch. "Almost noon. Can you stay for dinner?"

Florez shook his head and bowed. "No, Excellency. There are those who did not want me here."

A military adjutant in a white tunic embroidered in red and gold hurried in and whispered in the king's ear.

Ferdinand's eyes widened in puzzlement and fear. "Tell the general, please."

The adjutant stood erect and looked at Florez with contempt.

"Tell him, captain."

"There was an attack at La Moraleja. Assassins bombed a coach, and four of your carabiniers were shot dead."

Florez flushed with anger. His eyes became like daggers jabbing into the adjutant. "And the passengers?"

"Dead. The bomb left little of them, I'm afraid."

"What is the meaning of this?" asked the king.

"They were a decoy. I had word of a plot to stop this meeting. The carriage carried my secretary, General Suarez, and my provost, Colonel Rodriguez. They knew the risk."

Florez could not say that the British uncovered the plot. Nor that a British agent provided the counter plan.

"Those were brave men who died that you may live, General Florez."

"No, Excellency, they died that Spain may live."

"You do not think that I…."

"No, Excellency. I can assure you the plot was not hatched in Madrid. A British businessman, a Mister Robertson, overheard the plotters in a *taverna.* He is sympathetic to Spain and informed us."

Florez knew his story was weak. But he would deflect any questions. *Half-truths often work better than lies.*

"Then where? Who?"

"I don't know where it was hatched. But it was ordered by the Aulic Council."

"What is this, Aulic Council?"

"A secret arm of the Holy Alliance. Yes – Prussia, Russia, and Austria are meddling in the future of Spain. I am sure they will not stop here."

"Where is this, Mister Robertson?"

"He escorted me here but is now long gone."

"Then you will return under my Royal Garde's protection. After all, you are now the nation's leader and the Spanish Army's commander."

***

Chancery Annex, Baltimore, Maryland, March 1823

The long sleeve of Brother Bernard's cassock dangled as he held up the crinkled newspaper to get more light from the lamp. The latest edition of the *Neue Zürcher Zeitung* was always worth a little eyestrain. As a liberal centrist organ of a dynamic and thriving nation, it gave him some of the best insights into Europe's economic, political, diplomatic, and social currents. And as it was a discreet journal, he had to read between the lines when the editors wanted to address issues discreetly.

He zoomed in on an incident in Madrid that none of his other papers or sources had reported. *Interesting – the King of Spain signed a political agreement against his own interests. He signs it with his political rival, who survived an attack in public.*

He reached over and fumbled with his mug of tea, then made a note along the paper's margin. *One of the clerics will record this one.*

The door's lock clattered as a key was thrust into it. Only one other person had that key. The heavy iron banded door creaked slowly open, and the Bishop of Baltimore stepped into the chamber.

"Excellency, so good to see you. May I offer some tea?"

Archbishop Ambrose Maréchal nodded amiably and fell into an oversized chair near the cold fireplace. He glanced around the dark, windowless room. "You'll go blind yet, Brother Bernard. I should find you a room with a window. Ambient light is always the best. Especially for someone of your age."

Brother Bernard smiled gently. "Truth is, I never thought I'd reach this age. But windows are a security concern, so I'll muddle along and squint through these specs." He waved nickel-framed glasses at the bishop.

"What keeps you here this late?"

He waved the *Zurcher.* "News, excellency, news."

"Tell me about it."

"It seems there is skullduggery. "

"Affecting America?"

"Everything affects America these days, Excellency. The European powers have come to view us as a threat."

Bishop Maréchal chortled. "That's news?"

Brother Bernard shook his head knowingly. "Ah, but it is beyond the usual talk and posturing. Specific actions have been taken. An attack in broad daylight in Madrid. I am sure others are underway even as we speak."

Maréchal sighed. "I disbelieved you when you predicted the English assault on New Orleans. I won't make that mistake again. What do you think is in the offing?"

"My assessment in 1814 was based on information from many good sources. We had a vibrant network and a team of dedicated patriots. Now, it is just us, *Madame* Bonaparte, and a few others. My overseas contacts are ad hoc. Still, I believe, with maybe seventy percent assurance, that our friends of the Holy Alliance are up to no good."

The bishop rubbed his chin. "Do you have further details?"

"Not yet. I have sent a letter to Paris and another to Amsterdam. But there is no telling what our agents will report back, if at all."

The bishop lowered his head. "Then we must pray that the Good Lord will send us a message."

Chapter 2

The White House, Washington, DC, November 1823

An aide stepped into the office of President James Monroe. "Mister President, the Secretary of State is here."

Monroe nodded. "Please bring him in."

Minutes later, John Quincy Adams was seated across from the president. A servant brought coffee, and the two went right to business. Adams opened his worn leather valise and shuffled through his papers.

Monroe's eyes shifted to the young aide, Robert Buchanan, and then back to Adams. "What do you have for me, Mister Adams?"

The experienced diplomat and son of the second president expected the question—a standard opening for the plain-spoken Monroe. The two had made diplomacy a force for American expansion from Florida to Oregon. "More stirring in Europe. Agitation over our nation's success and anticipation of what transpires in the dwindling Spanish hegemony in this hemisphere."

"I am glad you have re-raised the issue. Perhaps another attempt by the continental European powers to implant their own colonies here? Russian imperialism seems to have no bounds."

"True, Czar Alexander is claiming his sovereignty over a large swathe of the Pacific Northwest. He banned foreign ships from sailing along the coast. And others have their own schemes. Imagine a Habsburg landing in Central America or a Prussian one in *Gran Columbia*."

"Then the demarche from the British Foreign Office suggesting a joint declaration against further European incursions seems like a splendid solution."

I did not expect that comment so quickly, Adams thought. "I think not, sir," he said.

Monroe's jaw tightened. "What do you mean? Two powerful nations acting in unison is a good thing."

"There is always an agenda, as you know. We are an expanding nation."

Monroe looked skeptical. "Go on."

"Just eight years ago, we were at war with the British. A war in which we came out looking rather weak despite General Jackson's victory at New Orleans. I believe it's time we show our mettle to the world. You shall issue your own manifesto warning against outside interference in this hemisphere. It will be brilliant and authoritative. And no one will dare gainsay or challenge it."

Monroe raised an eyebrow. "How can we be so certain?"

Adams drummed his fingers and leaned forward. "Because I shall write it!"

Monroe crossed his arms and sat brooding with his eyes fixed on the center of his desk.

"Mister President?" *Have I overstepped my bounds?*

"Very well," said Monroe. "But we need to do something to make this more than the bluster of a young republic. What say you, Mister Buchanan?"

The young clerk had been sitting quietly, pen in hand, jotting notes. "I'm not sure, Mister President. But the nation's fiftieth birthday is just a few years out. I have been toying with various modes of celebrating to recommend to you both."

Monroe nodded. "I was just a junior officer in the war, but there are still some brighter luminaries."

"I was a lad myself when I sailed on a diplomatic mission with President Adams."

"Learned at the feet of your father," said Monroe. A great man."

"What about the marquis? Buchanan asked. "Lafayette is legendary on two continents – bringing him to America would send a signal to both hemispheres."

"You are on to something, Robert," replied Adams. "American exceptionalism punctuated by a European republican and former aristocrat, a hero of two revolutions, an empire and a monarchy."

Monroe rose from his seat and strutted to the window, then spun quickly, and thrust his right fist into his left palm. "Yes! The marquis has written me of a desire to visit our country. And if we do this right, it might have political consequences here. The youth of America quickly forgot its origins and the sacrifice so many made for the noble cause. This visit can highlight American exceptionalism. And, of course, every place he visits has voters."

Adams stiffened. "Why, I suppose so, Mister President. But we want this grand tour to unite all factions and regions of the nation and signal our strength and determination to foreign monarchies."

"If the marquis accepts our invitation," Buchanan said.

Monroe slipped back into this seat. "Of course." He turned to Adams. "Place Mister Buchanan in charge of this. That will give you time to draft our manifesto. Also, send my regrets to Stratford Canning. But thank him for his proposal of a joint declaration. I want to keep on King George's Envoy Extraordinary's good side."

"I'll begin working on it. It shall be our sharpened sword against foreign intervention," Adams replied.

Buchanan smiled as he made the last stroke of his pen. "While the marquis shall be our burnished shield."

***

The British Legation, Washington, DC

Stratford Canning sipped his tea. He rubbed his tongue over his lip in disgust. *Even their tea is foul to the palate. I cannot wait to depart the United States.*

What should have been a plum in his career had become a flop. His cousin George Canning's initiative to jointly issue a proclamation on Latin America was, after such promise, shot down by John Quincy Adams.

He put down his cup and looked across the table at the British Consul, Godfrey Arthur. "When is this American proclamation to be issued?"

"My sources say any day now. Certainly, before year's end."

"Thank God I shall be glad to be gone then," said Canning. "My time here has served no purpose. Neither for His Majesty's foreign policy nor my career. These Americans are set on their own ways, not British ways."

"They are rambunctious, that is certain. They have whipped the Spaniards and driven the natives ever westward. They have extended settlements and have tilled farmlands exceeding our own England five-fold. And their merchant marine and fishing ships have the run of things far beyond the Atlantic coast."

Canning played with his fob chain and then glanced at his watch. "Our next meeting is in an hour. So let me say this. My successor will need a strategy to ensure they make no demands on our Pacific coast holdings."

"Well, perhaps their proclamation will still the Czar's incursions from that quarter," said Arthur.

"I hope you are correct, Godfrey. I certainly do. But I'm concerned. It might stir the opposite effect. The Holy Alliance cannot be trifled with. I was at the Congress of Vienna when the emperor, czar, and king joined forces. They are unscrupulous in their zeal for autocracy."

"What should I do, sir?"

"Beware of their agents in America. Keep up your friendship with that young American diplomat. It could prove valuable. And dispatch me a copy of Mister Monroe's statement once issued."

"I will, sir."

Canning grunted. "If I learn anything in London, I'll send a secret dispatch."

"Isn't that Lord Avondale's purview, sir?"

"Blast him and his skullduggery." Canning glanced at his watch again. "Now, let's go meet the New England Fisheries delegation, shall we? I've been anxious to learn how the scrod is doing."

***

16

The Yellow Oval Room, White House, Washington, DC, December 1823

Secretary of State John Quincy Adams entered the presidential reception room used by James Monroe for formal meetings. He went straight to the large desk just off the bow windows, draped in yellow damask curtains since the days of First Lady Dolly Madison.

"What do you have for me, Mister Secretary?" Monroe asked as he motioned Adams to the seat opposite. Despite their political differences, he liked the efficiency of Adams.

"The final draft of the speech for you to present to Congress next week."

"And then?"

My staff will send copies to all our embassies, consulates, and foreign delegations."

"And the public?"

"Release to the press will be timed with your presentation."

Monroe nodded and rose to glance through the drapes. "You remind me of that squirrel scurrying up yonder chestnut tree, Mister Adams."

Adams flushed and stiffened in his chair. "What do you mean, Mister President?"

Monroe knew he had struck a nerve. After all, he was not of his political party, and a little jibbing always kept them on their toes. "As with the squirrel, you appear scattered and harmless. But you are focused on what is to come, prepare for the hard winter, and set actionable plans in motion."

"I will take that as a compliment," said Adams. "With your approval, we are set for this to be your address to Congress next week."

***

Chancery Annex Baltimore, Maryland, January 1824

Bishop Maréchal nervously fingered his gold chain and cross. "Who would have thought the year 1824 would pose threats to the nation that rival those of 1812?"

Brother Maurice Bernard smiled wryly. "Or 1776. The troubles in South America and the Caribbean have the European capitals in arms."

"With Spain pushed aside, they are eyeing the void and the threat caused by the new world order," Maréchal replied.

"What some call a void, others see as an opportunity. And the only thing standing in their way is this nation, which is growing in size and population. They fear we will move in to exploit the void or, worse, the British will."

"I'll send secret correspondence to the Provincials in Europe. Perhaps they can provide more insight…."

Brother Bernard's mouth turned down in a frown, and his eyes stared nostalgically. "There was a time I could sort these things out directly. I'm afraid I am of little use to this country with my age."

Maréchal smiled. "Nonsense, Brother Bernard. And besides, even if your country may not need you as much as it did – the world does."

***

Château de la Grange — Bléneau, France, March 1824

The rider leaned forward in the saddle as he turned his pale charger up the winding, tree-lined causeway to the massive array of stone towers enclosed by a still water moat. The gray walls were the abode of France's greatest son of liberty, a man whose struggle for freedom spanned fifty years.

A servant took the bridle in hand as the rider sprang from the horse and mounted the staircase into the darkened chambers. Minutes later, Lafayette's valet, Sebastien Wagner, ushered George Washington Motier de La Fayette into his father's study. The gray-haired Lafayette tossed a bundle of fagots into the hearth, hoping to rob the room of the evening chill.

"I rode thirty miles from Paris without a pause, father. I hope your summons is worth it."

Lafayette motioned him to a sofa and stood silently before the growing flames. "You are but forty-four and in your prime, George. I am an old man. I need warmth. My years in Olmütz prison in Moravia left me with a permanent chill in my bones."

George nodded. His father was nearly broken by his Prussian and Austrian imprisonment. Only the presence of his mother kept his father from succumbing. All the while, George was in safety in America, the guest of his namesake and beloved friend of his father, George Washington.

"Yes, father, but you have the gratitude of France for your sacrifice."

Lafayette turned. "Do I? I tried to guide the Revolution, advise the monarch, suppress extremism, make peace with France's enemies, control Napoleon's worst ambitions, and spare France from Bourbon excesses. All for naught, eh? Now, I conspire with the *Charbonnerie* in the nebulous hope of returning a republic to France."

"Perhaps not a pipe dream."

"I am not getting younger." The marquis shrugged and smiled. "But I suppose the alternative is worse."

"Age is but an idea. You are still eyeing the ladies, I hear."

"None as fine as your *maman* was!"

"Well, you helped free America and gave the world a great republic. No one can take that from you."

Lafayette threw himself into a chair. "No, they can't. In fact, I am more celebrated there than in my own country. In some ways, America is our country."

"We remain in France only because you're more needed here."

"Perhaps no longer. I received a letter from the Americans asking me to tour the country."

"Like a grand tour of the continent?"

"No, not a feckless and romantic journey among ancient ruins. Instead, it is a celebration of a new land. A new people. For liberty. For democracy. I intend to depart in a few months. Arrangements need to be made. And the Americans are sending out broadsheets to all the major papers."

"But father, so many things here need your attention."

"Not at all. My visit to the United States will accomplish more than help the Americans celebrate their fiftieth year of freedom. As that nation does, it will serve as a beacon and signal to the oppressed to the world."

Chapter 3

Hohensalzburg Fortress, Salzburg, Austria

The rattle of drums summoned a score of white-jacketed fusiliers to the courtyard, where gloomy stone walls surrounded them. The yellow flame of a score of lanterns fought the ever-darkening gray sky. It was time to post the evening guard at the fortress, which served as military barracks, depot, and dungeon.

But this evening, it served as *Geheimtreffpunkt, a* secret meeting place for some of Europe's most powerful, dangerous, and least known men — Under Ministers for the Security Committee of the Holy Alliance. Known among its members simply as The Committee, it planned and executed covert operations on behalf of the Holy Alliance's political governance arm, the Aulic Council.

Hobnailed boots rattled across the cobblestones. A sergeant barked, "*Achtung*!" Twenty pairs of heels snapped, and as many fusils were crisply shouldered.

A servant closed the window and lowered a heavy felt curtain of rich burgundy. Some rapidly moved about the oaken walls, lighting lamps, while others stoked the twin fireplaces to drive off the evening chill and brighten the room.

Count Franz Esslinger, the Austrian Empire's under minister and the group's chairman, banged his gavel and called the committee to order. His counterparts, Russian under-minister Prince Vladimir Vassiliev and Baron Otto von Zoranski, the Prussian under-minister, stiffly sat in tall-backed chairs.

Three pairs of steely eyes narrowed and met as one. Although they served three distinct empires, all were chosen by the Aulic Council because they were clever, devious, and ruthless. As former military officers from the "petty nobility," they were zealous supporters of their respective monarchs and the upper nobility they slavishly served. But above all, they all shared a hatred for democracy, republics, and any constitution or system of governance not controlled by an autocrat.

"What do you have for us?" Vassiliev asked.

Esslinger expected the blunt opening. His eyes shifted to the paper in his hand. "The Aulic Council is concerned about the nonsense sweeping America and Europe. For now, it is directing the police to suppress things at home. Our task is to track down dissidents abroad, particularly in France, Spain, and Italy."

Vassiliev's voice rumbled, "Your plot in Madrid failed. What of 'The New World'?"

"We have allies there who will not give up," replied Esslinger. "Senior military officers and high prelates. The Madrid junta's days are numbered. But more importantly, the Council hopes to exploit the weakness of Spain. More of its breakaway colonies are ripe for the plucking. Imagine a Romanov realm including Chile, or a Hohenzollern New Columbia, or a Habsburg Mexico."

"Grandiose plans, Your Excellency," von Zoransky said impatiently. "But what are our specific tasks?"

Esslinger both liked and disdained the bluntness of his counterparts. It made things simple but caused him to fear they lacked the creative mind for such work. *They are merely assassins.* Esslinger favored a more nuanced approach. When he ordered a *Schlag*, a hit on an enemy, it was usually made to look like an accident or, better yet, a natural death.

But his new orders left little room for nuance, and he knew his associates would be like bloodhounds on a crippled fox. "The Americans have invited Lafayette to tour their country. A tour for democracy as much as for the marquis. And a signal from America to the world."

"A signal for what?" von Zoransky asked.

"It is unclear right now. Our consular office in Washington expects something is brewing. Their foreign minister Adams spends much time at the White House — their republican royal palace, with their president, Monroe."

Von Zoransky scowled. "Monroe — he's the fox that coaxed the Spanish lands of Louisiana from Bonaparte!"

"I met Adams in St. Petersburg when he was American Minister Plenipotentiary. Of course, I was just a young Chevalier Guards subaltern. He was just a boy himself. Very guarded and highly intelligent."

Esslinger tired of the banter. "Gentlemen, I hold a black envelope."

Von Zoransky tore the monocle from his eye. Vassiliev twisted his glove. The servants attending shuffled into the hallway and slammed the door closed. A heavy silence hung in the chamber.

"Now that I have your attention, I shall open it. As we all know, whoever is listed on the card has been sanctioned for death — an *Assassinat*! Since we three have been brought into this, I assume there are three *Sanktionen* — sanctions."

Von Zoransky's eyes narrowed. Vassiliev grimly frowned while Esslinger returned a knowing nod. Although they were all experienced at planning sabotage and assassination, they took their work seriously. Each sanction became the focus of all their power.

A slim knife appeared in Esslinger's hand, and he carefully slit the edge of the envelope and peered inside. *Mein Gott!*

***

Château de la Grange-Bléneau, France

"Bon pour les Chiens!" Lafayette tossed the last scraps of veal from their working supper to his mastiffs, who eagerly gobbled the treat.

Servants whisked away plates, dishes, and silverware and opened a sizeable leather-bound planner before him.

"I have most of the journey planned, *Monsieur* Marquis," said Auguste Levasseur, Lafayette's confidential secretary. "Of course, the Americans may insist on changes when we arrive."

Lafayette smiled nostalgically. "I served with them many years, Auguste. Improvision is both the weakness and strength of *les Americains.*

"The papers are all abuzz with the excitement of your journey, father," said George. "I brought a stack of gazettes, newspapers, and broadsheets for you to peruse."

"It's late, my son. I'll view them over coffee tomorrow. Are they favorable?"

George took a sip of brandy. "Well, let's just say the usual detractors had their say, although most French papers were positive."

"And the foreign press?"

"Not so much. As I said, the usual suspects had a field day."

Lafayette nodded. "I see. Let me guess: the Prussians bridled, the Austrians huffed, and the Russians growled."

"Indeed, how did you know?"

"My former jailers have long memories. And they continue to resist liberty at every opportunity. What of the *Anglais*?"

"As usual, quite guarded."

Levasseur smiled. "Perfidious Albion, eh?"

Lafayette cocked his head. "Sometimes."

***

The Saint James Club, London, March 25th, 1824

The waiter bent slightly forward and placed an opened bottle of champagne between the two diners. "Is there a problem with the soup, gentlemen? I can have the chef make adjustments."

Lord Avondale looked up and smiled. "No, it's quite tasty. We are just trying to catch up. Old military chums, wot?"

The waiter nodded and slipped off to attend to other guests at the club, one of the poshest in London.

Captain Richard Neall stirred his soup listlessly. He had just reported his latest activities on the continent, and Lord Avondale was not taking it well. *Sometimes, being too good at spycraft is a liability.* But he thought the head of the Foreign Office's "Special Accounts Section" (Secret Service) would be impressed with his coup. He had penetrated the Holy Alliance secret committee and scored several fantastic leads on their nefarious plans. As the British agent 'Mister Robertson,' he also connected to the Spanish military cabal, which was now controlling Spain. *What more can I do?*

"Your report is quite alarming, Richard. You've come a long way from the dragoon officer I met fighting Boney in Spain."

"We all have, sir. Europe is changing. The world is changing. I'm simply trying to give you a forewarning."

Avondale picked up his flute of the sparkling beverage and downed it. "You'll need to do more than that, I'm afraid."

Neall was stunned. *Do what?* "I think your Foreign Office friends will be overjoyed with my report. They can now take appropriate action."

Avondale lifted his spoon and quickly dropped it into the bowl. He reached for the bottle and poured another flute while he shifted his eyes left and right. "This is too hot for the Foreign Office! Or the Prime Minister. There are sinister politics afoot. And I cannot vouchsafe it might fall into the hands of nefarious people in the government sympathetic to the Holy Alliance. But I think the top agent of 'The Special Accounts Section' is up to it, wot?"

Neall drained his flute and poured another. "What do you propose, sir?"

"You go to America and warn the Americans. They must deal with the news. But you stay on and assist them. They are amateurs in such affairs."

"Then who do I deal with?"

"I'll provide letters of introduction to the President and Secretary of State. But you'll deal mainly with the bishop."

"The bishop? I'm sorry, sir. Is this a joke?"

"Oh, it is no joke. After all, the buggers have a global network almost equal to ours. Bishop Maréchal, the Archbishop of Baltimore, is a shrewd Jesuit with a knack for intelligence gathering. But you'll mainly deal with one of his secretaries, Brother Bernard."

"And a monk to boot? Should I become a papist?"

Neall smiled. "Yes, perhaps you should. Now, let's finish our meal before the waiter throws a fit. I'll give you the details later over coffee, brandy, and cigars."

***

Spanish Riding School Vienna, Austria
"Hoch!!"

The white stallion raised its forehooves to the rhythm of the whip and pranced like a dancing bear. The equestrian's knees firmly pressed as he put the horse through its paces while the riding students watched in awe.

From the dark recesses of the stable, a slim figure in a military-style suit watched with amusement. He patted the slender arm of the beautiful woman next to him.

"Weren't you once with the academy?" she asked.

Jan Nagy nodded. "I was a *Rittmeister*, a master horseman. But I took a musket ball in the leg at Jena and never regained the strength in my thigh."

He knew what the next question was. He had answered it too many times, rarely admitting the truth.

"Is that why you were cashiered from the service?"

"No, it is why I turned to the wine and gaming tables of Grinzing — they are why I was cashiered. "

She squeezed his arm gently. He liked her smell and touch. He found the attraction ironic and, in some way, poetic.

Madeline Pauline Goulet was a French noblewoman who had served Bonaparte as a spy in Vienna. She had penetrated the French aristocratic emigres in the Habsburg capital. Although Madeline did not admit to it, some had likely penetrated her. Now, she worked with him, cheating at the gaming tables, and killing enemies of the crown.

"I have a new *Sanktion*," he whispered while nibbling at her ear. "But we must travel for this one."

Her pert lips parted in excitement. "Rome? Paris?"

"*Non, mon cher.*"

"London?"

"Much farther. And less glamorous. But if we succeed, the bounty will enable us to own our own gaming tables instead of hustling for others. And purchase an estate, becoming the daughter of a French *Vicomte*."

She nuzzled him and purred. "I go with you always, Jan."

"We can play tables if they exist where we travel. But we will employ our usual ruse."

"*Maestro* Pietro's magic tricks always capture your audience and your target."

"Indeed." He omitted to say he did not yet know the target nor that he knew she was the illegitimate daughter of the *Vicomte*.

***

La Scala, Milan, Kingdom of Lombardy, and Veneto

The orchestra pit was in a fever as the closing notes and waning voices signaled the end of the final performance of Rossini's *Il Barbiere di Siviglia*. Alexander Buxhowden favored darker works, but his interest in opera was not the music or the libretto. His eyes were fixed on the soprano, Carmen de Gioia. Carmen served him when not singing for the world's most renowned opera house. Not as his mistress, as so many suspected, but as a preparer of potions, potions made to render its drinker giddy, confused, depressed, asleep, or dead, as his masters wished.

An hour later, they were in a coach heading to the seacoast. Buxhowden sat meditating as the carriage bounced along the winding road. A defrocked Russian

Orthodox priest, Buxhowden still prayed but to a more sinister deity. He was a practitioner of the occult and a world-renowned writer and speaker on the dark arts.

After a long time, she turned to him and squeezed his hand. "I must be back in a month for my role in *La Donna del Lago.*"

"That is not possible, Carmen. We are traveling far and could be gone a year. Maybe more."

"Oh no!" Her ample chest heaved with excitement. The gold crucifix that adorned her cleavage seemed to mock him. Her tiny fists began to pound at him.

His bear-like hands crushed hers in his. "You know you must do this for me. You always do."

She lowered her head. "I know. But I don't know why I do."

"It is simple. You love making potions. You revel in the look when a victim senses something is wrong. When they choke or gurgle. Swoon or collapse in a heap."

"The effects are so enthralling to watch," she whispered. "I know it's wrong, but...."

One great hand caressed her throat. "That's precisely why you love it. It's a thrill beyond holding the most mellifluous note in an *Aria* before the King of Lombardy and all the noble people."

She nuzzled against his chest. "Oh, you are so right, Alexander. I enjoy the mixing and the watching. It's...."

"Your glimpse into the dark arts."

He knew she liked to be led like this. It excited her to be separated from the church of her youth. When her singing career ended, he would make his final seduction of the lovely songbird. This sanction could be that bridge.

The message from Vassiliev was ambiguous:

An Assassinat is sanctioned. Travel immediately to Genoa. Instructions to follow. Codex

Buxhowden chuckled every time he saw Vassiliev's cover name –*Codex*. They had never met and only communicated by paper. He had only seen him once. That was years ago when he was a priest, and Vassiliev was a soldier of the czar. They both worked for a cause that served the czar, but surely the czar knew little of it.

Suddenly, a strange thought surged through him, one of those premonitions. As soon as he had his instructions in Genoa, he would go to Paris.

***

Donat *Fechtschule*, Berlin, Prussia
"*En garde!*"

The words echoed through the hall of the Donat Fencing School.

The duelists sprung at each other like leopards. Gleaming blades snapped and spat, sending sparks with each scrape of steel on steel: feint, thrust, parry, thrust, feint, parry, thrust. Block and pivot—change the point of attack. Feet moved with the grace a ballet dancer would envy. They broke contact, and each paused for a delicious breath of air. Eyes bore in on their opponent.

"*En garde!*"

They moved like pythons, teasing and striking out, but neither could touch the other. At last, the larger duelist decided on strength over skill, committed full bore to a death strike, and sprang forward with a powerful thrust. But his nimbler opponent anticipated the move and danced left, then back, pivoted, and thrust cold steel at the larger fencer.

Both blades ran along their edges with a *screech* and a final *clang* as the polished hilts clashed. The two stood, shoulder against shoulder, breathing like wildebeests at the scent of the lion. Sweat covered their faces and stained their clothes.

"*Finito!*"

The blades dropped, and they bowed their heads in salute.

"I have slain over fifteen expert swordsmen in duels but never met one with your skill," said Ernst Emil Donat, the most notorious swordsman in Europe and expert in the German and Italian fencing schools. "Although I think I would have taken you in time. I'm not certain. One should never fight a duel in which the outcome is uncertain."

"In that case, it is not a duel but murder."

Donat smiled devilishly. "But of course, *mein Schatz.*" His style of fencing mixed the medieval German *Kunst des Fechtens*—the use of daggers, poleaxes, and broadswords, with the more contemporary *Ecole Francais*—the use of rapier, saber, epee' and foil.

His opponent removed her cap and let her luxurious golden mane tumble halfway down her shoulders. "You are a rogue, Emil."

Lilly Nordstrom was a former darling of the Swedish stage whose skill with the epee' could defeat most men in a fair duel. Although Donat had slain her husband in such a duel, she had no hatred of him and was all the more attracted to him. After all, they had fought over her.

"So, tell me about our journey," she said as she oiled and stowed her blade.

"It will be long. Perhaps difficult. But the fate of monarchy lies in the balance."

Lilly smiled and shook her flaxen tresses. "How much will we earn for this one?"

Donat's eyes narrowed. "More than from all the others combined."

***

Hohensalzburg Fortress, Salzburg, Austria

Von Zoranski stuffed a chunk of meat into his mouth. "The roast boar is quite juicy, Count Esslinger."

"Let us hope our plans are as exquisite as the gravy. The Aulic Council is making a bold gambit. For our prey is exotic, the Marquis de Lafayette is a hero on two continents," said Vassiliev.

Von Zoranski spat a piece of gristle onto the floor. "A traitor to his class and to monarchy."

"We must be cool and precise, not passionate about this task," said Esslinger. "The Aulic Council relies on this committee to make surgical strikes, leaving no trail."

When the servers swept off with the dishes and silverware, the head waiter set a frosted bottle of white *Schnapps* before them. Esslinger stood and filled their glasses. "Williams Christ pears make the best schnapps. *Prost!*"

They tipped their glasses and drank. Esslinger poured a second round and held a piece of paper before them. "Here is the plan. If you *Herren* agree, we will set it in motion. Have all your assets been notified?"

Heads nodded.

"*Ausgezeichnet*. Excellent. Three killer teams, one from each of our respective services, are moving to go into action. The marquis must die in America."

"Accident?" Vassiliev asked.

"No. The world must know he was killed. The black hand of the Holy Alliance must be evident but not provable from a legal standpoint. Locals can be hired. But then that assassin must be quickly and discreetly eliminated."

"Emil prefers to go right to the point," said Von Zoranski.

Esslinger eyed him disdainfully and then realized it was not a pun. "Whatever works. The biggest problem is preventing our teams, who know nothing of one another, from getting crossed and disrupting each other."

"What do you suggest?" asked Vassiliev.

"I have given the matter some thought," said Esslinger. "One team will get to America and set up for action at a future venue. I understand they are widely publicizing his travels for propaganda purposes."

"The American system is built on democratic fantasy, not the holy right of a ruler," Vassiliev sneered.

"Another will trail him. Depart for America later. If the last leg of his journey does not result in his death, a team shall make a final strike, even if it is as he is boarding for his return voyage."

"We'll cut him down before that," hissed Von Zoranski.

"In any event, the third team has the most difficult task. Embed themselves with the marquis's entourage. Get to know him, if possible. Kill him when the opportunity strikes."

"I wish I could do this myself," Von Zoranski said.

Esslinger leaned forward and wagged a long finger. "*Nein, mein Herr*, this needs to be done, as I said, by cold professionals, not hot-blooded amateurs. Regardless of their motivation."

Silence filled the chamber. Each knew that this was more than murder and, in some sense, more than assassination. After all, Lafayette was a public figure, not a governing ruler or official of any country or regime. But they were not out to kill a citizen, a royal, or an official. They were out to kill an idea.

Chapter 4

The Chancery, Baltimore, Maryland, April 1824

A servant entered the bishop's study and bowed slightly.

Bishop Maréchal smiled. "Yes, Robert?"

"Your Eminence, a gentleman is here to see you. But he doesn't have an appointment. Should I send him away?"

"What is his name?"

"He did not give his name, but he said Lord Avondale sent him, and you would know what that means."

Maréchal's mouth tightened. "Very well, send him in. Then fetch Brother Bernard and bring some wine, Robert."

The man they ushered in had a military bearing. He wore a distinguished but practical suit of gray with knee-length boots and carried a walking cane. Maréchal noted his bronzed complexion and brown sun-bleached hair. Marechal surmised the visitor had spent many hours on deck.

Richard Neall introduced himself, and they were soon sipping fine French wine and making small talk. Minutes later, Brother Bernard joined them.

"So, what skullduggery has Lord Avondale sent you to engage us in, Mister Neall?" Maréchal asked. He was almost afraid to hear the answer.

"No skullduggery, excellency," Neall replied. "I have information that is both sensitive and urgent."

"Indeed?"

"It is all over the papers in Europe about your president's invitation to the Marquis de Lafayette. And his acceptance has stirred things up in certain quarters."

Maréchal glanced at Brother Bernard. "What quarters, may I ask, *Monsieur*?"

Neall took in a breath and hesitated. "At Hohensalzburg Fortress, for one. And in the halls of the Aulic Council itself."

Brother Bernard looked at the bishop, who nodded in approval.

"What is the Holy Alliance's interest in such a visit?" Brother Bernard asked. "Other than they view anything that celebrates democracy as a threat."

"You are correct, Brother Bernard. They have made plans to terminate the visit."

"How?"

"By assassinating Lafayette during the journey. Killing him on American soil – thus sending a message to the people on both sides of the Atlantic."

Brother Bernard nodded. "And how will they do this? Moreover, where and when will they attempt this?"

"I wish I knew. All I know for certain is that each member has engaged killers, skilled and experienced professionals. They may already be on their way to your country."

"We can alert the authorities at the major ports: Boston, New York, Philadelphia, and here in Baltimore," said Maréchal.

"My understanding is that your customs officers are adept at finding contraband but are not very good at police work. And you have no other police than the night watch, local sheriffs, or constables. Perhaps your Navy..."

"Most ships are decommissioned with officers and sailors on half pay," said Maréchal.

"Which means Mister Putnam is without a ship," Bernard said with a twinkle in his eye.

Maréchal's eyes widened. "*Oui, Monsieur Putnam est libre.*"

"He's free and experienced," said Bernard.

Maréchal could not reveal to Neall that he and Bernard ran an intelligence network that included the young naval officer. While commanding a small schooner, Lieutenant Kent Putnam served as an intelligence officer during the late war with Britain, serving mainly on the Great Lakes.

"*Madame* Patterson has many social connections up and down the Atlantic coast. She may be of some service," Maréchal said. "Reach out to her as well." Maréchal watched for Bernard's reaction but noticed nothing.

Bernard turned to Neall and slightly cocked his head. "So, Mister Neall, you must have some contacts here in America we can draw upon? Contacts remaining from the last war?"

Maréchal drew a breath. *Mon Dieu, he's still the bold one!*

Neall's eyes lowered as he scanned his right boot.

"Well?" Bernard said like a schoolmaster scolding a boy.

"I was a dragoon captain in that war, Brother Bernard. Wounded on the Spanish Peninsula but able to serve at Waterloo by God's grace."

"How did you come to this line of work?" Bernard asked.

"No need for cavalry officers policing our empire. That's more for the infantry and artillery officers. Lord Avondale plucked me from a life on half-pay with no real property to fall back on."

"Why, you?"

"Gentlemen, I come here to offer information vital to your nation and you..."

30

"You are entering *our* circle, Monsieur. Brother Bernard is simply doing his diligence."

"Lord Avondale knew I spoke Spanish and passable French and German. He knew I needed a meaningful diversion, or I'd dissipate with women, gambling, and drink or, more likely, get hung for dueling."

"How would he know such a thing?"

Neall straightened in his seat. "Because his daughter, Evelyn, is my late wife. But you knew that, didn't you, Brother Bernard? You look the type who would not ask a question he didn't already know the answer to."

Maréchal interjected to avoid any more unpleasantness. "You are correct, *Monsieur*, although Brother Bernard asks questions when he suspects the answer. The English society pages provide quite useful bits of information to the discerning eye. And I assure you, *Monsieur*, Brother Bernard has a most discerning eye."

***

The President's Office, The White House

John Quincy Adams finished his report. "All embassies, consulates, and legations report your letter to Congress has created quite the stir. You have everyone's attention, Mister President."

"What about the note from the archbishop?" asked Monroe.

"Ah yes, interesting developments, as it turns out."

"Interesting from that quarter usually means something unpleasant is afoot."

"Your instincts are correct, Mister President. Simply put, there seems to be a threat of some sort to the marquis."

"What is the source of this news?"

"The British."

"Mister Canning?"

"Not Stratford. He's departed. From an unofficial emissary from Lord Avondale."

"Can we trust this information?" Monroe knew that Lord Avondale's department, a secret service within the Foreign Office, was covert in mission and clandestine in its operation.

"No. But I'm afraid we must, for now. I am assigning young Buchanan to sort this out. He is, after all, my lead for the visit."

"Makes perfect sense. Keep me apprised."

***

Fells Point, Baltimore, Maryland

Neall stepped out of the entrance to his modest hotel and into the late morning sun. He raised his cane and signaled the hackney coach. The large bay pulling it snorted as the coach halted in the street's thick mud. He whispered his destination and the hackney rolled through Old Town Baltimore before turning north past stately homes and through increasingly verdant gardens and orchards.

The ride gave Neall time to think through his way forward. *Did the Americans believe him?* He thought so. But his visit to the bishop and his monk unveiled a surprise to him so great he had to sort out its meaning if his mission were to succeed. The coach rolled to a stop before a small, freshly whitewashed Palladian-style home.

An enslaved servant in a white livery jacket that contrasted with his dark skin opened the door. He escorted Neall into the grand entranceway and pointed him to a parlor where a beautiful woman sat waiting on a divan across from a fireplace.

Neall removed his hat and bowed. "*Madame* Bonaparte."

Elizabeth Patterson rose from the seat, took his hands in hers, and then offered her cheek for a kiss.

Neall noted the slight trace of lines from her lips only added to her beauty and charisma. "Betsy, you are lovelier than ever," Neall gently whispered. His arm circled her waist. He lifted her from the carpet and passionately kissed her.

***

The evening twilight bathed the room in a faint copper tint. Neall's leg shifted, stirring the silken sheets.

"Don't go. I'll have the servants prepare supper," Betsy murmured.

"I have an appointment at the chancery at eight. I was made to understand by Bishop Maréchal that you do as well."

"Her face flushed. What would I have to do with the Archbishop of Baltimore? In fact, what do you have to do with the Archbishop of Baltimore?"

"Indeed, darling. It seems we each have explanations to make." He ran his hand down her spine.

Betsy sat upright and held the sheets to her pale throat.

Their eyes locked in a gaze of longing mixed with doubt and fear. Each longed for what they once had while fearing and doubting their future and shared interests. Both were spies, after all.

"Ladies first," he said with a mischievous grin.

Betsy's bright eyes gazed at his muscular chest as if to measure him and sighed. "If I must."

Neall still found her the most fascinating of women. Since 1819, Elizabeth had spent much of her time traveling Europe hoping to find closure to the embarrassing affair and marriage with the youngest brother of Europe's most powerful ruler, Napoleon Bonaparte. Napoleon annulled her marriage to Jerome and married him to a German princess for dynastic advantage. But Betsy was already pregnant and bore the feckless Jerome, a son.

They met during her travels through many of the continent's most fashionable seats of power, and she became his lover and spy. The socialite's beauty, influence, and connections were ideal for keeping tabs on Europe's elite. Her brilliant mind and charm provided Neall with nuggets he could never obtain from a male informant. And the debriefings were much more pleasing.

But Lord Avondale was not confident of Neall's high-placed informant and told Neall using her would backfire. Although he did not know it, Avondale was right. Betsy's journeys to Europe were organized, planned, and controlled by the Secretary to the Archbishop of Baltimore, Brother Maurice Bernard.

"So, our first encounter was no accident?" Neall asked, dismayed but not surprised by her revelation. *I let myself be played the fool.*

"No less than your interest in me, Richard. I believe we mutually benefited from our liaison. We were a team."

"But I was unaware you served another side, too."

"Would that have changed anything?" Betsy rose and began sliding her lithe figure into her petticoats. "All the information I provided you was true. I just provided it to the chancery as well. I suspect your Lord Avondale was aware or at least suspected. He made you break with me rather suddenly. Don't you agree?"

She is a very insightful woman. Avondale must have known! And he sends me to meet her through her American handlers. He sat up, pulled on his breeches, and reached for his boots. "Just as long as we truly are on the same team now, my darling."

Betsy made a face, bent over him, and slid her arms around his neck. The twilight had turned to darkness when they ended their kiss.

***

Lieutenant Kent Putnam dug the faded brass spurs into his horse. He needed to arrive at the chancery before dusk. Putnam's note from Brother Bernard included the code word "Kilkenny." He did not know why the monk used the name of the Irish town as a signal for action. But it meant something was afoot. And since overseeing the repair of cordage in the swamp-like miasma of the Washington Navy Yard did not amuse him, he was glad for the summons.

Captain Blaine, his commanding officer, understood. A letter would follow authorizing his departure. Blaine was not too pleased, though. Putnam's last call to action lasted almost a year, and he spent three years away during the war with Britain, patrolling the Great Lakes and dispatching spies and scouts across the Canadian littoral. He longed for that kind of work. But any job would do.

***

The Chancery, Baltimore, Maryland

A dozen lanterns hissed, glowing dimly in the struggle to illuminate the large meeting room. Neall sensed tense anticipation of something familiar yet unknown. *These people have done this before.*

Maréchal called the meeting to order and introduced all the parties but promptly turned it over to Brother Bernard. "I must celebrate Mass, but the good brother has my blessing and instructions. *Adieu.*"

When the servant bolted the door closed, Brother Bernard addressed the group. "From here on, the archbishop will distance himself from our circle and its proceedings."

Neall thought he detected a hint of an Irishman in his voice. "Who knows these proceedings? Besides those in our circle."

Neall gestured to those around the table: Betsy, Kent Putnam, Bernard, and Mister Buchanan from the State Department, a surprise addition.

"The secretary and the president, as far as I know," said Bernard, who glared at Neall. "And who on your side knows?"

"Just Lord Avondale, as far as I know. He felt this was too sensitive for the Foreign Office. They might go off half-cocked with demarches and press releases. For some reason, he trusts the archbishop and, by extension, this circle."

Neall did not trust the circle, however. His own beloved Betsy had deceived him. *Who could he trust among these Americans?*

"'Tis important we trust one another. 'Tis why I call such teams a circle. A circle cannot be broken," Bernard said. "Our prime objective is to protect the marquis from harm and ensure his journey has the desired political result both here and abroad. I believe Lord Avondale concurs, Mister Neall?"

Neall nodded. "It's why he sent me." He wondered if this were the right time to say more and decided not.

"This is Mister Robert Buchanan, a clerk at the State Department."

Buchanan nodded in greeting. "I'm an Assistant to the Clerk of the Consular Service. Thus, I work for Secretary Adams and am appointed liaison for the Secretary and the President in this affair."

"Is Mister Buchanan's inclusion necessary?" Neall did not like the complication of *official* oversight. He and Lord Avondale agreed that sensitive matters were best left out of the eyes and ears of *official* government.

"In this country, the president has final authority in all such matters. He and Mister Adams will neither know nor want details, but such is our way."

Neall glanced at Betsy and the naval officer in his dark blue uniform. "Very well, sir."

Bernard motioned toward the young diplomat. "What do you have for us, Mister Buchanan?"

"It seems the marquis has requested the services of a packet ship's master by the name of Francis Allyn."

Neall grew suspicious. "Not an American ship of war?"

"Seems he knew the Allyn family from his time here during the war. Against the Brit...." He quickly drew his eyes from Neall, whose nation had been their enemy.

"British, Mister Buchanan. The war is long over."

Brother Bernard cast a smile. "'Tis, 'tisn't it?"

"I'll make contact with Allyn once on board. Can you provide a letter of introduction?"

"Of course," said Buchanan. "It will solicit his cooperation with you on behalf of the US government but not provide the reason."

Neall nodded. "Better that way."

Bernard raised a hand. "Now that we have the preliminaries, let me lay the plan."

Bernard's plan was succinct. Betsy would begin tapping into her network of acquaintances. She had contacts in the three Holy Alliance countries – men of some means and sometimes notoriety. Neall would return to Europe and try to book passage on the packet ship *Cadmus* to ferret out danger. Buchanan's note would alert its master, a ship's captain who was friends with Lafayette, to be vigilant, but not why. Putnam would travel to key venues to meet with local constables and sheriffs and provide Bernard with a report on each.

"One last item, Mister Buchanan," said Bernard in closing.

"Of course, Brother Bernard."

"Is it possible to contact the embassy in Paris and secure the services of a certain Marine Corps sergeant seconded to our Naval Attaché there?"

"Who? And to what purpose?"

"A sergeant by the name of Daniel Riley. He did service in Canada with Lieutenant Putnam. I'd like him to be given a support role on the marquis' entourage. But he will be a personal bodyguard."

"Will the marquis know of his role?"

"Prepare papers informing him that this is standard protocol and not in response to a specific threat."

Buchanan's eyes widened. "Why wouldn't we inform the marquis of a threat?"

Neall had heard enough. "Because, Mister Buchanan, we cannot ensure the marquis will not talk of it. He enjoys talking, I am told."

"Yes, he does," said Betsy, lowering her long lashes.

Neall noticed a slight flush to her pale skin. "He may tell tales out of school, and we must assume the assassin or an accomplice will be in his party."

***

Fells Point, Baltimore, Maryland

The carriage rolled through the heavy gray mist and slowed to a halt at the quay. Betsy lifted her head from Neall's chest but held his hands tightly. She feared it would be their final kiss. Their eyes locked, and they kissed longingly, each drinking in the last taste of their shared passion.

35

She had numerous lovers since her marriage to Jerome Bonaparte was dissolved, but none like Neall. Although a few years her junior, he had the demeanor and self-assurance of an older man. Although not wealthy, he moved among the rich, like the most powerful magnate. And to her greatest delight, his muscular frame gave her no rest.

"So fortunate you booked passage on *Cadmus*, dear," she said breathlessly.

"I've learned preparation mixed with fortune brings success – unless bad luck intercedes."

They smiled and kissed once more.

Betsy slid an envelope from under her blouse and placed it in his hands. "Post these letters once you reach Paris. They will be carried to contacts in a half dozen cities."

"Your spider's web of contacts must include very powerful men?"

She understood his meaning but was not angry. It was understandable for a man like him to be jealous. She entwined her fingers in his. "My destiny was to be abandoned by my husband and left to raise his child. Powerful men were necessary to disabuse society that I was a jilted woman. And it helps protect my son. One never knows what those Bonapartes may do."

"The Ogre is dead, my dear Bess."

She liked it when he called her Bess. No one else did. "But his shadow looms large over Europe — perhaps reaching America. We are in an eternal fight against despotism."

The sound of a Bosun's pipe whistled in the fog. It would soon be time to board.

"Is that why you allied with the archbishop?"

"No, I allied with Brother Bernard."

"Speaking of Brother Bernard, is he Irish? I detect a certain lilt to his...."

Betsy placed her fingers on his lips. "Hush, darling. The only man I am interested in right now is in this carriage."

Chapter 5

Hohensalzburg Fortress, Salzburg, Austria

The mallet struck the oak table with a *thud*. "This meeting is called to order," said Count Esslinger. "A report of activity will be entered into the record." The tall aristocrat nodded at a scribe. "Take precise notes, Uzeir."

Esslinger did not like having Uzeir privy to such delicate proceedings, but the Bosnian clerk had served him well for two decades. *His name, he who helps, is most apropos.*

"I'm not authorized to have details of our effort recorded anywhere but St. Petersburg," said Vassiliev.

"I must remind you, this is Aulic Council business. As such, it can only be recorded here. As a matter of the utmost security," Esslinger replied icily.

The room grew silent. Esslinger's eyes shifted to the scribe, who sat patiently with his pen. "Now, our strategy is threefold. You Russians will place a team onboard the marquis' ship if possible. That's our prime method of liquidation, preferably in American waters."

Vassiliev straightened himself in his chair with an air of pride.

"You Prussians provide the pursuit team. If Prince Vassiliev's efforts fail, they will move in. Action should be discreet but swift."

"My report is quite brief. A team of the most astute professionals has been dispatched according to our agreed action plan," declared Baron Zoranski. "They travel as we speak and will only report when the task is accomplished."

Esslinger smiled. "Let's hope the frantic newspapers will precede them with the news. What about you, Prince Vassiliev?"

"The same. They will attempt to book passage along with the marquis. If not, they board the next ship with the same destination, which we assume is New York."

"Where does he sail from?"

"The papers and our informants do not yet know," replied Vassiliev.

"Most likely Le Havre," said Zoranski. "I suggest you inquire there."

Vassiliev nodded, his suppressed anger exposed by the veins bulging at his thick neck.

Esslinger was not impressed with Vassiliev. *Are these the kinds of princes Muscovy sends us?* He glanced at the scribe. "Make a note of that, Uzeir."

"As you say, *effendi.*"

"Baron?"

"Our team is making sail from Hamburg. They travel to New York and learn what they can of the itinerary. Then select a locale from which to strike when the marquis arrives."

Esslinger motioned toward Vassiliev and Zoranski. "Do your teams understand the backup plan? If the mission fails or they must abort, they must find another venue and strike again. No matter what the cost!"

Vassiliev glanced at Zoranski.

"Well?" Esslinger needed to press them.

"Our normal protocol is one strike and clear, Count Esslinger."

"I will get word to my team," said Vassiliev.

***

Chancery Annex, Baltimore, Maryland

Brother Bernard hunched over the stacks of newspapers, magazines, and broadsheets cluttering his desk. He held his reading spectacles with his left hand and made notes with his right.

Putnam paced impatiently before the fireplace with his hands folded behind his back like a ship's captain at sea. He appreciated the brother's attention to detail and extensive research, which had made his exploits on the lakes even more successful, but he wanted to depart.

"How much longer will this take, Brother Bernard?"

"Just a few more minutes. I believe I've captured the marquis' proposed itinerary thus far." Brother Bernard moved from the table and slid into the chair at his desk. "When a copy is made, I'll send it to you. Foreknowledge saves work and, in this case, perhaps lives."

Putnam had missed his service with the cleric, who was not a cleric back then. After the second war with Britain concluded, he went into the clergy. No one knew why. Major Maurice Bernard, as he was known, ran a network of agents and informers tightly intertwined with the Jesuits and other religious orders during that struggle. His background was a mystery to all, but the rumors were legendary.

All Putnam knew was that he was meticulous, well-prepared, courageous, and trusting of those he selected for his service in his "Circle."

Bernard drew a bottle from under his desk and poured each a whisky. "Do you miss being at sea, Kent?"

"I do. Do you miss being in action?"

Bernard hesitated and then shook his head. "No. My time is past. And besides, 'tis more important to research, analyze, and plan. That's my value now. Fieldwork is for youngsters such as yourselves."

"I'll be a forty-two-year-old lieutenant next month. The way the Navy is going, I'll be a sixty-two-year-old lieutenant when I die."

"Well, the archbishop and I are well acquainted with Mister Southard. I suspect you'll die at least a commander."

Putnam took a sip of the liquor. He was not sure if that was an exaggeration. "With a ship?"

Brother Bernard smiled. "That you'll have to wangle for yourself."

They discussed his travel north, his general plans, and most importantly, his means of communication.

"How can Mister Neall, an obvious Briton, get anything done on his own?"

"There is a man in the mayor's office who oversees police functions, such as they are, in the city. And the militia commander can always call on a few of his lads to assist, in or out of uniform." He handed Putnam a slip of paper. "But here's the person Neall's to be wary of."

"Martin Van Buren?"

"He heads the Albany Regency. Powerful men who control the Tammany Society, New York politics, and thus the city and state. But you'll work with the other name on the paper."

"Mick Flynn?"

"He runs day-to-day operations for the Regency." Bernard stifled a laugh. "Ironically, they are also known to some as The Holy Alliance."

Putnam was stunned that Bernard had so many contacts of that sort. "These are factionalists and gangsters! Is the bishop aware of your connection?"

Bernard's eyes narrowed. "Now look, the government barely provides enough money to buy the newspapers and supply my ink. The archbishop provides this place and his vast network. But that's just the minimum to keep track of the world and its intentions regarding our republic. Without connections such as these and their funds, we'd have had little enough intelligence in the last war."

***

Office of the American Envoy Extraordinary and Minister Plenipotentiary, Paris, June 1824

The reception was drawing to its conclusion. Scores of French dignitaries had mixed with the American expatriates of Paris to line up and wish the Marquis de Lafayette *bon voyage*.

Sergeant Dan Riley, an American Marine, stood silently and watched. He was just informed he would accompany Lafayette on his journey. The girls of

Montmartre had taught him passable French, among other things, but he struggled to comprehend amid the background noise of several hundred drunk guests.

A dainty French lady in a dark green gown with stuffed shoulders and a mildly scooped décolleté clung to Lafayette's arm. "So, tell me, *Monsieur*, how will you stand being so far from Paris for so long?"

The crowd around him all nodded and cooed their own versions of the question. Lafayette accepted the flute of champagne offered by a servant and exposed them to his most disarming smile. "It will be difficult. But not so difficult when I spent years in foreign prisons with few in Paris to lament me."

The crowd murmured protests.

"But *Monsieur*, that was a different time."

"Was it? And what of my first journey to America — a journey to champion the cause of liberty? Why I had to slip away secretly lest the *comte* de Vergennes had me thrown in irons for defying the royal decree to remain. Sometimes we must dare all for liberty, *n'est pas*?"

A chorus, *oui, oui*, and here, here erupted.

"What is your greatest memory, General Lafayette?"

Lafayette played with the stem of his glass. "There are too many to count. My arrival at Congress. My first encounter with General Washington."

Oohs and *aahs* erupted.

"Standing my ground on a dozen battlefields."

"You were wounded once?" someone from the rear of the crowd said.

"Wounds are but a means to an end. Many never recovered. It is to hold their memory that I travel. And to celebrate the nation that is my second homeland."

"Do you support the liberation movements in the new world?" someone asked.

"Of course."

"And here in the old?"

Sensing a trick, Lafayette placed his glass on a passing tray and bowed his departure.

Riley pushed his way through the crowd and up the winding marble stairs where Lafayette would spend the night at the vacant quarters of the American Envoy Extraordinary and Minister Plenipotentiary. The new envoy, a Virginia planter friend of President Monroe, was due to be appointed by year's end.

Outside the room, he saw a young woman of around thirty, fashionably but not fancily dressed, slip from the room. Riley had been warned Lafayette wanted to bring his mistress — something the American government would not abide by. Besides the moral implications, the woman, Fanny Wright, was a philosopher and writer from Scotland with some unusual political beliefs.

Her strawberries and cream complexion framed in dark auburn locks set against gray eyes proved Lafayette had a good eye for women if not politics. Riley knew nothing of politics but had a good eye for beauty, so as she passed, he nodded.

When Lafayette's valet removed his jacket and boots, Lafayette sat in a chair and stared at the fire. His son and his secretary joined him, and soon a bottle of brandy was uncorked.

"Come join us, Sergeant Riley. You are off duty, yes?"

Riley had fought the Barbary Pirates at the turn of the century and the British during the War of 1812. He was Irish and liked a drink but could not get used to the idea of drinking with officers.

"Thank you, General, but my orders are to avoid alcohol so long as I am at your service." He was surprised at how easily the French rolled off his tongue.

"What are your orders, Sergeant? Besides those?"

"I'll sleep in the room next to yours and accompany you whenever you leave. In addition, I will ensure local security and ceremony are appropriate."

"Did you serve in a war, Sergeant?"

"*Oui*. At Tripoli and against the pirates in the Mediterranean. Also, against the British, while they were taking a break from Napoleon." Riley regretted the quip.

But Lafayette laughed. "Yes, a break from Bonaparte was always a good thing. It is a shame his ego took advantage of his better nature. He was a genius and had he stayed true to the republic, France and Europe would have had a fifty-year peace."

The son of a teacher, Riley was well-read in history, politics, and culture. He knew Lafayette and Napoleon Bonaparte had a checkered past.

Riley snapped to attention. "I will leave you, gentlemen, to yourselves. But will be in the next room."

"I appreciate that, Sergeant Riley. But I do not see the need for an American bodyguard. There is no threat to me. Especially in America. They know me as one of their first patriots."

"That you are, General. I believe it's only a mere formality."

***

Montmartre, Paris

The walls were heavily draped, and the open space was packed with religious icons. A score of red candles bathed the room in a crimson hue, and heavy incense filled his nostrils with its sickening sweetness. It reminded Buxhowden more of a Russian monastery than the salon of a celebrated yet mysterious woman.

The once beautiful and still comely sixty-year-old woman poured a cup of tea and handed it to Buxhowden. The bangles draping her arms chimed rhythmically. "Drink this, Alexander. And tell me why you are here after all these years. I'm too old to be of use as a mistress."

Her laugh was mesmerizing, as was everything else about her. Barbara Juliane, Baroness von Krüdener, was the celebrated mystic visionary of her age. Once, kings, princes, barons, and dukes sought her seances and her charms.

Born in Livonia, the daughter of a descendant of the Teutonic knights, the baroness was a mystery within an enigma who attracted men of power and wealth. And sometimes, men like Buxhowden yearned for power and wealth but pursued the occult with even greater yearning.

"No, Baroness. But as you know, you are my muse. My guide to the occult when I was but an Orthodox seminarian."

"If I led an impious seminarian from the priesthood, that might make me a saint," she said with a smile of satisfaction. "Do you still dabble in the dark arts, Alexander?"

"More than dabble, Baroness. But I have other pursuits as well."

"The Alliance?" she asked with a laugh.

"The Holy Alliance," he replied. Her tone of ridicule annoyed him. He would walk out but needed her to reveal a dark secret.

"If you say so. What is it you want?"

"You once told me you visited Lafayette when the Austrians imprisoned him at Olmutz."

The baroness leaned forward, letting her pendulous breasts entice him. "I revealed that to you under the dark spell of mysticism."

"I should call it eroticism, but as you wish. I want to know what transpired between you and *Monsieur* Lafayette."

"Why is that a concern?"

"I cannot say."

She closed her eyes and drew a breath. "You don't have to. I know General Lafayette is in danger. I sense it. And I sense you present that danger."

Buxhowden stared impassively, but his mind raced. *This witch senses more than most know.*

"You want me to help you and the Alliance. Destroy him on his journey." Her eyes opened and locked with his. "Why do you care about Olmutz?"

Ah, I've touched a sore point. "Were you and *Monsieur* Lafayette lovers?"

"Why should that matter?"

"You once said you'd never betray a lover."

The baroness' eyes narrowed. "I foretold his death!"

"And how and when will he die?"

She laughed dismissively. "Don't you want to know where?"

"Begin with the first two, Baroness."

Her eyes closed, and she murmured words he could not decipher. Then she intoned, "...at four... a liquid will choke the life from him... in a great city... surrounded by his son and friends."

The son travels with him. We must strike him in a city — with a potion!

Buxhowden reached out and wrapped his fist around the baroness' plump hand. *"Merci beaucoup, Madame."*

He stepped into the night chill and jumped into a cab. Armed with a way forward, he had neglected to ask Baroness von Krüdener if his plot would succeed.

***

Aboard the Bark *John Howard*, Atlantic Crossing

Richard Neall gazed into the fog thick as jelly as the *John Howard* slowly set south by southeast from British waters. He could not believe his luck, finding a ship to Plymouth with a follow on to Le Havre, France.

He ruminated on his journey and what lay ahead. It impressed him that Lord Avondale had connections to a secret intelligence network so confidential even the American presidents were scarcely aware. And he could not get over Betsy's connection to the group. Although she had deceived him, he loved her even more for her commitment to a cause.

Hours later, the *Cap de la Heve'* appeared on the starboard. Neall turned to go to his berth and retrieve his bags.

"We'll be at the quay in short order, sir," said the diminutive porter. "I can fetch your kit now if you'd like."

He had an Irish brogue. And he looked vaguely familiar. And despite his size, he was hauling an oversized trunk on his back.

"You look like you served his majesty."

The porter shot a wide grin, and a look of pride crossed his face. "That I did, sir. 'Twas at Waterloo, the luck."

"You carry yourself like a cavalryman."

The porter lowered the trunk effortlessly and stood erect. He was not as diminutive as Neall had thought, maybe five-foot-six. "Trooper Tom Lynch, 6th Inniskilling Dragoons, at yer service."

"I was at Waterloo as well. With the Royal Dragoons. So, we both charged with the Union Brigade?"

Lynch's face beamed. "Ah, one of your lads took a French eagle during our charge!"

***

Mont St. Jean, Belgium, June 18th, 1815

Neall's mind transported him to the hot June day eight long years ago. The barley was chest high, and his troop waited impatiently in a sea of it. Over the crest, they could smell as much as hear the battle. Gunpowder drifted into their nostrils. Both eager troopers and anxious horses stirred. "Easy now," sergeants chided.

Napoleon had broken from Elba and retaken France. His 100,000-strong *L'Armee du Nord* marched north and placed itself between the Anglo-Allied and Prussian forces, desperately trying to close before facing the "Corsican Ogre."

Word reached them that Napoleon smashed the Prussians at Ligny just a few hours' march east. The day before, the army fought Marshal Ney to a standstill. Still, the commander-in-chief of the Anglo-Allied Army, Arthur Wellesley, the Duke of Wellington, decided to retreat to the undulating hills of Mont St. Jean, just south of the town of Waterloo.

After a night of heavy rain, Napoleon came for them. Now they waited in reserve, the Union Brigade under Major General William Ponsonby with this own 1st Dragoons, the 2nd North British called the Scots Greys, and the 6th Inniskilling Dragoons fresh from garrison duty in Ireland.

The pounding of Napoleon's grand battery of over 100 heavy guns seemed to sweep everything before them. But the thick mud clung to the massive iron balls meant to roll and bound, tearing limbs and crushing spines and skulls.

Suddenly, the guns ceased. There followed the *rat – tat – tat – tat* of hundreds of drums, and even with the ground soggy from the rain, the tramp of over 50,000 shoes shook the earth.

Neall had scouted the field earlier and knew the French had to march down a long slope, enter a narrow defile, and climb another to reach the waiting British ranks.

Cries of *Vive l'Empereur* filled the air. The *pop* of muskets followed. The musket fire grew to a crescendo when Ponsonby received the order to advance. Bugles sounded the charge, and a thousand powerful horses bounded as one. They streamed over the ridge and faced a sea of blue jackets – a block of French infantry that looked like the populace of a small city.

But the troopers dug their spurs, and their neighing horses lowered their heads. In seconds, they were skewering fusiliers, slashing voltigeurs, and trampling grenadiers. The French were struck in the flank and could do little against the scythe of sabers glistening in the sunlight.

Neall faced down a burly French sergeant defiantly holding his regimental eagle – the soul of his regiment. Neall called for him to surrender, but a trooper struck him before the proud veteran could reply. His barracks mate, Captain Alexander Kennedy Clark, snatched the 105th *Regiment de Ligne's* standard.

Neall rode on, swinging left and right as on the playing field. The slaughter only ended when the French broke or surrendered. But the horses sped on and through the rows of guns that minutes earlier had terrorized their infantry.

The gunners resisted, and many of these strong and proud men fell to the heavy sabers. But many troopers were down, and the horses began to slow. Their mounts were blown, and their sweat-foamed flanks heaved as the horses struggled for air. Neall knew they had gone too far. He turned to his trumpeter. "Sound recall, now!"

The trumpeter put the horn to his mouth and blew. But it was too late.

"*Vive L'Empereur!*"

A wave of green with spear tips glinting in the sun galloped straight at them. Squadrons of French lancers fell upon the disorganized troops and winded horses.

Neall waved his saber. "Fall back and regroup!"

Some did, but most fell to the nine-foot lances, stuck like pigs. By the time Neall had counted his troop safely behind the red-coated ranks of British infantry, he was down to a dozen men with horses of his original forty. Ponsonby had fallen along with most of his brigade. The remnant of his regiment was sent into the reserve, and Captain Richard Neall's day of battle had ended.

***

Neall's mind returned to the present. He looked at Lynch and asked, "I'll double your pay if you agree to enter my employ. I need someone I can trust. An Irish dragoon is just the man."

Chapter 6

Le Havre, France

The hotel was small and full of the pungent aromas of fish and seafood dishes Neall had never experienced. The food comforted his stomach if it did not tantalize his palate. But its location was perfect for checking the ships entering port and making inquiries at the Customs Office, where he told them he was a maritime insurance agent with Lloyd's of London. No one questioned that.

Lynch's job was to seek a position on the ship returning the Marquis de Lafayette to America. Neall's job was to get on board without attracting too much suspicion. He had briefed Lynch on the bare bones of the operation — protect an important man.

He stepped out onto the *Rue de Paris* and strode toward *the Grand Quai* where he found the *Port Centre*.

"Bonjour, *Monsieur* Locke," greeted the clerk.

"*Bonjour*," Neall replied. "Any news?" He slipped a coin into the clerk's palm.

The clerk shifted his feet, slid his eyes from side to side, then nodded and slipped a piece of paper to Neall.

Neall scanned the note: *Cadmus, arrive' circa 7th Jul. 1824.*

His eyes shifted to the clerk. "I'll return tomorrow and want to see all this ship's logs of visits to this port. And any other unlogged visits as well." He slipped another coin to the clerk.

The clerk nodded. "*Merci, monsieur. Comme vous le souhaitez.* As you wish."

Neall strode along the quay, watching dozens of tall ships with sails spread against the wind like the wings of large birds of prey. *They soar over the sea like great Albatrosses.* Scores of smaller craft filled the estuary and lined the channel into the inner harbor. Finally, he ducked into a small café for his daily meeting with Tom Lynch.

Lynch had gotten a room over a bakery, and the two met each day as he trained the former soldier to be an agent of His Majesty's Secret Service, better known as the "Special Accounts Section" of the Foreign Office. So far, Lynch had taken to it like a fish to water. A native of Donegal, he had moved to Derry as a boy and learned the ways of ships, mostly fishing smacks. Tiring of the smells, he jumped at the king's shilling when recruiters came through the pubs looking for new troopers to sail to Spain.

"My luck, I joined a regiment that never left the island until Boney returned to power," he had said laughingly.

Neall taught him the essentials of spycraft. He learned how to spot a follower and how to follow. Then came the rudiments of communication using hand signals, secret notes, and secret drops to service. Drops were carefully selected locations to hide messages for pick up.

"Once you get aboard, act normal. Do whatever job you're hired to do. I'll set up our activities around your schedule. We'll have three meeting paces, likely spots for crew members and passengers to interact. And we'll have an emergency signal."

Lynch's eyes widened, and a slight smile crossed his face.

"You like danger," said Neall. "That's good up to a point. The key is the mission. And mission follows discretion."

"I see, sir."

"Don't get me wrong, when we have an emergency, then 'Hannah bar the door.' And that's the signal."

"Signal for what, sir?"

"If there is an immediate threat, we fight." Neall slipped him a knife and a pistol.

"Don't need any of that, sir. I was my regimental boxing champion. I'm not a heavyweight, mind ye, but I laid even the largest mick low, I did."

Neall smiled. "Well, we don't usually have time for fisticuffs. The latest weapon specially commissioned by the section is this Forsyth percussion-cap pistol. These aren't yet available to the public, but I managed to acquire a pair for each of us."

The Forsyth pistol was slightly larger than a man's hand, just half the size of a standard gun. And it had two .54-inch over-and-under barrels. The barrel and fittings were darkened steel and mahogany hand grips.

"Don't let the size fool you. These weapons have rifled barrels and can fire a quarter-inch ball accurately up to forty paces. They don't misfire in rain or snow like our flint firelocks did.

"More importantly, it's got two barrels, over and under. Look, you squeeze once." *Click.* "Slide the primer to the second cap. Then squeeze again."

Lynch worked the weapon. *Click.*

"Very good," said Neall. "But this here knife is quieter, and the pommel designed to crack even the thickest Irish skull."

The tempered blade was razor sharp on both edges and less than an inch across at the heel of the blade, while the point tapered quickly to provide an almost needlepoint to penetrate efficiently.

Lynch smiled broadly. "B' Jeezus, sir. I like the way ye think."

***

47

Neall pulled up his collar to better shelter against the cut of the October wind. He sat at an outdoor café, sipping hot chocolate, and surveying the scene as coaches and carriages dropped off or picked up travelers. Several tall ships bobbed along the stone quay.

Across the street, Lynch did the same. He made no eye contact as each had his role well-rehearsed. Neall looked for potential assassins. Lynch watched for anyone showing undue interest in Neall.

They had done drills like this at various venues along Le Havre's waterfront. But the exercises were also a means to understand the city's rhythms and its people and to identify suspicious persons. Not the seamen, thieves, whores, and assorted scalawags organic to a thriving port, nor the high and low-born travelers embarking and debarking, but the out-of-place look of someone intent on being unnoticed.

He chuckled silently. *Someone like Lynch and me.*

A sudden shriek rose above the clatter of hooves and rattle of wagons on dull pave stones. He saw a very well-dressed woman push two men from her. They stepped back and forth with hands raised and heads bobbing, showing they meant her harm.

He glanced at Lynch. The Irishman was leaning forward, fighting his every instinct not to intervene, for he was only to act on a signal from Neall. The woman struggled as the two groped at her, dragging her down a narrow alley. Lynch's jaw was tight, and his pale Irish face was beet red. He curled his forearms and clenched his fists tight enough to turn coal into a diamond.

Easy now, Lynch.

The woman was crying, but her cries turned to sobs, then moans.

Neall lifted his hat and flipped it upside down on his head as if to catch raindrops. The signal sprung Lynch into action. As taught, he left a coin at his table. And without running, discreetly but swiftly moved to assist the woman.

Her assailants turned to meet the interloper. One picked up a board and brandished it like a club. He took several swings at Lynch, who danced left, right, and back. The second assailant had circled to Lynch's rear and moved to grab him in a neck lock. But Lynch spun about and landed a crunching blow to his jaw, sending him down in a heap.

The man with the board sent it crashing into Lynch's back with a sickening *thud*. He then lunged at the Irishman with hands outstretched. Lynch turned and slipped the point of his dagger into his assailant's throat, poking just enough to draw a trickle of red.

"Enough!" Neall's voice echoed down the alley, and the fine lady scampered off.

"You can lower your poignard, Mister Lynch. Noah's a friend."

Lynch lowered the blade.

Noah wiped the blood from his throat with a dirty kerchief. "You did not tell us he was a master boxer, *Monsieur*. I think he killed Dugard."

Dugard moaned.

"He'll live. I just tapped him once," Lynch said. "Now, would ye mind telling me what in blazes is going on, sir?"

Neall smiled and handed Lynch his flask. "Just a test. You passed."

"A test? You can't be — why a second later, and I'd have skewered him like an apple."

"Needed to know how quickly you'd respond and how you'd handle things. You may take Dugard and go now, Noah."

Noah lifted Dugard across broad shoulders and scampered down the alley like it was nothing.

Lynch took a long swig of the flask and handed it to Neall. "That's foin brandy! A test?"

"Yes, you passed. But it's Armagnac, an exceptional brandy."

***

A coach rumbled down the cobbled avenue that led to the harbor, but Lafayette and his companions remained focused on the cards they held while finishing a quick game of whist.

"Did you make arrangements for *Madame*?" Auguste Levasseur asked.

Lafayette thought he was trying to distract him from playing his trump card. "*Oui*. Fanny and her sister Camilla will sail on a later vessel."

George's lips twisted slightly.

"My son does not approve, nor do my American hosts. But *Mademoiselle* Frances Wright is a brilliant mind, close confidante, and dearest of friends. Why would I not want her with me on a journey such as this?"

"They say whist was Bonaparte's favorite game," Levasseur said as he played a card on the small pull-out table, bouncing on their knees. "I think I won this trick!"

"But hopefully not in the Napoleonic way." Lafayette's eyes scanned the cards. Napoleon Bonaparte was notorious for cheating at Whist, among other things.

"Whoa!" The driver tugged the lines, and the carriage wheels screeched as they came to a halt.

Lafayette stuck his head out the window, taking in the port's salt air and other, more unsavory, smells. He hoped to be out at sea as soon as possible. He looked out in the harbor where a neat packet ship danced in the light swells, its stern adorned with a flag – the stars and stripes that warmed his heart with pride. *The journey begins soon.*

"Sergeant Riley, can you help with the baggage?" George Lafayette asked.

"Of course, sir."

49

"Nonsense, George," Lafayette said. "Sergeant Riley is not here to serve as our porter. Go fetch a stevedore."

When George was gone, Lafayette smiled at Riley. "You must excuse my son, Sergeant. He is unaware American sergeants hold a special place in my breast."

"How so, sir?"

Lafayette gazed out the window. But he was not seeing the bustling quay. He was looking at a skirmish line of redcoats emerging from a stand of trees.

***

Brandywine, Pennsylvania, September 11th, 1777

General Washington had arrayed his forces along the Brandywine River, its last line of defense if it were to prevent the capture of Philadelphia, the new nation's capital. British General William Howe's redcoats and Hessians had turned the Continental Army's flank and harassed its center. Units began to fall back in disorder, and General Washington tapped Lafayette to help steady the men. He rode into a scene of hellish pandemonium.

Smoke seemed to surround Lafayette as the *whizz* of lead filled his ears, almost drowning out the desperate voices of Brigadier General Thomas Conway's Third Pennsylvania Brigade, who began wavering and abandoning the line.

"Stand fast, boys!" Lafayette pointed his saber at the oncoming wave of crimson. "We must stop them here, or the Army is in danger!"

His leg suddenly snapped from under him like from a hammer blow, and he tumbled into the wet grass with blood staining his stockings.

"The marquis is hit!"

Lafayette was helped to his feet by a Pennsylvania sergeant. "Get over here, boys! We can't leave the marquis to the lobsters."

A few of the Pennsylvanians halted in their tracks and rejoined what remained of the line. Bayonets flashed as a file of British light infantry descended on them. The sergeant discharged a blast into one, ripping his guts from his body. A private swung his musket like a club, sending a pair of them fleeing.

Lafayette managed to regain his feet and retrieve his saber, which he slashed at a hungry enemy bayonet. "Away with you!"

While the British regrouped for another charge, the sergeant grabbed Lafayette and ushered him down the narrow path through the woods.

"Form division of companies and fall back in order," Lafayette commanded as the sergeant took him away.

Inspired by the young general's tenacity, the brigade's rear-guard companies had formed a cordon that ensured an orderly withdrawal.

The sergeant had him on a wagon with several other wounded officers sometime later. The pain from his wound hurt terribly, but Lafayette maintained a calm demeanor. Thanks to the gallant American whose name he never learned. He had survived his first test of battle.

Chapter 7

Packet Ship *Cadmus*

The lights of Le Havre began to fade as the *Cadmus* rounded *Cap la Havre*. The brisk channel gusts filled her sails with a sudden snap, and the wind's power now fully stressed timbers, which emitted a subtle creak.

Neall watched the marquis and his entourage strolling the deck. *They seem totally captivated by his repartee.*

Flynn had managed to gain employment as a porter, and the two used a series of dead drops on the ship to pass messages. Neall slid his hand under the fore lifeboat and found an envelope. He opened it and scanned its contents: a manifest of the ship's passengers.

Excellent work, Tommy!

Neall tucked the envelope into his waistcoat and strolled to his cabin. He lit a lamp, read the list, and then read it twice more to commit the names to memory, in addition to the marquis' entourage, a half dozen Americans, a Swiss diplomat, a Mister Pavlov, and *Senora* Carmen de Gioia. He was amused that Lafayette's mistress was not on the manifest.

Carmen de Gioia! Neall knew the last name as he was an opera buff. It would be good to have a celebrated opera singer on board. *Overall, nothing too suspicious.*

There was a sudden knock on his door. "Dinner is at seven, sir. Captain Allyn likes all his guests there."

***

The captain's table was large enough to seat half the guests, including Lafayette, his son, his secretary, the Swiss diplomat, an American banker, and *Senora* De Gioia. Neall managed to slip between the *senora* and the banker, Claude Barnes. Across from him were Lafayette, Captain Francis Allyn, and the Swiss diplomat.

After introductions, Captain Allyn stood and raised his glass. "I propose a toast to the Marquis de Lafayette. A true friend of America and liberty for all."

Glasses rose, and all stood.

"Hear, hear!" Neall said.

"To the marquis!" declared the Swiss.

"To Liberty!" proclaimed Barnes.

"To America!" said De Gioia.

Neall assessed the group as they conversed. He noted the Swiss diplomat's attention on the *senora*. Not that he could blame him. Her dark eyes, olive skin, and ample figure would attract any man.

The banker spent most of his conversation with Levasseur, peppering him with questions about the itinerary. "Will your party be visiting Virginia? I own two banks there — one in Alexandria, the other in Norfolk. I'd love to handle your banking while in America. No fees. It's the least I can do."

Levasseur shrugged. "I believe the American government will see to our expenses."

Barnes smiled patronizingly. "Yes, but in America, there are no government-owned banks. You'll need private banking to pay your bills and provide ready cash."

"If you say so, *Monsieur*," replied the secretary.

"Your manner of speaking is not that of a Virginian, Mister Barnes," Neall said.

"Very perceptive, Mister?"

"Locke, Raymond Locke."

The banker smiled. "My family changed its name from Bornstein. Barnes seemed simpler and more American. Better for business. And you?"

For a moment, Neall thought the banker realized Locke was a pseudonym. "Always Locke. But the e is silent, and I have toyed with dropping it."

Laughter filled the table.

Neall noticed a man at a nearby table listening to every word. *Curiosity? I think not.*

The Swiss banker wiped his mouth with a soft white napkin and looked up at Lafayette. "So, Marquis, tell us about your first voyage to America. Was it in as pleasant company as this?" He waved his hand at the guests.

Lafayette's eyes widened. He put down his knife and fork, and a whimsical look crossed his face. Then, a dark look.

"King Louis forbade my passage to America. I was under an interdict, for *Monsieur* Gravier did not want to offend the British, at least not yet." A smile crossed his face.

"Who is *Monsieur* Gravier?" Allyn asked.

"*Comte* de Vergennes. The French Foreign Minister. He ran the government for King Louis, who was, at heart, a simple soul."

"So, what did you do?" Carmen asked.

Lafayette gave her a knowing look and slid his hand over hers. "It was simple. I acquired a ship, *Victoire,* but my relatives and the government delayed me. I even feared arrest. However, our government secretly supported the Cause as early as

1776. So, I contrived for *Victoire* to sail to Spain and secretly load arms and munitions for America. I traveled separately and joined it at Pasaia on the Basque coast."

"How exciting!" Carmen gazed at him with evident admiration.

"Perhaps now. But for a feckless young idealist, it was a trifle. And the two-month voyage was a bore. Certainly, it lacked the charming company of this journey."

***

A crewman decked out as a waiter deposited brandy on the table. Lafayette glanced longingly at De Gioia and asked, "Could the lovely and talented soprano honor us with a song?"

She batted her eyes. "Of course. But without an orchestra or piano, it must be a *Siciliana*. And, of course, *a Cappella*.

As the gentlemen sniffed and sipped brandy, Carmen rose and strode to the center of the room. "A Siciliana is somber music. It hesitates. And portrays loss or longing-grief. This is from Mozart's, *Die Fledermaus*." She raised her eyes, closed them seductively, and began.

"*Ach, ich fühl's, es ist verschwunden…*"

When she finished, the room was silent. Neall noticed the man at the other table was gone, as was the banker, Barnes. Neall made his excuses and slipped out.

On deck, he passed Lynch, who seemed busily swabbing. "Down that gangway," he whispered.

At the far end was a door. He watched the stranger exit and swiftly push past him. Neall shoved the door open and found Mister Barnes indisposed.

"Food get to you as well, sir?" asked Barnes.

Neall nodded. "But on second thought, the railing might prove better."

On deck, Neall grasped the railing along the top of the gunwale. The stranger was there as well. Barnes exited the door and proceeded toward the guest cabins. The stranger waited a few moments and followed. Lynch was still swabbing. As Neall passed him by, Lynch barely looked at him but gave a subtle headshake.

***

The door to *Senora* de Gioia's cabin creaked, and heavy feet made the flooring squeak. Carmen was in a flimsy shift, removing her makeup.

Bear-like arms pulled her close, and plump lips wet her ear. "I was able to pour a vial into the marquis' brandy snifter while he was enthralled with your performance. I hope you mixed it properly."

Carmen spun about and pulled away from him. "Why did you tear me away from *la Scala* if you don't trust me?"

Buxhowden smiled. "I trust you. But Mister Barnes is a skeptic."

Carmen laughed. "You mean Mister Bornstein?"

54

He pulled her to him and sunk his face into her shift. She laughed and ran her hands through his hair. Although she found him physically ugly, he was a hard man for her to resist. She sometimes wondered if he had one of his spells placed on her.

"I thought this was reserved for the marquis?" she murmured.

"I just learned his mistress will join him soon after his arrival."

"So, I won't seduce him?"

"Maybe with your voice and your potion. We have one more night to ply him with your marvelous concoction. Then, you will provide the final dose at his first banquet in New York. For all the world to witness."

"For all the world to witness. How do we avoid capture?"

He lifted her in his arms. "Leave that to me."

***

Lynch made out only half of what the banker and the singer said. And from the non-verbals, they were lovers. The word potion struck him. He needed to inform Neall. He squeezed the gray water from the mop into his bucket and turned to leave. But standing before him was the banker Barnes.

"You were listening in on us. Eavesdropping. Why?"

"Just mopping, sir. My job, it is."

Lynch turned to leave as a mighty blow from Buxhowden's fist turned out his lights.

He awoke with his head swirling, his hands and feet bound, and a gag over his mouth. From the sweet, perfumy smell, he figured he was in the soprano's cabin. His mouth was dry as toast. *Sucker punched by a whore's son!*

His eyes opened to the singer stirring some sort of concoction.

"I hope you are thirsty. I made this special for you. It is aromatic and delicious and will make your head stop throbbing."

He shook his head.

She smiled seductively. "Drink, my sweet."

"How long have I been here? Where's the sod that pasted me?" He said the words, but they did not come out.

"Please drink. You have been sleeping. And don't bother trying to speak. You can't."

Lynch realized a potion followed the sucker punch to keep him out. And it rendered him incapable of coherent speech. *But why?*

There was a sudden rap at the door.

A ship's officer named Thompkins entered. "Pardon me, ma'am, but we are about to reach our dock. How's he doing?"

"He would do better if he'd drink this. He needs nourishment, dear fellow."

The officer wagged a finger at Lynch. "You're a lucky sailor to have *Madame* de Gioia nursing you. That fall would have killed most men. Thank God Mister Barnes happened to see it and summoned help."

Lynch suddenly ached all over. *They dropped me to fake a fall. Where was Neall? Of course, he can't acknowledge me without giving up the game.* He shook his head and pointed at Carmen, grunting as best he could.

"I must go now." The officer tipped his hat and stepped from the cabin.

***

Staten Island, New York, August 15th, 1824

Cadmus rocked gently off the quay. The passengers were to suffer one last meal as guests of Captain Allyn — the marquis' farewell.

Levasseur and Buxhowden lifted their whisky to their mouths.

"So, it is settled. You shall represent our finances, Monsieur Barnes. We'll tell the marquis all about it at the farewell banquet. Captain Allyn wants to honor him one last time."

"I'll need to sit near him to share details. Explain things."

"The marquis doesn't bother with details. That's why he took me along. But I'm sure he'll want you to sit with him."

Buxhowden nodded. "It would be my honor."

Around them, the guests were downing the final before-dinner beverages and shuffling to their seats. Buxhowden saw Lafayette was in a heated conversation with the captain. *There's the target.*

He watched as Carmen de Gioia took Lafayette's arm and gently guided him to his chair at the captain's table. It was agreed she would sit opposite their target and distract him while Buxhowden slipped the poison into his bowl when the soup course was served. He felt his waistcoat pocket to make sure the potion was there.

As soon as they were all seated, the waiters began to serve an appetizer of smoked fish soufflé. Buxhowden had purloined a copy of the menu and knew the soup was the third of a five-course meal. Dry white wine was poured.

He rarely made eye contact with Carmen, allowing her to focus her charms on the distinguished man across the table. The room hummed with banter as the wine flowed. After dinner, the passengers would gather things and depart the ship. Buxhowden had a tight timeline. Once he slipped the potion into the target's bowl, Carmen would excuse herself, never to return. He would depart for a toilette break. They would meet at the stern, where the First Officer had a skiff waiting to row them to another quay, where they would board a schooner bound for Cuba.

Then he noticed something odd. The insurance agent, Raymond Locke, was not at his seat — no time to check why. The waiters began delivering steaming bowls of soup. Barnes knew it was potato leek. Lafayette was explaining to Carmen why

France embraced and then shed itself of Napoleon. She leaned forward, generously exposing her ample cleavage, which had Lafayette's eye.

"So you see, a nation that fought all of Europe for twenty years and gave its most precious commodity, its young men, decided a king in peace was better than an emperor at war."

As Lafayette spoke, Buxhowden deftly moved his hand to remove a handkerchief from his waistcoat and, with the sleight of hand of a Persian magus or a Parisian street hustler, squeezed the vial within over the target's bowl. Then, he wiped his brow.

"You must expand on this, as most of Italy felt betrayed when he was deposed." She gave him her most beguiling smile. "But first, I must excuse myself."

As Carmen sauntered off, Lafayette turned to the captain and began to regale him with tales of his time in prison.

Now's my chance. Buxhowden slid from his chair and wiped his forehead with the handkerchief.

"Too much whisky before wine, *Monsieur* Barnes?" Levasseur chided.

"I think the fish souffle was too much for me."

As Buxhowden turned to leave, his ear caught Lafayette saying, "I don't know why chefs insist on inserting a soup course in meals. I came to detest soup. For many months in an Austrian prison, all they fed me was soup! Barley soup! Cabbage soup! Potato soup! Pshaw!"

A cyclone of thoughts coursed through Buxhowden. *The ploy failed.* As a professional, he knew not to improvise. Lafayette's journey would last over a year, and they could strike at another time and place. But first, he would crush the neck of the prisoner in Carmen's cabin and toss his carcass into the murky harbor waters.

***

Neall had searched every inch of the ship for Tom Lynch. He had jimmied the lock on nearly every cabin and searched the hold, kitchen, crews, and even the bilge. Only one place was left—the soprano's cabin. He had little time to waste if he were to return to the dinner on time.

One kick sent the door to splinters, and he bolted in to find a figure tied to the bunk—Lynch! Neall tore the gag from Lynch's mouth, slipped his knife from his belt, and sliced through the bonds.

"Are you all right?"

Lynch nodded and started to speak, but his tongue seemed unresponsive. His words were a stew of vowels and consonants, sounding like an infant.

"What have they done to you?"

Lynch took a deep breath and seemed to spit the word from his mouth, "Assassins!"

He knew Lynch had stumbled on the plot, the killers. This was her room. Carmen de Gioia was at the center. *But who else?*

"The singer did this? She must have an accomplice. Who else was here?"

Lynch's eyes widened in fear, and he babbled at Neall. A word gushed out at last. "Him!" Lynch pointed to a figure lurking behind Neall. As Neall turned, Buxhowden's massive fist plunged at him like an enraged musk ox, sending him crashing to the cabin floor.

"I don't have time to beat you like a drum, so I'll make it quick," Buxhowden roared.

Neall reached for his knife, but the large man stomped on his wrist, sending it across the floor.

He pulled Neall to his feet and shook him like a rag doll.

Then Lynch snapped out of his haze. "Let Mister Locke down, you bloody ape!"

Buxhowden tossed Neall aside like a doll, turned, and growled. "How did you recover from Carmen's potion? No matter, I'll crush you!"

Before he could finish his thought, Lynch whaled in on him with a barrage of blows. *Snap, snap,* sent his jaw turning. *Pop, pop* collapsed his belly.

Lynch slugged him relentlessly. But Buxhowden recovered from the onslaught and came at him like a wounded bear. His huge paws crashed in on Lynch's shoulders, collapsing him. The enraged Buxhowden reached for Lynch's neck, intent on snapping it.

Neall pulled himself on all fours and sprang for the lost dagger. Buxhowden saw the move and turned on Neall. But Neall retrieved it and, panther-like, pounced on Buxhowden, driving the blade deep into his chest.

Buxhowden's mouth opened as if to make a final statement but collapsed onto the soprano's bed.

Neall slipped the blade back into its sheath.

"I thought you were shark food. They said you had fallen, but when no one would admit where you were, I assumed it was overboard. Obviously, I could not show too much concern for a lost swab. Still, I must have searched every rat-infested inch of this hulk the last three days."

"It's the woman. She concocts potions that can numb ye or kill ye as she wills. They kept me dumb and senseless. I think one of the ship's officers is in on it, sir."

Searching Buxhowden revealed a polished silver coin with a three-headed eagle clutching a globe in its talons. The reverse had three crowns superimposed on each other, surrounded by the words *Aulic Concilio*.

"Pretty penny, this, sir," said Flynn. "But what does it mean, *Aulic Concilio*?"

Neall slipped the coin into his pocket. "It means this fellow was not Mister Barnes but an assassin sent by the Aulic Council."

"The what?"

"The operational arm of The Holy Alliance."

"The what?"

"No time to talk. If the soprano is his partner, the marquis's life is still in danger."

***

Murmurs filled the captain's mess. The buzz of heated conversation among the guests sounded like a bee hive. They were huddled in a corner while Francis Allyn, his first mate, his chef, and a pair of able-bodied seamen huddled over a corpse carefully laid out on the carpet.

A sick feeling went through Neall. *By God, I'm too late!*

He approached the captain, who stood between him and the body covered with a tablecloth.

"What is going on?" Neall asked, feeling stupid for the question.

Allyn's face grew grim. "Murder, I believe."

"Or bad soup," the first mate said.

"My soup was not bad," the chef protested. "Someone slipped poison into the marquis's bowl. No one else is sick!"

"Join the others, Mister Neall," ordered Allyn.

"I'm an agent of the firm that underwrites your ship, Captain. Affairs such as this are subject to a claim. A claim I must investigate."

Allyn nodded at the first mate, who slipped the makeshift shroud from the victim's body. The eyes stared wildly, and the corpse's hands gripped its neck as if it were trying desperately to breathe.

Neall was stunned. "It's not the marquis!"

"No. The marquis loathes soup, so he passed his bowl to the Swiss diplomat, who loves it," the first mate said.

"Loved it," Allyn said. "I have notified the New York harbor authorities, who are sending police and a doctor to examine the body."

"Well, one of the would-be assassins is dead. His body is in *Senora* de Gioia's room," Neall said. "She is the poisoner, and her partner was Mister Barnes, who I think the police will find is not Mister Barnes. I'm also afraid one of your officers is involved."

Allyn turned to the first mate. "Where is Mister Thompkins?"

"He was taking the skiff across the harbor to purchase items. You don't think?"

"The schemers tied up one of your crew after he overheard them plotting. She drugged him with a potion, and they faked a fall."

"Thompkins found him, sir," the first mate said. "I'm sorry. He convinced me to keep it quiet so as not to alarm anyone. Said he'd find a safe and comfortable place to recover."

"That would be *Senora* de Gioia's chambers," Neall said. "She's likely absconded with your officer."

Allyn grew agitated and glared at the first mate. "I'll deal with you later. Meanwhile, we need to alert the port authorities."

"You should. But I suspect the soprano and her new accomplice are heading somewhere that does not conform to international norms."

Chapter 8

The Chancery, Baltimore, Maryland

Brother Bernard pulled back the weighty sleeve of his cassock and carefully slid the blade along the seam of the envelope. "There seems to be more than paper in this message from Mister Neall, Your Eminence."

Bishop Maréchal leaned forward and rubbed his hands, anxious in anticipation. "What could it be?"

"A coin," Bernard declared. He raised the silver piece to the lamplight. "I have only seen one of these before." He handed it to Maréchal and pored over the report from Neall.

"Does the report explain this odd medallion?" Maréchal handed the coin back to Bernard.

"He found it on the body of a man he killed—an agent of The Holy Alliance."

"Killed!"

"There was an attempt on the marquis's life by an agent of the Alliance. At Staten Island, of all places. I've actually been to Staten Island, although decades ago."

"Where on Staten Island?"

"On board the marquis's ship, the *Cadmus*. Seems our agent had a female accomplice, *Senora* Carmen de Gioia."

"The famed soprano? Of *la Scala*?"

Bernard rubbed the coin. "The very same. Neall believes she concocted a potion that the agent, who called himself Barnes, administered at a dinner, unsuccessfully, thanks be to God."

They both made the sign of the cross.

"The pair captured one of Neall's agents, and when Neall found him, there was a struggle, which Neall ended with a dagger to the soprano's accomplice."

"I'll pray for his soul. What else does he report?"

"The lady escaped with an officer of the *Cadmus*. Likely she seduced him with her potions or her charms."

"We'll soon see what the newspapers say about this."

"No, Eminence. Mister Neall has arranged to hush this up. The passengers and crew are sworn to silence, and he has reached out to Mick Flynn to arrange things with the papers."

"So, we have succeeded."

Bernard rubbed the coin with his thumb. "I don't believe so, Your Eminence."

The bishop pursed his lips. "Why not?"

He handed the coin back to the bishop. "These three eagles represent the three members of the Holy Alliance: Austria-Hungary, Prussia, and Russia. Only one of the three eagles has tried to sink its talons into the marquis."

"What shall we do?"

"I am hoping *Madame* Bonaparte can help us."

"That's not funny, Brother. Miss Patterson was Napoleon's victim. A victim we exploited. We owe her respect."

Bernard straightened his sleeve. "I stand corrected, Your Eminence. Of course, Miss Patterson is a wonderful and gracious lady." He could not tell his bishop he once had a close connection to the lady. Only his confessor knew of that.

"What next?"

"Mister Buchanan just provided me with a partial itinerary. Unfortunately, it will be released in the newspapers in a few days. General Lafayette will spend most of August in New England but will be back in New York by the first week of September."

"And then?"

Bernard scanned a paper on his desk. "Let me see. Late September has him on a journey south through Philadelphia and Washington before traveling to Virginia."

"That is a lot of traveling to provide protection through. What do you propose?"

"Some prayers will help."

"And in the non-spiritual realm?"

"I am asking Mister Neall to cover the northern journey. Lieutenant Putnam will make arrangements here. Neall is also going to reveal himself to the marquis's bodyguard. A Marine sergeant from the Paris embassy named Riley. Riley needs to understand there is still a threat graver than a soprano with a beaker of laudanum."

***

The Battery Hotel, New York City, August 19th, 1824

Neall sat in the corner of the lobby with a newspaper held before him. His eyes scanned the large room with its vaulted ceilings and smooth, deep green paneled walls. He watched Lynch enter the lobby and casually stroll into the dark barroom to the left.

After waiting the five minutes agreed upon, Neall folded the paper under his arm and strolled into the dark bar filled with bad piano music and acrid smoke, which cloaked the equally bad singers. But he soon found Riley sitting at the end of the bar. Neall slid quietly onto the stool beside Riley and placed his paper on the bar.

"Whisky, please," he said to the barman. "And one for my friend."

"We are headed north tomorrow," Riley said as he stared straight ahead, checking the scene behind them through the mirror.

"How's Catullus holding up?" asked Neall. Catullus was the nickname Brother Bernard had selected for Lafayette. Neall was pleased to learn he and the Brother liked Latin poetry, although he was surprised the monk favored a poet known for sensual writing.

There is more to Brother Bernard than meets the eye. When this Lafayette affair was over, Neall decided he would investigate Bernard and his American secret service that no one admitted to.

"Seems fine. After all, Catullus survived years of warfare fighting for the Cause. Was wounded too. Then, all the craziness in France and their revolution and wars. Plus, years in prison followed by some interesting political fluctuations."

"His time in prison may have saved his life," Neall said, remembering his distaste for soup. "The soprano is at large, so watch who gets near his vittles."

"I could if he were one of my marines. And there is some news. He has a doxie, it seems. Well, a mistress. British, too."

Neall's eyes widened. "You have my attention, sir."

"Scottish lass named…."

"Fanny Wright. Is she here?"

"Arriving shortly. Son isn't too happy about it, of course. She's pretty, they say, and decades younger than him."

Neall was not happy with the complication of a woman joining the entourage. His mind filled with the implications.

Neall sipped at his whisky, but Riley threw back his head and downed it.

"Any indication we have an inside man?" Neall asked.

"No. I don't like any of them particularly, but they seem genuine lovers of Catullus and what he stands for."

"And what does he stand for?"

"Freedom, a better world, and the rights of men. And in some ways, he stands for America. The new America."

"New?"

Riley's eyes narrowed. "Look, sir. I don't want to cross with you, but America is not the same collection of Englishmen who rebelled fifty years ago. It's expanding westward. More non-English are arriving here every month. Germans, French, and such. But mostly Irish. We'll be more than a nation in a few decades."

"More than a nation?"

"Isn't England more than a nation? America will be a continent."

"Won't the Spanish and Russians have something to say about that?"

Riley smiled gently, and his eyes twinkled, but he did not reply.

Neall's eyes roved Riley's waistcoat and pockets. "Are you armed? What kind of weapon are you carrying?"

"Embassy wouldn't let me take my fusil on this mission. But I have these." Riley's hand slipped into his pocket and emerged wearing a wicked-looking set of brass knuckles made of polished steel with four barbs covering them.

"How do you take out a sniper? Or fend off a saber or knife?" Neall laughed.

"If the first shot doesn't get me, I'll be pounding on the shooter in a moment. And I've fended off many knives with these." Riley softly stroked the barbs.

"Where? How?"

"At Tripoli. It was August. Hot as a furnace but surrounded by gleaming blue water. The harbor swarmed with Algerian gunboats. I was just sixteen. Barely a marine private, they attached me to Captain Stephen Decatur's ship. I was the only marine with him."

"I read something of it in the papers."

"The papers don't give you the sounds — cannons roaring out a terrible fire — the non-stop crack of muskets and the sting of lead balls. Black smoke so thick you could chew on it. The stench. The war cries of angry men and the terrified screams of the dying."

"What did you do?"

"The battle was at its peak when a ship pulled up, and the commander told Decatur his brother had died when a surrendering ship turned on him. Decatur was a hard-ass on a good day. This news sent him roaring at the sky and our vessel in hot pursuit.

"When we pulled up on the Tripolitan ship, Decatur sprang over the gunwale, swinging his cutlass. A midshipman and I were right behind him. A giant Tripolitan captain, large as an ox and angrier than a bull, charged him with a spear as large as a flag pole. Decatur blocked the stroke but broke his cutlass.

"I saw one of our officers taking a blow intended for the captain, who had his hands full with the hulking Tripolitan commander. I saw a long dagger coming down on Decatur, but the captain drew his pistol and shot the big Turk dead. Mad as hornets, his crew rushed us with war cries I can't repeat but still make my blood curl.

"We stood shoulder to shoulder as their bare feet padded across the blood-stained deck. I emptied my fusil into the onrushing Turks. That's what we called the Barbary corsairs. But behind him came two more. I thrust my bayonet into one, but the other slashed my side with his curved sword. My fusil slipped from my hands. I tried to draw my short sword, but he was on me before I could reach it.

64

"I dodged his next slash and pulled these babes from my pocket. I slugged him so hard that his face collapsed. I spun around to face three more. Before I could think, I had leaped at them, swinging these in a frenzy. I tore open flesh and crunched bone and was going for more when a sailor pulled me off the last one. Their ship had surrendered."

"The horrors of combat constantly challenge its glory for control of our beings," Neall said. "Anything else?"

"Just this: I'm done with the trappings and festivities of this city. I'm looking forward to visiting America's countryside and small towns."

Neall slapped a coin on the bar. "Have another on me. And keep your eyes peeled and your brass knuckles ready."

***

Tammany Hall, New York, September 1st, 1824

Neall sipped the whisky but declined the dark, torpedo-like roll of tobacco offered by Micky Flynn.

"I see from the newspapers that Frenchie is having quite the time in New England. My boys could barely keep up with him in Westchester. There are two or three daily stops, plenty of speeches, and handshaking. Of course, he's on his own in New England."

"Your State Department has a marine sergeant guarding him. He seems pretty good."

"Oh yes, that would be Sergeant Riley. Dan grew up near Five Points. So I suppose, in a way, I suppose we are covering him in New England." Flynn took a puff of his cigar and filled the room with smoke.

"Any word on the woman?"

"Oh, his gal and her sis were sticking pretty close but are back in the city now."

"I meant Carmen de Gioia."

"No."

Somehow, Neall did not believe him. He had a real sense that the Albany Regency was only half supportive of the effort. *Not enough money or graft for you.*

"Well, please have your men at the docks pay extra attention. She may not have left the city. All she needs is to figure out which restaurants are feeding the marquis when he is in town."

"Sure thing. Let me know if I can get anything for you while you're in my town — booze, steaks, girls. Whatever."

"Just keep looking for the soprano — and any other suspicious foreigners."

"Like the one sitting before me?" Flynn broke into peals of laughter.

Neall did not allow the barb to ruffle him.

"The Holy Alliance has three teams of killers on the hunt for the marquis. It would not bode well for your city and your political cronies if one of them succeeds in your town."

***

Bolton, Massachusetts, September 2nd, 1824

The clatter of hooves and rumble of wheels rattled Riley's ears. A score of blue-clad dragoons lined either side of the carriage, and the torches spitting flames on either side of the entrance to the estate cast their shadows along the road. Riley was impressed by the show of force but thought such large numbers brought confusion and made it easier for a determined killer to strike.

"Who do we visit, *Monsieur?*" Riley asked.

"An old friend, Sampson Stoddard Wilder," replied Lafayette. "He convinced Mayor Quincy that he would be able to provide us suitable accommodations."

"And keep us on our schedule," said Levasseur.

Lafayette waved a hand dismissively. Riley knew he disliked tight schedules, which resulted from his years following those set by his Austrian jailers.

"Your friend is quite well-off," Riley remarked.

"He made his fortune in France but saw fit to take it to this fair land. So that makes him wise as well as well-off."

The carriage rolled under an arch over the front gate.

"What are the words inscribed on the arch, Sergeant Riley?"

Riley squinted. "*The Sword of Jehovah, of Washington, and Lafayette.*"

Lafayette sighed. "Too kind."

The large entrance of the mansion was aflame with torches that made the black night seem like noon. They stepped from the carriage, and Sampson Wilder leaped from his horse and pointed at the assembled militia. "These are the Bolton Guards, who, in your honor, renamed themselves the Lafayette Guards."

"I want to inspect them and ensure they are fit to provide security for the night," said Riley.

Wilder motioned toward their commander. "I think their colonel can...."

"Mister Riley is an American marine in charge of my security."

The colonel bowed at Lafayette and Riley. "Say no more, *Monsieur.*"

They entered the parlor, where servants greeted them with trays of refreshing sherbet.

"I do not drink, so I'm afraid there will be no wine this evening," explained Wilder. "I wanted to offer you your own house for the night, but I thought the mansion was better since you need to depart early."

"My own house?" Lafayette replied.

66

"An agreeable wooden cottage. Quite roomy and well-appointed. Too late and too far tonight. But I'll point it out on the way out tomorrow. It's nestled in a small wood. I built it as a refuge for *L'Empereur*.

Lafayette looked aghast. "Napoleon?"

"I once had hoped he would escape to America and be my guest until other arrangements could be made. You know I am a supporter."

Lafayette stroked his chin pensively. "As are many. As was I. I tried to save the nation as a sovereign republic. But things changed."

"The king returned," said Wilder.

"Thanks to the machinations of Fouche and some disingenuous Marshals of France," said Levasseur.

"And the Allied powers," said Lafayette. "Let us not forget."

Lafayette knew he would never forget.

***

Chamber of Representatives, Paris, June 21st, 1815

The great hall echoed with the murmurs of a score of heated conversations. The Secretary of the Chamber, France's nominal legislative body, called the assembly to order. "The esteemed leader of the Liberal Party has requested the floor. He says it is a matter of some urgency…."

Lafayette rose and paused as he scanned the faces before him and finalized his thoughts. He had worked hard to support Napoleon Bonaparte when he thought he was in the right and even harder against him when he believed him wrong. Recent reporting from a confidential contact in Napoleon's Cabinet Council confirmed suspicions that the emperor planned to seize dictatorial powers and force the Chamber to grant them. If he were to stop it, Lafayette had to act boldly.

"Representatives! For the first time in many years, you hear a voice that the old friends of liberty will yet recognize. I rise to address you concerning the dangers to which the country is exposed. The sinister reports circulated during the last two days are unhappily confirmed. This is the moment to rally around the national colors — the Tricolored Standard of 1788 — the standard of liberty, equality, and public order. It is you alone who can now protect the country from foreign attacks and internal dissensions. It is you alone who can secure the independence and the honor of France.

"Permit a veteran in the sacred cause of liberty, in all times a stranger to the spirit of faction, to submit to you some resolutions which appear to him to be demanded by a sense of the public danger and by the love of our country. They are such as I feel persuaded, you will see the necessity of adopting."

Lafayette went on to say the Chamber must declare the nation's independence menaced and that its sessions were now permanent — and opposition to it was treason. He praised the Army of the Line and the National Guard for bravery and

67

devotion to France. The general called for the rearming of the Parisian National Guard and charged it with the defense of the representative government. And he invited the Ministers of War, Foreign Affairs, Police, and the Interior to sit in the Chamber.

An uproar rolled through the Chamber, and Lafayette's proposals were immediately accepted. As the Secretary's gavel pounded, Lafayette surveyed the room and took stock of what he had just done.

I have just put the saber to the Empire, but perhaps it will save the nation and its democratic institutions.

***

Sturbridge, Massachusetts, September 3rd, 1824

Voices strained as each singer strove to deliver the best hymn ever. The choirmaster, Reverend Blake, lifted his hands and then dropped them in a flourish as the last notes drifted to the church ceiling.

Nancy Keating closed her leather-bound hymnal and turned to her friend Felicity White. "I'm so excited the mayor chose us to sing for the marquis. I haven't slept in two days."

Felicity grinned mischievously. "I wonder what he looks like. I've never seen a French officer. I hope he's handsome!"

"I bet he's old," replied Nancy, feeling just a pinch of jealousy. She had a crush on the gallant French nobleman since she read of him when she was just ten. But the reality was sinking in that he was older than her papa. Much older.

"I read in the broadsheet that he has a son! I bet he's handsome. And younger."

"Now, singers, we have fifteen minutes until our guest arrives — time to troop out to the green and wait," announced Blake.

They assembled on the green with scores of other onlookers. Folks from every farmstead between Sturbridge and the surrounding villages stretching as far as Southbridge.

Nancy looked at the crowd with great interest. She had wanted to teach grade school and write music, but people always fascinated her. The townsfolk were dressed for Sunday church while the farmers arrived as if right from the fields in homespun. Most of the women wore pretty white dresses and gloves. The men sported dark suits and freshly polished shoes.

"They say Sturbridge is his twelfth stop in two days!" Felicity exclaimed. "He's been through Newburyport, Boston, Cambridge, Lexington, and Concord."

"Of course, Lexington and Concord, silly. Those were the start of the war. He's also been through Bolton, Lancaster, Sterling, West Boylston, Worcester, Leicester, and Charlton. Now, he'll soon be here."

Felicity elbowed her gently. "You are always the smart one. I could never remember so many names. My older sister has a beau in Worcester. I may get to visit there someday."

"This is his last stop in Massachusetts. From here, he continues south through Connecticut and then back to New York."

"All roads lead to New York," Felicity said.

Nancy eyed her. "Not Boston?" She knew Felicity had a crush on a cousin in Boston.

Felicity's pale cheeks turned rose.

The cry soon ran through the assembled crowd. "Here they come! Here they come!"

Reverend Blake raised a hand to prepare the choir as the street seemed to shake with the pounding of hooves and rumble of wheels that had seen too many miles.

Nancy pushed dark curls from her oval face. Her blue eyes twinkled with excitement as a pair of dust-caked coaches screeched to a halt. The mayor said something indistinguishable, and the Sturbridge town band played "*La Marseillaise*," followed by the very popular American tune, "General Washington's March."

After much clapping and cheering, Blake's hands went into motion, and the choir belted out its best rendition of *Amazing Grace*. When the reverend's hands made their final move and the last syllable was sung, the town folk were still with reverence and wonder.

A middle-aged man climbed the small wooden platform and greeted the throng in perfect English.

Felicity tugged Nancy's arm. "It's his son, George Lafayette!"

Lafayette's son spoke of his love of Washington and America—and his father, weaving the three in a mosaic that touched all. When he finished, an erect and impeccably dressed man in his sixties joined him.

The crowd burst into a frenzy of cheers, the likes of which Nancy had never heard in the quiet, almost silent village. "He hasn't even spoken yet."

Felicity giggled.

Lafayette began to speak when the town folk grew quiet, thanking the mayor and citizens for their warmth and friendship. He told of America as he knew it and saw it as a model for the world. When his words turned to George Washington, his eyes welled with tears.

"He was more than a father to me. I was more than a son to him. I joined his service a feckless boy and finished a man—a man of the people!"

Felicity whispered to Nancy, "I think his son is looking at me. And his father at you!"

Nancy said nothing. Lafayette had locked his eyes on her for a moment. But then they rose and gazed into the distance as though he were looking at something beyond time and space.

As the speech finished, Felicity ran forward with arms outstretched toward Georges, and the rest of the townfolk erupted in huzzahs as they followed in a wave that swarmed the general and his entourage. The carriage doors slammed shut, and the coachmen touched the lines, sending the horses bolting down the street in a cloud of dust.

Nancy and Felicity sighed as the wheels rumbled down the road.

A collective sadness overcame the crowd, slowly returning to the mundane world they inhabited. Each seemed to realize this was the most significant moment in their lives. The last great hero of the War for Independence had visited their humble town. He had seen them and embraced who they were and what they stood for. And now it was over.

***

Dark eyes peered down on the crowd angrily as the rifle's hammer clicked back into place. This was the place and time to send a ball into the marquis's breast. But a silly girl rushed to greet the son, and others swarmed the platform, denying a kill shot.

I would have had him!

He let his hand stroke the smooth wood of the rifle's stock. Aulic Council agents had stolen plans from the English-American artist and inventor Joshua Shaw. Then, skilled Tyrolean gunsmiths engineered it to perfection. The sniper slid a gloved hand across the side-by-side barrels and down the elephant walnut butt of the specially-made weapon. With expressly designed grooves and front and rear adjustable sights, the rifle was modified to kill men from a distance — and not just in wartime.

The shooter tucked the rifle into a bag and slipped down the back stairs to the horse tethered behind the church. He leaped into the saddle and galloped south, hoping there was a suitable venue where he could make another attempt.

Chapter 9

Brooklyn Narrows, September 8th, 1824

Choppy waves slapped the prow of the longboat, making the crew struggle with the oars. Ahead lay a small land mass, Hendrick's Reef, with scattered scrub trees and a squat diamond-shaped fortification recently renamed "Fort Lafayette" in honor of the great Revolutionary War hero.

A fleet of pleasure boats, ferries, and a squadron of naval vessels bobbed in the fast-moving waters of the Brooklyn Narrows, the inlet between lower New York Bay and the Upper Bay, both estuaries of the Hudson River.

The longboat's passengers included Lafayette's entourage plus Mayor Stephan Allen of New York. Sergeant Dan Riley sat near the coxswain with eyes peeled for suspicious activity.

Riley noted with amusement that Lafayette's indifference to timetables and spontaneous movement changes would vex any stalker. Several times over the past few days, he thought he spotted something lurking—a public itinerary made tracking the marquis easy for a would-be assassin.

A blue and white pennant on a small sloop from the Brooklyn Navy Yard fluttered against the stiff breeze. A smile crossed his lips when he saw a marine on the main mast with a musket cradled across his arms —*only the best to protect you, Marquis.*

A *thump* shivered the boat as it hit the wooden dockside. A platoon from New York's militia regiment stood rigidly as an honor guard, and a band from the local coast artillery struck up *"La Marseillaise."*

Lord, am I tired of that tune. Riley suddenly felt a tingle at the back of his neck. He had felt that tingle before, and it always meant no good. *Where is Mister Neall?*

The mayor began his introductory speech, citing Lafayette's contributions to America's and the world's liberty. He droned on with a laundry list of achievements and then thanked the numerous business, academic, and political note-worthies who were there to pay homage.

"And, of course, we stand on a distinct patch of land—America's first line of defense against a foreign foe. This island and this fort are named Lafayette to honor our distinguished friend and to deter an enemy, for the name Lafayette is synonymous with victory over tyranny!" Allen extended his arms toward Lafayette, who seemed to stammer a *merci beaucoup.*

The marquis's shoes clattered as he crossed the rigged platform, and his hands firmly pressed Allen's.

Lafayette turned his gaze toward New Jersey, took in the array of ships, and thrust his head forward to address the crowd silently awaiting him.

"*Citoyens!* American friends, it seems that I only rode the hills, fields, and valleys of your Jerseys yesterday. Sometimes at the head of gallant soldiers, sometimes alongside dedicated officers. Always, it was the sincerest wish of His Excellency, General George Washington, to throw the Continental Army at New York and Long Island.

"Not just to drive out the British occupiers but to bring the citizens from captivity and return America's most important lands to the nation's bosom."

Hats flew into the air, and men cheered, whistled, and whooped in appreciation. It never ceased to amaze Riley how the older man could melt a crowd or send them into a frenzy of delight with just a few phrases and a French accent.

"But the Royal Navy owned the water, and its guns provided the bulwark preventing such a gallant and righteous endeavor. So it doubly pleases me to see an American navy now fully possesses this harbor and an American fort guarding its entrance."

The crowd roared, and the band began to play "Yankee Doodle."

Riley's eyes scanned the crowd and wandered toward the water, where a small whaleboat slid into view. His eyes narrowed in on it. He squinted, then blinked. A dark figure rose at the bow and lifted a long rifle, snapping it into his shoulder, and the hammer clicked to full cock. Riley had no time to think. His legs sprang like coils, and he was on the marquis as the dull *crack of a rifle* cut through the music.

***

Tammany Hall

Neall's highly polished boots echoed through the hallway, which seemed like a tunnel to hell. A servant, who looked more like a guard, turned the brass lever, and the heavy wooden door swung open. Neall choked on a cloud of tobacco smoke and the smell of men who had not washed in a fortnight.

"We're just finishing lunch, Mister Neall. Help yourself to a porkchop, and we'll get you a beer," said Flynn, licking fat from his thick fingers.

"No, thank you. Well, maybe the beer."

Someone slapped a tankard of frothing beer into his hand, and he ushered him into a stiff-backed chair. Neall eyed Flynn as he took a sip. *Pisswater.*

"I'm glad you could come." Flynn waved a hand, and his cronies scattered.

The door slammed shut.

"Your note said this was urgent. I should be with the marquis. He's speaking on his island. Nice, you Americans named a piece of ground for him."

"Your girl may have been sighted."

Neall stiffened and nodded. *Finally, a breakthrough.* "Go on, sir."

"Well, she's a singer, ya see. So, I thought she'd know some singers here in the city. Seek them out. So, I had the boys check every place in town: playhouses, auditoriums, and saloons. At first, we found nothing, but then I realized the connection we needed wasn't singing. The soprano is Italian."

"Sicilian," Neall corrected.

"Sicilian is Italian, right? Anyway, one of my guys has contacts with the Italian fishmongers by the docks. A beautiful woman with a full figure was seen a few times. And get this — in the company of a man of military age."

Neall was impressed. "Excellent news. Did your man round them up?"

"No."

"Where are they?"

"At a hotel on MacDougall Street."

"Well, let's get some of your boys and have a go."

Minutes later, a carriage rumbled along cobblestoned streets, turned up MacDougall, and screeched to a halt. Two of Flynn's biggest toughs sat across from Neall and Lynch.

"You take the back, Jimmy," the older one said. "I'll go in the front with Mister Neall."

"You cover us and watch the street," Neall told Lynch.

"Aye, sir."

The older man grinned. "You ain't no English diplomat, are you, sir?"

"I was in the army once," Neall replied.

"Thought so."

They entered a four-story dark brick townhouse and found a tawny-haired sixteen-year-old boy at the hallway desk. "May I help you, sirs?"

"We are looking for a foreign lady, Italian-looking. Elegant dresser. Possibly with a gentleman," Neall said.

"Well, I don't know."

Flynn's tough snatched a fistful of the tawny hair and lifted the boy across the desk. A heavy left hand smacked him, and he dropped to the tiled floor, flopping like a fish."

He turned and smiled at Neall. "The trick is not to break anything like teeth or bones — the first time."

The boy curled into a ball as a mud-splattered brogan thudded into his stomach.

"Oof… She left! They left!"

"When?" Neall asked.

"I don't remember exactly. Maybe last night. Maybe early this morning. I wasn't on shift."

The brogan lowly pressed the boy's neck flat against the onyx-colored tile.

"No!" he screamed, whimpering, "They left at midnight. Said something about meeting a boat is all I know."

"What pier?" asked Neall. "I don't have much time."

"South Street Pier."

"Catching a boat to Brooklyn," said the old tough.

"Or Lafayette Island."

***

Lafayette Island, Brooklyn, New York

The band's last tune trailed off as several dignitaries pulled Riley from Lafayette's prone body. Murmurs flowed through the crowd. Something had happened, but no one knew quite what.

"There was a rifle trained on you, sir," stammered Riley. "Stay low, and I'll see what it is. Keep him covered," Riley glanced at Levasseur and George. "Act like it was a pratfall."

Riley glanced toward the whaleboat, but it was slipping over the waves of the lower bay. He saw the sloop coming about to pursue it. Riley's eyes rose to the topmast, where the marine reloaded his musket. A shiver and a feeling of pride went through him. A brother leatherneck had saved the marquis — or maybe him.

"I think it's clear now. The ceremony can continue." Riley's finger got in the mayor's face. "The marquis's valet stumbled into him. Make sure that's all that gets into the papers."

***

The .69 caliber lead ball hit its mark, and the sniper's rifle tumbled to the whaleboat's deck.

"Get us out of here," the shooter exclaimed. "Hard to port and heave with all you've got!"

Strong hands gripped the oars, the crew straining muscles with each tug. They had the vessel sliding over waves as it turned toward Staten Island. The shooter grimaced as Carmen staunched the blood with her perfumed kerchief.

Another *crack* sent another ball at the whaleboat, but it splashed harmlessly behind the stern.

"Keep up the pace, boys! The wind is against them, and the sloop is too far from us to launch longboats," said Millard Thompkins.

"You are fearless, Millard. I like that in a man," said Carmen. She tied the wound and softly stroked his hand. "You will have another chance soon enough."

"I hope so. I need the money to buy my own ship."

Thompkins was a former light infantryman—an expert shot who saw much action against the British in the late war. Thompkins liked his work but realized he could make more money at sea. He entered the American Naval Service as a Petty Officer in charge of the rigging and earned renown for training his sailors to snipe from the masts like marines. The war's end saw him sign up with a merchant ship and soon became a ship's mate.

"Alexander was wise to recruit you to the Council, *Cara Mia*."

Two more shots came their way, but Thompkins now realized they had made their escape. His dark eyes narrowed as he glared at Lafayette Island fading in the distance. "I still need to prove my worth."

***

Lafayette paced the hotel room as he and Neall talked. Levasseur and George were downstairs at the bar. Riley stood by the window, peering through heavy damask drapes and eyeing the street below. Lafayette's valet poured their brandy and quietly closed the door behind him.

"Your next few days keep you local, *Monsieur*," said Neall. "That makes you easier to protect and for this shooter to find you. What do you think, Sergeant Riley?"

"I think wherever the marquis travels, he'll face danger. I spoke with the marine who took out the sniper. His shot struck the hand, so the sniper is still at large. He also noticed a woman lurking on the boat."

"A woman! That might have affected his shot, *n'est ce pas?*" Lafayette quipped with a wink.

"Yes, General," Riley said. "Quite good-looking. Course, to marines, all women are good-looking."

"Our soprano, I'm sure," Neall said.

"*La belle chanteuse?* I thought she specialized in deadly potions?"

"Apparently, she just specializes in deadly, *Monsieur*," Neall replied.

"Treachery," said Lafayette. "It seems my life has been witness to treachery."

***

Monmouth Court House, New Jersey, June 28th, 1778

The heat and humidity seemed to dull the senses and the sounds. Puffs of smoke began to cloud the far end of the green fields to their front. The occasional cannon boom and the increasing *pop* of musket fire blotted out shouts of angry and frightened men.

The regiments ahead seemed to scatter, with bands of men retreating more rapidly than the desultory fire they were receiving from the British rear guard.

Lafayette's spyglass fell from his eye, and his lips were pursed in anger and thought. "Something is wrong, gentlemen. General Lee has enough men to punish the English rear guard even if it has been reinforced."

A fast rider galloped up, his horse frothing. "Sir, the British are appearing in numbers. Several of our regiments have pulled back. General Lee wants an orderly retreat."

"Were I still in command, we would stand firm and counter this attack," said Lafayette.

But he was not. After his initial appointment to lead the advance guard against the British retreating across Jersey, General Charles Lee, who had declined the command, insisted on reclaiming it at the last minute. As Lee was the senior officer, General Washington had no choice but to agree. Lafayette wondered why an officer who argued against a strong attack on the British would insist on leading it. After all, British dragoons captured Lee in December 1776, and rumors of his cooperation while in custody abounded. Lafayette could not abide rumor, an innuendo, but perhaps?

Lafayette turned to an officer. "Go find General Washington and inform him his steady hand is needed at the front."

The summons saved the day. Washington took charge himself and led an hours-long series of firefights that filled the heavy air with dark smoke. By dark, General Lee had left the Continental Army, and the Continental Army had shed its legacy of retreat and ignominy. At dawn, the British regulars had ceded the field.

***

Chancery Annex, Baltimore, Maryland, September 1824

Brother Bernard rubbed his fingers in a vain attempt to stop the scratchy itch in his eyes. He wiped the teardrops with a handkerchief and readjusted his spectacles.

Even with sunlight, this becomes an increasing struggle.

The reports from New York disturbed him. But those from Europe even more. The Berlin, Vienna, and Saint Petersburg papers printed increasingly strident articles attacking President Monroe's letter to Congress and Lafayette's celebrated visit.

But most disturbing to him, he learned through a confidential correspondent in Paris that The Holy Alliance might have recruited agents in America, perhaps within the government.

Bernard stared out the window and watched the ships sail up the Patapsco River in the warm Indian summer light. *Things should be clearer.*

He knew he needed to warn the Circle. He dipped his nib into an ink well and began a series of short notes.

A *knock* on the door broke his concentration. "Come in."

Betsy Patterson slightly lifted her dress and stepped through the doorway. She said nothing but quietly approached him, lifted his hands to hers, and softly kissed them. "I was hoping to find you alone, Brother."

"I was hoping not," replied Bernard. "Something about the near occasion of sin." She smiled and plopped into a seat. "I could use a drink."

Nodding, he rose, retrieved a wine glass, and filled it with red liquid.

She received the glass with a grateful glance. "Thank you."

Bernard poured himself several fingers of whisky, took a sip, and raised the glass to her. "No regrets, but no looking back."

"Perhaps that should be the Lafayette Circle's motto. No, what we once had was special to me. God knows I have had so many less-than-special things in my life."

"How is your son?" he asked.

"Bo finished Harvard Law School but declined to sit for the Bar. I hope he finds himself."

A soft smile crossed Bernard's lips. "He will, *Madame* Bonaparte."

"He often asks of you, Maurice. I think he thought we would marry."

"No father could replace the one he never had."

"Jerome would have been, or is, a terrible father. You would have been a brilliant father. But the war, your work, my work."

"You were my best spy, *Madame* Bonaparte."

"And you were my best lover."

He knew that was mere flattery. "But now I have taken vows, and you?"

"I vowed never to fall in love again, certainly not twice with the same man. Oh, do not worry. I'm not here to seduce a monk."

"An old monk who seems to be losing the battle against time and gravity." He saw she did not understand his meaning.

"I just wanted you to know Richard and I were once lovers, and his appearance here in Baltimore rekindled old flames."

He did not tell her he suspected as much. As she spoke, the flush to her face revealed her unrestricted beauty. "And why not? You are still the most beautiful woman at thirty-nine than most at twenty-nine — in Baltimore and the nation."

Peals of laughter. "Are you flirting, Maurice?"

"No." But he knew he was. "Have you anything for me?"

"Now I know you are flirting. Oh, work-wise, yes."

"You have my attention, *Madame*."

"Are you familiar with The Albany Regency?"

This should prove interesting. "A little. It's a powerful machine controlling New York Democratic politics, right?"

She nodded. "Do you know William Marcy?"

"Now you have my attention, *Madame*. I knew him as a New York Militia officer during the 2nd War against England."

"And he's now a well-connected New York politician and member of the Regency, originally dubbed The Holy Alliance," she said.

"Go on, please."

"Marcy recently remarried, and I am good friends with his new wife. She was in town, and we had lunch. I used the occasion to solicit information. Old habits die hard."

"They do, indeed."

"She overheard discrete conversations among Regency members when her husband hosted a meeting."

Bernard took another dram. "Go on."

"Seems there is a connection between The New York Holy Alliance and that of the Old World."

"Thus, the name change?"

"Yes. It seems the Regency does not favor the President's new policy."

"You mean the one written by Secretary of State Adams?"

"Exactly. They loathe Mister Adams. And they did not favor the invitation to the marquis. She overheard them speaking of visitors from across the sea — I assume The Holy Alliance."

Bernard put down his drink and leaned forward. "How many?"

"She did not say. I couldn't push too deeply anyway. But she did advise that there are three discrete teams. For some reason, New York came up a lot."

"Naturally, they are New Yorkers. Anywhere else?"

She nodded and whispered, "Here, Washington, and maybe Richmond."

As Betsy left, she kissed Bernard on the cheeks in the French way she so often affected and whispered, "*Merci beaucoup* for taking me once more into your Circle."

Chapter 10

Alexandria, Virginia

Madeline Goulet stretched languidly, allowing the silk sheets to caress her long legs. "I have not slept so well since we boarded ship for that awful voyage."

She sat up, spread the curtains, and gazed from the hotel window. Across the river was the ramshackle village the Americans called their capital. To her, it looked more like a work camp with tents and various wooden buildings interspersed with the occasional brick or stone structure.

Jan Nagy pressed his lips to the nape of her neck and ran his hands along her slender form. "I would like to think I tired you out, my dear."

She turned up to him with a gleam in her eye. "Perhaps."

Madeline jumped up and took a wet cloth to her body. "Why are we here and in Washington?"

"More secure, easier to escape, yet a simple ferry drops us anywhere in that collection of hovels across the water."

She giggled and began brushing out her hair.

"And we can travel to various venues once we know where Lafayette is going."

"And when," she replied.

"Yes. But we have time."

"Time for what?" She knew Jan always had two or three schemes in motion.

"For the widow of Le Duc D'Ambrosien to meet influential people in Washington and Baltimore. Both places Lafayette will visit. It will be best if you can gain me close access to him. Although I can shoot a gold Louis d'Or at fifty paces, I prefer five."

Nagy retrieved a soft leather saddlebag from under the bed and took out a pair of elegant dueling pistols wrapped in felt. "I must find a place to practice, however. And you must meet people."

Madeline did not like the sound of his voice. "What people, *mon cher*?"

"Diplomats, senators, generals will discover your charms. But I prefer a more direct approach."

Jan's schemes were sometimes overly ambitious and often vague. She was confused. And suspicious. "Go on, *mon cher*."

"You told me you had made the acquaintance of Bonaparte's sister-in-law, the disgraced mother of Jerome's son. She lives in Baltimore. Renew your acquaintance."

"Why?"

"The woman, this Elizabeth Patterson, fancies herself still as *Madame* Bonaparte. We know she and Lafayette were once acquainted. You will play up to that senseless vanity and that acquaintance."

***

Commodore Hotel, New York

Neall was growing weary of the fox hunt. Mickey Flynn and his network had come up with five leads in as many days. Each time, they were just a step behind the would-be assassins. Once, they were just an hour away from catching them in Morrisania.

The hotel bar was quiet, but it was not even ten a.m. Neall sipped black coffee while Levasseur laced his with Pernod and worked on his first cigar of the day. As usual, Tom Lynch sat in a corner booth watching them and the door.

"Perhaps you are trying too hard, *Monsieur*," said Levasseur. "These people failed twice."

"Which means they'll try harder next time. We must stop them at every attempt. They only have to succeed once."

Levasseur nodded, "*Eh, bien.*"

"It would help if the general's schedule were lightened a bit. Rallies, speeches, luncheons, and dinners nonstop provide a vast array of venues for assassination."

"A man who sailed to America at nineteen, defying the wishes of the King of France, the king's foreign minister, his powerful father-in-law, and his beautiful young wife. One who fought valiantly for two countries stood up to the mob, the European monarchies, suffered years in a dank cell, and helped overthrow Napoleon Bonaparte would not temper things to avoid an assassin's bullet."

Neall drummed his fingers on the polished maple counter. "I'm not sure there is much to be done, then." *Just the second month of the Lafayette visit and two attempts that could have easily succeeded.*

"Bah, the general has a star greater than Napoleon's. His good fortune will foil his assassins' most devious plots."

"I can't rely on luck forever," said Neall.

"But he can."

"Riley will have to be extra alert," replied Neall. "I am going to change my approach. Instead of waiting in the wings on the chance I can intercept an assassin, I'll arrive at likely locales early. Perhaps the day before."

"How can that help?" asked Levasseur.

"Perhaps if I act like an assassin plotting a crime, I can detect one." Neall nodded and picked up his hat. "Good day, sir."

Lynch followed Neall out the back door, scanning the barroom one last time for prying eyes.

***

Carmen de Gioia stirred slowly, slowly humming, "*Nacqui all'affanno... Non più mesta*" an aria she once performed as Angelina in Act 2 from Rossini's opera, *La Cenerentola, ossia La bontà in trionfo* ("Cinderella, or Goodness Triumphant").

Music helped her in her secret craft. She poured a spoonful into a bowl of milk and placed it on the floor, where a gray cat eagerly lapped it up.

"Three minutes," she said.

"And then?" asked Thompkins.

She did not answer until the feline collapsed at precisely three minutes.

"We are sending a message. If the marquis collapses of what could be apoplexy or some other natural cause, we will fail, and the Alliance will kill us."

"Not if we write letters to a prominent New York paper dated precisely one day before the deed," she replied with a knowing smile.

"But that will provide a warning."

"Exactly, and his team of misfits will be checking every bowl of soup, glass of wine, and snifter of cognac in New York. The distraction will make it easy for you to get within gunshot range for a kill. Lafayette will attend a ball in two days at Castle Garden. You can hide in Battery Park across the street."

"Very good!" His eyes shifted to the limp body on the floor. "So why the potion and the cat?"

"The cat will accompany the note to show we are serious."

Thompkins wrapped the animal in brown paper and tied it up securely, then took ink to paper as Carmen began the aria again, serenading him.

"You might keep it *pianissimo*, or someone might report us."

"We have friends tracking our trackers. They will warn us again."

***

Commodore Hotel, September 13th

Lynch handed Neall a note. "A messenger just ran this over, sir."

He scanned it. "I need to go."

The hackney cab dropped Neall off at a nondescript brick and stone edifice with a name carved over the doorway:

The New York Patriot

Selleck Osborn, the editor of the tabloid, wasted no time. "I understand you provide security for the Marquis de Lafayette."

Neall was surprised his connection to Lafayette was so well known. "Yes. The note said you had something for me."

81

Osborn slid a brown paper bundle across his desk. "Take a look."

As he opened the paper, a stench sickened Neall's stomach. He glanced at the stone-like body of the gray cat. Neall closed the paper over it. "What's this about?"

"Read this," Osborn handed him a letter.

Neall's eyes rolled across each word.

So shall the Marquis de Lafayette be within forty-eight hours. Bon appetit!

He *crunched* the paper in his fist. "*Bon appetit*, indeed."

"I'll not print anything about this if you grant me the exclusive story when you save the marquis," Osborn said.

"My employers might disagree. But I'll see what I can provide once all the threats to him are accounted for."

"Threats? More than one?"

Neall nodded. "Not a word leaks out, or you may wind up stiffer than this poor feline."

"Lafayette is attending a ball tomorrow night at Castle Garden. I have a reporter covering it."

"Tell him not to touch the soup."

"Ye received a note from your pal, Flynn, sir," Lynch said when Neall arrived at the hotel.

Neall tore open the envelope. "He has a lead for us. Someone suspicious is nosing about a place called Verplank's Point. The marquis sails past there on his way to West Point in two days."

"I'll pack a few things," said Lynch.

"No, boyo, this will be our fourth chase. I think we are being played."

"By Flynn? He's Irish, B'Jeezus. He wouldn't—oh shit!"

Neall tore up the note. "Or one of his cronies. Either way, we should stake out Castle Garden and the Grand Ball. There's a threat of poisoning, and the ball is the most likely place."

Lynch smiled. "Sometimes the most obvious things."

"Are too obvious. You go and inspect Castle Garden. I'll warn the general to bring his own bottle of wine."

***

Castle Garden, The Battery, New York City, September 14th, 1824

By no means as lavish as anything like it in Britain, yet Castle Garden was decked out with all the finery New York could muster. From the outside, the stone and brick edifice looked like a giant three-tiered cake, each round layer bristling with windows once meant to serve as gun embrasures. The exterior gardens were decorated with French and American flags interspersed among torches, turning the autumn evening into a spectacle of light.

Neall and Lynch had inspected each entrance — before each stood a pair of New York Militia in gray uniforms with muskets handy.

"Nice o' the governor to give you this company of soldiers, sir," Flynn quipped. "Not Inniskillings, but they seem ready enough."

"The unit never saw combat, but I understand many served in the last war."

"Against England?"

"Yes." Neall found it somehow ironic to be inspecting his country's former foes. "They were coastal artillery but are being organized as an infantry regiment. The general should be pleased."

"The general? Why so?"

"General Lafayette commanded the *Garde Nationale* in France during their revolution. They were much like the American militia. Let's check the reserve squad."

They entered the building and walked through the grand and elaborately decorated theater with a large stage adorned with red, white, and blue flowers, scores of American flags, and various New York State and City flags. A gray-clad soldier stood at each wing of the stage.

"There's a dozen more behind the stage," said Lynch.

A Second Lieutenant snapped to attention when Neall approached. "Are you Mister Neall?"

Neall nodded. "We'll need a man on each tier overlooking the stage. Mister Lynch and I will be moving about, checking your men, and keeping an eye out for danger."

"Can I know what we are looking for?"

Neall was glad the attacks on Lafayette had been squashed from the pervasive New York press corps. "A sniper. Expert shot. Your men should try to subdue him quietly." Neall glanced up into the seats above them. "But deadly force is authorized."

The sharp staccato sound of strings and horns filled the chamber as the bandsmen tuned up for the event.

"In two hours, this place will be filled to the brim and noisy as a battlefield," said the lieutenant.

"Excellent cover for a shot," said Neall.

"Or two," said Lynch, fingering the Forsyth pistols tucked into his belt.

***

The music enthralled the crowd. Whistles and thunderous clapping followed each song. As it turned out, the State Militia Band and the New York City Band had set up before the stage and were competing in a battle of the bands.

Promptly at eight o'clock, both bands joined in a stirring medley that included "Yankee Doodle," "*La Marseillaise*," "General Washington's March," and other patriotic tunes that had the audience on its feet. Men in long tails and women in jewel-bedecked gowns were prancing like youths at a May Day Fair.

At last, Mayor Allen signaled, and the final notes drifted through the cavernous hall.

"Ladies and gentlemen, it is my pleasure to introduce America's favorite adopted son, unfortunately, for the last time. I give you, citizens of New York, the man who eschewed a life of ease as the wealthiest man and head of the noblest aristocratic French family to risk all in a fight for America's freedom and man's liberty from oppression."

Hands clapped, and feet stomped as shouts of bravo filled the great hall. Neall's eyes scoured the crowd for trouble, but he realized anyone could be waiting to strike among the frenzy.

"A man who shed his blood for our cause and lost his fortune and health in France's cause. Who risked the wrath of his privileged class in leading France to liberty and equality but also gained the wrath of the tyrannical mob of Jacobins and crowned heads of Europe."

More shouts of bravo and "*Vive'* LaFayette" swirled through the air. Neall's mind raced nervously. *What have I left uncovered?*

The mayor continued, his voice beginning to crack from the stress and excitement at what would be his last speech before any crowd so large. "Who could do such a thing?"

"Lafayette!" the crowd replied.

"The man who stood up to Napoleon Bonaparte himself. The man who forced the abdication of the most powerful man since Charlemagne. To this very day, the man who is the epitome of selfless devotion to the liberty of all men, whatever their status or color!

"Ladies and gentlemen, I present to you the most remarkable man in two countries, on two continents, and since the death of the late great George Washington—in the world. General Marie-Joseph-Paul-Yves-Roch-Gilbert du Motier, and although I know he hates the sound of it, The Marquis de Lafayette!"

Men and women were on their feet as one. The roar of their voices mixed with the two bands, which went into a rousing version of "The World Turned Upside Down."

Lafayette rose and slowly made his way to the podium, grasping the hands of well-wishers with each step until the sweat stung. He slipped a hand in his vest pocket and swabbed his beaded forehead with a red, white, and blue handkerchief.

"My dear friends… my dear friends. How can I ever thank the American people, the people of New York, for the warm reception given me at each step of my progress across your wonderful land?"

Neall gazed across the hall, where Lynch seemed squinting at something above the stage. *The balcony!*

"Now, I must say, the band is wonderful, is it not?"

Clapping ensued. When it died off, Lafayette continued.

"'The World Turned Upside Down' — since your brave friends in New England stood at Lexington and then at Concord, it most certainly has. But the brave men of America shook the world. I was only glad to assist — at Williamsburg."

***

Williamsburg, Virginia, October 1781

The piping of fifes and *rat-tat* of drums filled the air as the Life Guards snapped to attention, and Lafayette entered General Washington's pavilion. The young division commander snapped his head and bowed twice: once to Washington and once to *Comte* de Rochambeau, commander of French forces of the allied army.

"Excellent work, General Lafayette," Washington said. "You and General Wayne have caged the fox in a near-perfect campaign of maneuver. Now he is ours for the taking."

"Thank you, Your Excellency. But it is the hard work and courage of the soldiers that made this possible." He turned to Rochambeau. "And thank you, *Monsieur*. A year ago, I would not have had the forbearance to let the enemy make such mistakes. I learned when you chastised me for suggesting a headlong attack on New York."

"It is a wise officer who learns from experience," Rochambeau replied.

"*Comte* Rochambeau tells me Admiral d'Estaing had proposed your forces combine with his to storm Yorktown. From the look of Lord Cornwallis's defenses, you may have succeeded. At least driven him from his lair. "'Tis a rare man who eschews glory when laid at his feet."

Lafayette smiled. "As a boy, my hunt master used to say, 'Why gallop after a stag when you can trot and bag two?' The combined armies before Yorktown will ensure his surrender to Your Excellency. Nor would I deprive you and your men of their share of the glory."

"Prepare your division," said Washington. "You and your men have earned a privileged role in this battle."

***

Castle Garden, September 14th, 1824

"Out of the way!" Neall pushed past people and ducked into the rear of the stage. His feet pumped as he twisted up the spiral staircase to the stage balcony. *Never checked this. A balcony over the stage. Damn, the idea!*

The area behind the stage was dark, but a pale light greeted him near the upper balcony. He thought he saw shadows moving. *Some of the crew?*

He slowed his pace, made his way carefully up the last twist of the stairs, and peered across the half-lit balcony. Something littered the floor. *Bodies!*

85

A dark figure crouched behind the marble balustrade. Neall approached slowly. His hand reached into his belt and drew out his pistol. His thumb pulled back the hammer while his left hand slipped the sharp dagger from his boot. A long barrel hovered over the crowd.

Neall spread his legs and slightly bent his knees as he prepared to spring at the sniper. A sudden crack across his neck sent him tumbling onto the lifeless forms littering the floor. Neall rolled over and looked up into the burning eyes of Carmen de Gioia!

She raised a heavy wooden pin used to secure the curtain winch and kicked away his pistol. "Drop the dagger!"

He tried to call for the militia guards, but the cries and cheering of the crowd drowned out all but the loudest sounds.

"You look thirsty, *Cara mia*. Try some of this delicate potion. Made for the marquis but equally refreshing for you. Just one drop, *Cara mia*.

Rough hands yanked him to his feet. "We've got him, Miss."

"He'll be happy to drink when we're done with him."

Irish brogues — *Tammany thugs!* Through the corner of his eye, he could make out the sniper waiting for his chance.

"Never ye moind that one! "

A blow to his gut sent Neall keeling over. A knee drove up into his face, and hands released him, sending him to the floor in a heap. His strength had sapped from him.

A jeweled hand grasped his chin and pushed a flask to his lips. "That is much better, *Cara mia*. Alexander Buxhowden would be so proud of you."

The toughs pinned his arms as she worked the flask's nipple closer. "You are tired. Drink and sleep."

His neck throbbed from her blow — the idea of sleep almost tempted him, but he fought it, letting his body go limp. At that, the toughs relaxed their grips just enough for him to kick his temptress in the shin. Carmen bowled over backward, her long dress spreading and exposing delightfully formed legs under petticoats.

"Why you!" growled one of the Tammany thugs.

"Take yer shot," the other called to the sniper.

Neall managed to pull loose from him and drove a fist into his side. He barely noticed and began a roundhouse to Neall's head.

"I'll send ye into next week, ya British bastard!"

Lynch's voice echoed from the darkness at the top of the stairs. "I'll say who's a British bastard and who isn't!" He sprang forward and slammed the thug's chin, his knuckles smashing through bone and teeth. *Crack!*

The second tough turned to run, but Lynch sprang on him like he was mounting his charger and ran the dagger blade across his gullet. The man toppled forward, gurgling blood.

Neall was on his feet and moving at the sniper, who turned toward him.

Millard Thompkins smiled grimly, lowered his head to the rear sight, and began to squeeze.

Neall launched a desperate leap, sending Thompkins's rifle tumbling between his legs.

Thompkins reached into his belt, and his fingers grasped the butt of a pistol. He thrust the barrel into Neall's belly and smirked. "Even with a wounded hand, I never miss from this distance."

As his finger drew back the hammer, Lynch's dagger flew, and its blade struck square between his shoulders. The sniper's eyes widened, and foamy blood painted his lips and chin. He sank to the floor, lifeless.

"I always was better with me knife than me fists, good as me fists are," said Lynch as he yanked the blade free and flipped the body over. "That's the officer from the boat."

***

Tammany Hall

Flynn's shoes scraped the top of his desk as the shoeshine boy struggled with his polishing cloth. His heavy eyebrows squinted as the Tammany boss read the evening broadsheet.

"Any news, boss?" a crony asked.

"Keep ya gob shut when I'm reading," barked Flynn.

The crony turned to another sidekick and laughed. "I'd say that was a no."

A commotion in the hall sent the shoeshine boy scurrying and the news sheet fluttering to the floor.

"What in the name of Jeezus is that racket?" Flynn barked.

Before Flynn's cronies could reach the door, it flew open, and Neall stepped across the threshold. His cravat was open, and his jacket hung loose, torn in the fracas at Castle Garden.

"Look what the cat dragged in," said one of the cronies, a heavy-set man in a green suit.

"Someone has bloody cats on their mind," spat Neall.

"Now, is that talk for a proper English gentleman? Not even a how-de-do?"

"I never said I was a gentleman or English, Flynn. But I know a few." Neall spotted the penny news sheet on the floor. "Have you read about what happened at Castle Garden tonight?"

Flynn barred his teeth. "I was just getting to it. Enlighten me, milord."

Neall picked the paper off the floor and jammed it into Flynn's hands. "Read it yourself. I'll wait."

Flynn motioned for the boy to leave and turned to his cronies. "Stand by. For now."

His eyes cruised along each line, hungrily searching for news of the event.

"Expecting something?" Neall asked. "Well, I can tell you this—don't expect to hear back from the two apes you sent to assist Millard Thompkins and his lady friend."

"What are you talking about?" Flynn looked at his men. "Have you fellas been up to no good?"

"Send them off so we can talk," Neall demanded

Flynn saw the bulge from Neall's pistol. "Go on, lads. Head down to the bar for a pint. I'll join ye soon enough."

Neall slid into an overstuffed chair. "Now, tell me about your connection to the foreign powers trying to assassinate Lafayette."

"What?"

"I searched your apes and Thompkins. Found each with one of these." Neall held up a silver coin — a Holy Alliance coin. "A few more days of this, and I'll have enough to buy an estate I've been eyeing in Surrey."

"Well, if 'tis money you're after, why didn't you say so? How about an estate near Saratoga?"

Neall crossed his arms.

"One call from me, and a gang of the lads will barge in here and crack your noggin for good."

Neall rose and stood over Flynn. "If that were the case, I'd already be dead. No, you're sworn to secrecy because if your superiors get word of this, you'd be joining me, and there is no room in Hell for the two of us."

Flynn's eyes lowered. "Whadya want, milord?"

***

West Point, New York, September 15th

The steamboat *James Kent* cruised slowly up the Hudson River, its engine *chugging*, its brace of smokestacks spitting plumes of black smoke with the occasional glow of embers shooting high into the darkening sky. The twin paddles churned the ever-sweetening waters of the Hudson, pushing against the tide.

Waiters set a tray of cold sandwiches and two bottles of fine wine onto the crisp linen tablecloth. Lafayette was gazing out the window, where the arching cliffs rich with autumn's red and gold attracted his attention.

"Where is Sergeant Riley?" asked George Lafayette as he reached for a chicken sandwich.

"With the ship's captain, checking the manifest since we departed West Point," said Levasseur.

The younger Lafayette's head snapped south where the gray embrasures overlooking the Hudson grew dim and distant. "I suppose one cannot be too careful after what transpired at Castle Garden. It is a good thing *Monsieur* Neall thwarted the killers."

Levasseur sipped a tolerable Bordeaux. "It is a marvelous thing that he kept it discreet. If word of all became public knowledge, we would likely be forced to cancel most of this journey and return home as fools."

"I hope father comes to the table soon. How long must one take to get reacquainted?" sighed George, who was unhappy when his father's mistress arrived unexpectedly in New York. Fanny Wright's presence pleased only the elder Lafayette.

"As long as she stays in the background, we should not hear too much from the journey's sponsors," said Levasseur. "Her sister being at her side helps."

Riley strode into the private dining room and took a seat. A waiter rushed to pour him a glass of wine, but Riley's fingers enclosed his wrist. "I'll take a beer if you don't mind."

The sudden *boom, boom, boom* of cannons erupted, drowning out the constant churn of the ship's engines.

Levasseur ducked under the table, and young George ducked for cover.

"The captain just told me there'd be a gun salute at New Windsor. I guess that's it," Riley said as he sipped the foam from his glass.

Smoke belched from the shoreline, and thousands of people ran, galloped, or rode carriages along with the boat as it steamed north. Suddenly, Lafayette appeared at the forecastle and doffed his hat, waving it madly at the well-wishers along the riverbank.

"*Vive* Lafayette! *Vive* America! *Vive La France!*" echoed across the water.

George joined his father, whose eyes grew moister with each chorus.

"It is too much," said Lafayette.

George felt touched for really the first time on the journey. "Come, papa, let us repair to the dining room and toast these wonderful people."

***

The 2nd Battalion, 2nd Artillery Regiment Armory, New York City

Neall's boots echoed down the long, cavernous causeway beneath Fifth Avenue. A gray-clad guard came to attention as Neall turned the handle and entered the commander's office.

"Please have a seat, sir," said Major Rodney Pettigrew, the acting battalion commander. "Your ward is quite secure now."

"Where is the soprano?"

"The boys repurposed an arms room as her personal prison cell."

Neall nodded. "I appreciate that. I can't rely on the constables. At least until I know who can be trusted."

Pettigrew's brow furrowed. "I'm not sure I quite understand all this."

"It's about keeping General Lafayette alive. I can't reveal much other than certain powers have issued a death warrant against him, and they may have friends in your country — powerful friends."

"We must protect him. As for the soprano, she shall receive good care and food from my family's private caterer."

"Just mind her. She likes to concoct poisons and potions." Neall decided to ask a question he had held back. "What do you know about Mister Van Buren?"

"Oh, he's well connected both here and in Albany. Washington, too."

"Can he be trusted?"

"I'm afraid to tell you this, but he's a New York politician. And a Republican-Democrat."

"Meaning?"

"I'd sooner trust a gang of pirates. But if you can accept him and his ilk for what they are, then I suppose he is an all-right sort."

"How do you know him?"

"Father has had him to dinner, and although my father was a staunch Federalist, he keeps contact with the other side."

Not unlike the British upper crust, Neall thought.

Heavy rapping on the door, and Lieutenant Tad Grayson stepped in. "The boys are ready for inspection. Then, I can place them at their posts. We'll give General Lafayette a grand welcome."

"He'll only be here a few days before shipping to Philadelphia and points south. Major, may I borrow a squad of your lads?"

Pettigrew's fingers intertwined as he lowered his head and then fixed his gaze on Grayson. "Very well. But they will be under Lieutenant Grayson's command."

Neall, a former professional officer, viewed all militia with skepticism. Yet he had no choice but to go with the hand given him. After all, the New York constables and the night watch reported to Tammany Hall.

"Very well. Lafayette's steamship will be back tomorrow. Soon after, we must head south."

Chapter 11

Baltimore, Maryland, September 22nd

The coach rolled up to an expansive house of fine alabaster marble. The early morning mist had cleared, and pale autumn sunshine filled a blue sky smeared with cotton puffs.

Madeline stepped from the coach and entered the home, wondering if its mistress would greet her. A survivor of the French Reign of Terror's guillotine as an infant whose parents were not as fortunate, her encounters with *Madame* Bonaparte were scarce and superficial. As a spy for the French émigré circle in England, she returned to France as one of the young aristocrats welcomed by Bonaparte when he became Emperor.

A dark-skinned servant led her into a magnificent drawing room, richly decorated with delicate curtains. Large oil paintings covered ornately plastered walls, and several sculptures of nudes adorned tables of mahogany and teak. *How fine to be an emperor's sister.*

"Thank you for receiving me on such short notice, *Madame* Bonaparte. But I will not tarry long in Baltimore, and who knows when I will return to this city of charm."

Betsy chortled. "Baltimore is not Paris or London, but then again, what is? Please sit by me so we can share some news and gossip."

Two pots of tea were gone by the time they had regaled one another with tales and exploits of Paris and London.

Madeline cleared her throat and began the story she and Nagy had prepared, a romance that would strike a chord and touch the heart of Elizabeth Patterson. When she finished, Madeline's face was flush, something she had learned to induce to deceive women and men alike.

"Oh, my dear, I can see just the telling of your travails has discomposed you. I wish we had spent more time together, Madeline. You and I would have had even more fun at the expense of the high-society types. A beautiful French noblewoman who thwarted Robespierre and an American woman who flummoxed the Emperor of the French!"

"Flummoxed? *Je ne comprends pas.*"

"Let's just say despite his efforts, I remain his sister-in-law. It is why I never remarried."

"But Jerome?"

"Let him live in bigamy."

Peals of laughter filled the room.

"I must depart. The hotel will not long hold my reservation."

"Nonsense, dear Madeline. You shall be my guest. That will mean only nine empty guestrooms."

Madeline sighed, another contrivance. "You are such a dear, *Madame* Bonaparte."

***

Scudders American Museum, New York City, September 1824

The musty five-story building could not be more different than the seat of American piety across the street—St. Paul's Chapel. John Scudder, Jr. moved his father's museum to the former almshouse to make a social statement while getting more square footage for less money.

Riley kept a respectful six feet from Lafayette as John Scudder, Jr. gave him a tour of the curiosity museum. Riley did not like the marquis coming to the dilapidated building. Besides being poorly lit, it had many causeways and too many ways to get in or out.

"This is an interesting collection of stuffed creatures," Lafayette opined. "It will amuse us before the dinner with your mayor."

"The next room has even more, and then there is the American Room," said Scudder.

"What is that?"

"Various mementos from earlier days in New York history."

"Why, that makes me a memento," quipped Lafayette.

"I don't understand, *Monsieur*," replied Scudder.

"My dear fellow, my family lineage stretches back a thousand years into France's history. That once counted for much in France, but now it is merely, as you say, a memento."

***

Bureau du comte de Vergennes, Versailles, France, February 1777

Charles Gravier, *comte* de Vergennes, closed the heavy leather-bound ledger and looked up at the thin, pale-faced cavalry captain who stood knock-kneed but proudly before him.

"State your business with the King's Minister," ordered Vergennes's secretary, an older man in the braided uniform of the King's *Corps Diplomatique*.

The young captain began to stammer but then snapped ramrod straight and announced, "Marie-Joseph-Paul-Yves-Roch-Gilbert du Motier, Marquis de La Fayette, Captain of Noailles Dragoons, wishes to speak with the Minister."

Vergennes turned to his secretary. "Leave us alone. This officer never saw me. Do you understand?"

"*Oui, Monsieur.*" The secretary vanished behind a panel.

"I should have you arrested," said Vergennes.

"Likely on the suggestion of my father-in-law."

"The *Duc* d'Ayen insisted on it. But I have seen fit to defer for now. Why do you insist on this charade of sailing to America? Your actions have the English spitting nails. We are not yet ready for war with them."

"The Americans are at war with them," replied Lafayette. "And I have spoken with *Monsieur* de Beaumarchais. You already have France deeply involved."

"What is done in secret is one thing — the affair of ministers. But overt actions have consequences for nations — the affair of kings. I must protect the king. You, of all, should understand that in your very bones. Your family on both sides has served France's kings for almost a thousand years!

"Why, your namesake, Gilbert de Lafayette III, was a Marshal of France. He raised a sword beside our beloved Jeanne *d'Arc* at Orléans in 1429 in our first war against the English. Another perished in the Crusades. Your great-grandfather commanded the Black Musketeers, charged with the personal safety of Louis XV. Your uncle died fighting the Austrians at Milan in 1734. Your father, Michel, fell at Minden."

"Struck down by an English cannonball," said Lafayette. "With all due respect, I know my family's lineage and history."

"So, *Monsieur*, is this about *revanche*?"

"No!"

But Lafayette was not so sure his answer was truthful. He wanted glory and honor. He wanted to fight for liberty and the rights of man, as espoused at his Masonic Lodge meetings. But he did indeed want to hurt the English. "I want to bring glory to France. Striking the English is the best way I can imagine."

"Did de Broglie put you up to this?"

How does he know about de Broglie? "No. It is my idea alone."

"Your lying needs improvement." Vergennes poured a glass of wine and took a gulp. "If you serve the Americans, you forfeit any chance of command when war does come with England."

Lafayette felt a jolt of hope. "So, France will wage war!"

"Only when she is strong enough. The weapons and munitions we send to America are paid for in farm produce and other raw materials that we sell and use the profits to rearm with the latest ordnance for the army."

"But this could take years."

"Or not."

"*Monsieur* Dean offered me a major general commission in the Continental Army."

"A boy general? The Americans will not defeat the English regulars led by boys." He poured a glass of wine and thrust it into Lafayette's hand. "Officially, you are under sanction if you leave France, and I shall have you arrested when you return."

"And unofficially, *Monsieur*?"

Vergennes dipped the nib of a long quill into the ink pot and began to write. "I am giving you a note for General Washington's eyes only. You will die before this falls into anyone's hands. They will never let you command their soldiers in the field, but this will ensure he keeps you close to the vest, eh? Learn what you can about them and their army. Write often to Marie Adrienne and keep me informed as best you can."

***

Scudders American Museum, New York City, September 1824

Riley heard feet shuffling, an unwanted intruder. "Stay close to your father," he whispered, jamming one of his pistols into George's belt. "Don't fire it. Just wave it."

George's eyes widened in surprise, but he nodded and stepped closer to Lafayette, who was paying rapt attention to his guide.

Riley ducked behind a collection of stuffed owls and ostriches, drew his other pistol, one of a brace taken from a Barbary pirate, and pulled back the hammer.

More shuffling. Then Riley picked up a scent known to many Irishmen: cheap beer. *My luck, they've been drinking.*

Two hefty men in dingy suits lumbered past him. Each carried a short club. *Enforcers for the Tammany rats Neall mentioned.*

Riley stepped out from behind the feathers. "Drop the clubs, boys, or the next sound will be the voice of your interrogator."

The two men spun about and stepped toward him but froze when they saw the pistol.

"Constables and the Watch are on the payroll, friend," said one.

"I didn't mean the police. I meant Saint Peter."

They edged toward Riley, who was deciding which one would get the lead ball.

The men raised their clubs in tandem. "You might get one of us, but your brains are getting scrambled one way or another. Then we'll get the Frenchman."

"But you already have the Frenchman, *Monsieur*. Or should I say he has you?"

They spun about.

George Lafayette stepped from behind a pile of boxes with the pistol held steady. The thugs bolted between another stack of crates and disappeared from sight.

"Stay with your father," Riley said, taking off after them.

He raced through the maze of crates until he reached a stairwell where the echo of footsteps met him. He closed the door, slid the bolt, and headed down the hallway where he had posted one of the New York militiamen.

He found the Guardsman sprawled at the entrance, clasping his head. "They jumped me, sir."

"So, they did. Well, it's just a crack on the noggin. Let it be a lesson. Next time, they'll split your skull."

***

Trenton, New Jersey, September 26th, 1824

The carriages lumbered along the post road from Princeton. Tom Lynch felt awkward wearing a fine suit to blend in with Lafayette and his entourage. Across from him sat Lafayette's valet, Sebastien Wagner, who bored him with stories of life in France. *He'd have a cow if he knew how many Frenchies I've killed.*

Next to him sat two of the New York 2nd Artillery. They had left New York by steamer on the 23rd, visiting Newark, where the Governor greeted them, then on to Elizabethtown, Woodbridge, and New Brunswick, boarding coaches for the overland journey to Philadelphia.

Lynch would have preferred to ride in Lafayette's coach, but Riley had that honor. After the incident at the museum, Neall assigned Lynch to back up the marine while Neall went to Philadelphia with the remainder of the squad from the New York militia, where Lafayette was most at risk.

"We're slowing down," said Lynch.

"The marquis asked us to pause at Trenton," said Wagner. "He wants to visit the site of General Washington's victory over the Hessians.

Hundreds of well-wishers jammed the narrow streets, calling out to the carriages as they rumbled past quaint shops and tidy homes. The alleys echoed with "*Vive Lafayette!*" "Huzzah!" "*Vive la France!*" and "God bless America!"

Lynch never saw anything like it. "The marquis is quite beloved."

"Indeed, he is," said Wagner. "It is my great honor to serve him."

Suddenly, the coaches turned off the road onto a cow path into a grove and then an orchard loaded with apple, pear, and plum trees, where the wheels churned through inches of mud until they halted.

Lafayette's door opened ahead of them, and he stepped from his coach.

"*Mon Dieu!* His boots will be full of mud," exclaimed Wagner.

"Give you something to do while we all sleep tonight," Lynch chuckled.

Wagner leaped out of the carriage and stomped through the mud after Lafayette.

"B'Jeezus!" Lynch stepped out and followed, his feet sucking with each tread. It occurred to him a sniper could easily hide in the trees. "Keep yer eyes peeled, lads," he said to the two Guardsmen.

Lafayette pointed across the meadow between the trees and the town. "The Hessians retreated to this place to regroup, but the brave patriots raked them with volleys that tore their ranks asunder and felled their brave colonel. The river crossing and night march through a dark winter night were even more impressive. His Excellency foiled the British conquest of Jersey with one bold act and saved the American cause. I wish I could have been part of it."

"But you did arrive and had equally glorious achievements," said George, who had joined him. He glanced down at his father's calf boots, now covered in thick slime. "We should go. Bastien will have much work tonight, I fear."

***

The next day took them through Bristol, where the Governor of Pennsylvania greeted Lafayette and his party. They rolled past the Frankford Arsenal that night, pulled by six cream-colored horses.

A pair of triumphal arches, newly erected along the route, welcomed the marchers and riders through Northern Liberties into the city. They entered the lamp-lit streets of Philadelphia, followed by a miles-long parade of ordinary townsfolk and country folk on horseback, pompous officials, some local militia units, and veterans who served with Lafayette in the war. The coaches and the procession rolled through imposing neighborhoods and past the city's landmarks. Crowds of cheering Philadelphia tradesmen and farmers from the countryside who had waited all day finally glimpsed the carriage and the gloved hand of the great man waving back at them. Lafayette and his entourage had onlookers with him all the way to the old State House.

***

Independence Hall, Philadelphia, September 29th

The gray early morning chill did not dissuade anxious people from gathering to see America's celebrated visitor at the site of the nation's birth.

The clock in the dining room said seven. Neall wiped his lips with a clean linen cloth and left a coin on the table. The rest of the squad should already be at their posts, and he would check out the area one last time.

He stepped into the damp morning air on Second Street and looked up. The glow from the sky over the Delaware River was pushing through a wall of slate gray. *Clouds should be gone by noon.*

Neall turned right onto Walnut Street. He walked briskly, crossing over Third and Fourth Street. After that, he melted into a wooded park-like area surrounding Independence Hall. The irony of it struck him. The brick building had served as the Americans' capitol and the site of the ultimate statement of resistance to Britain — The Declaration of Independence.

He soon encountered a pair of young men in fine suits, richly embroidered cloaks, and top hats. Add the walking canes, and any passerby would take them for

96

young men about town, possibly lawyers or businessmen. But a closer look might reveal rumpled cloth where each tucked a brace of pistols.

Neall nodded at the gentlemen. "Catullus will be here in a few hours if he's on time." Whenever his mistress was nearby, Lafayette's penchant for punctuality faded. "Older men need more time."

The young gentlemen, New York militia assigned to Neall, smiled knowingly.

"Be on your watch. We stopped one sniper, but we must stop all their snipers while they only need to succeed once," he said, stealing a line from Bernard. "I'm going to check on the others."

Minutes later, Neall looked up at the large brick structure where the Continental Congress debated and guided thirteen colonies toward nationhood. Modest compared to anything of its kind in London or other European capitals, Independence Hall seemed to fit the Americans just right.

By eight, he had checked his other teams. As hundreds on hundreds began their assembly, he realized they were hunting for an adder in a barrel of garden snakes.

***

Alexandria, Virginia

Nagy tugged and grunted as he pulled on his boots.

"I come all the way back from Baltimore, and you sleep in late?" Madeline teased.

"If I knew you were coming. Well, never mind. We'll take a morning walk, and you can tell me everything."

Alexandria was a bustling port made even more prosperous with the growth of the nation's capital across the river. The boats on the Potomac spread their sails like the wings of swans. At the same time, the longboats lunged across the water like ducks, their crews grunting with each pull of the oars. Somehow, it relaxed her.

They strolled along the riverfront, stopping now and again to stare longingly like lovers. They spoke in hushed tones, ignoring the cries of vendors and the rattle of carts dragging goods from ships exhausted from tacking up the long river delivering their goods via the Delaware Bay and the ocean beyond.

"*Madame* Bonaparte was most gracious. She took me right in. She insisted I stay with her and is already introducing me to her friends. The *creme de la crème* of Washington and Baltimore."

"Will she see Lafayette when he arrives? That is most important, my dear." Nagy stroked her hand and pinched her chin. He had done so a hundred times and more, but somehow it bothered her.

"I haven't asked that question. I don't want to appear too forward. Too obvious."

He reached his hand along her petticoats.

"Nor should you. Stop."

Nagy's lascivious smile twisted into a snarl. "You are not my mistress?"

"I am your partner. I'll let you know when I want to sleep with you."

His snarl flattened, and he nodded. "You're right. We'll have enough time when we finish our work and swim in a tub of the emperor's *Gulden*."

"As long as I get my 25,000," she said. She knew he would, in the end, try to cheat her. So many of her partners had.

"I did learn something, Jan. Lafayette will come to Washington before Baltimore. I suspect *Madame* Bonaparte will try to see him there." She glanced across the river. "Not an impressive place for a capital."

"It's a swamp," Nagy retorted. "But I hope to deliver him to his maker in a swamp. A swamp named for his beloved Washington."

He led her through a series of waterside sheds and shanties, finally halting at a clapboard building urgently needing paint. An old black man sat at the door, whittling on a piece of wood.

"What is this?" she asked.

"Greetings, Amos," Nagy said.

Amos grunted and went on with his carving.

He knows this man?

"Amos watches things for me," Nagy said as though he had read her mind.

The door's hinges screeched like a cat with its tail cut. They stepped in, and Nagy lit a lamp. The pungent smell of rotten eggs overwhelmed them — sulfur.

He pulled a canvas from a large crate and pried open the side. Inside, Madeline saw what looked like a barrel with cords, springs, and wheels.

"Are you going to open a brewery?"

Nagy smiled and, once more, stroked her chin. "You are endearing but ignorant of science and technology. It is a most powerful bomb."

"A bomb! You've been busy since I left."

"Nonsense. It was designed and built by some of the best scientists contracted by the Aulic Council. Capable of being delivered by boat, coach, or cart. Or with the hire of a few of these strong black men."

"But you are an experienced shooter. The pistol or rifled musket is your delivery choice."

Nagy sighed. "True, *Ma Cherie*. But they insisted. Count Esslinger wants to make an explosive statement." He smiled wickedly.

She did not like that about him. *He really enjoys inflicting pain.*

"But many others will die or be grievously injured."

"Precisely the point."

***

Hohensalzburg Fortress Aulic Council, Salzburg, Austria
The faint echo of marching feet and fading drums reverberated through the castle.

"I hate it when they have evening parades," said Prince Vassiliev. "You Austrians have too many long military ceremonies."

"Our soldiers are more professional. And our uniforms do not make them look like peacocks," snapped von Zoranski.

"Gentlemen, the Aulic Council expects its Secret Committee to work as one. Our success depends on operational unity. Has anyone heard back from their wolves?"

"Nothing," said Vassiliev. "I had expected a dispatch from New York. But our representative has seen nothing in the New York papers other than Lafayette's strutting about like a rooster."

"Baron?"

"My wolfpack sailed to Charleston or Savannah. But has orders to sail to New Orleans if things are not progressing. They were given the southern part of the journey. Donat was not pleased that two other wolfpacks were given the earlier destinations. "

"He'll be well reimbursed, regardless," said Esslinger.

"He wants the kill and the glory."

"What of Nagy?" asked Vassiliev.

"The device arrived, is all I know. But I hope Madeline Pauline Goulet can use her wiles, so the device is unnecessary."

"I thought our goal was to terrorize the Americans as well?" von Zoransky asked.

"It is the Council's wishes. But the archduke was informed of the plan, and he is a staunch Catholic who disapproves of unnecessary bloodshed."

"That is why I hope the beautiful Carmen can offer Lafayette a toast," said Vassiliev.

Wicked laughter filled the room.

***

Independence Hall, Philadelphia, Pennsylvania

Neall approached the final pair of guardsmen. "How goes it?"

"Catullus is in the building," replied Lieutenant Tad Grayson. I was able to rent a pair of horses. Well, borrow. My uncle is one of the wealthiest men in Philadelphia and has a decent stable of hunters. Can you ride, sir?"

"A bit, yes."

"Well, in case we need to pursue a fleeing suspect."

"I hope to stop the assassin, not arrest him for murder, but I see your point, Tad. Mister Riley and Mister Lynch are with Catullus. You will keep an eye on the well-wishers. Permission to act, but discreetly."

"Where will you be, sir?"

"Since you got the horses, I'll take one and roam the grounds."

The *clop-clop* of the hooves on roughly paved stones and the familiar smell of leather tack swarmed Neall's senses. *Good to be back in the saddle.*

His hand absently reached for the hilt of a saber before he realized he did not have one. *Old habits die hard.* He loosened the reins and halted the horse, taking in the morning air while scanning the open area before the hall. Crowds of well-wishers were going to make today most difficult.

He took a moment to contemplate the mission. The soprano was under lock and key. One accomplice rotted in an unmarked grave while her other accomplice fed the fish in New York Bay. *Senora De Gioia draws male accomplices like a Queen Bee — drones to do her work.* The assassins, however many, seemed not to fear striking among crowds and perhaps even preferred it. *Of course! They are making a statement to the world, not to Lafayette or even the American president. Death in the open is preferred to death in the shadows.*

He saw someone rustling the branches high up in a tall tree directly overlooking the entrance. *A sniper?* He spurred the horse for a closer look. As he approached, he saw the climber was actually two, a pair of teenage boys, and they had no firelocks.

His watch pointed to late morning. *Hours of this left.* Neall heard a voice calling his name. At the entrance, 100 yards away, he spotted Tom Lynch holding his hat upside down.

***

Well-wishers jammed the large drawing room to meet Lafayette, whose hands were sweaty from greeting so many good people of Philadelphia. He quickly went through the politicians and bluebloods and was knee-deep in tradesmen, shopkeepers, and local farmers. Occasionally, one would mention a shared event during the war, and he would nod and begin chattering away like the person was a long-lost friend. And indeed, in a sense, many were.

Lynch positioned himself against a wall and eyed the two doors for suspicious movement while Riley stood close to Lafayette, ready to pounce at the first sign of trouble. The two New York militiamen were at the doorways, nervously eyeing the crowd.

A sudden tumult erupted across the room, and the panicked legs of the crowd shuffled to spread themselves as cries of "Help this man!" and "Get a doctor!" filled the chamber.

Lynch pushed past confused onlookers and elbowed through a pair that would not budge. Several stood aimlessly around a man in a gray tweed suit writhing on the floor before a table strewn with bowls of punch.

The man suddenly groaned and gurgled, then lay still. His eyes bulged, and his tongue lay limp against blue lips.

Lynch pushed his way back to where Lafayette stood talking with some middle-aged men, oblivious to the events around him.

He tugged Riley's elbow. "A fella's been poisoned. Don't let the marquis touch a drop of liquid or let him out of your sight."

Riley nodded, edged closer to Lafayette, and motioned for the group to move on.

"What is the matter?" George asked.

Riley's eyes shifted.

George nodded. "Stay with my father. He has one more group from the Cincinnati Society to receive before we retire to the hotel."

George strode through the crowd and found Lynch directing the two militiamen to carry the man away.

"Too much to drink, I'd say," someone in the crowd wisecracked—the room filled with guffaws.

Lynch stomped to the table, pushing away the thirsty well-wishers, and tipped it over. The thud of the wooden table striking the inlaid floor and the crackling of glass shattering into hundreds of shards were masked by the babble echoing through the room.

Lynch breathed a sigh of relief. *Barely heard, thank Christ.*

***

Mansion House Hotel, Philadelphia

The clink of glasses and the clatter of plates combined with the hum of heated conversation in the dimly lit bar provided the backdrop for Neall's post-mortem of events.

Lynch nursed a beer. "'Twas a close one, sir."

"Excellent work, Tommy. I'll be with Catullus for the remainder of the evening. You get some rest."

"Righto." Lynch downed his beer, snatched his hat, and left.

Neall turned to Grayson. He had not trusted him at first but was warming to the scion of a wealthy New York family. "Tad, post a man in the lobby. Have him report anything suspicious to me alone. You and the rest of your lads get some food and rest."

Grayson nodded. "Will do. But I was wondering where this all ends?"

The question surprised Neall. "What do you mean?"

"I mean, sir. Whoever is behind this has all the opportunity in the world. Who knows how many assassins await the marquis on any given day?"

"I do," Neall said. When he had met with Lord Avondale, they discussed the likelihood that each member of the Aulic Council had dispatched a team. He did not want to tell him he suspected at least two different teams had struck thus far.

Grayson's eyes narrowed. "Well, sir? Is there a plan to get ahead of them?"

He's not the fool. "Yes, there is. But you raise a point. It needs some adjustment." When Grayson left, Neall motioned to the bartender. "A bottle of your best port."

He found Lafayette and his entourage finishing plates of chicken from a nearby restaurant—the first measure of his new mitigation strategy.

"Ah, *Monsieur* Neall, please join us. Not *Poulet au Vin Blanc*, but more likely the simple but excellent roast hen I enjoyed with the Continental soldiers."

"I ate in the bar, *Monsieur*, but I brought some after-dinner libations."

Neall talked as Lafayette, George, and Levasseur sipped the port.

"Whenever possible, we'll order food and drink from places not on your schedule. I'm mixing up the New York militiamen a bit. Some, in close to you, others a distance. And the numbers will vary. Also, we must adjust your timetable without informing local authorities. We cannot let newspapers and broadsheets provide a map for gaining access to you."

"I don't see how that can be. The people need to know where and when I go," said Lafayette.

"We must walk a fine line between public knowledge and your safety, but I see your point," said Neall.

"Anything else, *Monsieur*?" asked George.

"I may put Mister Grayson in charge of the day-to-day security. I want to get ahead of these plotters if I can. I may need to ride on once again and reconnoiter upcoming venues."

Lafayette put down his glass, strode across the plush carpet to the fireplace, and stared into it. He then pivoted and said, "I do not want this journey to put innocent citizens at risk. But Sergeant Riley is my personal bodyguard. *Monsieur* Grayson must take instructions from him."

"I understand. But your enemies can hide in a mob. And the mob itself can pose a great danger," said Neall.

Lafayette lowered his eyes at Neall. "I assure you, *Monsieur*, I, more than any living man, know the power and the danger of the mob."

***

Champs de Mars, Paris, July 17th, 1791

Lafayette's aide de camp halted his horse and handed him an envelope. "Sir, an order from the mayor."

Lafayette scanned it as the hoarse cries and a drumroll of epithets rolled across the broad, green, expansive parade field on the city's western fringe.

He looked up. The late afternoon sun was bright. A sea of angry Parisians filled the place where the Kings of France reviewed their most prestigious regiments. Now, a rabble filled it, and only a battalion of Lafayette's *Garde Nationale* stood by to protect what he and the Constituent Assembly hoped would be the official signing of a new constitution ushering in democracy under a constitutional monarch. Now, the Jacobin faction had stirred their forces to protest and stop the signing under the aegis of the king's aborted attempt to flee Paris.

"He wants the mob dispersed," said Lafayette. "Yet though loud, they are mostly peaceful." Lafayette was less than truthful. The mob scuffled with the *Gendarmerie* and *Garde Nationale* troops all day. Minor scuffles. Troops, even Lafayette, had been pelted with stones and things unmentionable.

"So, it was before the mob stormed the Bastille," replied the aide.

The crowd began to roar, "*Mort aux traîtres!*" "Death to traitors!"

"Look!" a sergeant exclaimed.

Across the field, several men were being hoisted on poles, dangling like puppets with ropes around their necks.

"Once the mob tastes blood, the deluge will come," said the aide.

A colonel approached, with his hand tightly gripping his sword hilt. "Sir, the men are restless. We must suppress this before even more are killed."

Lafayette squinted at the sight across the field. The limbs were being plucked from the torsos of the dangling corpses. "Clear the field, colonel. The *Garde Nationale* cannot stand idly by while French citizens are in danger."

"*Avec baïonnettes! En avant!*" The colonel's sword flew from his scabbard and glinted in the sunlight.

As one, the blue-coated ranks stepped forward with fixed bayonets and nervous eyes fixed on the angry crowd ahead.

"Spare the good citizens of Paris, Colonel," said Lafayette.

Lafayette watched anxiously. He remembered the Liberty Pole fight in New York City and the Boston Massacre that sparked the American Revolution. *Minor scuffles can explode into a maelstrom of violence and open rebellion.*

Rather than break and run, the mob rushed the outnumbered soldiers. Lafayette watched his troops move piles of angry men for over half an hour, only to retreat when large numbers descended on them. Bayonets jabbed threateningly. But Jacobin rabble-rousers who secretly salted in the crowd urged the mob to "attack and kill the soldiers of tyranny."

Stones flew through the air, crashing down on the heads of the soldiers.

Along the line, muzzles suddenly flashed, and the *pop* of musket fire erupted, at first sporadically, then in a crescendo. Lafayette stared in horror as the mob broke and his men cleared the field. In less than an hour, it was over.

His aide galloped up to report. "Sir, the mob has left fifty dead on the field. More than that lay wounded."

Lafayette knew even more wounded had shuffled away to safety as he had at Brandywine and that they would live to fight another day.

"What are your orders for the colonel, sir?"

"Tend to the wounded and collect the dead. Then return to barracks."

Lafayette knew the Jacobins would now stir the city and all of France to reject a constitutional monarchy. The Revolution would now lurch left in what could only prove fatal to the king and perhaps the nation.

Chapter 12

Philadelphia, Pennsylvania, September 30th, 1824

Neall slid his boot into the stirrup and swung into the saddle like he was on parade with the regiment. He absent-mindedly reached for his saber and smiled faintly.

He glanced back at the carriages lining the street. *One last fanfare before the marquis heads south.*

Neall looked down at Lynch. "Anything at the post office?"

"Just this, sir." Lynch handed Neall an envelope.

His eyes scanned the contents. "Damn!"

Lynch blanched. "I've never heard you swear, sir. It must be bad news?"

Neall shifted his gaze to Grayson, who sat on the horse beside him. "What's with your lads in New York?"

"What's the letter say?"

"The soprano, *Senora* Carmen De Gioia, is at large."

"What? How?" exclaimed Grayson. "She was under lock and key in the armory basement."

"It matters not. That explains the tainted punch."

"What will we do, sir?"

"Stick to the plan, of course," Neall shot back angrily.

"And be on the watch for an exotic woman. The boys will be happy to oblige," Grayson quipped.

Neall's face softened. His anger was fading. "Yes. But our soprano seems adept at enticing foolish men to do her bidding. Keep that in mind."

Neall flicked the reins, and the horse began a slow canter down the road south of the city. His mind was racing with the implications of the soprano's escape. Someone had gotten her out. *Had she seduced one of the militiamen? Possibly. Had she a confederate in the New York City grab bag of corrupt politicos? Likely.*

As his horse's hooves stirred up small dust cyclones, his mind raced to what came next. New York was one thing. Had the black hand of the Holy Alliance and the Aulic Council reached as far as Washington? He had to see the one man who might know. A wry smile crossed his lips. Who in the Service would have reckoned Richard Neall's success would depend on the services of a papist monk?

***

The National Hotel, Washington

Carmen de Gioia pulled on a pair of silk stockings and slipped into her petticoats. A weary body stirred from the featherbed as she slid them up her well-shaped calves. "Don't get up on my account, my dear."

Carmen's English had improved since she arrived in America. The people were so ignorant. No one spoke even French. *Vabbè! Whatever it takes to avenge.*

"You speak English quite well now, "*Cara mia*," said her companion. Perhaps you should star in one of their operas."

"Do you know of any?"

"Venus and Adonis." he sprang from the bed and sank his mouth into her neck. His lips blew soft air into her ear, sending shivers down her spine. "By John Blow."

"You are joking!"

"Only a little." His arms encircled her waist, and he whisked her to the bed.

"I am half dressed!" she protested, knowing it was useless.

"We have time before our friends arrive."

"I have potions to make — chefs to meet. We can't serve the marquis his death cup ourselves."

His hands fumbled clumsily with her underskirts. "You may keep the stockings. The petticoats are mine!"

Carmen tried to push away from his massive form, but his strength, as she knew all too well, was irresistible.

Later, she was mixing a concoction, slowly pouring poisons and laudanum together in a cocktail, stirring gently. "This can go into anything. I don't want to depend on the soup course again."

"And your use of American traitors with firearms did not go very satisfactorily, either."

Carmen smiled softly. "But he was a gentleman."

"A gentleman who got you arrested. It took a not-so-gentleman to get you out."

"And I thank you for it. Who did you bribe?"

"Everyone! These Americans are obsessed with money."

Hoarse laughter filled the room.

"Seriously?"

"The Aulic Council has purchased the support of several prominent members of a cabal of politicians called, curiously, The Holy Alliance. Strings were pulled, and gold spread in the right palms."

"The Constables who released me from that awful armory seemed very well fed."

"I just need to feed the right people in the capital."

105

"Anyone in mind?"

"I'm meeting a friend who can provide me with names. After the fiasco on the boat and in Philadelphia, I think it's time we remove the marquis' attendants and guards. Then it will be a simple matter of my hands around his throat."

She knew he meant it. He reveled in inflicting personal physical pain just as she preferred the less personal use of potions. "The last time did not go well. It seems that Mister Neall was your match. How did you ever survive his blade?"

Buxhowden's face darkened, and he began to snort like an enraged bull. "Willpower, my dear. Baroness von Krüdener taught me the art of channeling it to control my corporeal condition. The blade sliced cleanly and missed vital organs. I willed myself to die. When they threw me into the harbor waters, I revived and swam to safety."

***

The Chancery, Baltimore, Maryland

Brother Bernard scrawled indecipherable notes across a page as Neall recounted the events of the past weeks. Bernard rose and retrieved a pair of glasses and a flask when he finished his report.

Only then did Bernard reveal a message from a priest in Austria containing more details of the scheme to get Lafayette.

Neall's eyes widened. "Our best agents in Austria and Prussia have learned little of this. How did you?"

"The garrison where they meet in Salzburg has a chaplain. Austria is a Catholic country. I can say no more," replied Bernard.

"You're sure there are three teams?" Neall asked.

"Yes. You have met one."

"With the soprano now at large, I still face three."

"*We* face three," replied Bernard. "But there's more. The Aulic Council has recruited agents in various American circles."

Neall nodded knowingly. "Flynn and his cronies!"

"I'm afraid it goes higher up." Bernard realized he needed to let Neall know more than he originally planned. "And sadly, includes people in Washington."

"Who?"

"Excellent question. I have some contacts in Georgetown. They are paying special heed to the delegations of the three nations. Lieutenant Putnam is talking to people."

"Meaning?"

"Making inquiries. Have you spoken with *Madame* Bonaparte?"

"I came right here, so no," said Neall.

Bernard lifted the crucifix from around his waist and rubbed it with his thumb. He found that soothing, somehow. "She has a guest — a French lady from her past. Perhaps yours as well?"

"Who?"

Bernard revealed some of what he knew of Madeline Pauline Goulet and her connection to Elizabeth Patterson. But he did not tell what he knew of Neall's connection.

"Do you suspect her involvement in this?" Neall's eyes narrowed, and his face darkened.

"Do you?" Bernard saw he had touched a sensitive area.

"I don't know. Why should I?"

"I think it's time for some brandy."

The brown liquid looked pleasing to the eye in the glimmer of the chancery lamplight.

"To the president," said Neall.

"To the king," replied Bernard with a wry smile.

They sipped quietly at the liquor for a few moments.

"What next?" asked Bernard.

"'Tis indeed the question, Mister Neall. The marquis departs Wilmington on time and should be in Washington by the twelfth. So, we have a few days to plan."

***

Ellicott's Falls, Maryland

Betsy Patterson gazed out the coach window at the steep, wooded hills surrounding Ellicott Falls, a small wood-milling village just south of Baltimore. The road winding through the narrow defile was thick with mud, and the coach's wheels jerked and screeched as the horses slowly slogged through the muck.

A cane made a sudden *rap* on the window. Richard Neall leaped onto the running board and twisted the door handle. Before she could react, he was beside her, his arms around her waist.

He kissed her tenderly before quipping, "It'll take a week to clean the mud from these boots."

"Does that mean you'll spend the week with me?" she asked, only half kidding.

"That depends. I understand Madeline Goulet is with you."

"You spoke to Brother Bernard? Well, yes. We are getting along now that she has dropped her Bonapartist and Royalist ways."

"Madeline always was torn between two worlds," Neall said.

"Aren't we all, Richard? I'm torn between being a Bonaparte and Patterson, between France and America. You between England and..."

He kissed her fiercely, and she gave in to his overwhelming magnetism. The most appealing man she ever knew.

The sound of a heavy draught wagon rattling with fresh-cut lumber broke the spell.

"Have your driver find someplace discreet. We have little time." Neall said.

Is he planning an assignation here, in my coach? She ordered the driver to follow Neall's directions, and soon, they were in a clearing behind the mill. She saw his horse tethered there. *No assignation.*

"Is Madeline at your house?"

"No. She left for Washington this morning with several letters of introduction from me."

"Letters to whom?"

"Various American officials." Betsy hated the swampy collection of huts that served as her nation's center. "Who else would live in such a place?"

"I'll need their names. Anyone else?"

"Yes, a baron I'm acquainted with." She hoped he would not probe further.

"How well?"

"Not as well as you. I was his companion at several social galas. His wife was back home."

"Where is home?"

"Vienna. You don't suspect collusion?" She suspected it herself.

"Perhaps."

"You're a terrible liar."

"Only to you. Send me a letter of introduction to the baron. I'll be staying at the Old Coaching Inn in Georgetown."

Betsy kissed him fiercely and pulled back. "If you promise not to behave, I'll bring it myself."

***

The Old Coaching Inn, Georgetown, October 12th

Neall tore open the envelope and scanned the letter of introduction. He smiled and looked up at Tommy Lynch. "It's what I suspected. Her baron is Franz Riedel, Assistant Envoy Extraordinary of the Austrian Sub-Consulate."

"Sub-Consulate?"

"The full Consulate is in New York City. The Americans still don't have full diplomatic relations with them."

"'Tis a fancy title, indeed, sir."

"Fancy title for an Austrian spy and possibly the lead Aulic Council agent in America."

"B'Jeezus, ye have hooked a big fish, sir."

"Haven't hooked him yet. He may merely be bait. Our fish may be one Madeline Pauline Goulet or someone she's connected to."

"What's the plan, sir?"

"Misters Riley and Grayson must be responsible for Catullus's immediate safety. You keep an eye on the Austrian Sub-Consulate for a visit by Madeline. It's at this address on Massachusetts Avenue. Most of the legations and consular offices are there, as it's central to the town."

"Avenue? I've seen better cow paths in Donegal, sir."

Neall described Madeline. "Middling height, dark hair, and eyes with fair skin. She dresses like an aristocrat, which she is, or rather was. Follow her. Note anywhere she stops and with whom she speaks."

"Should be a delightful task."

"Don't let her comely features lure you. She escaped the guillotine through her guile and spied on at least three countries. Betrayed others and even posed as one of Napoleon's hussars."

"A hussar? Not possible, sir."

"Rumor has it she cut her way out of a band of Cossacks near Paris in 1814. Although why she took up the saber is unclear, some suspect she was paid to get Bonaparte himself."

Lynch flipped his hat onto his head and slid from Neall's hotel room.

Neall scooped up his hat and cane and took his horse from the stable. He rode to Lafayette's hotel, a nondescript clapboard building near the White House.

"I've assigned Mister Lynch to other duties, so you'll be in charge, Mister Riley."

"Sergeant Riley."

"Sergeant Riley. Mister Grayson will control his men, but you are responsible for Catullus."

They discussed the next few days. Lafayette had no significant engagements but wanted to visit some people and places before continuing south.

"His impetuous nature is an advantage, sir," said Riley. "Difficult for an assassin to plan ahead."

"So he has to get close to Catullus's entourage or just get lucky," said Grayson.

"Keep your boys sharp. Be suspicious of everyone," said Neall.

Neall joined Lafayette at dinner. When the waiters cleared the table and pipes came out, the talk turned to the escape of *Senora* De Gioia.

"I find it astounding she hasn't yet been found," Lafayette said.

"The Americans aren't very keen on a large police system. Something they adopted from our English tradition," Neall said.

"I'd say the woman is charmed," said Levasseur. "I once saw her sing at *la Scala*. Magical!"

"As was her soup. I say she has had luck," said George.

Lafayette glanced at his son and rose from his seat. "When the Austrians had me in prison, I had terrible luck. An elaborate escape plan was arranged. I was, at the time, allowed daily rides in a coach. On returning to the prison, I asked to step out and walk the final mile for exercise. The sergeant of the guard obliged, joining me, of course. When the carriage was out of sight, two riders galloped up as arranged, subdued the sergeant, and gave me a horse."

"Brilliant, thus far," said Neall.

"Brilliant until misfortune struck. I took the wrong road, having misunderstood my instructions, and was soon captured. My rescuers were also arrested but later deported from Austrian territory — to their fortune! As for me, my confinement conditions became quite harsh due to my audacity."

"Let's hope we have better luck. Now, I have work to do." Neall tamped out his pipe and reached for his hat and cane. "*Adieu*, gentlemen."

As he reached the door, Lafayette said, "*Monsieur*, I must thank you for all you have done on my behalf."

"And will continue to do," said George.

Neall tipped his cane to his hat and slipped out.

***

Austrian Sub-Consulate, Washington

Lynch adjusted his collar to stem the cool breeze of the autumn evening. He had been observing the somber stone building for hours but did not see anyone fitting Madeline's description among the dozens of passersby. Neall did not say how long to stay in the area, but he feared someone had spotted him and decided to pack it in at dusk.

Six men in faded blue jackets and dark trousers stepped from the building and, with a series of military moves, lowered a yellow flag with a black two-headed eagle. The sun had begun its final descent over the western horizon when a woman exited the building.

Lynch strained his eyes in the dimming light, but her dignified gait and elegant clothing marked her as someone special — the woman in question. *That's you, me darlin'.*

She walked to the corner, where she barely paused, yet stole a glance back to see if she was followed before crossing the street where hackney coaches lined the curb in anticipation of an evening shuffling diplomatic personnel to dinner, the theater, or salons. As she reached the other side, evening shade descended on Massachusetts Avenue – the time between sundown and the city's lamplighters making their rounds to illuminate the capital's streets.

Lynch made for the line to hail a cab to follow her, but a pair of sturdy hands wrenched his shoulder and turned him about.

"*Nicht so schnell!*"

He was looking into the faces of two frowning men in the comical blue and black suits by the flagpole.

"Let me go," said Lynch as he struggled to break free.

"*Bleibt stehen,*" commanded one of them.

Lynch did not need to speak German to know what they meant. They wanted to give the lady time to slip away. He had a split second to submit or resist. He relaxed in their grasp, and they instinctively lessened their grip. Not much, but enough for him to slip free and unleash a barrage of punches to their whiskered faces and button-festooned bellies.

He was across the avenue waving for a hackney in seconds, but she was already in a carriage, quickly rolling into the blackening night.

***

When he left Lafayette, Neall rode to Massachusetts Avenue to check on Lynch and cover his post so he could have dinner. He arrived in time to see Lynch follow a well-dressed woman and get accosted by what looked like the Austrian Sub-Consulate's guards.

Tom Lynch can handle those two.

Neall's horse maintained a casual pace as it trotted south in pursuit of the carriage with the lady. The carriage rolled south on Fourth Street, heading toward the river. At Q Street, it slowed to a halt, and the lithe figure slipped out of the cab and into an elegant brick home with the speed of a nymph. The lamplight was dark, but he thought he recognized the face. *Good job, Tommy Lynch.*

He slid from his mount, slipped the reins around a lamp post, and edged close to the red brick townhouse. There was just enough light to make out the address: 211 Q Street. He toyed with the notion of a direct approach. Tap on the door with the cane and have it out with her, but he would need to learn who lived at the house or owned it.

Guess Tommy will spend tomorrow morning at city hall.

Then, he would decide his approach. Either confront the lady directly, force her to talk, arrange a more seductive move, or continue watching her. But he needed to act soon. He had little time. Lafayette would only be in Washington for a few more days, so they'd likely make their move.

The following day, Neall took a carriage for his morning business. He tapped his cane absent-mindedly while his eyes roamed over the smattering of simple wooden and brick buildings, meadows flush with grazing sheep, cows, and horses, and small stands of trees. Stacks of stone and lumber marked the site of future construction that he imagined would someday give way to more massive edifices.

At last, the carriage slowed to a halt before a gray Palladian-style building with a sizeable Union Jack fluttering in the morning breeze.

"British Legation," announced the driver.

Neall stepped into the dusty road and dropped a coin into his waiting palm. A sharp *crack* of the whip sent the hackney searching for another fare.

Two men in conservative suits opened the double-wide wooden doors, and a third escorted him to a small office crowded with books and maps. Neall was taken by its resemblance to Brother Bernard's lair in Baltimore.

These inside men live in the same world.

A man of about fifty with thinning white hair and a beak nose set over a small white mustache rose as Neall entered. A dwarfish hand greeted him. "I've been expecting you, sir. The lord highly recommended you." His smile revealed uneven teeth.

Neall had planned to see the British consul, Godfrey Arthur, but decided to check in with Lord Avondale's man, Robert Horan, at the legation. Neall had never met Horan, but Avondale insisted he was one of the Service's best "Special Accounts Clerks." So far, he was unimpressed.

"Do you know why I'm here?"

"The lord didn't allow as much, but I'm assuming it has to do with the Aulic Council and the Marquis de Lafayette."

"Your powers of deduction impress, Mister Horan."

"I've had years to work on them, sir. And I have contacts in both the Austrian sub-consul's office and the Prussian Legation."

Things aren't always what they seem. "Even more impressive. Not the Russian?"

Horan cast a sheepish smile. "Hard to get at their Legation. The Slavs are such a riddle. I might work ten years and not get close to one. Very standoffish."

"We'll work with what you have. Start with the Austrians."

Horan grinned, exposing his picket fence. "I always start with the Austrians, sir."

"What have you got?"

"They are very attuned to the marquis's visit. Seems they gather every paper, broadsheet, and bulletin reporting on his journey."

"That's to be expected. The world is watching."

"My contact informs me of an unusual series of parcels scheduled to arrive in diplomatic pouches. So whatever is in them is not meant for the eyes of the American customs inspectors."

"Must be something unique if the inspectors can't be bribed to look the other way."

"My thought exactly, sir. We seem to get everything we want through without a problem."

"Weapons and powder can be had here cheaply, so it can't be that."

"My contact has been instructed to take extreme risks to find out."

"What can your contact tell us about Baron Franz Riedel, Assistant Envoy Extraordinary?"

"I can tell you he is much more than a baron. He's an *Oberstleutnant* in the Austrian Service. He specializes in things that a real baron would never do."

"I know, gentlemen, don't spy."

"Spying is just the beginning. Riedel speaks several Balkan tongues, English, French, and Russian fluently. He has crushed several rebel movements in the Balkans. Kidnapped a Turkish general surrounded by his army. He engineered the plan to smuggle young Bulgars into the Habsburg lands to educate them and train and recruit them as agents to return and stir the populace against their Turkish overlords."

Neall took this in. "There must be something else about him."

"Hmm," Horan's fingers played with each other, and his mouth made curious shapes. His eyes closed, then quickly fluttered open, and he nodded. "Yes! He studied engineering as a cadet but began his career as an officer of the Artificer Corps."

Neall's eyes widened. *A bomb maker!*

"Anything else?"

"Just that, when this affair is done, I'd appreciate a report on all the doings at the Chancery."

Neall was surprised. "I thought we had an arrangement with the bishop. Lord Avondale sent me to him."

"We do, of a kind. Yet, it is an enigma to us. We'd like to know about its capability and how it operates. Plus, names. Will help in our assessment of the value of what they produce."

"I should think the result of their product would suffice. I'll see what I can do." But Neall had no intention of submitting a report.

***

Lynch could hear the rumble of heavy wheels from a two-block distance. After his unsuccessful query as to the ownership of the townhouse, he went back to keep an eye on things. His forbearance paid off. A large draught wagon pulled by a team of nags rolled down the street, occasionally stopping as two men leaped off and on.

What in the name of? As it drew closer, Lynch could see the men, burly types with arms bulging with muscles, hauling large ash cans positioned along the street. *Bloody dustmen — trash collectors.*

The wagon did not stop at 211 Q Street. Instead, it slowed enough for two figures to leap to the street and back onto the vehicle, which sped to the next home. Lynch eyed the house, where he thought he saw a flurry of curtains at a parlor-floor window. He had to decide: pursue or stay? His head turned in time to see the wagon pick up speed and turn down Fourth to the waterfront and out of sight.

His pulse raced. His eyes scanned the street for a clue. There was nothing there. Nothing! 211 Q Street was the only home without an empty ash can before it.

He decided to pursue it. At first, he moved down Q at a casual stroll, but when he turned onto Fourth, his feet pumped like pistons, and his heart pounded like one of the new steam engines. He caught sight of the wagon as it turned toward a waterfront warehouse.

The heavy wooden doors were just shutting as he arrived. *B'Jeezus!*

Sounds of hurried voices came from the warehouse. Lynch rushed to a window along the side. A solitary lamp provided only shadows, but they were moving something that did not involve waste. The shriek of heavily rusted hinges announced the doors reopening. Lynch crouched behind a water barrel, hoping to see what would emerge.

"Was ist los!"

Lynch turned to see a figure hovering, one of the trash haulers, coming at him with fists clenched. The man's eyes suddenly widened as if he knew Lynch. He reached for a large hunting knife tucked in his boot and waved it menacingly at Lynch. *"Komm mit."*

Lynch recognized the voice and the face, one of the thugs from the Austrian Sub-Consulate. Lynch began to reach for his pistol tucked under his vest but decided to play along for a while.

The thug shoved him toward the rear of the warehouse, where Lynch spotted a small boat rowing across the river toward a town just south of them. Another more forceful shove sent him into the bowels of the building. The dark cavern-like warehouse was almost empty. Just a few barrels and a crate lined up neatly on one side. A mix of straw and sand covered the floor.

Another man stood in the shadows. *The other Chucker – out from the Austrian sub-consulate.*

"Why in the name of Saint Patrick's snake are ye buggers following me?"

The two looked at each other and rambled in German. He thought he could make out the word *Tot* from the gibberish. "Now, where do ye think ye'll be toting me?"

"Ja, umbringen," said the other with a nod and a wink. "Kill."

The thug with the long blade nodded, turned to Lynch, and smiled. *"Tot ist besser."*

He stepped toward Lynch with the blade chest-high. The other drew a pistol from a box and pointed at him. *Click!* He pulled the hammer back to full-cock. As he did, Lynch gave a kick, sending a mix of sand and straw into the air while drawing his Forsyth pistol.

Boom! The thug's shot went deep into a heavy beam overhead.

Lynch leveled the Forsyth at the thug with the firearm and sent a ball into his chest. While his finger worked the action and the hammer, he pivoted right and squeezed just as the other thug lunged with the blade.

When the smoke cleared, the two Austrians lay dead.

Lynch pondered his next move as he dragged the bodies into the dark recesses of the warehouse and covered the bloodstains with sand and straw. Lynch made a quick check of the building to make sure no one was hiding. He needed to report back to Neall. *The Cap'n will know what to make of this.*

***

Northeast Executive Office Building, Washington

Kent Putnam strolled past the White House and turned east. About eighty yards before him stood a two-story brick building with an ionic portico harkening to ancient Greece. Putnam visited the facility often, as the Department of State Consular Service was on the second floor.

Since leaving sea duty, Putnam's ostensible job was liaison with the Consular Service, which assisted distressed American sailors, among other missions. He had once benefited from their services when his small vessel shipwrecked off the shore of a semi-hostile power. They quickly arranged his release.

Putnam's highly polished shoes echoed through the hallway of the spacious new building. Open doors revealed secretaries in somber suits scribbling away at ledgers, correspondence, and orders from the clerk in charge of the Service. Some were graduates of nearby Georgetown and other prestigious colleges, hoping for an overseas posting. But most were ambitious political men seeking bureaucratic advancement.

Robert Buchanan, a recent Georgetown graduate, rose from his desk and gripped Putnam's hand firmly. "What brings you here, Kent?"

"Our favorite Frenchman, of course. Brother Bernard asked me to provide you with an update for your superiors." His eyes shifted toward the White House as he slipped a double envelope into Buchanan's hand.

Among their other tasks, the two men served as a communication channel between the Archbishop's Chancery, the State Department, and the White House.

"They are always eager for news on this Catullus affair," said Buchanan.

"Mister Neall is aware of 211 Q Street," Putnam said.

"Really? How could he?"

"Once he left Sergeant Riley in charge of personal protection, he went to track down the possible assailants. It's a good bet someone at the British Legation tipped him off.

"Probably Robert Horan. Ostensibly a clerk of some sort, but I believe he works for their secret service."

"As does Neall," said Putnam. "Well, I suppose we should commend him for his initiative."

"Still, a possible safe house for the Holy Alliance or one of its member states is our affair."

"I disagree," said Putnam. "If Brother Bernard and the bishop brought him into the Circle, it is also his affair. Perhaps he can learn more about the goings on than we can."

115

Buchanan smiled mischievously. "And if the affair is exposed and something goes awry, we can leave him and his service responsible. Provide the Secretary with plausible denial. After all, we have diplomatic considerations to maintain."

Putnam pursed his lips. His friend was a true diplomat despite his foray into intelligence matters on behalf of the State Department and the White House. Putnam had heard rumors of shutting down the Chancery and assigning its mission to an actual government agency.

"Of course we do. But first, we must protect General Lafayette."

"At least while he's on American soil," said Buchanan.

"He's not on American soil now. He's on a steamer due to land at Petersburg."

"Yes, I know. I am supposed to join the general for part of his Virginia trip. I was packing to leave when you arrived."

"No son of the Old Dominion would pass on a chance to return to horse country," said Putnam.

The two smiled. Buchanan was the scion of wealthy Henrico County planters who had studied at Princeton. Putnam was born near Winchester to a small farm family but made for Alexandria, where he apprenticed on a small schooner at sixteen.

"Why don't you join me?"

Putnam nodded. "I'll send a note to Brother Bernard. He wanted me to spread our inquiries farther south."

***

Petersburg, Virginia October 19th, 1824

Lafayette sauntered down the gangway with the snappy step of a man twenty years his junior. Scores of Virginians began cheering the man who many still remembered led a small army that blocked the advance of Lord Cornwallis's regulars without fighting a major battle.

After a short speech, Lafayette waved his hat as his coach kicked up dust along the road to Yorktown, where another crowd was waiting. Hundreds lined the road this time, and thousands crowded the open field where he was to speak.

The horses slowed, and the coach gradually rolled under a large triumphal arch adorned with red, white, and blue bunting. Riley saw a tear roll down Lafayette's eye.

People of all ages climbed trees or trotted alongside the procession. The carriage halted, and Lafayette stepped from the coach. "Wish me luck, *Monsieur*," he said to Riley.

Mayors, assorted clerics, and dignitaries from the surrounding counties waited to greet him. Local Virginia militia companies and various fife and drum bands had assembled and now stood quietly at attention.

"To return to this place where our two nations united to defeat our common enemy is too much," Lafayette said. "My fellow Americans, I salute you!" A gloved hand rose to his brow.

The multitude exploded in cheers, and as one, the bands struck up *"La Marseillaise."*

***

Yorktown Siege Works, October 14th, 1781

The constant *boom* of cannons filled the night sky, and the *thump* of heavy iron balls shook the soft, loamy soil along the York River. Major General Lafayette stepped down from the parapet and turned to Christian, Count von Forbach, and Lieutenant Colonel Alexander Hamilton. He grasped each firmly by the hand.

"My sincerest hope for your success, gentlemen. My only regret is that I cannot personally lead one of your columns. But His Excellency has entrusted this to two of the boldest men in the allied armies."

Although a close colleague, he did not mention that Hamilton was not his first choice.

Washington and Rochambeau had entrusted Lafayette with the joint attacks on the two British redoubts protecting General Cornwallis's southern flank. Their fall would seal his fate.

"The firing will cease shortly," Lafayette said. "Soon after, a small battery will discharge a volley — your signal to attack."

Both men nodded.

"Redoubt Ten will swiftly fall," Hamilton pronounced.

Von Forbach, the Colonel of the Royal Deux-Ponts regiment, eyed him skeptically.

"They must both fall swiftly," said Lafayette. "You each have four hundred of the two armies' best men. The redoubts are weakly held, but the *Anglais* will reinforce if you don't attack with *l'audace.*"

"Weakly held in numbers, yes, but trenches, *fraises,* and *abatis* protect both," said Hamilton. "And as you said, they are English."

"Your sappers must be quick at hacking apart the tangled tree branches and cutting down the wooden stakes, and your infantry even bolder, for they must rush forward to fill the trenches with fascines. Then, your boldest will rush forward with ladders and storm the walls. You can expect your men will be under fire the entire time."

"My men work best under fire," replied von Forbach. His manner was confident, not arrogant.

"One last reminder. The storming parties will fix bayonets to their muskets but no flints. They must storm forward with *l'audace* and give the *Anglais* cold steel."

At eight o'clock, three successive cannon shots broke the stillness of the night. The signal guns belched fire, and 800 cheering men rushed forward.

Lafayette saw the night sky erupt with scores of fireflies — the British on the ramparts were firing desperately at the assailants. "*L'Audace!* Boldly, my friends!"

Quick flashes from musket barrels and explosions lit the dark. Cheers and roars grew so loud they drowned out the dwindling rattle of muskets. *Stay steady, my comrades.*

Ten minutes that seemed like an eternity later, a runner came gasping to Lafayette's post.

"Colonel Hamilton has the honor to report Redoubt Number Ten has fallen! We lost nine men killed and twenty — five wounded."

"And the *Anglais?*"

"Eight killed and twenty prisoners. Major James Campbell, the redoubt's commander, is among the taken."

Lafayette nodded, almost absent-minded. He was most concerned for von Forbach's men. Hoarse cries and the *pop* of muskets came from his direction. *Redoubt Nine clearly gives more resistance.*

Some twenty minutes later, a young ensign arrived from the *Regiment Gatinois.*

When Lafayette received the final report, it was from the French field commander, General Baron de Viomenil, who had galloped to the redoubt as von Forbach's regiments secured it. The French lost fifteen killed and seventy-seven wounded, while the British and Hessians lost eighteen men killed and fifty captured.

Lafayette turned to an aide de camp. "Report this at once to His Excellency. I believe the assaults on the redoubts have won this battle, the campaign, and perhaps even the war."

Chapter 13

Richmond, Virginia, October 27th, 1824

The last plume of smoke rose from the tree line as the steamer gasped its way up the river, careful to avoid the shallows and an embarrassing grounding. Thousands stood in awe, with palms sweating and hearts beating at the idea of meeting one of the last surviving leaders of the American Revolution.

Militia regiments stood erect in long gray and blue lines. Colorfully uniformed bands, decked in white, red, and even yellow, awaited the signals from the drum majors. Civilians, in their Sunday best, fidgeted with anticipation. The greatest spectacle to grace the state capital was unfolding, and young Edgar Allan Poe, a lieutenant in the Junior Morgan Riflemen, was ecstatic to be part of it.

Poe's outfit was the younger version of the militia regiment named for the famed Revolutionary War hero from Winchester, Daniel Morgan. Morgan led a corps of riflemen who were the most vaunted fighters and best shots on either side of that war and had defeated the British at Saratoga and Cowpens. Poe was proud to be a member and, at not quite fifteen, the youngest officer in the junior corps.

The Junior Rifles senior cadre officer, Captain Markham, paced back and forth before the color guard, where Poe usually served as the bearer of the American flag. But today, he carried a saber and stood behind the colors as the executive officer for this occasion.

Markham was not happy when Poe suggested this. But Poe had his reasons. A premonition of sorts descended on him several days earlier. At first, he did not know why, but things slowly began to form in his mind.

It began with dreams. It always did. Shadowy but distinct dreams — always the same. A crowd around a man, urging them to the love of liberty and country. Band music in the background. The *rumbling* and *hissing* of steam engines, the bosun's whistling, and the ship's bell *clanging* — all extinguished by the *crack* of a rifle shot.

To young Poe, it could only mean one thing. *The great General Lafayette was in danger!*

He dared not mention it to anyone lest they think him mad. He was already considered somehow different by the boys in the outfit. And he agreed. But he grew suspicious when Corporal Pretorius appeared as a new senior cadre, suspicions based more on intuition than any facts. He had a strange accent, but Richmond had begun to attract foreigners. *Why was he here?* Pretorius had told one of the cadets he worked at The Virginia Bank. But when Poe asked the name of several prominent employees there, men who had dined with his adopted family, the Allans, Pretorius shrugged.

On the rifle range, Pretorius fired a perfect score and then, at the urging of his young charges, did the same at 500 yards. Pretorius used his personal weapon, a .54 caliber Hawken percussion rifle, rather than the standard issue firearm, an 1803 Harper's Ferry rifle the Morgan Rifles carried. The large and powerful Hawken rifle did seem to match the man, who was large and burly, barely fitting into his uniform.

Poe became obsessed with Pretorius and his dreams and hardly slept as the day of Lafayette's visit drew nearer. *What to do?* Poe got out of color guard detail, at least color bearer, as the executive officer did not really have a job, so he could slip away and keep an eye for Pretorius.

The question plaguing Poe's fevered mind was how an assassin would strike.

***

The bands played *"La Marseillaise"* as the steamer bumped the Yorkville landing slip. The splendid military formations snapped to present arms, and the bands began a series of stirring marches. Lafayette and his entourage climbed into a luxurious barouche drawn by four magnificent horses glittering with silver.

At the edge of Richmond, the barouche began the grand procession, surrounded by cavalrymen whose warm-blooded steeds jingled rhythmically with each prance of their hooves. The Richmond Light Infantry Blues and a brass 23-piece band followed in crisp stride. Behind them rolled the caissons and guns, whose wheels seemed to lumber along in time. Prominent citizens of Richmond marched or rode with them.

"I don't believe my own Marines could turn out as sharply as these Virginia militiamen," Riley confided to Lafayette.

Lafayette smiled in assent. "Many turned out for the final march to Williamsburg and Yorktown."

Eager spectators crowded every door and window. Riley's ears rang from the hoarse cries of "Welcome, Lafayette! Welcome, Lafayette!" The main street of Richmond had a gradual rise up Shockoe Hill, so Riley could see plainly from Market Street as they rode up and reached the top. Riley saw an impressive stone building with a sign of white letters over blue: *The Virginia Bank*. They continued down this street and arrived at Capitol Square.

The entourage was overwhelmed by the goodwill and noise by the time the barouche rolled to a halt in front of The Eagle Hotel. *This may be the most challenging place yet*, Riley mused.

Riley jumped out first, pushing away some local police and signaling Ted Grayson to have the New York militiamen secure the building.

When Lafayette and Riley strolled into the grand lobby, they were greeted by Kent Putnam and Robert Buchanan. Riley's face flushed. *Neall mentioned nothing of their joining the entourage.* Riley did not like surprises. He was a Marine sergeant — everything planned in detail.

***

"Where's Corporal Pretorius?" Poe asked Captain Markham.

"He said the colonel gave him another mission."

"More important than this?" Poe's eyes scanned the crowds as they marched behind the furling standards: the stars and stripes, the Old Dominion flag, and the regimental colors.

Poe's senses tingled, and he took a slow breath. *What could he do?* The immediate answer was nothing. Nothing but hope he was either wrong or that Pretorius would not act before he could figure something out.

The rows of young Morgan's Rifles filed down the prescribed alley into a stable mews. After a quick roll call, Captain Markham dismissed them until the next day, when they were assigned to escort the general. Poe was hoping to sneak over to Linden Street and pay a call on a young girl of whom he had become fond. But the delicate and dreamy Elmira Royster would have to wait. He had a general to save and an assassin to catch — if he could.

Poe felt sure Pretorius was up to something. *But what? Attempt to get close enough to ensure a deadly strike? Or take his chances with a long-distance shot.* His mind returned to the range where he saw Pretorius fire a ball of lead and shatter a brick from 500 yards — three times!

But from where? The hotel was logical. So was Capitol Square, where the general was scheduled to speak to the throng and mingle. *He could use a pistol or sword there.* Maybe at The Richmond Bank, he could set himself up on an upper floor and pick his prey like a hawk.

Poe gasped to himself, "using his Hawken." He decided the least he could do was warn General Lafayette. *To hell with them all if they think I'm delusional.*

***

That night, they had a magnificent ball at the Eagle in Lafayette's honor. A large band played waltzes, and fireworks screeched over Capitol Square like the rockets' red glare over Baltimore's Fort McHenry in 1814.

No one paid any heed to the pimple-faced youth in the gray uniform of a cadet. Several constables stood guard at the entrance to the Eagle Hotel. The lobby had been cleared of all but those staying. Raucous noise and music from a player-piano drifted from the bar.

Poe approached the neatly dressed men at the reception desk. He was counting on the uniform to do its work.

"I have an important message for General Lafayette," he said.

"Leave it with us, cadet. We will send it up to his room."

"No, I *have* strict orders to hand it to him and answer any questions he has."

"Well, that's just not allowed...."

"That's all right. I'll take the cadet up," said Kent Putnam, who stood with two bottles of champagne procured from the bar.

"Thank you, sir."

Lafayette stood listening patiently to Poe. When he finished telling them his suspicions, he lowered his head, expecting ridicule, berating, and rebuke before being tossed out and a letter sent to Captain Markham. So he was stunned by the response.

Putnam placed his hands on Poe's shoulders and glanced at another man he learned was Robert Buchanan of the Dinwiddie County Buchanans. "Thank you for your concern, Cadet Poe."

"Cadet Lieutenant Poe, sir."

"You're from here. Can you spare the time to assist us in further investigating this matter?"

Poe's pale face beamed. "Yes, sir!"

"Excellent! I'm Lieutenant Putnam of the United States Navy. This is Mister Robert Buchanan of the State Department. We were sent here to help safeguard the general." Putnam turned to Riley. "This gentleman is a United States Marine placed in charge of the general's immediate security detail, a team from the New York Second Artillery."

Poe's gaze shifted to Lafayette, who stood calmly nodding. "It's my honor to do whatever I can to help one of the great war heroes of our Glorious Cause."

He did not mention the premonitions after Poe told them of his suspicions. The conversation turned to Corporal Pretorius. Poe did not know where he was staying in Richmond, so his only tangible link was The Richmond Bank.

"But I can go see Captain Markham. He'll know more about him."

"No," said Putnam. "This affair is very confidential. We don't want to alarm the public or cast a shadow on the joyousness of General Lafayette's visit."

"Does the name Claude Barnes mean anything to you, Cadet Lieutenant?" asked Riley.

Poe shrugged. "No, not particularly. Why, sir?"

"I'm Sergeant Riley. No sir needed."

"I'm sorry, Sergeant Riley. But who is Claude Barnes?" Poe wondered how a sergeant could be at the level of or superior to the others.

"He was a guest on the *Cadmus* and dined with General Lafayette at every opportunity," said Riley.

"Mister Barnes tried to interest the general in his banking services. He owned banks in Virginia, or so claimed."

Poe was confused. "Why not question him about Corporal Pretorius?"

"We would love to, except Claude Barnes is dead," said Riley, whose eyes shifted to Lafayette and back to Poe. Riley then related the events on the *Cadmus* with the crisp conciseness of a marine.

"Your associate, Mister Neall, shoved a blade into him, and you buried him at sea," mused Poe.

"Mister Neall dumped his corpse into the harbor off Staten Island.," said Riley. "Since then, we have captured his accomplice, but she has now escaped."

"Describe Corporal Pretorius," Putnam said.

When Poe did, in vivid and poetic detail, Riley and Putnam stepped out momentarily.

When they returned, Putnam spoke, "Although Mister Barnes is dead, this Corporal Pretorius fits his description and demeanor. The bank connection is an interesting coincidence. We must find this, Pretorius. I'm sending someone to ask your Captain Markham to inform us if he shows up for morning assembly. The general wants to visit a couple who assisted him and his army while operating around Richmond during the Revolutionary War. The Ege family lives at a place the general calls the old stone house."

"My stepfather is acquainted with the Ege family. They're one of the oldest families in town."

"Are you willing to come with us now and check the route we'll take tomorrow?"

***

Poe led Putnam and Buchanan down the route along Main Street past the capital district, not far from the river. Most of the way was lined with rows of two-storied buildings and private homes that appeared benign. The trees along the walkways were of concern, enabling an assassin to hide and spring at the general's coach. They strode through lamp-lit streets, occasionally halting to discuss whether a particular spot provided a vantage point for an attack.

"The boys from the New York militia will be armed and looking from the coach behind. And, of course, the local militia will be out in force."

"My outfit as well," said Poe.

They turned right on North 20th Street and saw a small gray stone two-story building with three gables on the second floor.

"The general says he and later General Washington used this as their headquarters. The Ege's must have done quite a bit for this excursion," said Buchanan.

Putnam wandered over to a three-foot-high post with a piece of paper attached. "Look, someone placed markers for the units to assemble tomorrow. You're with the Junior Morgan Rifles, young man?"

"Yes, sir."

"Here's where your lads will be," Putnam said. "Looks like you can take your place among them and still help. If you see Corporal Pretorius or anything suspicious, remove your hat and place it upside down on your head. That's the signal we use for danger."

***

The Old Stone House

Commands echoed in the predawn air as the Junior Morgan Rifles silently tramped down East Broad Street and made a right-column turn onto 20th Street. Captain Markham's gloved fist rose in the morning gray, and over 100 of Richmond's finest youth clicked to a halt as one.

Poe rubbed his eyes and yawned as he marched in the company's dust, an executive officer's fate. It had been a sleepless night. He dozed a few times and even felt another premonition surge. The large round face of Corporal Pretorius haunted him. *Would he join us? Is this all a coincidence?*

Poe saw a collage of images as hazy as they seemed real. *The shadow of a woman under a lamp post. Pretorius lurking in one of the many shops, where he emerged to leap on the general's coach. He saw a dark room and Pretorius lashing out with his rifle. A military tune echoed faintly in the background. Another shadow of a woman? Or something else?*

Pretorius smiled while a strange and sensuous woman offered the general a drink. When Lafayette refused, Pretorius growled like a bear and raised his large rifle at the general, who stood with his vest thrown open for the blast.

"No!" snapped Poe, who threw himself between them. The rifle exploded with a flash and a swirl of black smoke.

Poe sat up. His last imagining, more than a dream or a premonition, roused him in a sweat-soaked nightshirt, a thumping heart, and a pounding head. *Did I save him?*

***

Dust-caked shoes shuffled as the cadets formed ranks across from the Old Stone House. Poe reached for a scarf, dusted his brogans clean, and passed the cloth along the lines.

Markham rode up and slipped from his saddle. "Lieutenant Poe, have you seen Corporal Pretorius?"

"No, I haven't, Captain. I haven't seen him. Have you?"

"He told me he would meet the company at the house."

Could he be inside with the family? Poe was tingling inside.

124

"It's barely dawn, and General Lafayette's party isn't due here for several hours. See if someone in the house is awake and if they saw him. Not that he's needed. A rifle instructor is a bit redundant to a unit with unloaded arms."

Poe's check came up with nothing. Mister Ege and his wife were finishing an early breakfast and told him no one had come by.

"Have you seen anything unusual?" Poe asked.

"Not a thing," said Joseph Ege, who appeared fit an alert for a man of his years. "Martha?"

Martha Ege was a handsome middle-aged woman, clearly his second wife. Or his third.

"Why yes. I was dumping a basin. An hour before you boys arrived. I glanced at the street and saw someone lingering under a lantern."

Poe's heart began to thump. "A large man?"

"Heavens no. That was the odd thing about it. It was a lady. Quite well dressed. Elegant. Now, what would a respectable lady be doing about at such an hour unescorted?"

***

The Capital Square was jammed with eager well-wishers anxious to greet the hero that morning. When Lafayette was announced, he made some pleasant remarks.

"My dear friends, my countrymen, we should never forget those who fought and bled to give us such a republic. A republic destined to be one of the grandest in the world."

Hats flew into the morning sky as the crowd erupted in cheers. Then, a line formed to meet the general, who took the time to shake hands with each one.

To Putnam, it seemed like everybody in town wanted to shake hands with the general. When he finished, Riley escorted Lafayette back into his coach while Lieutenant Tad Grayson, Buchanan, and Putnam searched the crowd for suspicious signs.

Young Poe had informed him of the nocturnal visit. *Could Carmen de Gioia be in Richmond? Is she connected to Pretorius?*

"It is time to meet some old friends," said Lafayette to his son and Levasseur.

The carriage rolled down Main Street to 20th and turned right. This visit was personal, so few Richmonders filled the streets except those riding to the capitol for state business or others trundling carts to and from the waterfront.

A moderate crowd had gathered around the Old Stone House. After all, one of the oldest families in town was meeting the most celebrated man in America. The door to Lafayette's coach flew open, and he stepped out to a round of huzzahs. He bowed at the crowd.

125

Putnam left the entourage and rushed to find Poe standing at his post. "The general is taking tea with the Eges. Mister Grayson's boys are securing the home. Show me where Mrs. Ege spotted the mysterious lady."

Putnam and Poe stood under the lamppost. It did not provide a vantage point to assault Lafayette or his coach.

"Why was she here?"

"It is strange. I would have picked another spot. The route here has so many."

Putnam smiled. He was a good boy. "Thanks for your help, Cadet Lieutenant Poe. You may return to your post."

Putnam turned on his heels and headed for the waiting coach.

***

Poe watched Putnam for a moment and then pondered the mystery. The cadet band struck up the first notes of a patriotic tune. A shudder went through Poe, and he began to tremble, almost as though he were in shock.

When it struck him, he stopped shaking. The mystery lady was marking the way to the Old Stone House—checking the pace and timing! Poe heard Captain Markham's voice in the distance. They would be stepping off any moment to escort the general back to the Eagle. He had to decide. *Where would they strike?*

Poe spun about, raced up 20th, and pivoted left on Main Street. Then he halted. Something caught the corner of his right eye. He turned, and across the intersection stood what he suspected was the place—The Richmond Bank.

The bank's corner spot was perfect. An assassin in the bank had a clear field of fire on Lafayette's coach while the escorting cadets were still around the corner. *It's the perfect location! But what of the customers?*

Poe grasped his saber by the scabbard and trotted to the bank's double doors. *Locked!*

A handmade sign that smelled of fresh paint hung from the door handle. *Closed in Honor of General Lafayette.*

Poe jerked each handle, but they did not budge. The windows were barred. *It's a bank!* His heart began thumping, and he felt damp in the palms of his white gloves.

Poe raced down the alley in search of a back entrance, but it, too, was locked. *Of course, it is.*

Then he noticed it. A three-story building that catered to the public had to have a fire escape. His eyes raced across the whitewashed stone wall until he spotted a black wrought iron ladder bolted to it. His gateway to the top. The wiry teen yanked himself up and scrambled as fast as he could. The sound of marching music was getting closer.

He pulled himself onto the roof and lay panting and aching. When he caught his breath, he crawled to a skylight and worked it open with his blade. *Who said sabers were only for show in modern war?*

Poe swung down and dropped to the floor like a cat. The music was loud enough to mask his footsteps and his heavy breathing. Drawing the saber, he slowly edged down a dark corridor toward a room with a gable that faced the intersection of Main and 20th.

The room only received light from the gable's open window, almost filled by the bulk of a dark figure. Poe could hear him whispering.

"That's it, Marquis, just a little more, and I'll have you as your coach makes its turn."

Poe edged closer, barely daring to breathe for fear of giving himself away. He heard the *click* of the percussion hammer going into full cock. From hours on the range, he knew the next sound would be the bang of the hammer on the nipple and the *boom* of a heavy lead ball escaping the barrel and spinning into the unwitting general, splattering the flesh and bone of the hero of two nations.

He raised the blade and stepped forward, placing it between the shoulders of the sniper. He slowly pressed the tip. "Drop the rifle, sir. You are now my prisoner."

The figure turned, and the jowly face of Corporal Pretorius greeted him with a scowl.

"You left your post, cadet. I'll put you on the report," he snarled. Pretorius rose to his full height, but his head bumped into the low roof of the gable. "Damn, you! I can't waste my shot on you without alerting them. Pretorius flipped the heavy Hawken around and slammed the butt at Poe's chest, but the cadet fended it with a twist of his wrist. Poe's palms sweated profusely, but the cotton gloves helped him keep his grip.

"You little...."

Pretorius lunged with all his strength, but the lighter Poe sidestepped him again and leaned forward and right, using techniques he never thought he would need, sending the long blade through Pretorius's exposed underarm. He felt the edge rub something stiff but slid past it deep into the big man's barrel chest.

Pretorius's mouth widened as if to speak before he slumped forward, spiraling down onto the oak flooring.

Poe reached down to pull the Hawken from the grasp of his sausage fingers when he felt a sharp *crack* to his head. His knees buckled, his eyes blurred, and then all went black.

***

Putnam crossed the street and looked back, just catching the tails of Poe's gray uniform coat flapping in the breeze. *Where's the boy off to?*

He turned to Grayson. "I need to follow up on something. I'll catch up with you."

Putnam's longer legs kept him in sight of the quicker Poe, who sprinted around the wagons and carriages at the Main Street intersection and behind The Virginia Bank building.

But the fire ladder challenged him. He worked his way up rung by rung and struggled over the railing onto the roof. *It's been years since I went skipping up the rigging.*

He found the skylight and slowly lowered himself, dropping like a sack of potatoes to the floor. He rubbed his arms and legs. *Nothing broken.*

As he moved down the dim hallway, he heard voices and the sound of struggle that ended with the shattering of a bottle. Putnam stepped into the gabled room, now lit by the open window. Two figures lay on the floor, but his attention was on the woman. She did not notice him as she tried to steady a rifle on the window sill.

Putnam drew his pistol, a heavy naval pistol, and pulled back the hammer. "Turn around," he ordered as he stepped over Pretorius's body.

She turned and lowered the weapon at him. He could see it was too heavy for her to control. He stepped toward her and grabbed the barrel, yanking it from her hands before she could pull the trigger. The woman was beautiful, and her olive skin and stark eyes beguiled him even in the subtle light.

"You will not prevent me from finishing Alexander's work!"

"Alexander? Buxhowden? He's dead."

Her lustrous lips parted in a smile, sending a shiver down Putnam's spine.

"Alexander is a master of the black arts. Lord of the Occult. He willed himself back to life."

Putnam bent down to check Poe's pulse. *Alive.*

He yanked the saber out of Pretorius's limp form. He was not superstitious, but the woman's words made Putnam cringe in expectation of his revival.

Instead, a sickening sucking sound emerged as the blade slid from the corpse. Putnam felt Pretorius's jacket. He was in a civilian suit, not the militia gray. Under it, he felt a heavy leather vest that circled his entire torso.

He looked at the woman. "Easy to return from the dead when you're not dead."

She laughed. "My potion enabled Alexander to remain motionless as they tossed him into the water."

Putnam rose to his feet and stepped toward her. "You'll have to come with me, *Senora* De Gioia. I have to summon help for the boy."

"That boy killed the invincible Alexander Buxhowden. For that, he must die!" Carmen slipped a vial from her skirts and bent to pour the contents into Poe's ear.

Putnam kicked the vial from her hands. Carmen surprised him with a cat-like leap, pointing a small dagger right at his belly.

Putnam's naval reflexes kicked in, and he ran her through with Poe's saber.

Carmen's beautiful dark eyes widened, and her throat quivered as though she were going to begin an aria. But her song became a frosty gurgle of blood that spattered her chin and her laced décolleté.

Putnam lowered her limp form to the floor beside her lover. He released the hilt, picked the young cadet lieutenant from the floor, and carried him toward the staircase.

Chapter 14

The Chancery, Baltimore, December 1ˢᵗ, 1824

Sparks hissed and shot from the fireplace as Brother Bernard tossed another log into the hearth. "'Tis the chill of winter that numbs me bones in my old age. Don't ever get old." The monk chuckled to himself and shuffled to his seat. "Now, where were we?"

"You wanted to discuss my report," said Putnam.

"Yes, and discuss the way ahead. That's why I asked *Madame* and Mister Neall to attend. I assume Sergeant Riley has things around the general in hand?"

"With the aid of Lieutenant Tad Grayson and my agent, Tommy Lynch," said Neall.

Bernard felt slightly uncomfortable when he read Putnam's report, verified by Mister Buchanan of the State Department, who was with him in Richmond. After the encounter at The Richmond Bank, Putnam got medical attention for the young cadet they met there. Then, he, Buchanan, and two of Grayson's men cleaned up the scene, as knowledge of the threat had to be kept from the public. They donated to nearby Saint John's Church and saw to their burial without religious services.

Neall continued. "I find it hard to believe Buxhowden was able to live and feign death after I gave him what I thought was a fatal thrust."

Putnam opened a satchel and tossed the leather and mail girdle onto the table. "Pretty ingenious. Primitive, but it worked. Cadet Poe's saber thrust, perhaps the length of the blade and its edge, slid along two mail links and through the leather. That *was* a fatal thrust."

Neall flushed. "I'll endeavor to do better next time, sir. But I do appreciate your young Poe's efforts and his discretion."

"Young Poe is highly gifted. He told me he had premonitions before his encounter."

Bernard sat up in his seat. "What kind of premonitions?"

"He didn't say, Brother. But they were good enough to save General Lafayette's life."

"What next?" Neall asked.

"That's why we are here, Mister Neall. What does Robert have to say?"

Neall did not reply.

"Bob Horan. Your Service's man at your Legation."

Neall raised an eye. *This monk knows more than he lets on.* "If there were such a man, I would say, Brother."

"But what would he suggest if there *were* such a man?"

Neall cleared his throat as he pondered his response. Putnam and Betsy were looking at him in rapt attention. "Well, he'd probably agree to our keeping this discreet. He'd probably assess that we still have at least two teams to contend with."

"More if the team members split up," quipped Putnam. "Teams are risky business. Members must communicate, and that is always a weakness."

Neall was impressed with Putnam's knowledge of spycraft. "I see why the good brother brought you into the circle. Now, I believe Buxhowden and the soprano were the only two operatives in Virginia. The rest of that trip went without a hitch. General Lafayette will be in the Washington area for the next few weeks. Keeping him alive should be our focus. But... "

Bernard's eyebrows rose. "But what?"

"His biggest threat is next year. Likely somewhere in the west. The general will be traveling through the spring."

"Is that what you think, or is that what Bob thinks," Bernard asked.

"It's what His Majesty's government thinks."

"Good. Now, why?"

This monk is working me.

"I think I know," said Putnam. "Next year is an election year. Why not send the message then?"

"The general is leaving in May. The election is in November," said Betsy.

"Maybe," said Putnam. "But maybe not."

"The counting of votes will be over by the spring, Kent," Betsy said.

"I didn't mean the election. I meant General Lafayette could remain longer to meet the new president and say farewell to the old. And besides, Mister Buchanan advised there is talk of asking him to stay through the summer."

"Why?" asked Bernard.

"The fervor of General Lafayette's visit could affect popular sentiment in a new administration's favor."

Neall pondered this snippet of America's internal politics. This invitation was more than it seemed. He would make sure to discuss it with Horan.

Bernard finished making a note and glanced up. "Can you obtain a prospective list of the additional venues?"

Putnam nodded. "I'll try."

"Once those are known, I propose someone visit the most likely venues for a future attempt," said Bernard. "Meanwhile, we must try to identify the remaining assassins."

"There's likely four still at large," said Neall.

"Unless the Holy Alliance has sent others, and these are merely the ones they want us to know of," said Betsy.

You are more than a beautiful and sensuous woman, Dear Bess. Neall cursed himself for not realizing that. *How did she reach such a conclusion?*

"That's a possibility I had not as yet considered. We must take it seriously. Well done, *Madame* Bonaparte." Bernard smiled at her, and she returned it with a nod.

***

The Patterson House, Baltimore, Maryland

The tea sloshed in the cup as Betsy lifted the fine porcelain to her freshly painted lips and gently sipped. "Lovely, isn't it, Madeline?"

Madeline's lashes fluttered as she sweetly smiled. "*Oui, Madame.* I thank you for it and for allowing me to stay here occasionally."

"You seem to be spending more and more days in the capital. Do you find it to your liking?" Betsy knew Washington was an acquired taste. Few Europeans, especially ladies, took to the muddy streets and clapboard buildings. Swarms of laborers, mostly slaves, sweating as they dug the foundations and moved the brick and stone.

"*Comme ci comme ça.*"

"Just so, so? Well, it's still a town in the making. Did my contacts assist you?"

Madeline smiled suggestively. "*Oui. Merci.* These men of the diplomatic services are the only saving grace — such charm. I have been to the theater here, such as it is. Some diplomatic balls and dinners."

"Has anyone, in particular, caught your fancy?" Betsy was sure she would reach out to the French embassy at a minimum.

"This is *Très discret.* A certain baron."

Betsy hid her surprise. No barons were on her list. "Which baron?"

"There are so many who affect nobility in the knowledge the primitive Americans cannot distinguish commoner from a nobleman."

Betsy tilted her head knowingly. "Has your baron been a gentleman? Or more apropos, have you been a lady?"

Madeline placed her hand to her white throat and blushed. "Such a question! Of course not." She parted her lips in a knowing smile.

Betsy realized the possible connection. *This is disturbing.*

"After all, I do have to enjoy myself while in that tawdry village."

"A baron sounds like a fine way to enjoy oneself."

"Not quite the brother of an emperor or some princes of the blood you have known, *ma chère fille*."

Betsy was not insulted by the retort. It was both accurate and fitting. So long as Madeline Goulet kept her talking, she had the chance to lure her into an indiscreet remark.

"I really must go. Perhaps I will share the name of my baron when he delivers on his promise to grant my most ardent wish."

Betsy signaled to the servant for her cloak. "Most ardent wish? An estate in Europe?"

"I said most ardent, not most distant. No. It is as simple as it is fervent—to meet the Marquis de Lafayette again. His schedule is quite public. But there seems to be little time for personal visits. It seems he is guarded around the clock. Why would they do that to a man so beloved by all?"

Betsy found her comments odd, if not reckless. "Would your baron deliver you to a competitor, especially a ladies' man like the marquis? What lover would do such a thing?"

"Indeed. The baron is very fond of me."

"I would like to meet such a man of refined and sophisticated ways. Does he offer you an opportunity?"

Madeline put down her cup and reached for her things. "I have said too much, but yes. He says he has an invitation to an event and hints I may accompany him."

"Hints?"

"He is very teasing in his way. Part of his seduction of me."

"He must be French."

"Or someone who knows the French—French women, that is!" Madeline giggled and rose to leave.

***

Later that evening, the servant answered the bell and opened the door for an unexpected visitor. Betsy led Neall to the East Wing parlor, where the servants seldom went. A small fire spat yellow flames. They sat side by side on a small sofa facing it.

His hand entwined hers. "How did your visit go?"

She raised her cheek to him. "You won't even kiss me first?"

Neall slipped his arm around her and drew her lips to his. Minutes later, Betsy sat back and smiled. "Well, that was more like it, Richard Neall. Thus far, this visit is much better than my last."

Neall's face flushed. *What does she do?*

"Just a joke, my dear Richard. Madeline was gracious but only partially forthcoming."

"Partially is a good start."

Betsy narrated the details of her tea party with Madeline.

"You played her well as she played you well. Two professionals at intrigue locking horns."

"Stags have horns. They bellow and charge, smashing ferociously. But the female of the species, the hind, uses body language and subtle sounds in her combat. Only as a last resort do the female deer thrash each other with forehooves. And that is rare but often fatal."

Neall was bemused by the answer.

She smiled. "What? I have been on many a hunting party. One must learn the ways of the prey."

"Indeed. So how did the signals and gestures go?"

"She has a baron in tow. One who was not on my list of prospective connections."

"How do you know?"

She giggled and let her finger play with his chin. "Because I would save a baron for myself."

The comment seemed odd. But Neall went to other matters. "Keep pressing her on who he might be. And, as importantly, what event she expects to attend. That is a likely point of attack." He did not tell Betsy they had surveilled a woman fitting her description at the Austrian Sub-Consulate, which they believed was Baron Riedel's undeclared residence. *Some things the Service must keep from the Americans.*

***

The rapid knock, knock on the hotel door, was answered by Levasseur. A bellboy handed him a large sealed envelope. "Mister Buchanan sent this exclusively for General Lafayette."

Lafayette beckoned from the small desk near the window. "I am he, young fellow. Bring it here."

Weathered fingers tore open the seal, and Lafayette moved closer to the light from the window to see better. "What is this Levasseur?"

Levasseur glanced at what appeared to be a very official letter. "It's President Monroe's annual message to Congress!"

"Please read it to us," said Lafayette.

Levasseur adjusted his spectacles and cleared his throat.

"In conformity with a resolution of Congress of the last session, an invitation was given to General Lafayette to visit the United States, with an assurance that a ship of war should attend at any port of France which he might designate, to receive and convey him across the Atlantic, whenever it might be convenient for him to sail. He declined the offer of the public ship from motives of delicacy but assured me that he had long intended and would certainly visit our Union in the course of the present year.

"In August last, he arrived at New York, where he was received with the warmth

134

of affection and gratitude to which his very important and disinterested services and sacrifices in our Revolutionary struggle so eminently entitled him. A corresponding sentiment has since been manifested in his favor throughout every portion of our Union, and affectionate invitations have been given him to extend his visits to them. To these, he has yielded all the accommodation in his power. At every designated point of rendezvous, the whole population of the neighboring country has been assembled to greet him, among whom it has excited in a peculiar manner the sensibility of all to behold the surviving members of our Revolutionary contest, civil and military, who had shared with him in the toils and dangers of the war, many of them in a decrepit state. A more interesting spectacle, it is believed, was never witnessed because none could be founded on purer principles, none proceed from higher or more disinterested motives. That the feelings of those who had fought and bled with him in a common cause should have been much excited was natural.

"There are, however, circumstances attending these interviews which pervaded the whole community and touched the breasts of every age, even the youngest among us. There was not an individual present who had not some relative who had not partaken in those scenes, nor an infant who had not heard the relation of them. But the circumstance which was most sensibly felt, and which his presence brought forcibly to the recollection of all, was the great cause in which we were engaged and the blessings which we have derived from our success in it.

"The struggle was for independence and liberty, public and personal, and in this we succeeded. The meeting with one who had borne so distinguished a part in that great struggle and from such lofty and disinterested motives could not fail to affect profoundly every individual and of every age. It is natural that we should all take a deep interest in his future welfare, as we do. His high claims on our Union are felt, and the sentiment universal that they should be met in a generous spirit.

"Under these impressions, I invite your attention to the subject, with a view that, regarding his very important services, losses, and sacrifices, a provision may be made and tendered to him which shall correspond with the sentiments and be worthy of the character of the American people."

"President Monroe himself signed it." Levasseur looked up from the letter to see tears rolling down Lafayette's weathered cheeks.

"Father, this is quite the honor," said George, who was also welling up.

Levasseur remained composed. "There is also something else in the envelope. It's an official invitation to address the Congress assembled on the tenth of December."

"That's in three days. We must prepare," said Lafayette, dabbing his eyes with his handkerchief.

***

The Capitol, Washington, DC, December 10th, 1824

Riley stepped from the carriage and scanned the scene. "Who's in charge here?"

A burly man with a double chin greeted him with an extended hand. A pair of constables stood anxiously behind him.

"I'm the sergeant at arms. Are you Mister Riley?"

"Please call me Sergeant Riley. I'm a marine and will handle most of the general's security. Mister Grayson and his men will also assist. The next carriage has the general and his entourage."

The sergeant at arms glanced at Grayson and the other New York militiamen. In their plainclothes, they looked like accountants.

The sergeant at arms sneered. "Marines? I have a whole platoon of them around this building, plus two more on alert. A troop of Maryland Dragoons is also here." He pointed at the array of blue-clad men on horseback.

"See here, sir. Sergeant Riley is specially appointed by the State Department with the approval of the White House."

"Now, who are you?"

"I'm Lieutenant Todd Grayson, New York Militia—Second Battalion, Second Artillery Regiment. But Sergeant Riley directs security for the general."

The sergeant at arms nodded disdainfully. "Follow me, gentlemen."

Grayson's men spread out around General Lafayette and his entourage. They climbed wide marble stairs and passed under a granite portico into a dark-paneled hallway. An impressive winding stairway took them to the entrance to a larger room beyond the archway. Above the archway were stenciled the words: *Chamber of the House of Representatives*.

A tall, austere-looking man with searing eyes and a strong jaw approached Riley.

"I'm Henry Clay," the House of Representatives Speaker said, pushing past him to grasp Lafayette's hand.

They had met days earlier when the general visited both houses of Congress separately. The two spoke a few pleasantries. "I'll introduce you," said Clay with a grin. "If there's any time left, you get to speak."

Lafayette nodded pleasantly.

Riley saw the general did not understand the joke. American politicians like to speak ad nauseam, usually about themselves. And Henry Clay, the famed Kentucky politician, was one of the masters.

The sergeant at arms stepped into the chamber and called it to attention. "Gentlemen, the Speaker of the House of Representatives and General Lafayette!"

They stepped into the cavernous room jammed with members of Congress.

At the large podium decked with red, white, and blue bunting, Riley and his men took up positions agreed to with the sergeant at arms and eyed the crowd. Besides the Senators and Congressmen, scores of assorted wives and family members jammed the hall—a rare time when women were allowed on the floor of the House.

A military band struck up "*La Marseillaise,*" and a church choir pumped out the words in passable French.

Allons enfants de la patrie,
Le jour de gloire est arrivé !
Contre nous de la tyrannie
L'étendard sanglant est levé !
L'étendard sanglant est levé !

Let's go children of the fatherland,
The day of glory has arrived!
Against us tyranny's
Bloody flag is raised!
Bloody flag is raised!

They ended with the third stanza finally chanting:

De vils despotes deviendraient
Les maîtres de nos destinées !

Vile despots would become
The masters of our fate!

The crowd went into a frenzy of cheers and huzzahs. Feet stomped so hard the scores of chandeliers shook, sending sparks and flickering the lamps. Then they grew hushed as Clay went to the podium to render the speech of a lifetime in a lifetime of great speeches:

He cleared his throat and glanced toward Lafayette, sitting quietly.

"*General. The House of Representatives of the United States, impelled alike by its own feelings and by those of the American people, could not have assigned me a more gratifying duty than that of being its organ to present to you cordial congratulations upon the occasion of your recent arrival in the United States, in compliance with the wishes of Congress, and to assure you of the very high satisfaction which your presence affords on this early theatre of your glory and renown. Although few of the members who compose this body shared with you in the War of our Revolution, all have, from impartial history, or from faithful tradition, a knowledge of the perils the sufferings, which you voluntarily encountered, and the signal services, in America and in Europe which you performed for an infant, a distant, and an alien people; and all feel and own the very great extent of the obligations under which you have placed our country. But the relations in which you have ever stood to the United States, interesting and important as they have been, do not constitute the only motive of the respect and admiration with this House entertains for you. Your consistency of character, your*

137

uniform devotion to regulated liberty, in all the vicissitudes of a long and arduous life, also commands its admiration. During all the recent convulsions of Europe, amidst, as after the desperation of every political storm, the people of the United States have beheld you, true to your old principles, firm and erect, cheering and animating, with your well – known voice, the votaries of liberty, its faithful and fearless champion, ready to shed the last drop of that blood which here you so freely and nobly spilt in the same cause.

"The vain wish has been sometimes indulged that Providence would allow the patriot, after death, to return to his country, and to contemplate the intermediate changes which had taken place; to view the forests felled, the cities built, the mountains leveled, the canals cut, the highways constructed, the progress of the arts, the advancement of learning, and the increase of population. General, your present visit to the United States is a realization of the consoling object of that wish. You are in the midst of posterity! Everywhere you must have been struck with the great changes, physical and moral, which have occurred since you left us. Even this very city, bearing a venerated name, alike endeared to you and to us, has since emerged from the forest which then covered its site. In one respect, you behold us unaltered; and that is in the sentiment of continued devotion to liberty, and of ardent affection and profound gratitude of your departed friend, the Father of his Country, and to you, and to your illustrious associates in the field and in the cabinet, for the multiplied blessings which surround us, and for the very privilege of addressing you which I now exercise. This sentiment, now fondly cherished by more than ten millions of people, will be transmitted, with unabated vigor, down the tide of time, through countless millions who are destined to inhabit this continent, to the latest posterity."

The congregation broke into cheers again but quickly regained their composure as they awaited the man of the hour, year, and decade.

Lafayette rose and bowed to Clay and then the assembly. He ambled to the grand podium, halted, and gazed at the enormous American flag dangling overhead.

He glanced down at his notes to speak, but for a moment, whether it was age or the sudden return of a memory, his mind took him someplace else.

***

City Tavern, Philadelphia, August 5th, 1777

Raucous laughter filled a room dense with the smell of men in wool suits stained with sweat from the summer humidity. Soon, the aroma of pipe tobacco would combine with this to make the room intolerable. But young Gilbert Motier, Marquis de Lafayette, barely objected. His hand went to his waist and stroked the sleek purple silk of the freshly sewn sash that marked him among the most elite of the Continental Army – a Major General.

The atmosphere was pleasant, even though the man at the head of the table, General George Washington, had just finished updating members of Congress on the dangerous situation they faced trying to thwart British General Howe's move against the capital.

He watched Washington fend off questions. When he was formally received before the dinner, Washington's tall figure and steady eye impressed him, but his command of the situation, both the good and the bad, as he fended the Congress's tough questions impressed even more.

As the dinner ended and anxious waiters gathered piles of plates, the commander-in-chief's aide tapped Lafayette's shoulder. "His Excellency would like you to join him on an inspection of the city's defenses."

"Of course," said Lafayette, both surprised and flattered that he would invite a newly appointed officer with no knowledge of the army to accompany him.

The rattle of muskets at the ready seemed louder in the night's darkness. The air was still very humid. Nothing in France matched its stultifying effect.

"Who goes there?" a sergeant demanded.

"The commander-in-chief," Lafayette replied without thinking. Was he supposed to speak as the junior of the two? Then he remembered that a pair of strongly built men from Washington's Personal Guard rode a few paces to their rear—*no point in stopping now*.

"Have your officer in charge show us the forward lines, brief us on his patrols and sentries, and report on the state of your weapons and victuals." Lafayette had spent only a short time with his regiment in France but remembered their standing inspection protocol.

They rode from regiment to regiment until all the defenses were accounted for. Washington questioned officers and men, checked the lay of the few cannons they had, and peppered Lafayette with questions while asking his opinion of the responses he had received.

As they rode back to town, Washington turned to Lafayette. "I am very pleased to have you among my staff, Marquis. From now on, however, you are Major General Lafayette, my trusted advisor and senior member of my household staff."

Lafayette's stomach sank. He expected a brigade command, if not a division. "Thank you, Your Excellency. I am honored."

"I know this disappoints you, sir. But others are not so pleased with your appointment, and truth be told, you have much to learn of this army before I can entrust a command to you. But if tonight is of any indication, I am sure that day is not far off."

***

Riley's daze shifted back and forth as he observed the crowd. *Who is the threat among all these?*

Grayson was near the main entrance to signal the sergeant at arms and the Marine officer commanding the platoon. One of the New York militia had gone to the upper balcony and checked the visitors for signs of weapons.

Lafayette was almost finished with his speech, a thoughtful review of the sacrifices of the American Revolution, sometimes a sentimental take on the cause of mankind's liberty. Still, he finished it with a somber look at the future. America must stand firm against autocracy and support democracy wherever its seeds begin to bloom.

He caused an uncomfortable moment when he pivoted to a lifelong dream of his, an America where all men, regardless of their race or skin color, were free and equal in rights. Riley noticed Clay's lips tighten, and the southern contingent issued low groans.

A gentle smile crossed Riley's lips. *The general is like a dog with a bone on this topic.*

But when Lafayette finished, he paused and dabbed his forehead before exclaiming, "*Vive Liberte'*, *Vive* George Washington, *Vive* the United States of America, *Vive ma Patrie!*"

As one, the assembly members leaped to their feet, and hoarse cries of "Huzzah" and "*Vive* Lafayette" echoed for many minutes. Then, the band struck up a marching tune from the American Revolution.

Riley stepped forward, took Lafayette by the arm, and guided him to the entrance where the marine escort waited. Along the way, the marquis stopped to grasp every hand thrust his way, peppering them with thanks in French and English.

Riley only breathed a sigh of relief when the entourage was in the coaches and the carriages rolling at full speed toward the hotel.

***

Alexandria, Virginia

"How useful it is to have powerful men in the palm of your hand," said Nagy as he downed a shot of gold-tinted liquor. His eyes then went to Madeline's glass. "Drink, *Kedvesem*! My darling…"

She hesitated but then lifted it to her lips.

"Don't sip. It is our custom. Slivovitz must be downed at once!"

Madeline recalled the time she posed as a soldier and threw back her head. The plum brandy seemed to burn her tongue and scorch her palate.

"Very good!" Nagy drew an arm around her slender waist. "I missed you. Your baron must be very accommodating." His hands roamed. "Does he make love as I do?"

"No one makes love as you do." Madeline edged away. Her attraction to him was fast fading.

He poured himself another Slivovitz. "He was able to get me an invitation to Lafayette's speech to the American lawmakers. I met a congressman whose wife is in some town far away in Ohio. He wants me to accompany him to a grand ball honoring Lafayette."

Nagy put down his glass. "*Istenem!* My God, that's good news! What better place to eliminate him than surrounded by scores of drunk American lawmakers and their fat wives?"

Madeline stared into her empty glass.

"What's the matter, *Kedvesem*? It's perfect."

"I will not help you place your bomb. It will kill innocent people, including many women. Don't you see that even the Aulic Council will not abide such an atrocity?"

"They will give us accolades. The more heinous and public Lafayette's death, the better. Democracy snuffed out by fear." He smiled, and his eyes gleamed like a tiger seeing its prey in the jungle's dim light.

Her hand trembled. She reached for the bottle and poured another shot. She knew all too well that she could not back down now. She had faced many dangers, but nothing as terrifying as the Aulic Council. *They will kill me.*

Nagy's hand locked on her wrist like a vise. "Calm yourself, *Kedvesem*. When you hear my plan, you will realize it is as foolproof as deadly. A blast that will shake the world of these Americans and their notions of liberty."

***

The Chancery, Baltimore, December 20th

Brother Bernard's eyes narrowed, and his brow wrinkled. "When did you receive this news, *Madame*?"

"Yesterday," said Betsy. "I had tea with Madeline Goulet after shopping. She wanted my help choosing a gown. It took me a while, but I finally elicited it from her."

"Who knew her connection to the baron would lead to this?" Bernard asked rhetorically. He did not notice Neall flinch at the comment. "I had hoped she would seek a more discreet way to get to the general. One we could prevent."

Neall sat silently, hoping to read between the lines. *Could the baron be Riedel? How? Secret connections with the Americans? A spy in their midst?*

"Maybe we can," said Betsy.

Her comment intrigued Neall. "How is that possible, *Madame*?"

"I was about to ask that myself," said Bernard.

"Lafayette has a commencement speech in honor of your President Washington at the new university named in his honor. Then he roves from Annapolis to Frederick, Maryland, and God knows where in between."

"I'd prefer if you left God's name out of this discussion, Mister Neall," said Bernard.

"Sorry, Brother," quipped Neall. "But the marquis moves like a gypsy, traveling to Baltimore in January, where he'll board a steamer for the southern leg of his journey."

Bernard nodded at Betsy. "Please enlighten us, *Madame*."

141

"He indeed has a busy schedule, but Madeline, perhaps not so much," said Betsy.

"Meaning?" Bernard grabbed some paper to make notes.

"Perhaps Madeline has just one engagement — but an important one. As you say, that would make it easier for us to plan to interdict."

"Lafayette takes a rare break over Christmas and the New Year," said Neall.

"No. He returns from Frederick on Christmas," replied Betsy. "I am sure he'll take some needed rest, but he begins the New Year with his final event in Washington."

"He was invited to a banquet hosted by your Congress on New Year's Day but that invitation was closely held and not released to the press. How did you know of it?"

"I didn't. But Madeline did. She received an invitation from a congressman who needs a suitable escort."

"Of course," said Bernard. "A festive event with wine and punch flowing freely. Perhaps with security just a wee less alert. And succeed or fail, an attack on Lafayette that will embarrass the American government and send a message to the world."

"Begin the New Year with a bang," Neall quipped.

Bernard's eyes seemed to wander momentarily and then focused on Neall with an intensity that made him uncomfortable.

"Mister Neall, I believe you may be right."

Chapter 15

Alexandria, Virginia, January 1ˢᵗ, 1825

The cold of the dark morning chilled the room like a morgue. Nagy stretched his leg, reached for the woman at his side, and gripped empty blankets. His eyes adjusted to the shadows, revealing the figure of Madeline slipping into her petticoats. "Put a log on the fire and come back to bed, *Kedvesem*. The affair does not begin until this afternoon."

"Three o'clock begins the banquet, but my congressman has a coach picking me up at one."

"The more time to have you to himself. And who could blame him for it?" Nagy sprung from the bed and scooped her from her feet.

"Stop, Jan!"

He padded to the bed and threw her onto the comforter.

"No!" Madeline had hoped to slip away before he was awake. She cursed her tardiness.

"I'll have you one time before we consummate this affair."

"I'll not let you treat me like a Cossack treats a captive!" Madeline lashed out with her leg and caught him in the groin, sending him toppling out of bed and hitting the oak-planked floor with a thud. She slipped from the mattress and delivered another blow to his side with a solid thud that knocked the wind from him.

"Okay! But we will continue this tumble when Lafayette is dead and we are safely on our way to collect our reward. You will be my extra reward, *Kedvesem*."

Madeline stepped back and straightened her petticoats. "We have much to do, Jan. I, to make myself breathtaking, and you, to prepare your infernal machine."

"Just remember why you are going to his gala."

"Why can't you shoot him from a distance? You are a master with the musket, after all? Or has your taste for liquor robbed you of the skill you were once so celebrated for?"

He smiled and pulled a long wooden box from under the bed. "Open it."

Is his bomb under the bed? "I don't think I...."

"Never mind!" Nagy slid the top from the box and pulled away the oilcloth cover.

"Where did you acquire those?"

"While you were acquainting yourself with Washington society, I made a trip to Harper's Ferry, Virginia, with enough gold coins to coax an armorer at the Arsenal to part with a pair of these and one hundred cartridges and ball. It's accurate and loads through the breech. I tested it and can easily squeeze off eight in a minute. The armorer promised it could hit a target at four hundred yards—I managed six hundred."

"So why not use this and get away?"

"I like the idea of a blast. The rifles are merely my backup or to use if we have troubles during our escape."

"Now, come here, and let's go over the plan one more time."

Madeline nodded. But all she could think of was the bomb and what other damage it would cause.

***

Tommy Lynch sat quietly at the window of a café on 7th Street, carefully observing the comings and goings at The Blodgett Hotel. Now being used by the Patent Office, the Congress was using its grand ballroom for a catered dinner to usher in the New Year. For days, decorators and event organizers scurried in and out to prepare for the great event. Lynch saw them all and felt he should know them by name.

A tall figure in elegant street clothing slid into the chair across from him.

Neall placed his hat and cane on the table. "What have you got?"

"Not much, Mister Locke. Certainly, nothing that looks like a bomb."

"How about around back?"

"Back doors, if they had 'em, have been sealed. I did go in and look around, discreetly, of course. Guess the Customs Office doesn't like surprises."

"Or thieves making off with contraband. Perhaps that's why the sergeant at arms chose the location. Well, we only have a few hours before they'll begin to arrive. Sergeant Riley, Lieutenant Grayson, and his lads will be with the general and his entourage. "

Lynch smiled. "He bringing his doxie?"

"Miss Wright will be with him," said Neall.

"I've dropped some coin on the owner. He's keeping this table free for me. That way, I can take a closer look if I see something suspicious on the street."

"Excellent, Tommy."

Lynch could see the calm and controlled Neall was fidgeting. "Is there something I should know, Mister Locke?"

"Truth be told. I'm not sure what to do if we even find a bomb. We could still set it off."

"Have you thought of your Lieutenant Putnam?"

"Putnam? No. Why?"

"Well, ya see, sir. He's a naval officer. They know some things about guns, powder, and explosives."

"By God, Tommy, you're right. And, he might know of some artificers at the Navy Yard who can help us."

"Arteefissures, sir?"

"Artificers work with ordnance. Bombs included. It's our best hope. I best find him. We've not much time."

***

The Navy Yard, Washington

Kent Putnam had fastened his cape and secured his cap. It had been years since he wore the more formal naval uniform. Unlike his peers, Putnam avoided the heady social scene in Washington.

He took a soft cloth to polish the eagle on his cap when there was a sudden rap at the door.

"It's unlocked. Come in," Putnam said.

The door flew open, and Neall stepped in and closed it behind him.

"Mister Locke! What brings you here? I was just getting ready to find a carriage to the event. Speaking of which, shouldn't you be there?"

"I should be there. But I had forgotten something."

"What?"

"Have you worked with bombs?"

"I have some experience. Not a lot, why?"

"What if we discover the bomb? We need to be able to disarm it, or we'll have an explosion anyway, and if Lafayette isn't killed, others surely will be. Are there any artificers stationed here?"

"I doubt I could find one sober enough on New Year's Day," quipped Putnam. "But I'll go to the barracks and see."

"Thank you. Tommy Lynch is sitting at the café across from the hotel, keeping watch on things. I'll meet you there in two hours — no later."

When Neall left, Putnam removed his cape and grabbed an overcoat. He was working on a bomb in his finest uniform. At least he would be blown to hell in style.

***

K Street Boarding House, Washington, DC

Madeline waited anxiously at the window. She did not feel good about the mission. Her escort was due any moment, but he could not arrive soon enough for her. She wanted the evening over. For years, she worked with Jan, usually luring a

145

target into the sights of his rifle. Using a bomb was something alien, even unclean to her.

Finally, a carriage stopped in front of the house, and a short, plump man in formal attire stepped out into the cold, windy street. Madeline threw her fur-trimmed cape over her shoulders and met him at the top of the stairs. *No need for him to see the place.*

"You look lovely, my dear Madeline," said the congressman as he tried to plant a kiss on her.

She offered her cheek, but no more. As the carriage pulled away, Madeline's thoughts turned to the plan. At the right time, she would ditch the congressman by mentioning a desire to meet his wife. She was to accidentally bump into Lafayette and throw all her wiles at him. Nagy was sure her brief connection with the general so many years ago, during the time of Napoleon, would kindle a spark once more. She would coax Lafayette into a ride home when the gala dinner ended in the early evening. A cart would be waiting on K Street, stranded with a broken wheel. When she exited the carriage, it would drive by the broken-down cart, and one of the dockers recruited by Nagy would ignite a bomb hidden in it.

She shivered when she recalled Nagy's final comment with his insane chuckle. "The poor black devil will, of course, get blown to pieces with the general. But he doesn't know that!"

***

The British Legation

"I didn't think you'd be here on the New Year's holiday," said Neall.

"A Special Accounts clerk has nary a day's respite. Besides, it's quiet, and I can get more done when the place is empty of staff," replied Horan. "What brings you here?"

"We have reason to believe there will be an attack on Lafayette today — at the Congressional banquet."

"Your source for this?"

Neall decided to keep Betsy's role and relationship with Madeline from Horan for now. "I cannot say right now. It's second-hand knowledge, hearsay, I suppose, but credible nonetheless. I was hoping you had developed some knowledge of it as well."

"What kind of knowledge?"

"Minor things like the when, where, and how?"

"Seems you know the when and where. A man of your distinction in Special Accounts should be able to handle the rest."

"The fact the attack will be during an event flush with American politicians makes it difficult to determine specifics. And interdiction will be difficult if it is to be done discreetly."

"What are your defenses like?"

"Spare. The marine sergeant, the New York lieutenant, and a handful of his militiamen. The latter are in civilian attire and only carry pistols and brass knuckles."

"No police?"

"Just the sergeant at arms and a few more marines. No more than ten. Plus, my man, who is watching the locale."

"Has he spotted anything suspicious?"

"Not a bloody thing. He's been there since last evening."

Neall watched as Horan placed his head in his hands and pondered.

"We need a better mind than mine or yours. I did not want to expose you to this, but." Horan raised his head from his hands. "Let's go to the library."

The library was one street down from the legation. It, too, was empty, but to Neall's amazement, Horan produced a key and entered.

"Don't ask. And certainly, don't tell, Mister Neall." Horan led him down a corridor, where they entered a research room with lamps lit.

Who would be here on New Year's Day?

Neall stopped when he saw the older man seated with a pile of papers. *Brother Bernard!*

"You never saw him, Mister Neall," said Horan with the tone of a sergeant ordering a private on parade.

"'Tis a surprise, 'tisn't it?" remarked Bernard with a mischievous smile. "I decided to be in the capital today. Catch up on research and, well, meet with Mister Horan. We often exchange information and, more importantly, ideas."

"What have you got?" Neall asked.

"A map of the city and the design for The Blodgett Hotel. The only place a shot could be fired successfully is from the coffee house across the street."

"You know we are expecting a bomb," Neall said.

"And I always expect the unexpected."

Horan chuckled. "That's telling him."

Are these two older men conspiring against me?

"But I think you are correct. The diners will be leaving just after dusk. Difficult for a sniper of any quality. No, I think 'tis a bomb. But what type?"

"I have Mister Putnam searching for some navy artificers to assist with disarming it if we can find it."

"Where, is the question, Mister Neall," said Bernard.

Neall looked at Horan. "You said we knew the when and where."

"We do," said Horan.

"Only in a general sense if ye can excuse my choice of words."

"What do you mean?" Neall asked.

Bernard rubbed his rosary beads absentmindedly as he pondered before saying, "Bombs are usually used to terrorize a populace as much as kill the target. Yet this may be different. I recall an attack on Napoleon Bonaparte, the plot of the *Rue* Saint-Nicaise in Paris. Use of something called the Infernal Contraption was the method."

"The bomb in the wine cask," Horan said knowingly. "A nefarious device. Blew everything to pieces within fifty feet."

"Yes, but it failed. And you know why?"

"Napoleon wasn't within range."

"He got delayed going to the opera, and that delay put others, but him, in the radius of its deadly blast."

Neall was confused. "So, what are you suggesting?"

"I'm suggesting the bomb will go off on Lafayette's way *back* from the dinner," said Bernard.

"And how will the attacker ensure there isn't another delay like the one that saved Napoleon?"

Bernard's eyes narrowed. "I believe I know."

***

The Waterside, Alexandria, Virginia

"One last push! Quickly!" Nagy lowered his shoulder, and he and the four enslaved dock workers strained their legs and shoulders and pushed the small wagon onto the ferry with a barrage of low grunts.

"What you got inside there, boss?" asked Amos with a bright grin.

"Lead weights that I hope to turn to gold," snapped Nagy. He had no time for questions. The hogshead was stuffed with lead — lead musket balls from his visit to the Arsenal at Harper's Ferry supplemented by nails. But at the core, he had packed the barrel with enough gunpowder to blast anything within fifty yards and send the hot metal to slice anyone within 100 yards.

"All ready, sir," said the ferry's master.

Nagy jumped onto the ferry, followed by Amos. The small steam engine sputtered to life in minutes, and the paddlewheel slowly churned the cold Potomac water.

The cold January air felt good as it whipped Nagy's face. It would sharpen his senses for the most challenging task before him, setting the mechanical apparatus to ignite the charge.

Dark hands tossed ropes around the bollards when the ferry's cork bumpers slammed against the quay at the Washington inlet. Soon, the wagon rolled down the plank onto the pier.

"Fetch the horses, Amos," Nagy ordered. He wanted to light his pipe but could not chance the stiff wind sending a spark swirling into the cart and igniting the powder. Instead, Nagy pulled his watch from his pocket — three o'clock. In three hours, the Marquis de Lafayette would fertilize the land he loved, and Nagy would be on his way to collect his payoff. The ferry would not return to Alexandria but continue down the Potomac, into Delaware Bay, and to Norfolk, where he would catch the first ship back to Europe.

Amos led two mules and yoked them to the wagon.

"Just two horses to pull this rig? And they seem deformed. What nonsense is this?"

"They ain't horses, boss. They're mules. Slower than horses but stronger and more sure-footed. We breed 'em to pull a plow over rock-filled soil for over twelve hours. These two can do the work of four horses."

It was too late for Nagy to argue. "Let's get going."

Amos climbed up and snapped the whip gently. "G'yap, boys!"

Nagy sat beside him and scanned the deserted streets for signs of surveillance. He smiled. *No one wants to go out on a cold New Year's Day.*

The mules pulled the wagon east on Frontage Road and turned north onto 7th Street. From there, Nagy planned to ride north past K Street and make several turns through the sparsely settled streets to avoid surveillance and arrive just in time. Too early might draw suspicion to the wagon. Too late and, well, Nagy determined not to be late for the Lafayette to make his rendezvous with death.

***

The Blodgett Hotel

The afternoon wind that swept from the Potomac bit the skin and stung the eyes, making even the short walk from the carriages to the hotel's entrance unpleasant. The congressmen and their wives moved swiftly with heavy cloaks, vainly trying to shield themselves from the wind. But the marine guards and the New York militiamen at the doorway suffered through the bone-chilling cold and scanned each arriving coach with watering eyes.

Riley jumped from the carriage and extended his gloved hand to Lafayette, who did not take it.

"I am old, Sergeant Riley, but I can still climb from a carriage," Lafayette said as he turned and offered the same to Fanny Wright.

"Don't you think a woman can exit a coach without a man's hand?" Fanny quipped but took his hand with a smile.

The ballroom was surprisingly warm, and the tables were already filled. Riley moved gently through the crowd, making a path for Lafayette, Wright, George, and Levasseur. Riley noted the disdain the latter two showed toward the outspoken Scotswoman.

When the party slid into their table, Riley joined Tad Grayson and Tommy Lynch, observing the event from a balcony.

"See anything of interest?" Riley asked.

"Just a bunch of drunk politicos, if ye ask me?" said Lynch.

"Much business is done by successful men in their cups," said Grayson. "Father once made a one hundred-thousand-dollar deal at a dinner but could hardly stand by the time he got home."

Riley usually did not take to officers, but Grayson had proven a solid leader of his small squad and displayed little of the ego he had expected of a wealthy militia officer.

"Mister Neall wants me to look for the lady I followed from the Austrian Sub-Consulate. So far, no sign of her. Does he reckon she has a bomb in her petticoats?" asked Lynch with a grin. "If so, I'm happy to risk me neck and check for him."

Speaker Clay suddenly rose and began what became a long series of toasts: to General Washington, to General Lafayette, and the Republic. The Senate leader followed him with his own toast. Other prominent politicians also rose to offer toasts.

Lynch took advantage of the toasts to cruise the main floor, hoping to spot the lady who evaded him. Now that he thought of it, he really did not get a good look at her. And the room was flush with beautiful women dressed in their best.

***

Madeline's fingers ran across her congressman's hand, occasionally toying with the gold pinky ring. She made small talk, but her mind raced with schemes to lure Lafayette. Should she approach him directly or try something subtle? Nervous fingers opened her small bag to make sure the note crafted by Jan was still there. Try as she might, he would not divulge the contents. *Give him this, and make sure he reads it. He will follow you.*

The band was playing quiet music. *Now is my time!*

Madeline put her lips to the congressman's ear. "Have you ever actually met General Lafayette?"

His face reddened, and he stroked his cravat. "Not actually, although I...."

She took his hand. "Come with me, darling."

Before he could react, her fingers tightened, and she yanked him from his seat and edged her way toward Lafayette's table.

***

Lafayette rose to his feet when the tall man with the shock of hair approached. Lafayette attempted a gentile bow, but Clay reached out and took his hand in a vice-like grip.

"I hope you're enjoying yourself, General. And Happy New Year!"

"Happy New Year, *Monsieur* Clay. How could I not enjoy myself? The food and company are delightful."

150

"Splendid!" Clay leaned into Lafayette and whispered, "I want to thank you for delaying your sojourn to our great south and west until the election result can be sorted out."

"Most confusing to a foreigner, I must say," said Lafayette. "But I suppose you will have a new president when your electoral votes are counted next month."

"Well, it'll be close. Your visit has raised a patriotic fervor in the breasts of all good Americans. And the stakes are high."

"Many believe this Mister Jackson will win," said Lafayette.

"Well, it's a three-way race: Mister Adams, General Jackson, and me. The winner will need a majority of the electoral votes."

"Meaning?"

"Meaning numbers aren't everything. Enjoy your evening."

Madeline was standing patiently behind Clay, and before Lafayette could take his seat, she tugged at his elbow. "*Bonjour*, General. I'm delighted to see you here. May I introduce Congressman..."

Lafayette's face turned white, and he broke into French as he pulled her out of earshot of his son and secretary. "What brings you here, *Madame*? This is a most unfortunate moment to importune."

She knew she had him on the defensive. They once had been lovers. But more importantly, she once saved his life. "Are you not pleased to see me in America? You once said you loved me. Yet I proved my love. And in a most disgusting way."

His eyes were wide, and his mouth aghast. Napoleon Bonaparte had gotten Lafayette released from an Austrian prison in Olmutz, but a clique of disgruntled officers decided to take things into their own hands and prepared an ambush of his coach as he departed.

"Your arrival just when the three miscreants attacked me was indeed fortuitous, *Madame*."

"Fortune had nothing to do with it. I had a source in Olmutz. And I am handy enough with a saber and pistol."

"You did not have to kill them," Lafayette retorted.

"Oh, but I did. A message needed to be sent."

"A message? From whom?"

"Napoleon Bonaparte. Now read this note and heed! My carriage will be waiting at the corner."

"What do I tell my companions?"

Madeline cast an eye at Fanny Wright, who was heavy into political discourse with a politician.

"Tell them France summons you. You are still French, no?"

Lafayette nodded as she whisked her congressman away by the hand.

***

Grayson grabbed Lynch by the arm. "Who is that woman?"

"What woman?"

"Talking with the general. Never mind, she's heading off with a man in tow."

Lynch squinted. Despite the overabundance of lamps, the woman was in the shadows of an ornate column.

"Could that be the one?"

"I don't think so," said Lynch. "She is tall and elegant like the lass I saw. But the ballroom is full of tall and elegant lasses."

***

"Who was that woman, father?" asked George.

"Someone I once knew."

"In America? She seems too young for you."

Lafayette recognized the barb and smiled. "You are now middle age, George. Soon, all women will seem too young."

Fanny had overheard that remark and turned back to Lafayette with a quizzical stare. "So, where did you meet her, General?"

"In a place I had sworn to forget. A time I had sworn to forget. Yet a place that, in many ways, brought me to my senses and back to my first love."

***

Olmutz Prison, Moravia, September, 1797

The guard's footsteps echoed down the dark corridor. Lafayette took his wife's hands and pressed his forehead against hers.

"I can't live seeing you suffer with me so, Adrienne. Nor our children."

Adrienne Lafayette stifled a cough she had carried for almost a year. Lafayette felt something tickle his tattered shoe and kicked. A squeak filled the room as another rat scurried for safety until it could launch its next foray.

"My entire time imprisoned in France I thought of nothing but joining you, my husband. Have not the past two years been a blessing? At least we suffer as a family."

Lafayette took a breath. "Of course. I was near death and inconsolable until your arrival, but I would rather die alone among rats and Austrians than see you and the children suffer so."

"I pray for our release. I know our American friends have tried and are trying. Mister Monroe was most helpful in Paris."

"Would that I had escaped when Mister Huger and Doctor Bollman launched their plot to save me. But fate had me ride down the wrong road."

"Two fine men," she said.

"Francis Huger was the son of an American officer who died at Charleston. Bollman was simply a high-minded lover of liberty."

She lay her head on his chest. "This time with you is, in some way, the best time of our marriage."

Lafayette could not believe his ears. "How can that be, my love?"

"The Lafayette in America belonged to the people of the United States and their cause. The Lafayette of Paris belonged to the people of France and its cause. Meetings with strangers, travel to far-off dangerous battlefields, hours of writing and discussing politics at all hours. Here, no mistresses, supporters, or collaborators demand your attention. Here, you belong only to the two girls and me."

Lafayette's ears rang, and his eyes swam. The enormity of what he and his career had done to this wonderful woman landed on him like the collapse of the *Bastille*. "When we are free, I shall never leave your side."

She looked into his face with fierce determination. "Don't make promises you cannot keep, my love. Just hold me now. Here."

They embraced, and he smothered her face with his. Then, the hallway once more echoed with footfalls, followed by the clink of the keys and the scraping of the door as it slowly opened.

The bailiff stepped in, followed by a beautiful figure in a gray riding habit.

"Madeline!" exclaimed Adrienne. "I don't... what are you doing here?"

Lafayette's stomach churned. *Why is she here? How?* Madeline Pauline Goulet had been a lover once long ago. He rose to his feet, stood erect, and bowed his head. "You wear a uniform?"

"Of the 3rd Hussars. General Bonaparte pays me from their rolls. He sent me here."

"You?" Lafayette gripped Adrienne's hand.

"I have done some, let us say, sensitive matters for the general. A woman with the right motivation can often go where others are denied." Madeline tilted her head toward Adrienne. "Your devotion to the marquis is commendable, *Madame*. General Bonaparte is working hard to ensure your visit ends soon."

"How can that be?" asked Adrienne.

Madeline frowned. "Then it is worse than they say. You have no contact with the outside world?"

"Only what the Austrians allow. I'm convinced Kaiser Franz is unaware of our situation," said Lafayette.

Madeline grinned. "He is now. General Bonaparte has driven their armies from Italy and is at the gates of Vienna. He'll burn the city if they do not submit to his terms. Part of his terms includes your immediate release. I asked to bring word to you."

"That is astounding," said Lafayette.

Her eyes met his for a moment. Madeline pushed aside the short saber dangling from her hip, slipped her hand into her sabretache, and pulled out some chocolate bars. "I brought these for the girls. Take heart. Official notification will arrive at the walls of this hell hole tomorrow."

"Official? Then how are you here?"

"As I said, a woman using the right motivation can often go where others are denied."

"You slept with my jailer?" Lafayette was disturbed. "A noblewoman?"

"Jailers! And once a noblewoman. My husband, the coward, is dead, and his property belongs to the state. I now serve General Bonaparte."

***

K Street Boarding House, Washington, DC

The wind stung Nagy's face and cut through his clothes. Ahead, Amos plodded on with the mules in tow. They passed open fields interspersed by small government buildings and the occasional monument. *These fools think they can solidify their democracy with marble.* Finally, he saw the modest wooden house where Madeline was staying.

"Stop here, Amos." Nagy's boots dropped onto the street—mud frozen hard as concrete with a patina of snow. He walked to the front and patted one of the mules. "You were right, Amos. Very sure-footed beasts."

"How long we waitin', boss? Massa Frost only gets angrier if ya stand still."

"Isn't earning enough money to buy freedom for you and your wife worth the wait, Amos?" Nagy looked at the darkening skyline. The city was still a work in progress. He noted that there were only a few street lamps. All the better for his purposes. "They should be here within the hour. Show me again how you will ignite the fuse."

Amos went through the motions precisely as trained.

Nagy had attached a naval percussion fuse to the small gunpowder-packed canister, forming a narrow funnel through the three-inch thick lining of balls and nails. There, a core of even more explosive gunpowder would ignite, unleashing a deadly tornado of energy, lead, and iron in all directions.

Amos grinned. "Pretty simple, boss. Practiced a lot. Jes hope the wind dies down."

"At dark, it will, for a while. Just enough time for us to finish our task. Now, you stand behind that fence. When the carriage draws up, pull the lanyard. The hammer will set off the cap, and the rig will do the rest."

"What about the mules? Shouldn't we move them someplace safe?"

"No. The mules will stay. I don't want to draw suspicion to the cart." Nagy knew it would kill the mules and Amos. But the work needed to get done, and Amos was a witness who knew too much of Nagy's doings.

***

"What time do we have?" asked Lafayette.

Levasseur shot him a quizzical look and pulled out his watch. "It is five thirty-three. We have an hour left."

"No, we shall leave now. I have something to attend to."

"Really?"

Lafayette's mouth tightened.

Levasseur's face showed he found this odd. "The Marquis de Lafayette, General Lafayette, never tired of celebrating with the Americans and never left early."

Lafayette's eyes narrowed.

"As you wish, *mon General.*"

The security detail hurried to get to the entrance. Lieutenant Tad Grayson sent one to summon the coaches.

"What's going on?" asked Riley. "This ends in an hour."

"The marquis wants to leave now. He has a matter to attend to."

Lafayette's hands trembled as he glanced at the note again.

Your jailer at Olmutz is in Washington. He will be at the K Street Boarding House at precisely six o'clock if you want revanche.

Lafayette crumbled the note in his fist. The indignities heaped on Adrienne and his sweet girls were the one dark hole in his heart. That he, a man born to honor and sworn to champion the common man, had to stand helplessly in the face of the pain inflicted on his most beloved jewels sent rage coursing through him as he had never felt.

Jan Nagy! He had no idea how Madeline got involved with Nagy, the man she had to sleep with to deliver him Napoleon's message. But she would provide him a set of pistols to settle things with the Hungarian blackguard! Now was the time to pay him back.

The coaches approached.

"Sergeant Riley may ride with me. The rest of you take the other coach."

"What about Miss Wright?"

Lafayette knew she would never understand. "Tell her to meet as many politicians as she pleases. We'll send a carriage back for her."

Mumbling began among George, Levasseur, and Grayson as they climbed in the second coach. Lafayette saw Madeline's coach just ahead. She had left the congressman with a fresh bottle of cognac. He climbed into his and took the left side, rolling down the window.

"A bit cold for that, isn't it, General?"

"The wind has died down. I like fresh air." Lafayette stuck his head out and ordered the driver. "Follow that coach!"

He leaned back in his seat as the coach lurched forward. He knew dueling in America was illegal. But he did not care. He would take his punishment like any good American citizen. As they rolled along the street, a third carriage appeared.

"What is that, Sergeant Riley?"

Riley strained for a better look. "I believe Mister Locke has joined us, General."

***

Neall had instructed the driver to snap the lines and race in front of Lafayette's coach on his command. Neall and Putnam rode with the driver while the artificers huddled inside the coach. They would shelter Lafayette from the blast if they could not dismantle the bomb before it exploded.

"Where's he going?" asked Putnam.

"Wherever that other carriage leads him. And I'm pretty sure it's a trap," said Neall.

"Why not stop him now?"

"I have to be sure there is a bomb."

Neall did not, could not tell Putnam he was after bigger game. He shrugged off his feelings of doubt and guilt. If he could pin the attacks on Riedel, he might have a chance of turning him. The Special Accounts Section could profit from a highly placed asset in the Aulic Council. He was here to help the Americans save Lafayette, but a message from Lord Avondale pointed him in this new direction.

"I thought we were heading to Q Street?"

"So did I," said Neall.

The coaches rumbled down dark streets. Few lamps burned, and only a few homes were lit. The official buildings were all shuttered and dark, too. The lead carriage halted. Neall and Putnam watched Lafayette's coach edge alongside it. A package of some sort was passed to Lafayette's coach.

"This is odd," said Putnam.

***

Their coaches stood side by side for just a few moments as their eyes met in a moment of tension mixed with long lost emotions.

Madeline handed over the bag with two pistols to Lafayette. They were French-made and of excellent quality but with flintlocks. They were never intended to be used, at least not by the Marquis de Lafayette. Not that it mattered.

"Use these well, *Monsieur*."

Lafayette's eyes locked onto hers like a torch. "Maddy, *merci beaucoup. Je suis désolé pour tout ce que je t'ai fait.*"

Sorry for all he had done to me. Madeline signaled her driver to continue. The lines snapped, and the horses plodded along. The street was silent except for the *clip-clop* of the horse teams.

Madeline knew this night was the culmination of decades of waiting for retribution. She was still the teenage bride of the *comte* de Lyons when she allowed herself to be seduced by Lafayette. She swore revenge when the revolution, a revolution she felt Lafayette had started, sent her husband's head tumbling into a

156

basket. Serving Napoleon and then the Aulic Council was only a salve to a longing mixed with hate that consumed her. *But was he really responsible?* No one could quench the mob's blood lust, no one except Bonaparte.

The carriage turned onto K Street.

Maddy, merci beaucoup.

His words lit a fire long extinguished. A sudden sense of guilt swept through her. *My revenge on an old man fixes nothing.*

Her thoughts turned to Nagy. She realized that she had allied herself with a pig. A pig who had exploited her, as well as the marquis and his family. A pig who had to be stopped.

Mon Dieu, qu'ai-je fait? Qu'est-ce que je fais?

Her face sunk into her hands as she breathed small sobs. "My God, what have I done? What am I doing?"

Her head snapped erect. She knew what she had done, and now she knew what she would do. She opened the window to her right and looked up the street. One lamp fought the darkness, but she could see the cart and Amos crouching a short distance away from it.

Madeline opened the door and swiftly climbed beside the driver. "I am sorry to do this, sir." With all the strength of a veteran of the 3rd Hussars, she shoved her weight into the driver and sent him tumbling onto the snow-spattered road.

Her sweat-soaked gloves gripped the lines and snapped them hard. "*Allez!*" Focusing on only one thing, Madeline directed the straining horses directly at the cart waiting in front of the house on K Street. She had to reach the cart before it was too late.

***

Up ahead, Neall saw the two carriages side by side. Then, one rumbled forward at a fast pace. Neall grabbed the driver's shoulder when he saw the lead carriage rumble off. "Catch up with the lead coach. Quickly! Go, man, for the love of God!"

He and Putnam held on for life as the coach lurched forward and picked up speed. Neall's knuckles turned bone white as he gripped the rails, squeezing as hard as he could, fearing the sweat on his palms would make his hands slip. The coach slipped and swayed. He glanced at the ground and then averted his eyes. He knew they would surely be killed if they fell and went under the wheels.

They caught the carriage carrying Lynch, Grayson, and the others.

Neall shouted, "Stop the general's coach! We'll catch the lead carriage."

Grayson nodded, and his driver cracked the whip, and the horses bolted forward in a desperate attempt to catch Lafayette's coach.

Neall's carriage rumbled along the street. Sparks flew from the iron rims, grinding over the ice-encrusted pave stones. "We'll lose a wheel and flip if we go any faster."

The look on Putnam's face was resolute. Somehow, that calmed Neall. *He's got nerves of iron.*

"Mister Grayson's coach has blocked the general's!" said Putnam. "But we'll never catch that other one."

Neall feared he was correct. The assassins had realized the scheme had failed and were now rumbling up the dark street and would soon escape north of the city.

As they strained against the black night to maintain sight of the carriage, the darkness ahead burst into a red ball, followed by a thunderous *boom*. The *woosh* of hot air knocked them back and lifted their carriage from its wheels. The air rattled with the sharp *crack* of lead and iron on wood. The horses reared on their hindlegs and collapsed in a mangled heap.

Neall lay still on the cold snow-strewn dirt. He felt his arms and legs. *Good.* He struggled to his feet. "Mister Putnam!"

"I'm okay." Putnam staggered to him, holding his left arm. "A ball has nicked me. But the driver is dead."

Neall yanked open the coach and looked inside. "So are your lads, I fear."

Chapter 16

The Chancery, Baltimore, January 19th, 1825

Bishop Maréchal's fingers intertwined pensively. "When does the marquis leave?"

"A steamer departs tomorrow," said Brother Bernard.

"What's the plan for his southern journey?"

"Mister Locke, that is, Mister Neall, is staying in the area to recover before he joins the marquis in New Orleans. "

"That means he has other schemes to attend to. What's he up to?"

Bernard shrugged. "I don't know, Eminence."

Bernard did have a suspicion. It had something to do with Horan. But he would not trouble Bishop Maréchal with mere notions.

"There are still some newspaper reports on the New Year's Day explosion. I thought the cover story quashed further speculation."

"They'll die down once the marquis is touring in the south. The papers love reports on exotic places—beautiful and coquettish women, aristocratic gentlemen, dusky slaves with skin dripping sweat while breaking their backs in steamy tobacco, rice, and cotton fields."

"You sound like you want to be there, Brother."

"No, Eminence. I have already been there. I prefer to shiver in this library and see the world in print."

Maréchal broke into a rare smile. "Well, you did an excellent job in covering the affair."

After the explosion, Bernard appeared at the scene. He examined the remains of the coach. The body was ripped to pieces and burned by the inferno, but there was no doubt Madeline was dead. And based on what her injured driver reported, she deliberately rode her coach into the bomb, saving Lafayette. He had suspected the killers would blow themselves up to ensure the explosion killed the victim. So many other attempts at remote detonation failed. The tragic death of Putnam's artificers gave Bernard the idea of blaming the explosion on them smoking while transporting ordnance from the Navy Yard.

"It was fortunate Captain Blaine agreed to help cover this up," Maréchal said.

"'Twas indeed, Eminence. And Kent got Mister Buchanan to cover things with the congressman. Of course, he was only too happy to oblige."

"Guilt can be a powerful tonic."

"Indeed. So can money. Mister Putnam spread enough of it to assuage the coach owners and keep all the drivers quiet."

"Yes, I suppose money can be persuasive," said Maréchal.

Robert stuck his head in the door. "Services begin in twenty minutes, Eminence."

Maréchal nodded at the servant. "Thank you, Robert."

"One last thing before you go," said Bernard.

"I am listening, Brother."

"A request from the marquis. Although some might view her death as suicide, he would like Madeline Goulet's remains buried in the church."

"The church cannot sanction or sanctify suicide. You know that."

Bernard's eyes lifted to the crucifix on the wall. "Jesus placed himself in the hands of his killers. Was his death suicide?"

Maréchal's jaw tightened. "Why, no. He did so to save us all."

"Madeline sacrificed herself to save the marquis and the others."

***

British Legation, Washington, DC

Horan's fingers twisted the muffler tighter around his neck. "As cold as it is now, you would be amazed how like Africa this swamp is in summer."

"I've not been to Africa," replied Neall, who lifted his mug to his lips.

"If you are here in July, you'll be well prepared for your time in hell."

Neall had provided Horan an account of the action on the night of the first and wondered why he was now detained from joining the next leg of Lafayette's journey. There was every indication at least one assassin had escaped, and he suspected another killer might be in America. He wondered how Bernard had such good information, but for now, he would just accept it.

"Why am I here, Mister Horan?"

"Baron Riedel has reached out. I believe he can be turned."

"Perfect. That's why Lord Avondale sent you here, isn't it?"

"No. His Lordship sent me here to conduct research, liaise with the locals, and observe and report. And to spot potential recruits, which is what I have done. You were sent here to recruit. He is your second. You're doing well."

"My second?"

"Surely *Madame* Bonaparte is in your employ?"

"Sadly, no."

"Are you in hers?"

"I won't dignify that with an answer." Neall felt Horan suspected his affair.

"What would you say if I spent more than the usual amount of time outside the Austrian Sub-Consulate?"

"I'd say you were in danger of being indiscreet and possibly being pinched by their security."

"Correct, sir. So, I paid someone to watch for me, a local street type, young and athletic. I believe he may be mulatto. Anyway, he saw the baron, whom I described in detail, depart with a woman."

"Tall, refined, and very well dressed. They departed in what appeared to be her coach, a cream-colored carriage with a unique coat of arms on the door. He followed on foot. These mulattoes can run great distances. To a house at 211 Q Street."

Neall's mind raced, and his heart skipped a beat. "Brother Bernard was sure Madeline Goulet died in the explosion on January the first. Intentionally set off the bomb to save Lafayette while killing herself. If she didn't, who did?"

"That's where you are mistaken. Brother Bernard was correct. This was another woman."

"Who could it be?"

"You tell me. The coat of arms was a golden bumblebee."

Neall was stunned. "Perhaps it's time for me to meet the baron."

"Excellent idea. For I suspect you have already met the woman."

***

The President's Office, The White House, Washington

James Monroe finished reading, folded the letter, and handed it back to Robert Buchanan. "An excellent report and some excellent work by all. Thank you."

"Thank the team, Mister President."

"Of course. Has the Secretary of State read this?"

"No. He said I should take it straight to you."

Monroe twiddled his thumbs. "Mister Adams is an esteemed member of my cabinet. But I am sure his mind is currently fixed on the election results. As is mine."

Buchanan did not ask a follow-up question. He felt it inappropriate to discuss partisan politics with a politician. "Well, regardless of the outcome, you'll be home in Virginia in a few months."

Monroe's face lit up. "Yes! The main house at Oak Hill is finished. Elizabeth and I shall reside there when I leave office. We are both looking forward to it."

"You won't return to Charlottesville? You'll stay in northern Virginia?" Buchanan was very parochial toward the central and southern parts of the Old Dominion.

"Yes. In my humble opinion, Loudoun County is the most beautiful in the Old Dominion and the nation. Besides, Elizabeth loves it even more than I do. Former first ladies rule, you know."

Buchanan nodded. Monroe was an idol. He was a Revolutionary War hero, co-founder of the Democratic-Republicans with his friend Thomas Jefferson, former minister to France, Virginia governor, Virginia senator, Secretary of State, Secretary of War, and negotiator of the Louisiana Purchase.

"Tell Mister Adams to continue to keep security for General Lafayette discreet. Certainly, until April."

Buchanan noted the wry smile. *James Monroe would be at Oak Hill in April.* The question was, who would be in the White House?

***

Charleston, South Carolina, March 15th, 1825

The steamer chugged slowly behind the pilot boat, seamen lining the rail to ensure they did not strike a hidden shoal, the bane of ships entering the harbor.

In the ship's library, Lafayette folded his newspaper and slammed it on the table. "If this newspaper account is correct, George, the Americans have broken new ground. I just don't know if it is good ground."

"What do you mean, father? Was the election not fair?"

"Yes, it was by all accounts. But unorthodox. General Jackson will be furious."

Lafayette had known it would be a close election. With three candidates, how could it not be tight? However, when the votes were counted, the Western firebrand and war hero Andrew Jackson had the plurality but not the majority of the count. John Quincy Adams and Henry Clay split that vote, sending the election to the House of Representatives for just the second time. There, Clay threw his votes to Adams, giving him the presidency. Lafayette thought the two had a prior arrangement and overheard something of it while on the Washington circuit.

George shrugged. "*C'est la vie, non?*"

Levasseur paused his journal writing and said, "*Non, George. C'est de la politique!*"

"*C'est la politique en Amérique!*" exclaimed Lafayette. He felt better. Of course, America would have a way to break political gridlock. It was certainly better than the coup or the guillotine.

The harbor began to thunder with the *boom* of the salute from gun batteries on Sullivan's Island. Soft balls of smoke floated over the glistening water. As if on cue, the ship's bell *clanged,* and the horn let out a long blast, a deep *growl*. The steamer closed in on the harbor.

Lafayette's entourage gathered on the deck to watch. The colorful homes of the city could be seen from a half mile out, and as the ship moved closer, they saw hundreds of well-wishers gathered at the Southern Wharf.

"We'll have a devil of a time getting through that crowd without a speech," said Levasseur.

"We've done it before. We'll keep doing it," said Riley. "Mister Grayson and two of his men were taken ashore early this morning to prepare the way."

162

"I am looking forward to this leg of the journey, but it will not be the same without Fanny and her sister," said Lafayette. "I hope the villains are not seeking her, as well."

"Of course not, father," said George. "Our foes are gentlemen. Besides, Fanny is of no political importance when not at your side."

Lafayette noted the snide tone in his barb. But he realized George was correct. He gazed at the pier as they grew closer. Red, white, and blue were everywhere. The sound of the cheering crowd grew louder, and the brass bands began playing stirring marches.

"Welcome to Charleston, General Lafayette. The city and the state are at your beck and call," pronounced the mayor.

Lafayette stepped off the gangway and waved to a throng as loud as he had encountered in the crowded cities of the north. "I am pleased to have the honor of meeting the great people of South Carolina."

***

From a distance, several pairs of eyes zeroed in on Lafayette. The ladies of the Palmetto Club stood anxiously waiting to meet the general. Comprised of some of Charleston's wealthiest and most eligible ladies, the club provided unmarried women a venue for socializing while doing charity work.

"My, he is so handsome! I mean for a man in his sixties, anyway," said Dee Fitzgerald, a raven-haired planter's daughter.

"I've never met a French man. I hear they're very charming – at least with the ladies," giggled the daughter of a wealthy merchant.

Dee playfully slapped the tall blonde woman standing beside her. "Don't you find him attractive, Olivia? Of course, you are from Europe, so you've probably known many Frenchmen."

Olivia De Rydt smiled and shook her head. "I am from Belgium – Flanders. My family avoided the Francophone people of Belgium and, indeed, the French. My father died fighting Napoleon. But General Lafayette is different. I should like to meet him."

Olivia knew most of her recent friends in the Palmetto Club knew little of Europe. To them, it was a far-off place that produced stylish dresses that their fathers ordered in bulk. Since moving to Charleston in November, she had learned much about their society, a world of balls, hunting, cards, receptions, and gossip. A society carried on the backs of the numerous hard-toiling slaves who performed all their menial tasks.

"The Palmetto Club is throwing a reception for him. You'll get to meet him then. He'll want to meet you – tall with the figure and poise of a goddess."

Olivia smiled. "You flatter me so, Dee."

Olivia did not have long to wait. The Palmetto Club reception was the following afternoon. Although March, the weather in Charleston had already turned balmy, and the function was held on the lawn of Dee's father's estate, a thousand-acre spread with an enormous Palladian-style mansion and several other buildings.

Several hundred people mingled in their finery, sipping wines and sherbet, all served by gracious servants who were lucky enough to escape the toils of the sugarcane and tobacco fields that sent so many of their fellow slaves to early graves.

Olivia and Dee waited patiently in line as Lafayette grasped the hands of the men and kissed the hands of the women. When Olivia and Dee finally reached him, he smiled, bowed like a courtier, and took each of their gloved hands to his lips.

"To whom do I have the honor?"

"I am Miss Dee Fitzgerald, and this is…"

"De Rydt, Olivia De Rydt," said Olivia. "Please call me Olivia, General."

"Olivia? De Rydt? Yes, I detect the hint of a Flemish accent. Otherwise, I would think you are just another beautiful flower of this wonderful land. *Parlez vous Francais?*"

Olivia nodded, and they bantered while Dee stood smiling but oblivious to the conversation.

"May I call you after the reception, Olivia? I lack a female companion for the gala dinner tomorrow evening. I would be charmed to have you on my arm."

"My dear General. I would be delighted." Olivia batted her long lashes, placed a hand on her bosom, and shot Lafayette an endearing smile.

***

211 Q Street, Washington

The light rain pelted Tommy Lynch's hat with a soft drumming he found annoying. *Been watching this place for hours.*

His fingers rubbed the pipe in his pocket. He had hoped the rain would drift off so he could smoke.

Neall had him watching the house of the mysterious woman for the past two days. If he saw the Austrian baron arrive, he would hurry to the British Legation and inform Neall.

Just after dark, a hackney coach halted in front of the house. A short, barrel-chested man in an ill-fitting coat stepped out and proceeded to the door. *'Tis the baron, himself.*

Lynch hailed the same cab and hopped in. "British Legation, sir."

The coachman nodded, and the cab jolted forward. After five minutes, it pulled up in front of a somber gray stone building.

Lynch did not see a Union Jack flying. *'Tis an odd thing for a legation to be without a flag.* He got out and went to toss the driver a coin when he saw his face. "You look like…."

Bare knuckles struck his jaw with a heavy *thud!* Lynch staggered back as pain shot through him. A heavy fist had struck his jaw. Although his head was swimming, he balled his hands into fists and began to pummel in all directions. He felt a soft *thud* each time he struck. His vision cleared for a moment, and he saw several angry-looking men with broad shoulders and long mustaches. *No more belly blows.*

A powerful arm tried to grab him, but he sent an uppercut into the man's square jaw. *Crack!*

His assailant stumbled away, but two more jumped at him, this time with clubs that smacked him up and down. His vision blurred again, and he began to lose consciousness as they dragged him through the heavy iron gate and into the bowels of the building.

***

Charleston, South Carolina, March 16th

The orchestra struck another waltz, and dozens of couples began twirling across the ballroom floor. Lafayette held his partner gently as they glided among the other dancers.

"We don't want to show up your hosts, do we, General?"

Lafayette's mouth formed a mischievous smile. "I show them up by dancing with the most beautiful woman at the ball, Olivia."

Lafayette took in the soft scent of fresh flowers from her perfectly shaped neck. He was infatuated with the tall but elegant lady in his arms. From the moment he met Olivia De Rydt, he forgot his Fanny. She had a sense of humor but was still mysterious and beckoning. George and Levasseur were not happy to learn of her, but he knew she would be the perfect companion for the remainder of his journey if she would accompany him.

When the music stopped, the dancers clapped their hands in approval, and Lafayette escorted Olivia to the punch bowl.

Olivia accepted the cup he poured her. "What has been the most enjoyable part of your journey, General?"

"Apart from meeting the loveliest lady on two continents?"

She slapped his wrist playfully. "No, I'd really like to know. You have met the president, congressmen, generals, mayors, governors, and business magnates."

Lafayette put down his cup and rubbed his chin. "To tell you the truth, it was yesterday. Just after I had the great fortune of meeting you."

"The governor of South Carolina?"

"No."

"The mayor of Charleston?"

"No. A man. A private citizen. When I first came to America, our ship accidentally dropped us off the coast some fifty miles north of here. With nothing but the clothes on our backs, we made our way to the nearest estate, a plantation owned by Major Benjamin Huger of the South Carolina militia. He served with

General Moultrie, a hero of this state. Huger's hospitality enabled me to head north to meet General Washington and serve with him at Brandywine. Years later, when I was in prison in Olmutz, the major's son Francis risked his life trying to save me. He failed and spent some time in an Austrian prison."

Olivia's eyes danced. "What a delightful tale!"

Lafayette's finger stroked her delicate chin. "Alas, it is no tale, *Mademoiselle*, I assure you. But a testament to the human spirit. Meeting Francis and giving him my thanks has made this journey for me."

Lafayette saw George signaling to him. "Excuse me, my dear Oliva. My son beckons, but I'll return for another dance."

George's dark face and angry eyes told Lafayette all he needed to know.

"I know what you are going to say, George. She's too young. I am almost seventy, and she is barely thirty."

"Well, I 'm glad you understand that much, father. First, a Scottish woman with, shall we say extreme political and social beliefs. Now an American socialite."

"She is *Belgique* – from Flanders. Newly arrived in America. We have much in common. I am asking her to accompany me on the rest of the journey."

"Father!"

"Son! My beloved Adrienne has a place in my heart that can never be usurped. None of these women can replace the jewel who was your *maman*. Allow me one last dance with the charming Olivia before we return to the hotel."

Lafayette motioned to Tad Grayson.

"You need me, General?" asked Grayson.

"Mister Grayson, my son believes my memory of his mother, my beloved Adrienne, fades with each smile I exchange with a beautiful young woman. Therefore, I am going to introduce you to the beautiful Olivia de Rydt. Please escort her and tend to her every need as I would."

***

211 Q Street, Washington, DC

Neall searched every possible place where Lynch could be watching the house. When he never reported back, Neall grew suspicious. Now, he was more than suspicious. He was alarmed.

Where the devil has he gone?

Neall mulled over options. Watch the house himself? Knock on the door and demand answers? Neither would be fruitful. He was about to return to the British Legation when a carriage pulled up. The door at 211 opened, and a woman cast her eyes up and down the street. Then, a man emerged and casually walked to the carriage.

Neall made his decision. He walked quickly toward the other side of the coach, jerked open the door, and sat. The other door opened, and the man's eyes widened when he saw Neall sitting, walking stick in hand.

"Baron Riedel, I presume?"

"What is this? Who are you?"

"Raymond Locke, Esquire. I represent the man I believe you have illegally incarcerated."

Neall made a calculated gamble. Tommy Lynch *had* to be in the hands of the Austrians. There was no other reasonable accounting for his disappearance.

"What nonsense is this, sir?"

"You don't deny having him? How much?"

"The very idea!"

"How much for his release?"

Riedel reached for his pocket. "Arghh!"

A crack across his knuckles, and he withdrew his reddened hand.

"This cane isn't merely a walking companion," said Neall. "Now, slowly withdraw the weapon from your waistcoat pocket."

A small single-shot pistol emerged. Before Riedel could do anything, Neall snatched it and tucked it in his belt.

"What now?"

"I want to see my man, and I hope, for your sake, he's alive."

"I don't know what you are referring to. There is no man."

"Look, Baron. Tommy Lynch was assaulted by thugs outside your sub-consulate."

"What was he doing there?"

"Never mind that. I last saw him observing the house at 211 Q Street for me, and now he's disappeared. I say there's a connection."

"There might well be a connection, *Mein Herr*, but I am not it."

Neall gazed into Riedel's dark eyes, and to his surprise, they showed no deception. But he knew Riedel was a master spy, and that carried with it deep use of deceit and subterfuge.

"Tell your driver to head over to Georgetown."

"Georgetown? Why? What is in Georgetown?"

Neall's eyes narrowed, and his teeth ground together. "Nothing. I just need some time to get to know you. And for you to give me answers, I can accept."

***

The Legation Without a Flag

Lynch sat on a small stool in the center of a poorly lit basement room. Not quite a cell, but uncomfortable, nevertheless. His stomach felt like a toothache, painful and tender to the touch. The goons with mustaches took turns peppering him with questions and fists for twelve hours. Lynch stared at the rough rope binding his wrists and swore he'd teach them how to throw a punch if he ever got them loose.

Their questions were in thickly accented English and made little sense, something about Riedesel but what he could not decipher. He wondered what the game was. *Why don't they ask Riedesel these questions?*

Lynch decided these were mind games. Tricks like the little people would play at home on a whimsy-filled night. He wished Mister Neall had trained him for this.

The bolt slid open, and another man stepped into the room. He carried a bottle of whisky and two glasses. Without a word, the man, whom he had not seen before, pulled over another stool, filled the glasses, and carefully placed one in Lynch's bound hands.

"I hope yer not gonna start the same line o' discussion as yer goon-friends? I've no idea about Riedel. He's your baron, not mine."

His interrogator smiled and raised his in a toast. "To your good health and the truth."

His English was flawless, almost like a lord's. Lynch sipped the whisky — American. Not his favorite, but not bad. "'Tisn't my health yer interested in, innit? And I amn't sure what truth ye seek."

"Why were you watching Baron Riedel?"

"Maybe I was watching the lady."

"Who paid you? Who do you serve?"

Lynch knew he needed to say something. "I'm a secretary to Mister Locke, Esquire."

"You work for a lawyer? Does the lady have a jealous husband? I think not?"

"Maybe the baron has a jealous wife?"

The interrogator smiled and tilted his glass. "*Touche'*"

Lynch decided to take the offensive. "Who the B'Jeeezus are ye? What are ye Oostrians after?"

"Call me Captain Denis. I am here to ask the questions, not you. Tell me what you have observed about the lady."

"She's a threat to Lafayette, is all I know. You and your lads are out to kill him. So are others." Lynch realized he had said too much.

Denis nodded. "Tell me more. Especially about the others."

***

The Chancery, Baltimore, Maryland

The door to Brother Bernard's library swung open, and Neall strutted in, cane tucked under his arm in military style. Bernard could see from his face that something was wrong.

"This is an unexpected visit, Mister Neall."

Neall tossed his hat onto the desk and slipped into a chair. "They've taken Tommy."

"Who?"

"That's the question. He was watching our lady friend's house to see if Riedel would return and rummage through her things to take incriminating evidence. He never returned."

"Then how do you know he was taken?"

"I kidnapped Riedel for an hour and interrogated him."

Bernard's stomach sank. "Was that wise?"

"Tommy was accosted while following the lady from the Austrian Consulate's office in Washington. Who else was I to believe did it?"

"And do you believe that now?" Bernard feared the answer.

"No."

Neall's eyes bored into Bernard, who calmly poured them each some sherry. "What did Riedel have to say?"

"He said he worked for the lady, and she worked with a man whose description fits you. Have you met with Riedel?"

Bernard nodded. "Several times. Why do you think I made my way down to Washington? I hate swamps."

Neall sat upright. "Tell me more, Brother."

"The lady was bait to dangle at Riedel. We succeeded in recruiting him to our service."

Neall's eyes lifted in surprise. "Well played, Brother. You beat Bob Horan to the punch. Too bad a lady had to die in this affair."

Bernard ignored the remark. "And you?"

"Yes. But you used sugar, whereas I use salt. However, the baron was most cooperative in providing details of what he suspects the assassins are about. Apparently, he has some coordinating role through the Prussian and Russian legations."

"What else did he tell you?"

"He believes the next attempt will be in or near New Orleans."

Bernard exhaled a sigh of relief. "That's what he told us. The same report to two 'opposing' collection services makes for a form of confirmation—a test of his veracity."

"Because he doesn't know we are working together?"

"Exactly. The marquis is due to arrive in New Orleans around Easter Week."

Neall smiled. "The Pascal Lamb to the slaughter. Somewhat ironic, isn't it?"

"Yes, 'tis ironic as so much of this affair is. We've only a month."

"I can't leave without Tommy Lynch."

"I'm afraid you must. I'll put Mister Putnam on that. I already have some ideas. Now, here's what we shall do."

Chapter 17

Johnson Square, Savannah, Georgia, March 21st

The last notes of "Hail Columbia" trailed off, and hundreds of brimmed hats and beavers returned to bowed heads. Lafayette stepped up to the foundation marked for the monument to General Nathanael Greene. The Chief Architect of Savannah selected the cornerstone from the pile and handed it to the mayor, who, in turn, placed the smooth gray stone into Lafayette's hands.

Lafayette felt a surge of emotion, for Greene was one of the most beloved of the Revolutionary War's generals, second only to George Washington himself.

Lafayette turned and very gracefully laid the stone in its pre-marked position. Soon, the chief architect informed the crowd that a solid pedestal would be topped with a tall obelisk honoring Greene. The mayor then introduced Lafayette.

The marquis drew a deep breath and looked at the crowd. The American people never ceased to amaze him with their warm enthusiasm, respectful, even grateful demeanor, and full-throated patriotism that was exuberant but not overzealous. *Sad that the Paris mob and the supporters of Napoleon were not so.*

To the side, George, Levasseur, and his butler stood smiling. And why not? They had left the cold of the north for the balmy climes of the south, where the people were as pleasant as the climate.

Then, his eyes fell on Olivia. He felt pleased she joined him here, if even for a short interlude. His journey would take him inland and up roads and rivers of the south, but she agreed to meet him in New Orleans. He was overjoyed at her eagerness. It warmed his heart.

"My friends, my fellow Americans. We are here on this festive occasion to celebrate the life of a great American, a devoted father and husband, and a true friend of all who knew him. Nathanael Greene loved your land, and he would have settled in Georgia even if your state had not graciously provided an estate. It was an estate he worked and loved. And it became his resting place.

"Many say that we defeated the English at Yorktown. Now, I must admit I was fortunate enough to corner the great English General Cornwallis long enough for

His Excellency and the *comte* de Rochambeau to arrive with the combined armies of our great nations.

"But let it be clearly understood: Major General Greene's intrepid campaign in the Carolinas had already worn down the general's army like the hounds wear down the fox — like a dozen barbed darts wear down the angry bull for the matador's final stroke.

"General Greene and his gallant men of the south made the work at Yorktown merely *le coup de grace.* "

The crowd erupted in mighty cheers, and hats of all kinds filled the air. The dainty white gloves adorning the ladies' hands applauded softly, but the children jumped, danced, and cried out a world of exclamations evincing pride and joy.

The band struck up "Yankee Doodle," and the mood was jubilant.

Riley took Lafayette's elbow. "Time to go, General. The boys have checked everything out. Your coach will be ready in the morning."

Lafayette's glanced at Olivia. She was more beautiful than any woman in the Court of Versailles or the salons of Europe. Possibly the most beautiful he had ever known.

"Of course, Sergeant Riley. But know that I prefer to dine without my friends tonight. One of your men may accompany me but must be discreet." Lafayette could tell Riley was not pleased. Neither George nor Levasseur would be happy with his decision. But he was, after all, here to mingle with the people.

***

Washington, DC

Putnam looked on anxiously as Buchanan finished the letter and handed it back. "Fascinating theory, Kent. Is Brother Bernard sure?"

"He is. I have watched the place for the past two days." His lips formed a smile. "A couple of off-duty ensigns owe me. And it's good training for standing watch."

"Do you want help from the constables? I can talk to Mayor Carbery."

"He's too busy packing up. He'll be out in a few months. No, we don't need to expand our knowledge of this affair. I'll be discreet. And I'll have an ensign and a pair of tars help."

"I'll go with you," said Buchanan. "If nothing else, you will have a witness to support you at your court-martial."

"Tommy Lynch has been in the place for weeks. Mister Neall was promised I would get him out."

"Why isn't he helping get his man?"

Putnam wondered that himself. "Brother Bernard said that things could get testy, and as a British national, a commotion could cause an incident discommoding the State Department and the Foreign Secretary."

Buchanan retrieved a whisky bottle from the cabinet and poured them each a finger.

Putnam raised his palm. "I'm not so sure. We're going in there tonight."

Buchanan smiled. "In that case, I'll pour two more fingers."

***

The dull tramp of feet filled the streets as the shadowy figures hurried under dimly lit lamps. They halted in a small copse of trees left for a future city park. Ahead was a gray building that appeared shapeless against the dark.

Putnam checked the cap on his pistol and slowly lowered the hammer. The rest carried cutlasses and boarding knives, sharp blades on a hilt that doubled as brass knuckles. Only he and Buchanan took a firearm. He did not want to risk an accidental discharge. From experience, he knew surprise was better than firepower in such situations.

"We have only rehearsed this once, so I'll go over it again. Ensign, you and the boys will stay behind at the gate. Mister Buchanan and I will knock at the door."

"How're we getting through the gate, sir?" one of the sailors asked.

Putnam produced a handful of skeleton keys. He had mastered them over the years. "One of them will do the trick. Otherwise, we're climbing."

With a few twists and turns, the lock *clicked*, allowing the gate to swing open. Bending low, Putnam and Buchanan lurched forward while the ensign had his men take positions.

Putnam worked the door with his keys, *click, click*. "Not working. Time for another plan of action."

Buchanan turned and raised three fingers — the signal that sent the ensign and two sailors scurrying to their feet to join them at the door.

"We'll need to put our collective shoulders to this and pop it. Then be prepared for action."

The ensign nodded, and the men formed a tight knot.

"Ready?" whispered Putnam. "One, two, three!"

With voices joined in a single *grunt,* they barreled into the door. A loud, crisp *crack* was followed by the center panel snapping clean open. The tars slashed aside the boards with their cutlasses, and Putnam jumped through, followed by the others.

The main hall was a dark, two-story room with a vaulted ceiling holding a large chandelier with lamps dimly lit. Suddenly, several lanterns along the walls began to brighten, and two burly men with pistols confronted Putnam and his men.

Putnam pulled back the hammer on his pistol with a *click*. "We are here to retrieve someone you are holding."

A third man entered the hall. "If you are speaking of Mister Lynch, he is no longer here. We released him yesterday."

"Do you mind if I look around to verify?"

"Not at all, but you would be wasting valuable time."

Putnam motioned with his head. The ensign and a tar ran down the hall, checking each room, and then found the basement stairs.

"I'm Lieutenant Putnam, United States Navy. Who are you? Why isn't a flag flying here? All legations and consulates are required to...."

"My name is Captain Denis. And this is not a legation nor a consulate."

"I know that," said Buchanan. "I'm with the Consul Service and just checked the official list. This address isn't on it. I reckon you are with the Czar's Special Bureau."

Denis smiled. "I tried to get it listed, but your State Department does not register secret headquarters for spy operations." He broke into a deep laugh, and his henchmen joined in.

Putnam snarled. "I don't see the humor in this. An undeclared foreign presence in a nation's capital is a serious breach of international law. I could have a company of marines here in an hour."

"Except we are not a foreign presence. We are, in fact, opposed to a foreign presence."

"What does that mean?" asked Buchanan.

"Although I am a Russian officer, as are my friends, we are here to stop the Czar's Special Bureau. At least those working with the Aulic Council."

Putnam looked at Buchanan. This was getting complicated, and he deferred to the man from State. "What say you?"

"I'd say we need to know more," said Buchanan.

Denisov motioned to a large parlor. "Let me explain over a drink. I can only offer vodka."

The ensign returned. "No sign of anyone, sir."

Putnam shot a skeptical look at Denisov. "Very well. I'd rather drink than fight."

Denisov poured them each a shot before downing his and smashing the glass into the dark hearth. "We are followers of the great Count Mikhail Mikhailovich Speransky and belong to a secret wing of his adherents called the Northern Society."

Then he began his story. He and his men were Russian officers and members of a secret society aimed at reforming the empire. Their enemies were the Russian reactionaries, the Russian General Staff Special Bureau, the Czar's secret police, and the Aulic Council.

During their occupation of Napoleonic France, many young Russian officers had become convinced that the Revolution's ideals were good and some were needed to reform Russia. They likewise supported many of America's approaches to democracy and a republican form of government. They were in America to thwart the Special Bureau and the Aulic Council in their quest to assassinate Lafayette.

When Denisov finished, Putnam looked at Buchanan. "What do you think?"

Buchanan poured himself another vodka. "You are Russians. Why watch Riedel? Where is the Russian assassination team?"

"We knew Riedel was the Aulic Council's coordinator of this operation. When the Special Bureau's agents failed to appear in Washington, we focused on the Austrians."

"So, where is the Russian team?"

"They followed the marquis to Virginia. We lost them there. And they never returned." Denisov smiled. "Perhaps you can tell me?"

"How many were they?" asked Buchanan.

"The Aulic Council wants the teams small. Just two, but two of their best, Alexander Buxhowden, is a vile, defrocked priest and occultist. He is an excellent shot and very skilled and powerful in the art of killing. He has tracked down and killed several from our Society. I wanted to get him for personal reasons alone."

Putnam's eyes narrowed. He was anxious for the answer. "You said two."

"Of course! The other was a woman. All Aulic Council killer teams pair a man and a woman. The Council does not want external dalliances, so this provides, how do I say it, companionship."

"The name of this woman?"

"The beautiful opera star Carmen Di Gioia. Perhaps you have heard of her?" Denisov's face broke into a broad grin.

Putnam took a deep breath and paused to take it all in. It was always more disarming when you had a name for a person you killed or caused to be killed.

"I see you know the pair from your face," said Denisov. "I know you cannot say it, but it would be most helpful if we knew they were out of the way."

Putnam stared blankly. "They won't bother anyone, Captain Denis."

***

The Chancery, Baltimore, Maryland

"An excellent report, Brother. It seems that all the world is simmering with unrest. Another pocketful of sorrows to pray for, I suppose."

"The sad truth of this work is successful collection often brings us detailed knowledge of our woes, Excellency," said Bernard.

Maréchal smiled wryly.

Robert stuck his head in the door, "Mister Putnam has arrived, Excellency."

Kent Putnam bent forward, placed his lips on Maréchal's ring, and sat across from the bishop and Bernard. Bernard had never seen him look so out of sorts. And Putnam was a man who courted many dangers during his service to the Navy and the bishop.

"What did you bring us, Kent?"

Putnam's eyes went from Bernard to Maréchal and back. "Trouble, I think."

Maréchal smiled. "This entire affair is fraught with trouble, Mister Putnam. Just relieve yourself of this one."

Putnam related the events at the "Legation" that turned out to be the secret hideout of the even more secret cabal of Russian officers.

"This man called himself Captain Denis?" asked Bernard.

"Yes, Brother. He had a military bearing and spoke very good English. Clearly an educated man."

Bernard looked at Maréchal. "That's Captain Alexei Denisov."

Putnam sat upright. "You know of him?"

Bernard nodded. "We had no idea he was in America, nor any members of his of Society. But it makes sense."

"What should we do? Buchanan and my naval team are aware."

"Keep an eye on him. Go back and convince him it's in his interest to report anything he learns to you. Meanwhile, what else did he reveal?"

"He said the other team is Prussian. He said many of the Aulic Council's Prussians belong to something he called the *Tugenbund*."

"We could assume so. A quasi-Masonic secret society—such groups seem to sprout everywhere in the wake of war and disruption. They were formed in 1808 after Napoleon defeated their army. Anything on the Austrians? Assuming Madeline Goulet died in that explosion, that leaves her partner on the loose."

Maréchal pursed his lips. "That tells me we have made little progress. A pair of Prussians primed to go after the marquis and an Austrian agent still on the loose."

"I'll draft a warning and instructions for Mister Neall and Sergeant Riley. Ask Captain Blaine if he can dispatch a packet to deliver this to them."

"Deliver where?" asked Putnam.

"New Orleans is where I'm thinking?"

"I'll include a special note for Bishop Louis Du Bourg. He just moved his Chancery from Saint Louis to New Orleans," said Maréchal. "He might have resources to help."

"Anything else?" asked Bernard.

"Oh, it's in my report, but Denis, or Denisov as you call him, mentioned they tracked Baron Riedel with a beautiful woman."

Bernard threw him a leading question. "Did he indicate that would be the unfortunate Madeline Goulet?"

"No, Brother. Another woman. They tracked her to the house at 211 Q Street."

***

New Orleans, Louisiana, April 10th, 1825

The muddy waters churned in a whirl of brown and green as the steamer *Natchez* chugged up the winding river. They had departed the Gulf coast port of Mobile two days earlier and had made good time.

As they rounded the final bend, Lieutenant Tad Grayson could see the outline of the city, with its colorful homes of various shades of pink, blue, and mustard. Many were three-storied affairs with ornate iron balustrades, freshly painted shutters, and boxes of flowers dangling gaily at each level. Palm trees and semi-tropical vegetation gave off a scent few northerners would experience.

Cresting the skyline was the white stone façade braced by two massive towers — the cathedral of Saint Louis, which overlooked a vast open area of fresh grass surrounded by more beautiful homes and lush tropical flowers. They were looking at the city's most prominent location, the *"Vieux Carre"* or Old Quarter, where on December 18th, 1814, General Andrew Jackson reviewed his troops before the great battle to save the city – and America.

"It's like a city in paradise, isn't it, Sergeant Riley?" asked Grayson.

"Not quite, Mister Grayson. Take a look there." Riley pointed to the docks along the riverside, where dark-skinned slaves hauled great cotton bales and sheaves of tobacco onto ships and barges. "Chattel slavery in paradise? I think not."

"This is a complex country, Sergeant. The more you see of it," said Grayson.

"It's a complex world the more I see of it. At least the Algerians enslaved everybody equally and freed you if you turned Turk."

Grayson was confused. "What do you mean?"

Riley laughed. "It's a mariner's term for Christians who accepted the Prophet rather than suffer enslavement. Some did. Probably still do. Slavery is worse than death."

"Mother would agree with you. She is an abolitionist."

They stood at the railing as the gangplank swung over the quay and slowly dropped onto the heavy oak planking before a pair of muscular slaves secured it. Thousands of voices cried out in French, but for the first time in the journey, they called to Lafayette in his language — their language.

"Vive la France! Vive Lafayette!" Echoed over the water, drowning out the military band's attempt at ruffles and flourishes.

The rapturous faces greeting them contained a mixture of white, brown, and copper hues, interspersed with dark black and mocha of the free Negroes who populated the city. Many well-wishers had stood bravely at the ramparts with General Andrew Jackson in his 1815 victory over a large and powerful force of British Napoleonic War veterans.

Grayson marveled at the mix of people, sights, sounds, and smells. He glanced over towards where Lafayette, George, and Levasseur stood, hands held high over their heads and waving their broad-brimmed hats at the crowd. He found the connection between Lafayette and this polyglot mix of races and ethnicities astounding in a journey that had often astounded him. *How can we keep him alive in this vast sea of people?*

"Time to go into action," said Riley.

Grayson stirred from his thoughts. "Sir?"

"Take a team with you to the hotel and check on things. The others will stay with me. We'll escort the general through the town while he gives a few speeches."

Grayson smiled. He and Riley had things pretty well worked out.

***

Hotel Maison de Ville, New Orleans

The high-stepping horse gracefully pulled the hired cab up Toulouse Street. It halted before a salmon-colored, two-story building with dark marine green shutters and railings. A servant in livery opened the door, and they stepped into a small but elegant lobby.

Grayson signed for everyone's rooms and then began to pump the concierge for information. "How many rooms do you have?"

"Too many, *Monsieur*. But the marquis will find it quite comforting here. A little bit of France *en Amerique'*, no?"

Grayson smiled. "He'll like that, I'm sure."

After checking all their assigned rooms, he placed one of the teams outside the general's suite and the other in the lobby. He was surprised when the concierge tapped him on the shoulder and handed him a small note.

"A young lady asked me to give you this. She says she knows you. Mister Grayson."

"But I've never been to this city before. Very well." He figured the concierge was pimping high-end prostitutes and slipped the note into his pocket.

Grayson entered the hotel dining room an hour later to inspect things before it filled for dinner. Of the dozen or so tables, about half were filled with guests lingering over café or chocolate or sipping a cold aperitif. He did not notice the beautiful woman watching him from across the room glide elegantly through the guests and run a long and slender arm around his.

"Mister Grayson, I am delighted to see you again."

Grayson was not that delighted. At least not to meet her then and there. Shortly after Lafayette had introduced them, they danced and fell into each other's arms. He spent the night in her room. A night he should have spent on the business at hand. But he had fallen for her.

"I told you and the marquis I would try to join you for part of the journey." She scanned the room. "New Orleans is magical. Don't you think?"

"But I never really thought...."

Olivia kissed him once on each cheek and then fully on the lips.

His feelings for her grew more intense with each moment. He let it linger before pulling back. "Not in public."

"Well, if you want more, check the note in your pocket. I am going to freshen up. Tell the marquis I would be delighted to join you for dinner."

"Well, you won't be joining us here."

Her long blonde lashes rose in surprise.

"We do this now. A backup location in case there's a problem. One team and I occupy it. Works well thus far. Are you disappointed?"

"Not really. It will give us more time alone. But where is the marquis staying?"

Her smile was beguiling.

"He's a guest of the people of New Orleans. The Cabildo will be his home. It's the seat of the city government. They have fixed him up a splendid apartment. I'll suffer here. But I'll escort you to some of the diners if you would like, my duties permitting."

"And those duties are?"

"I have my men from New York. We try our best to safeguard the general and his entourage."

"Who would want to harm the marquis? Everyone loves him."

Grayson knew he had already said too much. "Well, it is just a precaution."

***

The Cabildo, New Orleans, April 11th

Lafayette felt like he was in France as he stood on the steps outside the imposing three-storied stone building enclosed with arches. Hundreds of men in dark blue French-style uniforms stood in straight ranks. As one, they hailed the new territory's most distinguished guest with whoops of *Vive la liberté! Vive l'ami de l'Amérique! Vive Lafayette!*

A military band struck *"La Marseillaise."*

When they finished, Lafayette dropped his hand from his hat and climbed into his coach.

"Olivia will be at the gala tonight, General," said Grayson, who sat across from him.

"I heard she was in New Orleans. You must have impressed her, Mister Grayson."

"How did you hear it?" Grayson asked.

"She sent a note to my suite at The Cabildo. She had a wonderful night with you."

Riley listened to the talk quietly. He did not like the complication of the young lady's presence. Whether she was after a handsome young officer or an old general made no matter. In his military career, Riley had learned that officers were fools when it came to the fairer sex.

The carriage passed through the *Place d' Armes* and took a road straddled by high magnolia trees. Finally, the procession stopped at Chalmette, just outside the city, where Andrew Jackson saved New Orleans and the New World.

Lafayette scanned the open field flanked by the Mississippi River and the cypress swamp.

"Andrew Jackson was a mere boy when he first fought the British, as was I. They are a people who opposed liberty in America and France."

Riley wondered what Neall would think if he heard this.

"And they were a brave and implacable foe in two wars."

Riley smiled. *That's more like it.*

Lafayette continued, "The great General Jackson learned on this field what I once learned at Yorktown. The Americans and French are unbeatable when they stand together in the cause of liberty!"

The crowd erupted, *"Vive la liberté! Vive l'ami de l'Amérique! Vive Lafayette!"*

Lafayette waited for the din to subside. "This territory of Louisiana was once part of France, then a property of Spain, and once again a possession of France. Now, thanks to the sacrifice of so many on this field and the indomitable will of Jackson, it is forever part of the great United States of America!"

Cheers once more erupted, and the band broke into a series of military marches.

Riley checked his watch. *Almost time to go.* He turned to ask Grayson about his teams and saw the young lieutenant deep in conversation with Olivia.

How did she get here?

The ride back to The Cabildo was quiet. The escort maintained its distance. Lafayette read his correspondence. Riley thought through the next day's plan. He needed to have a discussion with Grayson about the girl. But he would keep it quiet with the general.

"I have two invites to the theater for this evening," said Lafayette over his reading spectacles.

George arose from his dozing. "Two?"

Lafayette smiled. "There are two theaters in this city, one Francophone, the other Anglophone."

"A difficult choice," said Levasseur as he gazed out the window.

"Not at all," said Lafayette with a wink. "I shall visit both!"

***

The Orleans Theater

The hoots and clapping of the audience covered the sound of Lafayette's entourage as they snuck into his reserved booth just before the third act. *Lafayette in New Orleans* was a specially produced homage to the general and the city.

A pair of sharp eyes from a nearby booth zeroed in on the general, not the show. *One shot from here should do it.*

Ernst Emil Donat was a patient fencer and an even more patient killer. *Let your opponent give you the opening, then strike quickly.*

180

Donat waited patiently for Lafayette earlier that evening, hoping to bag his prey at James Cadwell's Camp Street Theatre. But the general's security men seemed to have all the entry points covered. And it somehow disturbed him seeing the beautiful golden-haired woman sitting between Lafayette and one of his security men.

Killing Lafayette would be easy. Escaping would be difficult as he would have to evade the security men stationed at the doors. So a grim-faced Donat quietly moved to the second venue and positioned himself before security arrived.

The show's lead singer, Jacques Bellevieu, began the third act with a stirring rendition of "*Un Héros pour Deux Nations.*" *A hero for two countries, indeed!*

Donat scoffed at the doggerel. The long barrel of the heavy dueling pistol felt cold to the touch as he pulled from his jacket and wiped it with a soft cloth. In moments, *Monsieur* Bellevieu would end the song with a flourish, and Lafayette would be required to stand and meet the applause of the theatergoers.

In the frenzy of adulation, his shot would go unheard. Lafayette would clutch his chest and stagger. Many would think it was his heart or, more likely, indigestion from consuming too much rich food as the boorish Louisianians stuffed him with their dreck from the muddy rivers and brackish bayous.

Donat would slip the weapon under a pillow and rush to the general, offering aid as *Herr Doktor* Kessler. Of course, it would be too late. They would thank him and escort him from the theater. He would be on the first steamer south by midnight. Donat smiled. *An excellent plan.*

A knock on the booth's door brought him back to his senses. A young man in the uniform of an usher handed him a note.

Donat quickly tore it open and read it. "Who gave this to you?"

The usher shrugged. "*Mon patron, Monsieur.*"

"Your boss? Are you sure?"

The usher shrugged and left.

He glanced at the note a second time. It read in German, *Jemand hat dich bemerkt.*

Donat scanned the audience. *Who could have noticed me? Lilly! How does she know?* But it did not matter. He was a professional agent of the Aulic Council but not a martyr. Donat slipped the pistol into his jacket and left. As he reached the alley exit, an American in a plain suit stopped him. "Sorry, sir. We have orders to check anyone leaving early or coming in late."

"I am *Herr Doktor* Kessler. A patient has summoned me. It's most urgent."

"This will only take a mo—whoa! What do have we here?" He began to draw the pistol from Donat's jacket.

Donat brought both fists down on the man's shoulders, momentarily stunning him. He snatched his pistol from the guard and brought the long,

blued steel barrel down onto his skull with a dull *thud.*

***

Neall and Lynch's steamer reached New Orleans late that same afternoon. Lafayette greeted him with warmth but was dismissive of the need for more security. Riley finally convinced him they could always use help.

"There's a Prussian team stalking you, General," Neall explained.

"Prussians, now?"

"It doesn't take a bomb, either."

Lafayette's face softened, and he grew sad. "Madeline was once a good woman of France."

"Perhaps she died that way, in the end," said Neall.

When it was time to secure the theater visits, Neall directed Lynch to the Camp Street Theater while he went to the one on Orleans Street. After checking the entry and exit points, he waited at Lafayette's box and enjoyed the first two acts of the show.

That's when he became suspicious. The place was packed with well-wishers of all stripes, and the loge and balcony filled with viewers, except one. A private box with just one viewer was at an oblique angle to the right. *Why?* He made a note to have Lynch tail the viewer when he arrived from Camp Street.

When Lafayette and his entourage arrived, he was surprised to see a beautiful golden-haired woman clinging to the arm of Lieutenant Grayson. She sat between Lafayette and the young officer. He did not bother introducing himself but took a position to watch the watchers, as he often did. But mostly, his eyes were on the lone man in the booth.

***

"The doctor says Mister Grayson's man would have died if you had arrived a minute later, Tommy."

"Just some Irish luck, sir. I had just arrived, and a tall, hawkish man pushed past me. Mumbled something about being a doctor in a hurry to see a patient."

Neall felt guilty. He had taken his eyes off the target in many ways. When the lady excused herself for ablutions, Neall followed her, introduced herself, and tried to vet her. He lingered near the ladies' toilette but returned to his place after deciding to talk to her after the show.

"He's not fit to travel. The doctor suggests he stay here and rest for two weeks," said Grayson.

"How many does that leave you?" Neall asked.

"One got the fever in Alabama. If he can find us, he may join us later."

"Well, the schedule is published and updated weekly by your beloved press corps."

Grayson smiled. "Hard to have a grand tour no one is aware of."

182

Neall knew he was right. But now, the New York militia was down to just four men. "We'll need at least two more men for security. I'll recruit them, but they'll work for you and Sergeant Riley."

Riley cleared his throat. "Excuse me, Mister, ah, Locke. They'll work for Mister Grayson. I'll just guide him from time to time."

They laughed at the cut. Lafayette still insisted his security be under the guidance of Sergeant Riley.

"Probably good to add a couple of locals to the team," said Riley. "The trip up the rivers will be hazardous. And now we'll have Indians to worry about."

"Indians! Are you serious?" Neall had only read of them in magazines and newspapers.

"Oh yes, Mister Locke. Scalpin' savages, they are—cannier than the canniest Algerian Corsair."

"Maybe we should hire a squad of them," said Grayson.

Riley shook his head. "I don't think so. Not easy to control. Not patient enough in crowds."

Neall rose and placed his hat on his head. "I'll put my insurance agent hat on and canvass the docks. They must use security men for their trips." He flashed a wry smile. "Locals work best. Why, I'll even consider an Indian."

Chapter 18

The Old South Building, Georgetown College

Brother Bernard's eyes twinkled as he poured a considerable measure of brown liquid into each glass. "My uncle, also called Maurice, taught me to drink cognac. I often prefer it to whisky."

"Interesting choice of words, often," replied Horan, who glanced around at the dark paneled walls and bookcases. "And an interesting place to meet."

"The faculty and some students travel from time to time. I like to hear about their experiences firsthand. This provides a suitable venue."

Horan's lips cut a playful smile. "I suppose you chat with them before they travel as well? You know, tell them what information you need."

"Sometimes I do. But often by letter. I'm getting too old for the journey."

"It's only a day's journey by coach," said Horan. "A little less if you mount a horse."

Bernard smiled. "I only have so many days left. So, I ration them carefully."

They sipped an ample portion of the cognac and let it linger for a quiet moment. Bernard waited for Horan to start.

"Now, why did you call me here, Brother? I have whisky in my office."

"Certain things I won't discuss in a foreign legation. No offense meant."

"I understand. And I'm listening."

"Neall made it to New Orleans. One of our lads was injured. We think the blow was meant for the marquis."

"I am sure it was," said Horan. "I wonder why Neall didn't inform me?"

"I don't think he likes you, Robert."

Horan's eyes widened, and his lips flattened.

"'Twas just a joke. Your Lord Avondale sent him to see us, not the British Legation."

"Why am I here?"

Bernard smiled. "Because I like you."

Horan drummed his fingers. "Either tell me more or at least pour another cognac."

"I shall do both," said Bernard, satisfied he had toyed with him enough to get his interest. "We have the baron."

"Under arrest?"

"No. As an asset."

"Curiously, I also receive reports from him," said Horan.

"I know. He's a reporting source for your purposes, but Baron Riedel is now in our employ. We pay him. We task him. We collect from him."

"Why are you telling me this?" asked Horan.

"I know he provides you with nuggets. That should continue. It will make him feel better about things to think he is double-dealing. Such types need the thrill."

"What do you want from me, Brother?"

"To meet from time to time and compare notes."

"You want me to help verify his work?"

"Simply put, yes."

"I'm flattered. The man who once placed a spy on Sir Edward Pakenham's staff, the spy whose reports helped destroy a magnificent British army in the swamps outside New Orleans, needs my help."

"I won't comment on the veracity of what you say, but I want your collaboration, not your help." Bernard knew the distinction made all the difference in how Horan reported this to his superiors.

"In that case, pour us one more cognac."

***

The Cabildo, New Orleans

Plates and glassware *clinked* as scores of servants spread across the Chapter Hall, known as the *Sala Capitular*. The size of the gathering impressed Olivia, but she needed to get to a more private setting.

The mayor ordered the main meeting hall in the government building cleared of seats and filled with tables for a grand dinner in honor of Lafayette, who would depart the next day.

The bunting and flags swarmed the room with red, white, and blue. Two orchestras engaged in a musical battle for the attention of the guests, which included only the most prominent politicians, businessmen, planters, and merchants.

Olivia's lean form hugged Grayson while she playfully toyed with the cuff of his jacket. Her large, light eyes scanned the room. She had already met the territorial governor, the mayor, and several militia officers whom she impressed with her beauty. Their ladies were equally impressed by her gold silk gown of the latest design.

But her eyes never failed to wander back to Lafayette, for she was most interested in him. During a lull in the music, she got his attention with a wink and a wiggle of her nose. She put her lips to Grayson's ear. "Would you mind if the general showed me around? This is a fascinating building."

Grayson cast his gaze toward Riley, who was engaged in a heated conversation, then turned back to her and smiled. "I think a government building filled with important people is secure enough."

Grayson took her hand and led her to Lafayette's seat. "Olivia is fascinated by the building, General. Would you mind escorting her around? You have been staying here."

Lafayette's face lit up. "Such a pleasant interlude from all the bombast and ceremony is more than a delight, Mister Grayson." He put his finger to his nose. "But will Sergeant Riley allow it?"

"Let me deal with him," said Grayson.

Lafayette's arm entwined hers, and they slowly slipped from the din into a long, dimly lit hallway covered with lush carpets and adorned with paintings and sculptures. Lafayette regaled her with interesting bits of trivia interspersed with glimpses of his political thinking.

They paused in a small library with walls of cherry shelves stuffed with finely bound works of literature, art, and science. A miniature painting depicting enslaved Africans at work somewhere in the West Indies caught her attention.

"This is an interesting thing to celebrate in art. What is your opinion of the slavery issue in a country founded on liberty?"

Lafayette's eyes narrowed, and his jaw stiffened. He lowered his head and then lifted his eyes to meet hers. "It is my greatest disappointment. Both here and in France. I implored all the leaders, even the great Washington, to consider immediate manumission. But they said the nation was not yet ready to shake its foundations to rid itself of something that would, by its nature, wither and die."

Olivia leaned forward and took his hand. "It's my great disappointment, too. I may leave South Carolina because of it. Except for the weather, and people are so pleasant." She saw the way he looked at her. She liked that. "Tell me more."

"I saw blacks fight well for America. Only to be disappointed. Why, one gentleman served me in Virginia with deeds more daring than a charging hussar."

***

Near Yorktown, Virginia, October 1781

Lafayette bent over a map, making notations on areas he was interested in.

An orderly entered his tent, "General Lafayette, there is a man here to speak with you. A runaway slave. He insisted that...."

"What is his name?"

"Junius, sir."

"Send him in."

James Armistead stood before Lafayette in tattered work clothes and a ragged jacket. Months earlier, he had offered his services to the Continental Army and became a spy in the traitorous Benedict Arnold's camp. His secret reports enabled Lafayette to wage a brilliant campaign to check, if not repulse, the renegade Arnold, now a Brevet Brigadier General in British employ.

"Is spying on Lord Cornwallis the same as spying on Arnold?"

Armistead's coal-black eyes flashed. "It's always more satisfying to deceive a deceiver, sir."

Lafayette smiled mischievously. "Well put, *Monsieur* Armistead."

"Sir, it's better if you just call me Junius." His eyes shifted left and right. "You know, just in case."

The comment impressed Lafayette, and he nodded in agreement. He eyed the papers Armistead had drawn up. The spy's reports were always concise and precise. "Are you sure of this, Junius?"

"Indeed, sir. If you move forces to that position at that time, you will deny General Cornwallis his last chance of reinforcement and, more importantly, replenishment. His men also suffer miserably from lack of food and other vitals. Even their officers mumble about it."

Lafayette nodded. "How fitting, as the Americans have gone all these years of struggle on empty bellies and wearing...." He paused as he eyed the rags on Armistead's back. "Insufficient clothing."

"It will be dark soon. I must return as soon as I have the cover of the night."

Lafayette eyed the man with wonder. "You have risked your neck for many months. That is commendable enough for any man, but for a slave, it is a thing of wonder."

"I believe in the cause and that I will justly earn my liberty."

Lafayette's head moved slowly from side to side. "I truly hope so."

***

"A beautiful tale, *Monsieur*," said Olivia. "Did Junius receive his freedom?"

Lafayette's eyes narrowed. "Not right away. A technical reading of the emancipation law for serving soldiers was a block to it. In this land and in many others, spies, regardless of cause, are viewed no differently than pimps and prostitutes."

"The poor man!"

"In 1789, his petition was finally approved. Both his owner and I gave testimonials on his behalf. The ending was happy. I just saw him in Virginia, and we embraced like the brothers in arms that we are."

He took her hand, and they strolled, discussing everything under the sun. His gentle manner took Oliva by storm. She now realized why he was beloved on two continents.

***

A pair of slit-like eyes went unnoticed behind the dark cherry wood bookshelves. Donat scurried after them, ready to finish his work. Although his pistol was jammed snugly into his waistband, the fencing champion dangled a saber at his side. Better to kill quickly and, more importantly, without the boom of a firearm to alarm the building.

Lafayette led Olivia into what appeared to be his suite. No security guards stood outside. *Is he going to seduce her?* Donat hoped so. A man in *flagrante delicto* is easier to kill and less sympathetic to his investigators.

A shadowy form moved down the hallway, forcing Donat to duck into a small room.

"Is everything all right, General?"

Donat recognized one of his guards.

"Yes, I am showing *Mademoiselle* this wonderful building."

The guard nodded. "Mister Riley said you must be back in an hour to give your closing remarks."

"Very well," said Lafayette, who took Olivia into the suite and closed the door.

Donat waited tensely as the guard passed by, then stopped, turned back, and began jiggling the door handle.

Does he hear my breathing?

The door opened, and the guard stepped into the room. "Anyone here?"

Donat's saber flew from the scabbard. He stepped from the corner where he had hidden and ran the guard through in one swift move.

He struck the heart. The guard was dead on impact and slumped onto the carpeting in a heap.

Der Leichnam ist nicht leicht! These Americans are heavy. Donat dragged the limp form to a closet, but the trail of blood on the carpet would quickly reveal its resting place.

Donat moved quickly. They might come for the guard. If not, he knew he had an hour to kill — literally.

***

Olivia sat with Lafayette on a small settee for two near a smoldering fireplace. As he regaled her, her eyes roved the room, the most European-looking she had seen in America.

The walls were bedecked with artifacts from the Spanish and French rule of Louisiana: shields, halberds, swords, and sabers hung from the walls. Ornate murals broke up the display of militaria while heavy drapes adorned the entrance to a large portico with a view of the *Place d' Armes* and, beyond it, the *Vieux Carre*, the Old Square.

"So, to prove my case regarding free blacks, my beloved Adrienne and I bought a plantation in the French colony of Cayenne. Its chattel servants were promised that they would be freed and own the land by demonstrating hard work and the right capacity. Proving that if done carefully, emancipation would benefit the whole of society as well as the Africans."

Lafayette's words captivated her, driving thoughts of a night with Tad Grayson from her mind. *He's truly the remarkable man they say he is.*

She took his hand in hers and stroked it as he talked. She knew he had a Scottish mistress but that, in the end, he was a Frenchman of a certain upbringing.

The drapes suddenly swirled from the slight movement of air. She knew what that meant. *The door is open.* But she kept her eyes fixed on Lafayette and stroked him more intensely. Yet she wanted his attention in more ways than she realized.

A voice with a harsh Prussian accent broke the spell. "Enough of your banter, General Lafayette! Say something more eloquent before you die."

Donat stepped from the drapes with his saber at the ready.

Lafayette rose and lifted Olivia to her feet. "Run, my dear! Save yourself. It will be too late for me."

Donat grinned a mean grin. "So gallant, *Monsieur.* But your young lady will not run from me. Will you, Lilly?"

Lafayette looked at Olivia. "Lilly? This is Olivia De Rydt."

"She is Lilly Nordstrom—my accomplice in luring you to your death. The company of a beautiful woman is a fitting farewell to the world, though. A parting gift from those soft-hearted barons in the Aulic Council."

Lafayette straightened. "Aulic Council, that means…. Olivia? Is this at all true?"

Lilly felt torn. She had come to admire Lafayette with a truly ardent fondness. What woman would not? But her duty and her livelihood were killing. In the end, this remarkable man was another victim to dispatch.

Lafayette dropped her hand and backed away.

Donat put himself into the attack position: saber held at an angle, feet forward and aft, body slightly turned. She knew the marquis would lay dead in seconds. Emil was the best of the best.

Just before Donat sprang, Lafayette tore a sword hanging on the wall. It was more of a cutlass from a century long gone, with a heavy blade and hilt.

She marveled at Lafayette's pluck. But at his age, such a weapon only delayed the inevitable.

"*En garde,*" said Lafayette, who took the stance and moved at Donat.

He's stolen the advantage of surprise from Emil!

The two men came together in a rasping of steel on steel. Parry, strike, parry, retreat. A change of angle. Neither man spoke. Lilly knew every breath was vital to maintain the fight.

Finally, Donat flicked his wrist and slashed the heavy blade from Lafayette's hand. He had struck like a viper, stinging the hand but making no cut. The cutlass went spinning across the floor and rattled against the baseboard with a *thud*.

Lafayette crouched, ready to spring forward to retrieve his weapon.

"Ah, ah, ah, *Monsieur*! The time for chivalry is over. You fought gamely, but I have a contract to fulfill. This blade will slice open your heart before you make your next move. I am sorry, *Monsieur*."

"As am I, Emil," said Lilly. She had searched the wall until she found the perfect weapon, a light dueling saber with a tasseled hilt. She tore the tassel free, and the blade rose slowly into the *en garde* position.

"*Das ist ein Witz!*" sputtered Donat.

"No joke, Emil. I decided it is better to risk the wrath of the Aulic Council than assist in the murder of the world's greatest man."

"*Weiber!*" spat Donat.

"Women indeed!" exclaimed Lafayette.

In a flash, Lilly leaped forward, and the two assassins traded blade thrusts. The *clang* of steel was rapid, making almost a constant ringing sound that filled the room.

Lilly drove Donat back to the drapes. She knew she only had seconds before his superior strength and speed would turn the duel in his favor. *Must maneuver him back and over the balcony.*

As she worked him, the easy calm left Donat's face. His eyes did not show fear, however, just the liquid evil of the trapped wolf.

He realizes my gambit! Must move now.

Lilly leaned into her stance and used her hilt to edge Donat further toward the rail. She had to drive him before his riposte countered her.

"Strike!" she called as she lunged with all her strength.

Suddenly, Lilly's forward movement stopped, and she toppled awkwardly before finally regaining her footing. Her gown had snagged a divan.

"*Weiber!*" she cursed ironically, knowing it would be her last word.

Donat's point plunged into her side before she could raise her blade. He drew it from her quickly, making a sucking sound, and the blood-soaked steel came free as a deep red stain formed on her shimmering gold gown.

"I am sorry to do this, my dear. You were a lovely partner in every sense. But I have the comfort of knowing the Aulic Council will include a bonus for dispatching a traitorous whore!" He brought back his arm for a final thrust.

The heavy cutlass struck Donat's arm with a sluggish *whoosh*, bludgeoning it into a mangled appendage. Lafayette stepped forward and kicked away the saber. "You have a rendezvous with the hangman, *Monsieur*."

Donat's eyes showed nothing but raw hate. "But you shall not live to see it!" He drew his pistol from his belt and cocked it. As the barrel zeroed in on Lafayette, Donat shrieked.

Lilly staggered forward and plunged her blade into his shoulder with a desperate swipe. It sent the point at an angle that pierced his heart and lungs.

The Prussian fencing master sputtered and collapsed into the thick carpet, his eyes staring blankly at his student.

Lafayette caught Lilly as she swooned to the floor.

She gazed at the hazy form of the Marquis de Lafayette. She could not hear his words, but they were comforting nevertheless.

"It's all right, *Mademoiselle* Olivia. I have you safely in my arms."

Chapter 19

Nashville, Tennessee, May 5th

The steamboat chugged its way up the Mississippi waters to Baton Rouge. Lafayette used the time to work on correspondence and reflect. The encounter at The Cabildo seemed a strange dream. Not like the horrible dreams he experienced in prison, but disturbing nonetheless.

"Still thinking of Olivia, father?" George asked.

"*Oui*. She was a noble girl."

Neall and Riley found him still clutching her lifeless form when they arrived. Although they may have suspected it, Lafayette never told them she was really an assassin named Lilly. It was the least a gentleman could do. She had, after all, saved his life and given hers up for his.

"Well, today we meet the great Jackson," said George.

"I met him at the Capitol. And his wife in Alexandria. But I look forward to seeing the home of the most popular man in America."

"I thought you were the most popular man in America, father."

"Haha! Perhaps of the old America. But the new America needs a man like Jackson. He is their Old Hickory, as they say."

"But he lost the election."

"He had more votes than the others. He lost to politics, not the will of the people." Lafayette felt a trace of guilt, for he liked John Quincy Adams and adored his father. "He lost to a good man. No shame in that."

The city of Nashville was still just a frontier town, with ornate wooden buildings, half of them saloons and boardinghouses, but all freshly painted in shades of gray, white, and occasionally blue or red.

Hoot! Hoot! The steamer blew its horn, and the early morning crowd began clapping and jumping for joy at the great man's arrival. Thousands of Nashvillians lined the docks in high anticipation.

"Pretty good crowd for eight in the morning," said Grayson. "You'd never get a New York crowd to turn out before eleven, if then."

The comment startled Lafayette. The young man hardly said a word to him since Olivia's death. He had fallen for her and seemed just a bit jealous. Lafayette, who had wooed scores of women, single and married, was always amazed by that American attribute.

The party leaped into coaches and joined a procession to the public square.

Neall had hired two new security men in New Orleans. A pair of Creek Indians named Piqué and Sam. They were about forty, solidly built with the rough copper skin of the Indian. They wore leather and carried hunting rifles, a hunting knife strapped to their side, and a tomahawk stuck in their belt.

Some forty men in blue and brown uniforms cheered lustily at the public square.

Levasseur smiled. "Revolutionary War veterans from all over Tennessee have assembled to greet you."

Lafayette sent the crowd into a frenzy of patriotic fervor in his speech, covering everything from the two revolutions. He praised his fellow veterans, including George Washington and Andrew Jackson.

"A dinner with over two hundred guests is planned for this evening," said Levasseur. "Andrew Jackson will preside and honor you."

Lafayette shook his head with a smile. "No. It is I who will honor him."

***

The Hermitage

The *thump* of leather soles on loose planking resounded as Lafayette and his party climbed the narrow wooden gangway onto a small steamer bound for Andrew Jackson's plantation, The Hermitage. After a whirlwind visit to Nashville upon their arrival and a late morning lunch the following day, Riley was anxious about the next leg of the trip.

Riley decided that after the attack in New Orleans, one of the principals, either he, Neall, or Grayson, must always be in earshot of Lafayette. Grayson's New York militia was down to three, but they were experienced hands now and would handle crowds and entry points. Neall gave Lynch charge of the two new hires, Piqué and Sam.

The journey provided them a bird's eye view into the beauty of Tennessee's Cumberland River, passing stands of drooping willows, majestic chestnuts, and grand oak trees, plus fields lush with spring. But all was marred by the glistening backs of slaves working the fields.

"Do you think your planter class will ever give up their chattel?" asked Neall as he puffed a cigar at the steamer's bow.

Riley removed his hat and ran his hand through his hair. "Yes, I do. But it'll take a donnybrook to do it."

"Right," said Neall. "Maybe better that way. Keep an eye on Grayson. He'll take a long time to get over that girl."

"As will the marquis," said Riley. "After all, she died saving him. Strange, the amazing effect he has on women."

"What do you mean?"

"She hardly knew him, but he quickly turned her from murderess to heroine," Riley replied.

"That may be, but she was in on it from the start and, according to the baron, one of the Aulic Council's best." Neall flicked the still-burning cigar into the thick, muddy water and pulled two silver coins from his pocket — each with a three-headed eagle clutching a globe in its talons. "Emil Donat and Lilly Nordstrom each carried one on them — proof of their link to the Aulic Council."

"Glad we were able to sink their bodies into Lake Pontchartrain," said Riley. "Shame though that Mister Grayson's man had to join them."

"You know the rules. None of these attacks on Lafayette ever happened."

"Funny he never accused her as an accomplice. Does he know you know?"

"I think he does," said Neall. "He just won't admit he was duped."

"I think maybe he respected her turn of heart. She saved his life, after all," said Riley.

The steamer's whistle was followed by the engines slowing, and the ship floated to the quay and stopped with a solid bump.

***

Andrew Jackson grabbed Lafayette by the hand as they shuffled down the gangplank. He looked stark and imposing in a dark suit, a shock of gray hair, and eyebrows framing a stern visage. The war hero and would-be president led them to a pair of coaches for the excursion around his expansive estate.

Grayson climbed in with Lafayette, Jackson, Levasseur, and George. He had drawn the morning task of shadowing the general. They rode past fields lush with spring planting, sapphire blue ponds, stands of hardwoods, and magnificent rows of myrtles, redbuds, and other flowery trees.

"*C'est magnifique*," said Lafayette more times than Grayson could remember.

The coach turned down a long road with cypress trees, chestnuts, and maples forming an arch that led to the large but simple and understated structure that Jackson called home.

Greek-style columns dwarfed the large veranda and the gray stone front, making the eight-room, two-story home appear stately yet modest.

"Hard to believe America's greatest hero lives in such a simple home," quipped Levasseur.

Grayson found the comment out of place. "Even our greatest man, George Washington, favored comfort over glitter, *Monsieur*."

"You have developed a tongue in your sorrow," replied Levasseur.

Grayson knew he was right. "It's a way of coping."

Jackson escorted Lafayette down one of the two parallel halls. The others followed, their shoes tap-tapping along the highly polished parquet floors. Grayson took note of every painting, curtain, and piece of furniture. If he ever made it home to New York, his mother would question him on every detail.

"*Mon Dieu*! What have we here?" exclaimed Lafayette as Jackson opened a walnut case.

"I believe these once belonged to you, sir." Jackson showed a pair of exquisite dueling pistols with a walnut finish and nickel fittings.

Lafayette fell into Jackson's arms and sobbed. "These were my gift to great Washington himself. How?"

Jackson appeared a bit embarrassed. "One of his relatives gifted them to me last year. How could I refuse?"

"I am delighted you didn't."

Jackson snapped the case closed. "Time to stroll the gardens before dinner. Mrs. Jackson takes particular pride in them. "

After the country-style dinner, the coaches hurried them to the quay.

"We never have time to linger and enjoy," Levasseur complained to the marquis as the coach bounced down the road.

"There is so much of America to see and so little time, *Monsieur*," said Lafayette.

"There will be time to rest and reflect when we board the steamship from Nashville after tonight's ball," said Grayson tartly. He still was in no mood for festivities. "We'll have several days of steaming back to the Mississippi and then up the Ohio River."

"How far will the water take us?" asked Levasseur.

"I think at least as far as Pittsburgh."

"That should make for an interesting journey," the secretary said. "For my journal."

"Hopefully, not too interesting, *Monsieur*," quipped Grayson.

***

The *Mechanic*, Nashville, May 5th

The four grunting black men in the boiler room barely heard muffled voices clambering onboard. The stokers shoveled pails of coal darker than their skin and hauled armloads of hardwood that rubbed their bare chests raw.

"We've some distinguished passengers for the next week, boys," said Erik Weiss, the *Mechanic's* engineer. "The famous General Lafayette is traveling with us. The first leg to the Mississippi is down the river, so we'll need only half our wood and coal. But once we hit the Mississippi and then the Ohio River, we'll be swimming upstream. You'll need all your strength then. The general is on a tight schedule, they tell me."

Homer glanced at the other firemen, who did not seem to heed what the engineer had just told them. He figured the fire's roar, the pistons throbbing, or the bellows pumping blocked their senses. They often did his.

Weiss clambered back down the ladder into the boiler room when the horn blew. "You've stoked her enough, for now, boys. Now, I need one of you to stand by while the others rest. The Cumberland's current will do most of the work on this leg. But you'll be busy when we head up the Ohio."

Homer did not know much about Weiss other than he had grown up in Cincinnati and that his parents were Germans from a town named Speyer in a place his parents called the Rhein Pfalz, but Weiss called the Rhineland-Palatinate.

"I'll stay," said Homer. He was the only freedman of the crew and felt it his duty to do just a little extra. Besides, he hoped to be an engineer like Erik Weiss one day.

***

Two days later, *Mechanic* turned into port at Cairo, Illinois, to refuel for the final push up the Ohio River to Louisville. "Come on! We don't have all night. You have two hours to finish."

The men grunted and continued hauling wood and coal. Coal was preferred as it burned hotter, according to Weiss. But wood was cheaper, and there was plenty of it. So coal was used to start the engines and to carry through particularly tough waters.

Homer glanced out the hatch and saw Weiss clamber down the gangway. *Probably looking for a beer hall.*

It occurred to Homer that he could do the same as a freeman. Assuming he did not pick the wrong beer hall. Everyone knew freedmen weren't very welcome in certain quarters. He could quaff a quick beer and maybe bring a pail back for the boys.

Minutes later, he was on the quay and strolling along the row of bars. He was listening to the music and laughter streaming from the open doors when something along the water caught the corner of his eye. *Mister Weiss?* It was, and he was not drinking. Instead, he was smoking a pipe along with another gentleman. Homer edged along the trees to get closer and listen. But the conversation was in German. Homer shrugged and soon found a beer hall that took his business.

An hour later, he was back on board. The men quaffed the beer with gusto and then tossed the empty pails overboard.

The whistle shrilled.

"We'll be going soon," said Homer.

The wooden ladder shook as Weiss clambered down into the boiler room. "How hot is she, Homer?"

"She's ready, boss." Homer had it ready for twenty minutes while the boys sipped their beer. "Have a good time?"

Weiss gave a strange look. "What do you mean?"

"You know, the beer halls here are good."

"Oh, yeah. Right. Ottos's Bierhaus was full of lively ladies and frothy brew. Had some of both."

"And a nice smoke, huh, boss?"

Weiss's eyes narrowed. "Nonsense. You know I don't smoke. Anyone who works with engines ought not to smoke. He might inadvertently light up in here. You know how that would go. Don't you let me catch you smoking, Homer! Ever!"

***

The *Mechanic*, on the Ohio River, May 8th

Neall held a pair of Jacks and Queens. The ladies thrilled him, but he would trade the two boys for a third girl. He slapped the hand on the table. "I'm out."

"Mister Neall, you are the most risk-averse poker player I've met," said Riley. "No self-respecting marine would fold that."

"I only stay in if I know I'll win," said Neall. He was lying—just setting them up for the big bluff when he needed it. "Better to live and fight another day."

"Good plan," said Grayson.

"I think I'll go check on the new men," said Neall.

He strode up to the tower near the bridge. The captain gave him a hello wave as he passed and sidled next to the two Indians, stoically scanning the river with their Hawken guns cradled in their arms like infants. "Anything to report?"

"The waterfowl are winging north in great numbers. But they fly too slowly. And not straight. Bad omen," said Piqué.

Just what I need. "What does that mean?"

"Danger for great white general," said Sam. "And all of us."

"What could happen here? On the river? Surrounded by guards?"

The pair grunted and continued scanning in silence.

"Canoes safer," Sam finally said.

Neall smiled. He never knew Indians had a sense of humor. He realized now they were kidding him.

As *Mechanic* turned another bend in its serpentine journey up the Ohio, Piqué suddenly pointed. "I see it."

Sam grunted and shifted his Hawken.

"See what?" demanded Neall.

"Again! Now gone."

"A flash of sunlight."

"So? Isn't that what the sun does?" Neall knew the Indians liked to speak in riddles. At least, that is what the books and periodicals reported.

"But not in forest," said Piqué. "Someone signal."

Neall scanned the trees, heavy with green leaves, for a sign but saw nothing. *But if what they say is true? There could be a collaborator on the Mechanic.*

Neall placed Grayson and one of his men near a lifeboat to be ready to move Lafayette off the ship. He alerted Riley and the others, hustled Lafayette's party into the captain's cabin, and locked the door. A pair of Grayson's men stood watch while Riley stayed with Lafayette.

"Come with me, Tommy."

Neall and Lynch climbed up and joined the stalwart Indians.

"Keep your eyes peeled, lads," said Neall.

He and Lynch checked their pistols and daggers. These were mere precautions. But now he and Lynch would need to scour the ship for anyone suspicious.

The helmsman kept his eyes fixed forward when Neall and Lynch stepped onto the bridge.

"Find anything?" asked the captain.

Neall shook his head and stared out across the roiling water. "Ever have trouble here?"

"Just the usual shoals and shifting silt," said the captain. "When I was a mate, a ship I served on ran aground just a few miles upriver. Of course, it was a keelboat, a shallower draft. But this lady will do just fine. We should be in Louisville in two hours."

"What do we do, sir?" asked Lynch.

Neall felt they had done all they could, for now. Sometimes, it was just a matter of watchful waiting. "You join Piqué and Sam. I'll stay with the skipper a bit longer."

***

Homer watched the marquis' security men take him to a lifeboat. It was then he noticed the other boat, the skipper's skiff, was missing. He went to ask the ship's engineer about it but found Weiss's cabin door ajar and empty.

He raced up three sets of ladders to the bridge. Knowing he was not permitted to enter, he slyly peered over the window. *Boss ain't here.*

Homer felt something was wrong. He had just left the engine room. *Where you at boss?* Then he remembered the strange encounter at the river. It bothered him that a man who claimed he did not smoke, who disapproved of it, was smoking with a stranger. *What could it mean?*

A thought struck him like an overseer's lash. Homer raced down the ladder into the dark of the engine room. The pistons pounded, and bellows belched. The engine fire was at a feverish pitch.

"Why so much heat, boys?"

One of the boilermen turned and stood panting with a hand resting on his shovel. "Boss came down and said to fire it to the max. We're just doin' what he says."

Homer stared at the Cornish boiler. It heated water in a cylinder with a fire tube in the middle, through which flue gases flowed. The outside, usually black, was beginning to glow red. Once the glow turned white, the entire contraption would blow.

The other boilerman continued to toss packed hardwood and chunks of coal.

"Did he say to use the coal? That's just for high speed and pushing through the strongest currents."

"Guess he spects something up ahead, huh?" The second boilerman turned to shovel.

Homer's mind raced. If he crossed the boss, he'd never be an engineer. His life would be relegated to hauling faggots of wood and shoveling coal till his lungs collapsed or he caught the fever. He remembered the figure smoking with the boss. *They spoke a foreign language!* The boss was up to something. *But what? Why blow the ship?* Then it struck him — *Lafayette!*

***

Weiss slowly turned the winch, lowering himself quietly into the churning waters in the wake of *Mechanic's* great stern paddle. The swirling river's current quickly separated him from the ship. In minutes, he was almost a half-mile downriver and paddling to the embankment smothered with ferns and scrub trees.

He opened his bag and gazed at the fistful of coins. The $500 was a half down payment, the rest to be paid in full when he arranged a boat for them to take south when they met in Cairo.

But Weiss selected one of them and rubbed it tenderly before slipping it into his vest pocket. His payer told him it was unique and would open more doors than the American gold pieces. The face side had a three-headed eagle clutching a globe in its talons. But the reverse side really got his attention, three crowns superimposed on each other, surrounded by the words *Aulic Concilio*.

***

Sam nudged Piqué, who tapped Lynch on the shoulder.

"What?" Lynch had trouble communicating with these Indian hunters. But he knew they only spoke purposefully, unlike his barracks mates and bar friends who gobbed on ceaselessly and uselessly.

"See," said Sam, pointing at a cleft in the rock overhang at the bend up ahead.

Lynch's eyes focused harder than if a French cuirassier were barreling down on him with a flashing broad sword. "I don't see — wait! I do. A flash of sunlight."

Sam lifted his hands to his eye and curled his fingers to mock a spyglass.

"Someone is watching us with a scope! Keep a bead on it, and I'll tell Mister Neall."

He raced down the ladder and pounded on the door of the bridge. The First Mate opened it, and Lynch pushed past him and stopped next to Neall and the skipper.

"What is it, Tommy?"

"Sam and Piqué spotted the flash of a scope. I did, too, up on the rocks ahead.

"That's Buzzard's Point," said the captain. "Could be a hunter up there. They say bears can still be seen there in the heavy woods. Winter hibernation is long over."

"I'm thinking the hunt's for something else," said Neall. "Okay, Tommy, go warn the others and get back up there with the lads."

***

The pounding of the pistons had become a whining that ripped through Homer's ears like a swarm of hornets. The mantel of the Cornish boiler was turning white-hot.

Where's the boss? Homer had waited long enough for Weiss to return. Even if there were a good reason to run so hot, the ship's engineer 's job was to oversee it.

"Where's the boss?"

The three strapping and sweating men with glistening chests just shrugged. Their rippling muscles strained with each shovel dumped into the furnace.

The whining grew shrill, and it was impossible to think between the fire's roar, the valves pumping, and the bellows blowing. But Homer knew he had to make a decision, or they would all be dead in minutes.

"This is about to blow, boys. Run for safety! Get out of here!"

Two of them looked at the boiler, then at Homer, and then scrambled up the ladder.

When Homer tried to take the shovel from the third, he turned and glared at him with lifeless, bloodshot eyes.

"Bossman said he'd sell us to a sugar plantation on the islands if we didn't shovel till he returned. I ain't dying in the hot son of a distant island. No way!"

A sick feeling plunged through Homer's belly. Every slave lived in fear of being sold. Worst of all was being sold to the sugar planters. But he knew now that Weiss would never return.

"Give me the shovel and go. I'll try to cool the boiler down before she blows."

With a low growl, the stoker rammed the shovel's blade into Homer's belly, blowing the wind from him and sending an ache that shook his spine.

He turned back to his labors as though Homer wasn't there. Homer drew a breath as he pondered what to do. He had worked hard too long and hard to stay a mere stoker, a boilerman. He took pride in the engine and the ship. He would not let anyone stop him from saving it.

He grabbed one of the other shovels, lifted it high, and slammed it with a heavy crack into the stoker's right shoulder, snapping his clavicle and sending him rolling to the engine room floor, writhing in pain.

Desperately, Homer began scraping burning piles of coal and wood out of the hearth. But the fireball had already reached its peak intensity. The mantle was glowing white.

He grabbed one of the nearby water buckets and tossed it onto the boiler, hoping to cool it. Instead, the water vaporized on contact, filling the room with a hiss and cloud of hot steam that choked and blinded him.

Realizing he had failed, Homer grabbed the moaning stoker and slowly dragged him toward the ladder. Before he could lift him up, the room filled with a ball of fire, followed by what Homer thought was the boom of a battery of cannons.

***

Piqué turned to Sam and chattered in their language.

"What is it?" asked Lynch.

"We must go now," Sam grunted, and the two clambered down the side rails toward the main deck. Lynch knew these men would do this only if danger lurked. He had learned to trust their instinct. *No time to consult Neall.*

"Abandon ship!" Lynch cupped his hands to his mouth a second time. "Abandon ship!"

Then he felt a rumbling. He searched for Neall and spotted him. Remembering the emergency signal, he desperately cupped his hands to his mouth and shouted, "Hannah, bar the door!"

Neall was now on the deck, getting Lafayette and the party into the boat. Sam and Piqué threw their kit into the boat, but it was jammed with people, and they leaped into the swirling waters.

Lynch ran to warn the skipper, who was now the only one on the bridge. Suddenly, the keel heaved, then *rumbled*, followed by a blast louder than Napoleon's Grand Battery at Waterloo. *Vaboom!*

A wall of energy lifted Lynch from the ship and pounded his eardrums till they burst. The force of it tossed him from his feet and sent his stunned body flying into the air before tumbling into the bowels of *Mechanic's* shattered and burning hulk, which slowly sunk under the swirling waters.

***

Neall had just made it into the boat when *Mechanic* began to rumble.

"Heave those oars," bellowed the First Mate, who the skipper put in command of the small boat. The four sailors lucky enough to join him pulled hard to gain separation from the steamship. Their desperate grunts and groans showed they realized the danger.

Fifty yards distant, *Mechanic* blew up in a thunderclap that pounded their ears and a fireball that seemed to sear their faces. Men covered their heads as ship pieces plunged into the waters around them. Neall saw that some of the pieces were human remains.

"Who was left aboard?" Neall snapped.

"The skipper, about twelve deckhands. Your man Lynch."

Neall's heart sank.

"Anyone else?"

"I saw your Indian scouts leap into the water after they left us their kit," said Grayson.

"Such a tragic accident to befall those men," said Levasseur, wiping his head.

"That was no accident," said the First Mate.

Neall's eyes narrowed. "Anyone else?"

"The engine room crew. Weiss was the engineer. So, it was just him and his pack of blacks. A gang of slaves and a freedman named Homer."

***

Buzzard's Point

Spyglass firmly against his eye, Jan Nagy watched the show from the rocks just upriver. A rumble, followed by a deep *boom* and a fireball, lifted *Mechanic* from the water and broke her keel. Shards of metal and chunks of wood flew in all directions.

The spyglass scanned the water. Bodies floated. He even saw the form of one poor soul in Indian dress bobbing near the shore with the sharp end of a spar implanted between his shoulders.

"Excellent!" The smile drifted from his face when he realized a boat had launched just before the explosion. *Lafayette was still alive!*

"What must I do to kill you, you French rooster?" he muttered.

He snapped the spyglass closed and opened his long leather bag. Nagy slipped a long, elegant-looking rifle with side-by-side blackened barrels and black walnut stock.

Johann, you crafted another masterpiece. This rifle had been made to Nagy's specifications, with an extra twist to the grooves, a unique site radius, and customized individual single-set triggers that were adjustable. The percussion cap firelock with a .63 caliber bore was the first designed by the gunsmith.

Johann Springer crafted special weapons exclusively for his only customer, the Aulic Council. Nagy knew Springer was under strict orders not to produce for the public until his secret contract expired.

He spotted the boat, jammed with people. It rowed hastily upriver to the safety of a small island flanked by some short trees. Once more, turning to his spyglass, he scanned the group until he spotted Lafayette. *Aha! I have you now.*

Nagy placed the rear sight to his right eye and let the soft feel of the stock give him a good spot weld. The rifle felt like a woman in his arms. He chuckled at the thought. *Let's see if your tongue lashes louder than a woman's.*

He thumbed back the first hammer and zeroed in on the older man in uniform. The hammer struck home, and the percussion cap flashed, igniting the fine-grain powder. *Crack!*

Screams came from the boat as a man toppled over the gunwale into the river and began bobbing downstream with the current.

He quickly put the scope to his eye. Lafayette was still there. Now, they had dragged the boat to the island and had flipped it to provide cover.

"*A macska rúgja meg!*" Nagy cursed silently in Hungarian. *May the cat lick it!*

He quickly shifted to the second trigger and scanned the water for a better look.

***

The boat thumped the shore just as a rifle cracked. One of Grayson's militiamen toppled into the fast-running water and began drifting quickly downriver.

"Roll this damn thing over to cover us!" Sergeant Riley commanded.

A second crack took down one of the sailors before he could duck behind the boat.

Neall's mind raced to piece things together.

"What's going on?" Riley asked Neall.

"Someone blew *Mechanic* out of the water and will now shoot us down like dogs. But it's Lafayette he wants. It must be the Aulic Council. Stay close to him."

Riley pulled Lafayette to the ground and threw his body over him. "He'll have to put one through me to do it."

Out of nowhere, a form in buckskin rose from the river and came at them. One of Grayson's militiamen reached for his pistol.

"Don't shoot! It's Sam." Neall pulled the Indian scout to the shelter of the boat. "Where is Piqué?"

Sam shook his head.

"I'm sorry. What about Lynch?"

Sam's head shook again.

"Damn! What shall we do? He has a powerful rifle, and we have pistols. He'll pick us off one by one."

"I say we wait till dark and creep in on him in the dark," said Grayson. "I'd love to plug one of those Aulic bastards who led Olivia astray."

Neall did not have time to explain Olivia's actual role in the affair. "I understand. But the mission is to protect General Lafayette from getting plugged first."

Sam pointed at a pair of leather satchels cast off on the riverbank and bolted forward to retrieve them. A sailor ran to help, and a shot rang out, sending the sailor toppling into the muddy bank. But Sam grabbed the bags and was behind the boat before a second shot rang out, cutting a chunk of wood.

Sam pulled a long Hawken from one bag, quickly poured powder and ball into the barrel, and rammed it home tight. He pointed to the other bag. Neall opened it and withdrew a second Hawken.

"Piqué," said Sam solemnly.

"You fire. I go." Sam slid the back of his hand along his throat.

Neall nodded.

"Discharge your pistol at the rocks while Sam makes for the woods."

"We're on an island," said Grayson.

"Not exactly," said the First Mate. "Behind those trees, there's a small sandbar connecting to the riverbank. You'll need to distract whoever is mad at us up there."

Bending forward at the waist, Sam took off.

"Cover him. At least we can distract the shooter," Neall ordered.

Grayson and his two remaining men stood and pointed their pistols at the rocks above.

A series of shots flew harmlessly into the air, but when Neall shifted his gaze, Sam had already disappeared across the sandbar.

***

Nagy saw the leather-clad figure running and lowered his barrel to draw a bead on him.

Pop, pop, pop suddenly filled the air.

Nagy shifted his gaze in the direction of the firing. He saw a man with a pistol, and he squeezed the trigger. *Crack!*

The pistol flew through the air, and his target clutched his chest. *Will I have to shoot half of America to get Lafayette?* Nagy found the thought intriguing, but he had neither the time nor the powder and ball to do it.

And now he had a leather-clad man with a rifle to take care of. *"A macska rúgja meg!"*

He reloaded and moved to a new position, a safe spot with a pair of gray and black boulders to provide him maximum cover. He then moved back and waited silently for his prey.

The sun was halfway to the western horizon when he heard something rattle. He clicked back both hammers and waited. The birds had all gone, but swarms of annoying black bugs, unlike any in Europe, began to swarm him and sting his eyes. The heat and humidity soaked his clothes and occasionally wiped his weapon so his sweat did not affect it.

He thought he saw something across the small clearing. Nagy squeezed off a round. A *pop* exploded across the clearing, and he saw the yellow muzzle flash. He began to slither to another vantage point just before his opponent's equally powerful blast struck his position. A lead ball splattered on the rock next to him. *A macska rúgja meg!*

Leaves rattled just twenty-five yards distant, and he thought he saw the leather. Another leaf moved, barely. Nagy squeezed the trigger, and a return blast struck his shoulder. A flash of movement regained his attention.

Out of the bushes rose a copper-skinned man in deer leather, brandishing a smoking rifle in one arm and a tomahawk in the other. *I found an Indian!*

"*Yeehiih! Yip, yip!* The charging figure unleashed a war cry last used when Sam and his braves fought with General Jackson against the Spanish and the English.

The terrifying cry sent a cold chill through Nagy, who managed to cradle the rifle with his good arm. The Indian was just above him with the deadly war tomahawk raised high for the kill.

Nagy squeezed the trigger. *Boom!*

The close-range blast blew the Indian off his feet. He lay in the tall grass clutching his chest and reaching maniacally for the tomahawk, just out of reach. His breathing was labored, and Nagy knew he could not live long.

A smile crossed Nagy's face. He rose from the rocks and stood over his victim. "I'll save the next bullet for that pig, Lafayette. You, my fine red friend, will die like your ancestors."

Nagy stepped on Sam's outstretched fingers and grabbed the tomahawk. "One blow and I'll take your scalp as a trophy. The ladies of Budapest will be quite amused, if not charmed."

Sam's eyes were wide. But Nagy saw he was not afraid but filled with the anger of losing.

"You die a noble warrior. I admit that is a consolation. Look, you even nicked me. But in the end, I win, and you die."

Nagy straddled the nearly motionless form of Sam and lifted the blade for the final blow.

***

A boom filled the meadow, and a .54 caliber Hawken ball split Nagy's spine and exited through the three-inch hole it blew through his stomach. Neall stepped from the bushes and rushed to check on Sam, who was lifeless.

"Damn!"

He turned to the lifeless form. Dark hair in a queue, wide sideburns, and a long black mustache – he was clearly an Eastern European type. *He's missing only the hussar boots.*

But the hussar stirred, and his hand reached for his vest.

"You'll not get another shot!" Neall drew his pistol and plugged him with both barrels into his chest.

The hussar's head flew back, and his arms and legs jerked in spasms. Neall reached into his vest for the weapon. But instead of the firearm, he pulled out a shiny silver coin with a three-headed eagle.

Chapter 20

The Chancery, Baltimore, June 17th

Raindrops pattered against the window pane, and brief wind gusts occasionally swirled through the library.

"Excellent work," said Bernard.

"But a damned near run thing," replied Neall.

"As Wellington said about The Battle of Waterloo," replied Bernard with a twinkle in his eye.

Neall's report was dismal. Although Lafayette survived a saber attack, an exploding steamship, and a deadly sniper, several had died during the events: three of Grayson's militiamen, the two Indian scouts, and Tommy Lynch. But Lafayette was safe, and when a steamship arrived the next day, he continued his journey.

He made his way to Louisville, Cincinnati, and Pittsburgh, with several towns and many speeches and ceremonies along the way. On June 4th, his party arrived at Buffalo, New York, where he headed east after more festivities. Neall was amazed at how resilient the old man was and how he handled everything with cheerful goodwill.

"Mister Grayson and his men accompanied Sergeant Riley and General Lafayette's entourage to Boston. He's giving a speech at Bunker Hill this very day. I decided to head south and arrange things for the final months of the visit."

Bernard rubbed his chin. "Can Grayson handle it?"

"He's distraught at the loss of the men but determined to see things through."

"Good. I'm asking His Excellency to say a special Mass for the departed and their families. Also, for the Aulic Council agents."

"What?"

Bernard expected that response.

"Jesus taught us to love our enemies as well as our friends."

Bernard cast an anxious eye at Neall. "Are you visiting Betsy while in Baltimore?"

"Why, uh, perhaps."

"She may not be there. She has been quite busy while you were out west. Her part of this mission has kept her in Washington most of the time."

"Where would I look for her in Washington? Is she staying at the Blodgett Hotel or the Willard? I bet she favors the Willard."

Bernard thought it was time to open up a bit more to Neall. "She stays in a house. It's at 211 Q Street."

***

Bunker Hill, Charlestown, Massachusetts

Anxious spectators filled the open hillside and streets of the town like ants swarming on an ant hill. Riley had never seen so many people since New Orleans. Although several militia regiments stood erect with arms ready, he wondered how he could keep Lafayette safe for the next few months with just Grayson and one man.

The keynote speaker, Daniel Webster, strode to the podium, gazed at the silent crowd, and began:

"This uncounted multitude before me and around me proves the feeling which the occasion has excited. These thousands of human faces, glowing with sympathy and joy and from the impulses of common gratitude, turned reverently to heaven in this spacious temple of the firmament, proclaiming that the day, the place, and the purpose of our assembling have made a deep impression on our hearts..."

Webster went on in a rich tone that recounted America's early challenges, the gallantry and righteousness of the cause, and its impact on the world. He closed with a final flourish of his hands.

"Let us extend our ideas over the whole of the vast field in which we are called to act. Let our object be our country, our whole country, and nothing but our country. And, by the blessing of God, may that country itself become a vast and splendid monument, not of oppression and terror, but of Wisdom, of Peace, and of Liberty, upon which the world may gaze with admiration forever!"

The opening speech by the famed orator-politician had kept the multitude spellbound. Then, it aroused them to a zeal of patriotism that embarrassed even an old marine.

Ruffles and flourishes signaled the transition to Lafayette, who graciously hugged Webster and ambled to the podium.

Lafayette lifted the cornerstone and gracefully set it in the place marked by the architect. His address was shorter and more to the point, but he captured the crowd with his very presence. Riley saw the awe as they hung onto each word spoken by the great hero.

"Would that I could return for the day when this stone becomes a mighty monument to the sacrifice of the Americans, not just here, but everywhere they fought for liberty. But, failing that, I take a spade full of this sacred earth and will, at length, have a small part of American soil on my grave."

Riley watched the reaction: a moment of respectful silence followed by a wave of cheers and huzzahs that spread across the hillside.

"They can probably hear this crowd in New York," Grayson said.

"I certainly hope so," replied Riley, pointing at the large coach with six white horses waiting on the other side of the multitude. "Let's get ready. Friends or not, there's a sea of people to get through to the carriages."

***

Navy Yard, Washington, DC

The thud of wooden nails driven into oak plank reverberated across the long stretch of piers on the Anacostia River.

"I'd shut the window, but the heat is rising," said Putnam, sitting at a small desk in the office he shared with two other officers, both lucky enough to be at sea.

"Do you ever get used to that racket?" asked Buchanan.

"Used to it, no. But it does provide a sense of ease knowing the nation is investing in the maintenance of our ships, if not their replacement."

"Anything new on Captain Denis?"

Putnam shook his head. "He has found no trace of other Aulic Council agents. Nor have I." Putnam lifted his foot, displaying a worn-through sole. "But I think I need new shoes. I've tramped through every restaurant, coffee house, and gin mill where foreigners hang out."

Buchanan laughed. "No bordellos? What next?"

"I just received a note from Brother Bernard. Mister Neall is back. He is minus several men, but it seems they got the general out of a few scrapes."

"I read about the steamship running aground near Louisville."

"In reality, someone sabotaged it, and the boiler blew. Then, an Aulic Council agent with a finely crafted Austrian rifle tried to shoot them. Neall took care of things, but Tommy Lynch is gone without a trace."

"What's Neall's next play? President Adams and Secretary Clay are anxious Lafayette's last few months stay uneventful."

"That depends."

"On what?"

"On whether Brother Bernard clued him in on everything."

***

The British Legation, Washington, DC

Horan scratched out a few notes when Neall finished recounting his tale. "I'll have a report sent to Lord Avondale with the next diplomatic pouch."

"I feel better already," said Neall. He still disliked the clerk. "What news on the baron?"

"Doesn't seem up to much. I think the American gold has him in its thrall. He's their asset, bought and paid."

"Gold only buys so much loyalty. Did they test him?"

Horan hesitated.

Neall felt he was holding something back. "Answer me, please."

"I should not say this, but Brother Bernard and I have an arrangement. We compare his feed to make sure he's not two-timing."

"And?"

"The little we have gotten has proved accurate. But now we have a small problem."

"What could a nasty Austrian do to upset you? I'll step on his lip again for you."

"He insists there are no further agents in the country. Good news, but I'm skeptical."

"As you should be. Perhaps I shall pay the baron a visit at the Austrian Sub-Consulate. Or better yet, surprise him at his hotel."

"You'll have a better chance of finding him at his preferred location," said Horan with a smirk.

"Where's that?"

"That, I have not figured out."

***

211 Q Street, Washington, DC

The evening lamplight added a pale shadow to the townhome. Neall slipped the driver a coin and stepped out onto the street. He paused and took a few moments to scan the road for anything peculiar.

Bernard did not explain why he would find Elizabeth Patterson at the home where Madeline Goulet had been meeting the baron. *What was her connection, and why didn't they tell me?*

Neall ignored the knocker and tapped the door twice, then twice more with his walking cane, a signal he had used before.

The door opened slowly, revealing the slender Elizabeth Patterson in an elegant crimson evening dress. He marveled at her beauty.

"I was wondering when you would get around to this. Come in, Richard." She took his hat and cane and led him to a small side parlor with a gently burning hearth.

He took her hands in his, but she averted her eyes.

"Brother Bernard suggested I come. We had followed Madeline here and, of course, Baron Riedel. You being here surprises me. But I suppose it shouldn't."

Her eyes rose to his. He found them distractingly beautiful but full of sadness.

"I heard about the men. It's awful. I'm sorry for their loss. Even the one you had follow me."

Neall released her hands and cocked his head. "Follow you?"

"Yes. From the Austrian Sub-Consulate to this house. And he surveilled me."

"Some thugs detained him. I followed your coach—I thought it was Madeline."

209

Elizabeth smiled sheepishly. "She did borrow some of my clothes. And she introduced me to the baron. That was all. I never suspected her direct involvement in killing the marquis." She lowered her eyes. "He and I were once...."

"Well, by all indications, Madeline had a change of heart and died in a blast intended for him. Now, dear Betsy, tell me about the baron."

"Excuse me." Betsy rose, retrieved a green decanter from a cupboard, and poured two sherries.

They each took a long sip and paused, their eyes exploring each nuance in their somber faces.

"The baron and I are lovers."

Neall controlled his emotions. "I thought Madeline was his lover."

"Maybe she wanted to be. But she introduced me to him at a coffee house, and I took it from there. I forget where and when now. It is not something I am happy about, but it was the quickest way to ensnare him."

"Ensnare him? Is he a hare?"

She smiled meekly. "More like a jackrabbit, I'd say."

Neall could not control giving her a smile in return.

Elizabeth sipped her sherry and gazed at the fire. "He's not the first person I have trapped, as you well know. But you must believe me when I say it was not something I took any pleasure in."

Neall nodded. He felt guilty challenging her. But he felt betrayed by not being in on the scheme. He realized there were things Brother Bernard would never share with him, at least until he was ready.

"He has provided good intelligence on several networks in Europe and the scheme to kill General Lafayette. The marquis is safe — at least while in America. The attack you faced in Ohio is the last, he says."

He smiled and stroked her cheek. "Kentucky, the attack was in Kentucky. You Americans know so little of your geography."

***

Baltimore, Maryland, July 30th

The teams of horses *clop – clopped* along the cobblestones in the early morning fog. Lafayette peered from his window and sighed. For once, no well-wishers were cheering or running behind the couch to catch a glimpse of him.

He was tired — the cross-country trip at a near record pace, the attacks that cost the lives of good people. The crowds were everywhere and always welcoming and joyous. He loved it all, but he was feeling his age.

Since his speech at Bunker Hill, Lafayette's schedule took him through New Hampshire, Vermont, New York, New Jersey, and Pennsylvania with multiple stops and numerous ceremonies and testimonials.

"Why are we in Baltimore if we have no official events?" asked George.

"To meet the archbishop. Bishop Maréchal is a good friend from earlier days. And he is French," replied Lafayette.

In the chancery, Lafayette bowed respectfully and kissed the bishop's ring.

"Your friends may enjoy some refreshments while we meet with Brother Bernard," said Maréchal.

Lafayette followed the bishop down several corridors until a heavy oak door blocked their way. Maréchal retrieved a key from under his cassock and opened the door, exposing a large but musty room where a man a little older than Lafayette sat at a desk.

Brother Bernard rose to greet the visitors. "Welcome to Baltimore, General Lafayette."

Lafayette nodded and took his seat. The monk looked somewhat familiar. "Have we met, Brother?"

"'Tis possible. Life is full of strange twists of fate," said Bernard.

Lafayette noticed a twinkle in his eye. *Where? When?*

"I wanted Brother Bernard to update you personally. He has been supervising our circle of patriots, shielding you from the Aulic Council."

"Is an English agent an American patriot?" quipped Lafayette. "And I noticed an Irish twist in your speech, Brother."

"Ah, but 'tis said that anyone who loves and serves America is American. You, of all people, should know that, General."

"*Touche'* Brother."

They switched to French, and Lafayette rapidly revealed his side of the events out west. "Mister Neall was fearless. He seized the dead Indian's rifle and hunted down the killer. A man who possessed the same coin as the others."

"The coin with the three-headed eagle."

Lafayette nodded. "I should like to keep one as a souvenir."

"After we attend noon Mass, we can get you one," said Maréchal.

Bernard pulled some papers from his desk, scanned the contents, and peered over his spectacles at Lafayette.

"Does the name Captain Denis or Denisov mean anything to you?"

Lafayette pondered. He had met so many allied officers when Paris fell.

***

Château de la Grange-Bléneau, France, July 9th, 1815

The clatter of horses came from the courtyard below Lafayette's library window. He stuck his head out and was surprised to see three young cavalrymen in dark blue hussar uniforms. *Are the allied armies here so soon?*

A servant soon led the three visitors into Lafayette's study.

"To what do I owe the pleasure, gentlemen?"

Their leader twisted his long, dark mustache and smiled. "We wanted to be the first to meet the great Lafayette. Our armies are bivouacked outside Paris, but we were allowed to enter the city two days ago. Our duties there done, we set out to find you."

"And you are?"

"Captain Alexei Denisov, 6th Hussars. These are lieutenants Nikitin and Orlov."

Lafayette motioned to a servant who returned with brandy.

"What can I tell you, gentlemen, to make your journey worthwhile?"

Lafayette figured the officers were part of a move to begin cleansing of revolutionaries and enemies of the Bourbons. That he helped depose Napoleon a year earlier offered little defense when it came to Royalist *revanche'*.

Denisov smiled broadly, sending his mustache tips pointing upwards comically. "We are followers of Count Mikhail Mikhailovich Speransky, a wise and great leader trying to bring liberal ideas to Russia. Tell us everything! Of America and liberty, of France and equality. We are eager to learn it at the feet of a great man."

***

"Perhaps, but it was long ago, and the memory fades."

"It is understandable. We all face such difficulties from time to time, *Monsieur*," said Maréchal. "Continue, Brother Bernard."

Bernard was afraid he would give Lafayette a false sense of security. Although Riedel's information had proven correct thus far, Bernard knew such things were fragile.

"I can't say much, but we have a high-level source in the Aulic Council who indicates no other plots against you. At least in America."

"Can this be true?" asked Lafayette. He was not fearful, but his life had too many downward turns for him to let up his guard now.

"Yes, but we must maintain vigilance. Sergeant Riley will stay with you for the remainder of the trip and return to France with you. Mister Grayson and his two remaining men will stay with you until you board ship in New York for your return voyage."

Lafayette stared at the monk. He was sure they had met. "Were you at Yorktown, perhaps?"

Bernard smiled. "It seems my memory, too, has faded."

"I am leaving tomorrow for Virginia. I decided to spend most of my remaining days at Mount Vernon. The family of our beloved President Washington are gracious hosts."

***

211 Q Street, Washington

The flicker of candles added a sense of mystery to the dinner. Betsy gazed across the table at her dinner guest. "Is the duckling to your liking, my dear Franz?"

Baron Riedel dropped the greasy leg into his plate and gave her a lascivious grin. "Almost as delectable as my hostess. I am very much looking forward to the dessert."

A pink hue flushed her porcelain features, and she batted her lashes modestly. Betsy hoped to slake his lust before it got the better of him, but she feared she had failed.

"In fact, I may take a sample now!" He leaped from his chair and was at her in a flash, running his whiskered face along her bare shoulder. "Your scent alone does me in, my dear."

Betsy went to a defense tactic often used in the Paris salons. "Oh, my dear Franz, be careful of my hair."

Riedel stood erect. "Of course, darling. We'll save all this for later."

When he returned to his seat, she smiled sweetly. "Franz, there is someone I would like you to meet."

"Of course! Is it a beautiful friend you wish to share me with? Or a powerful politician? You know, it helps protect me if I can report on politicians. It is, after all, why I was sent here. Perhaps a luncheon?"

A *rap, rap,* followed by another double *tap* at the door, alerted her. *He's early.*

A servant led the tall figure of Richard Neall into the dining room. Neall slid into a seat, casually threw his hat and cane onto the table, and poured himself a claret.

He lifted his glass and eyed the baron. "Please enjoy your meal, Baron. I'll sip this and listen until you are done."

Riedel bristled but then smiled in resignation. "I know you! You're the blackguard lawyer who accosted me, Raymond Locke!" He turned to Betsy. "Why is he here?"

She smiled sweetly. "Raymond is a dear friend. And I thought, well, having you perform such precarious work on our behalf, he could be of use."

Neall gazed at her and added, "We must ensure the payments are suitably protected from exposure. I represent a particular bank noted for high discretion and the ability to prevent the funds from being traced."

"Who would trace them?" Riedel was now listening attentively.

"Well, dear, your other employers. Don't they have internal controls to prevent..."

"Betrayal? Of course, they do. But in America, I am the internal control."

Betsy looked at Neall. Her eyes signaled him to take over.

Brother Bernard wanted to double-check on their new and prized asset and asked Neall to assist. Neall began a long narrative and a series of veiled questions to discover a flaw in Riedel. But Riedel had countered, explained, or clarified every issue.

"Are you sure there is nothing else you wish to advise me of?"

Riedel looked at Betsy. "I report to *Madame*, not you. I was saving something for after dessert." He shot Betsy another of his looks.

She knew it was time to take control. "We may skip dessert tonight, Franz. Tell me now." She looked at Neall. "Mister Neall works for me, just as you do."

The look on both their faces gave her a sense of calm. *I have their attention.*

Riedel gazed at the floor nervously. "There *will* be another attack, after all. The failures of the others have upset my superiors in Salzburg. I have been informed only of its existence, not its date and place."

She saw the look on Neall's face. She truly loved Neall but enjoyed seeing him surprised. *So, I have scooped you, Richard.*

"You are the senior agent in America. You must have some idea of when and where," Neall said.

Riedel rubbed his fingers together. "I believe the press has reported that Lafayette will celebrate his sixty-eighth birthday at a joint session of Congress. Your president will also attend."

Betsy's body tingled, and her stomach turned. It was a terrible thing to report intelligence that is both accurate and horrific. "How awful! Will they try to kill them all? What brutes."

Riedel smirked. "Such things are high risk, so why not make them of high worth?"

"Indeed," said Neall. "The Aulic Council is known for such things."

Riedel's bushy brows rose. "How do you know anything about the Aulic Council?"

"I don't much," Neall replied. "I was hoping you could enlighten me."

Chapter 21

Mount Vernon, Virginia, August 2nd, 1825

Tufts of white clouds blended with the azure sky to make a perfect but humid late summer afternoon. The veranda faced the Potomac, and Lafayette and his party had an enthralling view of the Potomac River, dotted with sailboats skipping along the dark water.

A dark-skinned servant, one of those emancipated on Martha Washington's death, announced a visitor.

"Who is it?" asked Levasseur, who was always anxious to meet new people to fill his journal.

"He only said he last met you at your home near Paris ten years ago in July."

Lafayette nodded amicably.

Minutes later, a tall, dark-haired man with the bearing of a soldier stepped onto the veranda. A servant placed a cold sherbet in his hand, and Lafayette motioned him to sit. Levasseur noted some confusion on Lafayette's face.

"Excellency, I am pleased to see you once more. I am Captain Alexei Denisov. I visited you at your home just after we occupied Paris."

"Yes! Now I remember. You wanted to hear of my experiences."

"Who wouldn't want to hear of the experience of the greatest of his age?"

Levasseur jotted down the name. This would make an interesting side note.

"What can I do for you now, *Monsieur*?"

"I am here in Washington on business and took the opportunity to learn of your experiences on returning to your second homeland. I have been reading newspaper accounts, but they lack a sense of your thoughts on all this."

"My thoughts? Interesting question, Captain Denisov."

Lafayette spent over an hour regaling his guest on his feelings and observances of the changes in America. Levasseur once more copied what he could. He would fill in the gaps later in the evening.

"I have met with nearly all the governors, mayors, and other officials at every level in many states. I have supped with wealthy men and military leaders, but I will say on reflection, my greatest joy has been meeting the ordinary Americans."

Denisov beamed with admiration. "Well said, Excellency. But you will have at least one last seat with the high and mighty. The newspapers report that you'll celebrate your birthday with the American Congress and President."

"Yes, papa's birthday will be a double event!" George said with a smile.

Levasseur interrupted. "This isn't in the papers. We asked for discretion, and so far, they granted it."

"But papa will visit Mister Monroe at his new home at Oak Hill," said George.

Levasseur glanced at Sergeant Riley, who nearly spit his sherbet.

"It will be a discreet visit to pay President Monroe a final homage," Lafayette said. "After all, he and then Secretary Adams invited me on this tour. President Adams will join us."

"A firm date hasn't been set, so who knows? Perhaps it will be canceled," said Riley.

Levasseur was amused at Riley's attempt to put the genie back in the bottle. "I certainly hope not. I plan to enter it into my journal."

***

The Chancery, Baltimore, Maryland

The open windows only let in the humid summer air, making the room steamier. But Brother Bernard hoped an afternoon breeze would stir the air to a tolerable level.

"How do you people live with summers like this?" asked Neall.

Betsy fluttered her fan in his face and giggled. "Lady's advantage."

Bernard was happy to see a little joy from her. The work with any spy is difficult, but Riedel was perhaps the master. He felt guilty for allowing her to use her charms to snare and keep him. Betsy's handling of the Austrian was brilliant. But at a certain level, he was ashamed of being a party to sin.

"I called this meeting to assess the way forward. We will have much to cover if what Riedel reports is true."

"We'll need outside help. I talked to Captain Blaine. He promised two platoons of marines plus a half-dozen of our best sailors," said Putnam. "They'll be under my command."

"Excellent, Kent," said Bernard. "Have we heard anything from the other Russians?"

"I asked Mister Buchanan to check on their whereabouts."

Bernard saw Neall's eyebrows arch slightly at the mention of Denisov. He kept the Englishman unaware of the Russians but suspected Horan knew of them and told Neall.

"Something bothering you, Mister Neall?"

"No, Brother, it's just I was unaware you had identified more Russians. Are they the Aulic Council or Special Bureau?

"Tell him, Mister Putnam," said Bernard.

Putnam explained the background of The Northern Society and the liberal movement among Russian officers and Denisov's role.

"I know about the Northern Society. I was tracking some of them during the Congress of Vienna. But I had no idea they had penetrated the Special Bureau and possibly the Aulic Council. Does Horan know of this?"

Bernard smiled. "I'll allow you to provide him that nugget. Meanwhile, we have new information from Mister Buchanan. It seems General Lafayette plans an impromptu and intimate visit to former President Monroe, and now President Adams will also attend. Monroe won't make the grand birthday feast, it seems."

"What's the plan?" asked Neall.

"We'll keep our presence discreet. It's in the country — about a day's ride west of Washington. An estate called Oak Hill, south of a town called Leesburg."

"That leaves us little time," said Putnam.

"Indeed. Mister Neall, I suggest you ride straight there. Get to know the place. I have a letter signed by His Excellency explaining your role."

"Bishop one to knight two?" Neall quipped.

Bernard smiled. Many years ago, he was a big fan of chess. "You play? We'll have to have a match when all this is over."

"Kent, you'll need to move quickly. Here is a letter for Captain Blaine. Also, you'll need to get word to Mister Grayson and Sergeant Riley. They'll be accompanying Lafayette."

"Yes, Brother."

"What about me?" asked Betsy.

Bernard hesitated. He feared her response. "I have to ask you to do something I know might be difficult considering past circumstances."

"Yes?"

"Lafayette requires a lady companion as *Madame* Monroe will be there. Baltimore's most prominent socialite is just what the situation requires."

"But I have the baron. What do I tell him?"

"Tell him you are visiting an old friend who needs your support," said Neall.

"Or something to that effect," said Bernard. "We are in a quiet time before the great event in Washington. Task him to keep extra vigilant."

Betsy's eyes showed her reluctance, but she nodded in agreement.

***

Leesburg, Virginia, August 5th

Neall's boots nudged the flanks of his bay gelding, sending it into a canter that spun a cloud of dust along the Leesburg Pike. Ahead, he saw a crossroads with several homes, a bank, and a small street with a few stores and a tavern. *This is Leesburg?*

The sign ahead confirmed it. Neall brought the horse to a slow walk, allowing it to amble along with a natural gait. He halted just in front of a small stable freshly painted gray and black.

A stableboy ran out. "Can I water your horse, sir?"

Neall dismounted and threw him the reins. "Walk him first, then water and oats."

"You know horses?"

"I was in the cavalry for ten years."

Neall strode into the tavern and ordered a beer. The bartender placed a mug overflowing with foam.

"How do I find Oak Hill?" Neall asked after he slaked his thirst.

"Just a few miles south on the North Carolina Highway."

A half-hour later, Neall rode south, hoping a dust-caked visitor would be allowed into the former president's estate.

The sign over the entrance road was also freshly painted — the bright red letters over a white background read, Oak Hill Manor.

Neall halted to survey the scene. Small stands of trees dotted the rolling fields of green, especially along a narrow creek meandering south through the property. To the west ran a line of verdant hills, and beyond them, the dark outline of mountains — a *paradise to rival the English countryside.*

Neall turned the gelding up the trail leading to the large two-story home with a massive portico buttressed by a front of five Greek columns. Meadows, sliced by small streams, flanked him. Several barns and buildings surrounded the main house. Herds of cattle huddled along the brooks, hoping to quench themselves in the heavy summer heat.

Neall wiped the sweat from his brow. His city hat did little against the hot sun.

A lanky black servant approached.

"I have a letter for the President," said Neall.

The servant signaled, and a pair of grooms took Neall's horse to walk and cool it.

"Must move quickly with the animals in the summer heat, sir," said the servant.

"I didn't see the same courtesy paid to the slaves toiling along the road," said Neall.

The servant impassively led him to the parlor. Minutes later, the figure of James Monroe greeted him. He took Neall to the portico, where another servant brought out a carafe of coffee over ice.

"Ice is a rarity this time of year, sir," said Monroe. "I read the letter. As you know, I was the sponsor of this journey. I would hate to see something happen to General Lafayette just as it comes to a close."

Neall realized Monroe knew nothing of the attacks on Lafayette. "We suspect a threat to the grand birthday celebration, but my visit here is purely out of an abundance of caution."

"They arrive later today. We'll travel to Leesburg tomorrow for a ceremony with the Loudoun County Militia. Although the county was incorporated just twenty years before the Revolutionary War, it provided the most men for the Virginia Line of any county in the state."

Neall's lip tightened. Bernard never mentioned this event at Leesburg. He would have made a thorough search of the town had he known.

***

The coaches creaked with every bump along the turnpike. All but the passengers in the first coach ate dust the entire trip. They had left Alexandria early that morning and were almost there.

"This new turnpike takes us almost directly to Oak Hill. It is the safest route," said President Adams. "We should be there within the hour."

Lafayette nodded politely. "Virginia is a most beautiful country. Even in the heat of battle or chasing the scoundrel Arnold, I always stopped to admire its beauty. Of course, it would be more beautiful if its field workers were freemen."

"You have no argument from me on that account, General. Like my father, I am an abolitionist."

Riley could not help but think Lafayette was at last tiring of these trips. Riley himself was. He preferred sailing the high seas in tall ships to creeping along dusty roads in coaches or chugging up rivers in steamers. *No snipers and bombs at sea.*

They arrived at dusk to find Monroe and his wife waiting with a large evening supper of cold chicken and iced wine.

The servants threw open the dining hall's tall windows to allow as much evening air as possible to cool the room. Betsy and Elizabeth Monroe sat together and engaged in gay conversation, not the least of it the sharing gossip about the capital's high society.

Riley sat across from them, occasionally questioned by Levasseur about this or that. Riley doubted if he ever really would publish his journal.

Lafayette sat between the presidents, and the conversation shifted from banal to high politics. But mostly, they spoke of Lafayette's adaptation of Virginia's Declaration of the Rights of Man to his own country's version.

"Getting it entered into our constitution took over a year. And despite what transpired thereafter with the Jacobins and Bonaparte, it still stands as the ideal of France and a fraternal counterpart to the ideals of America."

"I understand our friend Mister Jefferson helped you with it," said Adams.

"As he inspired the design of this home," said Monroe.

Lafayette nodded and hoisted his glass. "To the great Jefferson."

***

Neall lit a cigar on the portico and gazed at the darkened fields. The chirping of crickets and the buzz of talk from the dining room filled the night air. "Where is Mister Putnam?"

Tad Grayson shook his head. "Could be he decided to stop in Leesburg and await the entourage there. In the unlikely event of an attack, it will likely be there where an assassin can blend into the crowd. "

"You're getting good at this, Mister Grayson," said Neall.

"Good enough to lose most of my men is not good, sir." He motioned to his last two men, quietly eating some chicken at the end of the portico.

An hour later, the servants drowned the lanterns and candles of light, and the summer darkness enveloped most of the mansion, which had suddenly gone silent. The presidents, Lafayette, and his party had all turned in.

Grayson's men took turns standing watch under the shade trees.

Neall crushed the stub of his last cigar and wondered if Leesburg had a tobacconist, he could visit the next day. He gazed at the dark sky and marveled at the fresco of stars. Then he heard a rustling and turned to see Betsy.

She slid beside him and stared at the sky while taking his hand. "I suppose you are returning immediately to England when the General leaves?"

"Let's get through this week. I'm concerned about the visit to Leesburg tomorrow."

"It'll be the usual cavalcade," she assured him.

"How are you getting along with him?"

"He's ever the gracious Gilbert. I enjoy his company, as I have in the past, but it's time for him to go home." She gripped Neall's hand tightly. "But you can stay."

"Did you come out here to seduce me?"

Betsy smiled. "It was a thought. But no. It seems this grand home lacks internal facilities." She pointed at a large outhouse at the edge of the orchard. "Care to join me?"

"I need not go as far as the first tree."

"Ha!" Betsy rose and gathered her skirts.

***

The flies in the outhouse buzzed annoyingly, but at least they did not bite like the mosquitos outside. Betsy finished and slipped quietly out the door, carefully closing it behind her. A large hand covered her mouth, and another lifted her from her feet and dragged her behind the outhouse.

She twisted, tugged, and bit savagely into the hand, tasting the hair that covered it like a rug. "Let me go!"

Her elbow slammed into the side of her assailant, who shook her, sending her hair cascading down her shoulders. "Stay quiet, my dear. It's me."

She looked into the face. Despite the moonless night, she recognized him. "Baron! What is the meaning of?"

Riedel smothered her mouth again. "Listen—there is great danger here. I've come to get you out."

"What do you mean?"

"I got word of a new attack. Someone must have been observing the marquis and following him. We should go now." He dragged her over to a pair of horses tied under a tree.

"We need to warn the others!"

"No time." He lifted her onto the horse.

None of this made sense. *Why just save me?*

"Richard!" she hollered as never before. "Danger! Danger!"

The *pop, pop, pop* of muskets broke the night's stillness. Horses neighed and snorted as a half-dozen riders galloped up to the house, circling the entrance, waving rifles.

***

Neall leaped to his feet when he heard Betsy's cry. He felt like a coward, but prudence and experience demanded he not rush blindly into an unknown situation. *It could be a trap.* He drew his pistol and stood to watch from behind a pillar.

The *pop* of muskets erupted from the road, sending Grayson's man in the orchard tumbling into the high grass.

He saw shadows moving everywhere. *How many attackers could there be?* Several cried out in pain—stung by lead flying in all directions. Then he realized they were slaves fleeing their dwellings for safety in the night's darkness.

Grayson raced out of the building, followed by Riley.

"Riders are shooting up the place. I fear they have Betsy," said Neall. "They're here for the marquis, but a pair of presidents make this an even richer harvest. One of your men is down, Mister Grayson. I didn't see the other. Sergeant Riley, stay with the marquis, and I'll try to hold them off until you can sneak him out the back."

Riley scoffed. "Outrun horses with an old man? I'm standing here with you."

The *crack* of rifles and *rumble* of hooves grew louder, and six darkly clad horsemen galloped out of the orchard from the shadows.

Foreign voices chattered, and the riders broke into two groups. One charged the portico. The other circled the house. A saber swirled, and the last New York militiaman collapsed.

Grayson charged down the portico steps and discharged two pistols into the riders, sending one flying from the saddle. The other two spurred their horses at him, and a swift-cutting blade took Grayson's head from his body.

Riley stepped forward and leveled his pistol at the two. He fired his into the horse of one, sending it rolling onto the dirt, but the horseman leaped to safety and came at him with his saber whirling.

The marine sergeant stood his ground and side-stepped before the blow struck, grabbing the attacker's wrist and snapping it like a twig.

"*Ubl'udak!*" "You son of a bitch!" The horseless rider reached for a curved dagger with his good hand, but Riley sent his shoe into his groin and drove his fist squarely into his jaw with a *snap*.

Neall had reloaded during the struggle and had both barrels ready when he heard a click behind his ear.

"*Ruki verkh!*" "Hands up!"

Neall raised his arms and turned to see the smiling face of a man with dark hair and a long black mustache. "You must be Mister Raymond Locke. I am Captain Alexei Denis. Order the marquis to come out alone."

"You'll have the full power of the United States after you if you harm him or the president."

"Hah! Their guards are dead. Some power if they have no army to protect their leaders."

The three other riders circled back and reared their horses onto their hind legs. The riders jumped from their horses like acrobats and pinned Riley's arms.

"My men are impatient, Mister Locke."

"A shot erupted from the upper window. The riders scattered and then returned fire, sending splinters into the face of the shooter."

Neall thought he saw a glimpse of Monroe, the war veteran. "These Americans all carry arms for a reason, Denis. I know your real name is Denisov. But why would the Northern Society threaten the marquis and America?"

Denisov laughed. "Because we serve the Aulic Council. We joined the Northern Society to break it up. Destroy it from within. They sent us here."

Neall realized Riedel had masterminded it all. *What's he done with Betsy?*

"We'll start hacking pieces from your friend unless you go in and send out the marquis. I'll think about the presidents." He twisted his mustache with a smirk. "Maybe we'll just kill one."

A tongue of flame filled the darkness and a volley blasted from the orchard. One of the Russians toppled over like a marionette with its strings cut.

The low roar of enraged men erupted from the shadows as six sailors charged with cutlasses waving. At their head was Lieutenant Kent Putnam.

Neall swiftly ducked and lowered his pistol, firing a ball into Denisov's shoulder. Denisov smiled and stepped back. "You took your shot, Mister Locke. Now, under the Code Duello, I'll take mine!" He raised his pistol and carefully aimed at Neall. At three feet, he could not miss.

But a second flash erupted from the Forsyth pistol, hitting Denisov in the center of his dark brow. He collapsed with his grin still smeared across his face.

"Good Englishmen have two balls," sneered Neall.

The sailors crashed into the two riders, and cold steel met steel. Putnam drove his saber into one, and a pair of enraged sailors hacked the other to pieces before he could call them off.

"Thank God you arrived!" exclaimed Neall. "Shots were fired. Get your men upstairs and see to the president and the others."

"Will do," said Putnam.

Neall paused. "Are you all right, Sergeant Riley?"

Riley slowly rose to his feet. "I think so. But those sons of bitches from the Navy Yard need more practice shooting. One of them put a ball across my ass."

Neall's smile turned to a grimace. *Betsy!*

He grabbed a saber and pistol from the hands of one of the corpses, jumped onto one of the assassins' horses, and galloped into the dark.

***

Betsy struggled to free her wrists, but they were too tightly bound to the saddle. Her heart beat like a bellows, and her stomach churned like a storm at sea as she listened helplessly to the shots and cries of men in combat. She prayed for Neall and Lafayette and then remembered poor Elizabeth Monroe was also in danger.

Riedel watched the melee from behind some nearby apple trees. She cursed herself for being deceived so easily. She thought she had recruited him. Now, she realized such men would never turn from their evil masters. Evil men, like evil nations, cling together like packs of wolves.

She tried to kick the horse and flee, but he tied it securely to a tree.

"Don't try to escape, dear. I have shot four men in duels," said Riedel as he stepped from the trees.

"What's going on there?" she asked, trying to stall for time.

"Several have fallen, but it's too dark to see who. Regardless, this affair is over. I still have time to arrange another surprise for Lafayette's birthday. If he survives."

Riedel untied her horse and slipped his boot into the stirrup of his mount. "I was an uhlan colonel in the war against the godless Jacobins and Bonaparte, so be prepared for a hard ride."

He drew a crop from his boot, and a slash went across his horse's rump, sending it into a full gallop. Betsy bumped along on hers, which trailed his by several yards.

If I can somehow cut the rope.

But it was no use. They raced up the road toward the North Carolina Turnpike straight ahead. Suddenly, swarms of shadowy figures appeared in the fields.

Slaves are escaping this madness.

But not all were trying to flee. Two brave slaves leaped onto the road with pitchforks lowered.

"Hah," cried Riedel. "These poor devils are protecting their masters!" He pivoted in the saddle, and his horse bounded left, allowing him to strike aside one of the pikes and slash the outstretched arm of one of them.

A horrific cry sent the rest of them scattering, and Riedel laughed like a devil.

The main road was now only fifty yards distant. When Betsy heard the sound of more hooves, her stomach sank again. *Were his hirelings done with their massacre?* She twisted her head back to see how many. *Richard!*

Neall's horse edged closer until Riedel heard the hooves and looked back. Betsy thought she saw a malicious grin cross the baron's face. He let her reins fly loose and spun his horse at nearly full speed.

She had never seen such horsemanship. *My God, uhlans can ride.*

Riedel's horse circled her and Neall, who tried to adjust his angle. But Riedel maneuvered away with a mocking laugh every time Neall drew close. The sky was brighter now, but the two looked like shadows in the night.

She saw tongues of flame and heard the loud *pop, pop* of pistols as the two shadows collided with a thunderous *thump*. Blades scraped and rattled in the darkness. Bodies tumbled in the grass. She heard curses in German and English that made even the worldly Betsy blush.

She edged her horse closer and could now make out their faces and forms. Both men were huffing as they circled each other on foot with sabers ready.

"I will kill you slowly, Mister Locke! Or should I say, Richard Neall?"

"You have failed, Riedel. Surrender, and I can get you free with diplomatic immunity. Your plot failed, and Lafayette lives."

"*Ach, du dummkopf!* Lafayette was never *my* target. I used those fools from the Northern Brotherhood." He stretched forward, and his point cut into Neall's shoulder before he could react.

Neall stumbled back, blood dripping down his shoulder. Betsy could see he was tiring.

"Dragoons are clods on plow horses. You can't use the blade like a light cavalryman." Riedel's feet moved forward like a dancer's, and then the flat of his saber turned away Neall's thrust before sending the point into Neall's thigh.

Tears ran down Betsy's cheeks. *He's killing Richard before my eyes.*

"The Aulic Council placed a *Spezial Sanktion* on you! Your foul plots against them have gone too far. Madrid was the final straw!"

She saw Neall fumble for his Forsyth pistol. Seeing it empty, he hurled it at Riedel, slamming it against his chest. But the baron laughed.

Neall was losing blood and tiring.

Riedel circled him slowly. *"Apropos Espagne,* you are the bull in the ring. I have weakened you enough to make the final thrust quick and deadly!" Riedel's blade struck Neall's hilt, sending his saber to the ground with a soft thud and out of reach.

Must do something! In desperation, Betsy kicked at her horse's flanks, and it lurched forward and plowed into Riedel, sending him spinning to the ground.

But the baron rolled and was on his feet like an acrobat, blade in hand. He slashed Betsy's horse in the leg, collapsing the poor beast in a heap and pinning her to the earth. The terrified creature let out a terrific series of squeals and shrieks before Riedel's blade tore open its throat in a curtain of blood.

Betsy squirmed in pain as the baron turned back to Neall. The baron began to say something when the *crack* of a firearm sent a lead ball into Riedel, striking his side. The baron staggered a few steps and stood erect, his head searching for the origin of the shot.

"Betsy, my darling. I should have checked you for a weapon." He staggered toward her with his blade menacing.

A figure suddenly appeared from the shadows.

The baron gasped, "You! I should have killed you years ago. Prepare to die!"

Betsy looked at Neall, who had collapsed completely. It was too dark to reveal the shadowy figure that closed on Riedel. *Who is this?*

The two dark forms bent forward in a half-crouch, their blade points nearly touching. Steel struck steel. The *clang, clang* of the metal sent sparks in all directions.

"Argh!"

One of the forms suddenly stood erect and then toppled backward. The other went to check Neall, then turned and came toward her from the dark until the starlight revealed his face.

Betsy's eyes widened, and her heart almost exploded with shock and relief. "Brother Bernard!"

Chapter 22

The Chancery, Baltimore, Maryland, September 7th, 1825

Robert placed a tray with a brandy bottle and snifters on the table and bowed. "Can I get you anything else, Excellency?"

Bishop Maréchal shook his head. "Thank you, Robert."

Maréchal himself poured the brown liquid into the crystal and paused to smile when he got to Betsy's. "I always thought you preferred champagne, *Madame* Bonaparte."

"I think I prefer brandy now," she said. "And the preferred name is Patterson."

"How are your wounds healing, Richard?" Maréchal asked.

Neall rubbed the white linen on his arm and leg. "Excellent. The surgeon says these can come off in a week."

"I called this final meeting of the Lafayette Circle to thank everyone," said Maréchal. "Today, General Lafayette boards a steamer at the Navy Yard. He'll then catch a frigate, *The Brandywine*, farther downriver and sail to Le Havre."

"Is Sergeant Riley going with him?" asked Betsy with a sad face. Her heart was saddened by all the death and mayhem at Oak Hill.

"His wound was more embarrassing than life-threatening," said Bernard with a wink. "But you'll have to ask Commander Putnam."

"*Commander*? Congratulations, Kent!" Betsy was thrilled for him. He always served stoically, asking for no credit.

"President Adams said my name would be on the next promotion list. That could be in a year or more," said Putnam.

"I suspect sooner," said Maréchal. "Saving two presidents does sometimes have rewards. And responsibilities."

Betsy's soft gaze turned to Bernard. "Brother, I must thank you again for saving me." Her eyes shifted to Neall. "And thank you, Richard."

"I'd say I owe thanks to both Mister Putnam and Brother Bernard. It was a right mess I got us in. And poor Mister Grayson and his men paid the ultimate price."

Everyone bowed their heads for a moment of thought and prayer.

"I'm saying a special funeral Mass for them in New York next month," said Maréchal. "Bishop Connelly's death leaves New York vacant until the Holy Father approves his replacement. Until then, it comes under my pastoral care. I hope you'll all attend. Your faithful servant, Mister Lynch, will also be remembered."

Betsy finally got the nerve to ask what had bothered her since the deadly night at Oak Hill. "Brother Bernard, what exactly transpired? The arrival of Mister Putnam was a welcome surprise. Yours was, well, a welcome shock."

"I was about to ask the same," said Neall.

"'Tis a long and dreary tale. But His Excellency called you here to hear it."

Bernard's revelations flabbergasted them. A new confidential source exposed Riedel as a triple agent—fooling the Americans into thinking he was their double. But Bernard had never believed he had turned. The source also revealed the Northern Society agents were really serving the Aulic Council, which had long penetrated the liberal officers' cabal.

"I was suspicious of Riedel all along," Neall said, eyeing Betsy.

She lowered her head. *He always knows how to best me.* "I should have listened to you, Richard."

"And you should have told us, Brother," said Neall.

"No," said Bernard. "I kept all this from you intentionally. You might have behaved differently if you knew, and the baron might have gotten suspicious. He is a brilliant agent, their best."

"Thanks to you, we can say he *was*, not is," said Neall. "Just how did you wind up at Oak Hill?"

Bernard smiled. "'Twas luck. I reviewed the papers provided by my source and poured through our other reports. And the events of the past year. Simply put, it was time for an old dragoon to ride again."

"Dragoon?" asked Neall with a startled look.

Betsy could barely conceal her surprise. She had never known he had military service before the War of 1812.

"I served with Lieutenant Colonel Benjamin Tallmadge in the Second Continental Light Dragoons. Still have my saber and carbine. They came in handy."

"So that's it?" asked Betsy. She felt Bernard was still holding something back.

"We have come full circle," said Bernard with a mischievous grin.

"How so?" asked Betsy.

"The Lafayette Circle's time is done, and I'm afraid so is the Chancery's," said Maréchal. "The work of the church in this country is growing. Distractions such as this affair and our other service to the White House must end."

Betsy was stunned. She had already decided to leave their service but strongly felt its need. "That can't be."

Bernard smiled. "'Tis necessary to pass the baton to the next generation. One dedicated purely to identifying threats to the new nation. At almost fifty years old, America must stand on its own legs. And those will be the legs of Commander Kent Putnam."

All eyes turned to Putnam, whose face turned red. "But how?"

"It's all right," said Maréchal. "I sent Brother Bernard's plan to the president, who approved it. There will be two small offices: one at the Navy Yard, under you. You'll have a small budget, but Sergeant Riley will return from Paris as a Marine Corps lieutenant and be your number two."

"But you mentioned there would be two offices," said Neall.

"Ah, yes, the other office will be embedded in the State Department under the able leadership of Mister Buchanan. He'll focus on political issues, while Mister Putnam concentrates on the military. However, the President and Secretaries of State and War expect close coordination."

"Is Mister Buchanan aware of this," Putnam asked.

"You can tell him when you hold your first coordination meeting here next month," said Bernard. "I'll turn all my papers and files over to both of you then."

"Meanwhile, enjoy your month of rest," said Maréchal.

Neall rose, shook Bernard's hand, bowed, and kissed Maréchal's ring. "Farewell to you both. And all of you. I must render my final report and will catch the first packet ship to England."

When Robert closed the door behind Neall, Betsy felt a piece had been torn from her heart. She was hoping for a last chance to discuss things. After all, he was nearly killed trying to save her. Tears welled in her eyes. "I shall miss him."

Bernard smiled softly. "I'm not so sure."

***

The British Legation, Washington, DC

Neall's nib scratched out his signature on the report, and he handed it to Robert Horan. "I hate to submit an incomplete report to Lord Avondale, but I didn't learn the name of Brother Bernard's secret source. It would be most valuable for us to know who it is."

Horan pushed a strand of white hair from his forehead. "Not to worry. I'll tell milord myself."

"What?"

"I'm returning to London next week. Permanently."

"Really? I thought you liked it here."

"Long summers — too hot and clammy."

"When will your replacement arrive?"

"He's here already."

"Do I get to meet him before you go?"

"No need." Horan handed Neall a paper signed by Lord Avondale.

Neall's eyes scanned it once, then a second time. "This is outrageous. I'm no Accounts Section Clerk. "

"Reread it. No mention of a clerk. You are here as a special envoy with diplomatic status."

"Envoy to what?"

"To Mister Putnam and Mister Buchanan, I'm led to believe. They'll need all the help they can get standing up the new American service."

Neall was stunned. "Well, before you leave, I need to know who Brother Bernard's source was."

Horan dabbed beads of sweat from his forehead. "Simply put—it was me. I was helping the good brother analyze his reports as well as ours. Two came from Europe, which could lead to only one conclusion. You were a target along with Lafayette, and Baron Riedel was playing the Americans. So the brother and I decided to play him in turn. Sorry you could not be informed, but you almost gave things away when you accosted him the first time."

Neall was stunned, but he knew Horan was right. He decided he had underappreciated the quirky old clerk. "I apologize for any disparaging remarks I might have made, sir."

Horan flashed a rare smile. "Success is the best apology."

Neall knew he was right. Success was the only measure. Lafayette was safely on his way home, and none of the mayhem reached the press. The tale of the Lafayette Circle would go untold—happily.

***

Hampton Roads, Virginia, September 10th, 1825

Captain Charles Morris tipped his hat, and the First Mate signaled the coxswain, who turned the wheel two points. The wind stiffened the sails, and the 44-gun frigate *Brandywine* cut through the waves as it sailed into the open seas.

"With fair winds and following seas, we should turn the cape at Le Havre in less than three weeks," said Morris.

Lafayette folded the letter he was reading and handed it to his secretary, Levasseur. "Please keep this with your papers."

"What is it, father?" asked George.

"A dispatch from a Major Rodney Pettigrew. He is the commander of the noble New York men who gave their all to protect us. He says the state has renamed the Second Artillery Regiment, the National Guard, in my honor."

"Well, you did command the National Guard in France during trying circumstances."

"I'd rather these men lived, and my memory fade."

George Lafayette grinned. "Take heart, father. We shall be home by October. Isn't that grand?"

Lafayette stroked his chin and stared back at the rapidly receding shoreline, recalling so many memories, new and old. He would never see his second homeland again, and the thought of it pained him. The Americans had shown him more than hospitality — they had saved his life in the bargain.

"Your papa is already nostalgic, George. But not to worry. I will write an account of this he can enjoy by the fireplace at his home many times," said Levasseur.

Lafayette spun about and glared at his secretary. "Where is home? I return to a land under the thumb of that blackguard, Charles X. An ultra-Royalist — is he really any better than the Holy Alliance and the Aulic Council?"

Charles X was a long-term resister to all the reforms Lafayette and many others had fought for. He fled France, leaving Louis XVI to die. A death Lafayette had fought so hard to prevent.

A dark look came over him. "Why, I may have to lead another revolution."

"But father, that hardly means...."

Lafayette turned and stared out to sea. He thought long about the many old friends he had seen in America and the many new ones he had made. Once more, he was in a land of liberty, and once more, sadly, men had died for him. Even their former president had risked himself with his own musket — a relic of Monroe's Revolutionary War service.

Lafayette caught a glimpse of Riley standing alone at the rail, looking back at the fading coastline.

"There is a man we could use in France," said Levasseur.

Lafayette nodded. "Yes. I am honored to call him my friend and fellow American."

Epilogue

Office of the Historian, Navy Hill, Foggy Bottom, Washington, DC, September 3rd, 1954

Tolbert's eyes were glued to the provocative silk stockings adorning the long legs of the secretary who led him into Doctor Canavan's office.

"I'm right here, Mister Tolbert," Canavan said with a knowing smile.

Busted! He shifted his gaze to the white-haired man in the gabardine blue jacket and bow tie but immediately returned to the secretary, who lowered her lashes in appreciation.

When the secretary closed the door, he looked about and was depressed to see that it was not much bigger than the cramped archive room. *I guess it doesn't take much space to understand the past.*

Canavan lit his pipe and began to puff clouds of smoke. "Take a seat and tell me what you found."

"Think it would be better to read this first, sir." Tolbert rose and placed his written synopsis on Canavan's desk.

Canavan carefully placed his pipe down and thumbed through the neatly typed pages.

"Well, this explains some things," Canavan said when he finished.

"Leaves more things in question," replied Tolbert.

Canavan smiled and retrieved his pipe. "Like, why is none of this in the history books?"

"To begin with, yes. But who were these people? With all those deaths, how did they keep it from the papers?"

Canavan drew from the pipe and spoke as smoke spiraled upward. "Newspapers can be corrupted. Facts and events are hidden or modified, and stories can be spun — especially when it is a story the public wants to hear. So, an explosion on board a steamer becomes a simple grounding in shallow waters. Not unlike how we cloak things today. You'll soon learn to read newspapers differently in this business, young man."

Tolbert straightened in his seat. Now he could make his pitch. "That's where we historians come in, sir. We research and discover untold truths and bring them to public light. Our mission!"

Canavan slid his pipe into a wide glass ashtray overflowing with ashes. "Not necessarily."

"I don't understand, sir. It's what we do. This is a great story about some amazing people working secretly against all odds."

"We give the Agency the history it wants. These were amateurs—a motley assortment of old clerics, shipless sailors, and come-as-you-are spooks. Better the world thinks professional intelligence began in 1947, with the National Security Act."

Tolbert could not believe it. "But they helped instantiate the Monroe Doctrine and celebrate America's founding, bolstering the nation's exceptionalism. This journey by General Lafayette was the beginning of true patriotism in the nation. They saved our last hero of the American Revolution, enabling him to return and help bring democracy back to France. Every schoolboy knows of the Marquis de Lafayette, but no one knows this. It's a story that needs to be told."

Canavan shot him a condescending smile. "Like George Washington chopping down a cherry tree? We have enough myths. We don't want the world to know the origins of American intelligence—it might debunk accepted history and open not just a can of worms but a hogshead of worms. Miss Brooks will take the file from you."

Tolbert's face reddened. "And do what?"

"Put it with the others after carefully re-classifying it, Top Secret."

"Others? There are more like this?"

Canavan entwined his fingers but did not answer.

Tolbert rose to his feet.

"Sit down, young man. I keep a special set of files under my protection. Available only to me and the Director."

This is a power game. Tolbert decided then and there to quit the Historian Office and the government and go to graduate school. He could do research on his own and piece the story together from open sources — maybe write a book.

"I know what you are thinking — the DO has case officers searching newspapers and libraries nationwide, looking for things like this. In fact, you are going to help them."

Tolbert's eyes widened. "What?"

"I have signed paperwork reassigning you to the DO permanently. You'll go right to that task force as soon as you finish training."

Tolbert's mind raced. He had a moment to decide or resign. He figured he could affect things better from the inside than out.

"When do I start?"

Canavan smiled. "Miss Brooks is waiting to escort you to your new office. Your operational training starts in a week."

"What do they call this task force, sir?"

"The Office of Special Research." Canavan smiled as he picked up his pipe and lit it. "You'll like it there. All your predecessors do."

"All my predecessors?"

"You don't think you're the first young staff historian to stumble on unwanted history? Many of them go onto the analysis side of the house. But your skills, especially your curiosity and follow-through, mark you as an operator. I wish you great success."

As Miss Brooks closed the door behind them, Tolbert took a final glance back at Canavan, who was fastidiously cleaning his pipe.

— The End —

Author's Notes

Gilbert du Motier, Marquis de Lafayette, was one of those rare types who, by sheer willpower, thrust himself into the pages of history. He did it through the great sacrifice of personal comfort, wealth, and family. He was an idealist who acted on his ideals, seeking pragmatic solutions to complex and sometimes theoretical issues of the day. He was also a man of personal bravery and a great friend to many people of all stations in life.

He had many flaws and made many mistakes. He was not brilliant, nor did he pretend to be. But he had tenacity, a good heart, a sense of right, and an engaging personality. He was willing to stake everything on whatever cause he championed, whether it was American independence, a French constitutional government, the rights of man, and, last but not least, emancipation.

I knew I was taking a risk by inserting him into a novel of this type. How to portray him? Well, I simply took my understanding of him and applied it to the historical situation and then blended it into the fictional assassination plot swirling around him.

Lafayette's great tour of America is little known today, except in some of the towns and villages he visited in the early decades of America. In some of those precincts, his visit is still the most significant event ever.

Some comments on the story are in order.

The blend of fiction and fact can be daunting. Thus, the cast of characters, glossary, and gazetteer. Those who like such details can sort through them for more context.

The Holy Alliance was real, not quite an axis of evil but a pact by autocracy to secure their rights in the face of democracy and liberalism. The real Aulic Council was actually the Austro-Hungarian military's general staff. I bent its role, making it into the Holy Alliance's fictional covert operations arm—a Specter-like entity.

But the real Holy Alliance was not pleased with the American experiment, nor with the new democracies cropping up as Spain's American empire collapsed. Ironically, when Russia parted ways with Austria and Prussia (which became the

Second German Reich in 1870) for an alliance with France in 1891, it began a series of events leading to World War twenty-five years later.

The Monroe Doctrine was America's answer to this. Originally a letter to Congress, it set forth America's first national security strategy. For it, we can thank President James Monroe and his Secretary of State, John Quincy Adams. I thought trying to portray their interaction in doing so was necessary and kind of fun. Equally important is the controversial election of 1824, which threw an election into the House of Representatives for the second time in American history. Although frustrated by the outcome, America's heroic General Andrew Jackson would recoup and win the White House in 1828.

The December 1824 letter from President James Monroe to Congress on Lafayette's visit is used verbatim, as is Speaker of the House Henry Clay's December 10th, 1824 introductory speech to Congress.

My use of flashbacks was another item I wrestled with. Although they interrupted the flow of the main plot, I felt they added insight into Lafayette's life and character, a secondary intent of this book.

There were no attacks on General Lafayette, at least none recorded anywhere.

The secret intelligence operation run by Archbishop Maréchal of Baltimore is purely fictional, although there was a bishop by that name at that time. The "Lafayette Circle" and its members are also fiction or fictionalized.

Elizabeth Patterson is a fictionalized version of a real woman who briefly stepped onto the world stage through marriage to the youngest brother of the most powerful man in the world. Although jilted in an awful way, she lived her life gracefully and raised a fine son from the marriage. Her grandson, Charles Bonaparte, was destined to become Attorney General under President Theodore Roosevelt and would create what later became known as the Federal Bureau of Investigation.

Lafayette's travels are exhausting just to read. In a time when things moved at the speed of a horse or a primitive steamship, he swirled across the new nation in a whirlwind of activity that would tire a man half his age of 67-68. He often made several stops a day, mesmerizing crowds, embracing well-wishers, and engaging American leaders. He talked of the heroic deeds of America's past, the accomplishments of the present, and the American greatness that was yet to come. He inspired patriotic fervor and issued his own version of a call to arms. All this happened as America was approaching its 50th birthday.

For purposes of the story, I bent a few things regarding his itinerary and some of the venues. For example, the grand dinner in New Orleans did not take place at The Cabildo but at a nearby hotel. I changed the locale for the purposes of the story.

New York did rename the 2nd Artillery Regiment the National Guard in remembrance of the *Garde Nationale de Paris* that Lafayette commanded during the French Revolution.

Finally, those more interested in this event can satisfy it with the memoir published by Lafayette's secretary, Auguste Levasseur, whose *Lafayette en Amérique en 1824 et 1825, ou Journal d'un Voyage aux Etats-Unis,* work provided some background to this fictional version.

I have listed below a rough itinerary of Lafayette's travels across America. This is not an exact timeline in some areas, as there are days without a point-by-point account of his time. But its purpose is only to give the flavor of the breadth and scope of his daunting journey. At the time, no prominent American had traveled so wide and far. It took this adopted son to make such a prodigious effort. I think that says something about the spirit of the man.

Lafayette's Travels

N.B. There is no official itinerary of Lafayette's journey. Dates and places are approximate.

1824

July 13 — Lafayette leaves France. Le Havre France
August 15 — Staten Island and New York City.
August 20 — New Rochelle, NY
August 21-24 — New Haven, CT, Providence, RI, and Boston, MA.
August 25 — Cambridge and Quincy, MA. Visits former President John Adams
August 31 — Boston, Lexington, Concord, Salem, Marblehead, and Newburyport, MA.
September 1 — Portsmouth, NH
September 2 — Boston, MA, and Lexington, MA.
September 3 — Worcester, MA, and Tolland, CT
September 4 — Hartford, and CT, Middletown, CT
September 5 — New York, NY
September 11 — Celebrates the 47th anniversary of the Battle of Brandywine with French residents in New York
September 28 — Philadelphia, PA - speech at the State House (Independence Hall)
October 6 — Wilmington, DE
October 12 — Washington, DC
October 15 — Arlington House, VA
October 17 — Mount Vernon, VA
October 18-19 — Petersburg and Yorktown, VA
October 19-22 — Williamsburg, VA
October 22 — Norfolk and Portsmouth, VA
October 27 — Richmond, VA
November 4 — Monticello, VA
November 8 — Charlottesville, VA

December 1-16 — Washington, DC
December 17 — Annapolis, MD
December 24 — Frederick, MD

1825

January 1-18 — Washington, DC
January 19 — Baltimore, MD
January 21 — Norfolk, VA
January 22 — Richmond, VA
March 2-3 — Raleigh, NC
March 15 — Charleston, SC
March 18 — Beaufort, SC
March 19 — Savannah, GA
March 27 — Lamar County, GA
March 31 — Fort Mitchell, AL
April 3 — Montgomery, AL
April 4-6 — Selma, Cahaba, Demopolis, and Claiborne, AL
April 7 — Mobile, AL
April 10 — New Orleans, LA
April 11 — Chalmette, LA
April 16 — Baton Rouge, LA
May 4 — Nashville, TN
May 11 — Louisville, KY
May 14 — Frankfort, KY
May 15 — Lexington, KY
May 18 — Georgetown, KY
May 19 — Cincinnati, OH
May 21 — Maysville, KY
May 24 — Wheeling, VA
May 25 — Washington, PA
May 29 — Braddock, PA
May 30 — Pittsburgh, PA

June 1 — Butler, PA
June 4 — Buffalo, NY
June 7 — Rochester, NY
June 17— Charlestown, MA
June 27—Claremont NH
June 28—Montpelier, VT
June 29—Whitehall, NY
July 14 — Morristown, NJ
July 15 — Madison, NJ
July 20 — Germantown, PA
July 25 —Wilmington, DE
July 26 — Brandywine Battlefield and West Chester, PA
July 27 — Lancaster, PA
July 30 — Baltimore, MD
August — Mount Vernon, VA
August 5 — Oak Hill, VA
September 6 — Washington, DC
September 7 — Lafayette leaves Washington DC and returns to France on the frigate USS Brandywine

Historical Characters

John Quincy Adams — US Secretary of State and architect of the Monroe Doctrine, later US President

The Allans — Edgar Allan Poe's adopted family residing in Richmond, Virginia

Stephan Allen — Mayor of New York and last Federalist mayor

Francis Allyn — Sea captain and master of the ship Cadmus and friend of Lafayette

Jeanne d'Arc — Joan of Arc, the heroine of the 100 Years War and patron saint of France

James Armistead — Virginia slave who spied for Lafayette during his campaign in Virginia

Pierre-Augustin Caron de Beaumarchais — French polymath and an architect of the covert support provided by France to America before a formal treaty was announced in 1778

Bo — Jérôme Napoléon Bonaparte, son of Elizabeth Patterson and Jerome Bonaparte

Jerome Bonaparte — Napoleon's youngest brother and husband of Elizabeth Patterson

Napoleon Bonaparte — French general, first consul, and Emperor of the French

Broglie — Charles-François de Broglie, Marquis de Ruffec, the Army of the East's commander, and head of Louis XVI's Secret Corps Diplomatic

Martin Van Buren — New York politician, head of the Albany Regency, and later US president

John C. Calhoun — South Carolina statesman and Secretary of War under President James Monroe

Major James Campbell — commander of Redoubt 10 at Yorktown

Stratford Canning — King George III's Envoy Extraordinary to the United States

Charles X — ultra-Royalist King of France from 16 September 1824 until the July 1830 Revolution, caused him to abdicate the throne on 2 August

Captain Alexander Kennedy Clark — celebrated British cavalry officer who snatched the standard of the French 105th *Regiment de Ligne* at Waterloo

Lord Charles Cornwallis — commanding general of British forces in Virginia who surrendered to Washington in October 1781

William H. Crawford — Secretary of the Treasury

Duc d'Ayen — Jean-Paul-François de Noailles, powerful French nobleman, military commander, and father-in-law to Lafayette

Monsieur Dean — Silas Dean, the secret American representative in Paris and an early orchestrated of aid to the American cause

Stephen Decatur — renowned naval officer who served in the Quasi-War with France and the First Barbary War against the North African pirates

Louis William Valentine Du Bourg — French Catholic prelate and Sulpician missionary to the United States. He built up the church in the vast new Louisiana Territory as the Bishop of Louisiana and the Two Floridas

Joseph Ege — owner of The Old Stone House in Richmond, visited by Lafayette in 1824

Admiral d'Estaing — commander of the French fleet at the Virginia Capes in October 1781

Rafael del Riego y Florez — a Spanish general and liberal politician who played a crucial role in the outbreak of the Liberal Triennium

Kaiser Franz — Habsburg ruler and Holy Roman Emperor Franz II, after 1804 Franz I of Austria

Christian, Count von Forbach — Colonel of the *Royal Deux-Ponts* regiment, a unit recruited from Lorraine

Alexander Hamilton — aide de camp to General Washington, hero of Yorktown, and later Secretary of the Treasury

Major Benjamin Huger — South Carolina militia officer and plantation owner who provided Lafayette shelter on his first night in America.

Francis Huger — son of Benjamin Huger and failed liberator of Lafayette from prison

Andrew Jackson — General, War of 1812 hero and politician from Tennessee

Barbara Juliane, Baroness von Krüdener, née von Vietinghoff — celebrated Baltic German noblewoman and mystic visionary who visited Lafayette in Olmutz prison

Marie Adrienne –Marie Adrienne Françoise, wife of Lafayette and daughter of the *duc* d'Ayen

Marie-Joseph-Paul-Yves-Roch-Gilbert du Motier, Marquis de Lafayette — French nobleman, Continental Army general, abolitionist, French Revolution leader, French National Guard commander, and celebrated political figure emeritus

George Washington Lafayette — his son and godson of George Washington

Auguste Levasseur — Lafayette's escort, secretary and scribe, and a former military officer involved in the 1821 conspiracy against the French government who produced an account of the visit, *Lafayette en Amérique en 1824 et 1825, ou Journal d'un Voyage aux Etats – Unis*, first published in 1829

Louis XV – King of France from 1715 to 1774 and grandfather of Louis XVI

Louis XVI – last King of France before the French Revolution and victim of the guillotine

William Marcy – New York politician and member of the Albany Circle

Ambrose Maréchal – Bishop of Baltimore

James Monroe – 5th US President known for The Monroe Doctrine

Daniel Morgan – Legendary Revolutionary War hero who settled in Winchester, Virginia

General Moultrie – William Moultrie, Revolutionary War general from South Carolina

Selleck Osborn – Editor of "The New York Patriot"

Elizabeth "Betsy" Patterson (Bonaparte) – former wife of Jerome Bonaparte, Napoleon's youngest brother, Baltimore socialite and fictional intelligence operative connected to the bishop of Baltimore

Edgar Allan Poe – Richmond youth and future writer of mystery and the occult

Major General Sir William Ponsonby – commander of the Union Brigade killed at Waterloo

Josiah Quincy – Congressman, State Assembly Speaker, Harvard President, and Mayor of Boston

Elmira Royster – Edgar Allan Poe's girlfriend and later fiancée

John Scudder, Jr – owner of Scudder's American Museum

Joshua Shaw - English-American artist and inventor

Mikhail Mikhailovich Speransky – head of the liberal reform movement in Czarist Russia

Johann Springer - Austrian gunsmith

Samuel Lewis Southard – New Jersey lawyer and politician and Secretary of the Navy from 1823 – 1829

Comte de Rochambeau – General in command of French forces in North America

Comte de Vergennes – also known as Charles Gravier, Foreign Minister under King Louis XI of France and architect of support and alliance with the Americans rebelling against Britain

Sebastien (Bastien) Wagner – Lafayette's valet

Arthur Wellesley, Duke of Wellington – commander of the Anglo-Allied Army at Waterloo

Sampson Stoddard Wilder - wealthy businessman friend of Lafayette

Fanny Wright – Philosopher and writer from Scotland with extreme political and social beliefs and Lafayette's sometime mistress

S.W. O'Connell

Joseph C. Yates — Democratic-Republican governor of New York in 1824

Fictional Characters

Amos — enslaved dock worker

Godfrey Arthur — British consul in Washington

Le Duc d'Ambrosien — husband of Madeline Pauline Goulet

Lord Avondale — British Chief of the Special Accounts Section

Claude Barnes — cover name used by Alexander Buxhowden

Captain Blaine — commander of the Washington Navy Yard

Brother Bernard — Irish Christian Brother and former spymaster Maurice Bernard

Major Maurice Bernard — American spymaster in the period leading to and during the War of 1812

Reverend Blake — choirmaster in Sturbridge, Massachusetts

Robert Buchanan — young State Department Clerk

Alexander Buxhowden — Russian agent for the Holy Alliance, defrocked orthodox priest and occultist, AKA Corporal Pretorius, AKA Claude Barnes, AKA Bornstein

Doctor Raymond Canavan — CIA Chief Historian

Catullus — nickname for Lafayette used by the Circle

Captain Alexei Denisov — former Russian hussar officer and Russian "Special Bureau" agent, AKA Captain Denis

Ernst Emil Donat — Prussian agent for the Holy Alliance despite killing more than a dozen men in illegal duels

Dugard — French thug hired by Neall

Count Esslinger — Austrian Empire Under Minister of the Aulic Council Secret Committee

Dee Fitzgerald — raven-haired planter's daughter in Charleston

Mick Flynn — Albany Regency and Tammany operative

Madeline Pauline Goulet — a French noblewoman who fought for Napoleon and later Aulic Council agent

Carmen de Gioia — an Italian opera singer skilled at poisons and potions and teams with Buxhowden

Lieutenant Tad Grayson — New York Militia officer with the National Guard Battalion

Homer — freedman boiler worker on the steamship, *Mechanic*

Robert Horan — "Special Accounts Clerk" at the British Legation in Washington

Nancy Keating — choir member in Sturbridge, Massachusetts

Tom Lynch — Trooper 6th Inniskilling Dragoons turned intelligence operative

Captain Markham — commander of the Junior Morgan Riflemen, a Virginia militia company that attended Lafayette's visit to Virginia

Jan Nagy — Hungarian agent for the Austrian Empire and the Holy Alliance, former hussar officer, and expert pistol shot

Evelyn Neall — Richard Neall's late wife and daughter of Lord Avondale

Richard Neall — British agent of the Foreign Office's Special Accounts Section AKA: Raymond Locke AKA: Mister Robertson

Noah - French thug hired by Neall

Lilly Nordstrom AKA Olivia De Rydt — a Swedish actress and Aulic Council agent

Major Rodney Pettigrew — acting commander of the National Guard Battalion

Piqué — Creek Indian guide

Kent Putnam — US Navy lieutenant and skilled intelligence officer

Baron Franz Riedel — Assistant Envoy Extraordinary of the Austrian Sub–Consulate in Washington

Daniel Riley — US Marine Corps sergeant assigned to guard Lafayette

Robert — Bishop Maréchal's servant

Sam — Creek Indian guide

Millard Thompkins — Mate of the Cadmus

Jake Tolbert — junior staff historian at CIA

Prince Vladimir Vassiliev — Russian Under Minister of the Aulic Council Secret Committee

Uzeir — Bosnian clerk to Count Esslinger

Erik Weiss — engineer on Mechanic

Felicity White — choir member in Sturbridge, Massachusetts

Baron Otto von Zoranski — Prussian Under Minister of the Aulic Council Secret Committee

Glossary

Abatis — torn-up tree trunks and branches, strewn before defense works like barbed wire

Able-body seaman — experienced deckhand on a ship, usually a merchant ship

Albany Regency— elite group of influential politicians led by Martin Van Buren who controlled the New York State government, sometimes through the Tammany Society and, ironically, also known as The Holy Alliance

Ancienne Regime — pre-revolutionary Royalist France

Anglo-Allied Army — the combined British, Dutch—Belgian, and German forces under Sir Arthur Wellesley, the Duke of Wellington

Aria — solo performance within an opera

2nd Battalion, 2nd Artillery Regiment, late renamed the National Guard — elite New York militia unit made up of well-heeled New Yorkers of the best lineage, later renamed the Seventh or "Silk Stocking" Regiment

Assassinat — French term for assassination

Assignation— archaic term for a tryst or sexual liaison

Aulic Council — originally the name of the Holy Roman Empire/Imperial Austrian General Staff, a fictional intelligence organization for purposes of this tale

Barbary Pirates — raiders from the north African "Barbary" states, Algiers, Tunis, and Tripoli

Bark — sailing ship of three or more masts, the rear (mizzenmast) rigged for a fore-and-aft rather than a square sail

Battalion of National Guards — a New York defense force created from Coastal Artillery units and named in honor of Lafayette, former French National Guard commander during the French Revolution

Bolton Guards — a local New England militia unit

Boney — derogatory nickname for Napoleon Bonaparte used by British soldiers

USS *Brandywine* — three-masted 44-gun frigate that transported Lafayette back to France

Brogan — archaic term for workman's shoes

Cadmus — Atlantic crossing tall ship that took Lafayette to America for his grand tour

Carabiniers — elite cavalry sometimes used as police

Charbonnerie — French wing of the secret society the Carbonari

Chamber of Representatives — the equivalent (but with little real power) of the House of Representatives in imperial France

Chancery — administrative offices of a bishop

Chevalier Guards — the most elite cavalry regiment of Imperial Russia

Cincinnati Society — otherwise known as the Society of the Cincinnati, a hereditary association of former Continental Army and French officer veterans of the Revolutionary War

Code Duello — 18th-century rules for dueling

Congress of Vienna — series of international diplomatic meetings to discuss and agree upon a possible new layout of the European political and constitutional order after the downfall of the French Emperor Napoleon Bonaparte

Consulate — the office and residence of a consul, a state representation lower than embassy or legation, and primarily for representing business interests

Corps Diplomatique — French foreign service in the *Ancienne Regime*

Decembrists — secret societies of Russian officers interested in reform and opposed to the status quo

Effendi — title of nobility meaning sir, lord, or master, especially in the Ottoman Empire and the Caucasus

Envoy Extraordinary and Minister Plenipotentiary — a diplomatic head of mission (called a legation) ranked below the ambassador

Federalists — one of the original two parties in America, favoring the Constitution and a strong federal government at the expense of state autonomy in some issues

Flammande — term for someone from Flanders (Flemish)

Fraises — sharpened stakes used in defense works

Fusil — light musket favored by elite infantry called fusiliers

Fusilier — elite infantry who originally carried fusils but later switched to normal muskets

Regiment Gatinois — French Army unit that served in America was prominent in the Yorktown campaign

Gendarmerie — French police

General Washington's March — popular American patriotic tune before the adoption of an official national anthem

Georgetown — Catholic college founded by Archbishop John Carroll

Grenadier — elite heavy infantry chosen for their size and strength

Gulden — money of the Austrian Empire from 1754 to 1892

Habsburg — hereditary ruling house of Austria—Hungary and parts of Eastern Europe and Italy

Hall Rifle — Harper's Ferry Arsenal breech-loading rifle modified later with a percussion cap firing system .552 caliber

1803 Harper's Ferry Rifle — early 19th-century military forearm manufactured at the arsenal of the same name

Hawken rifle — one of the first large caliber percussion rifles favored especially by Western hunters

Hohenzollern — hereditary ruling house of Prussia and parts of eastern Europe and northern Germany

Holy Alliance — political and diplomatic entente of Austria-Hungary, Prussia, and Russia aimed at buttressing traditional monarchy against the forces of democracy

Jacobins — hard-left French Revolutionaries in favor of a Republic versus a constitutional monarchy

James Kent — Hudson River steamboat takes Lafayette to Albany and back

John Howard — vessel termed a bark that sailed the Atlantic trade and used by Neall in this story to travel to France

Junior Morgan Riflemen — a youth militia unit in which Edgar Allan Poe was a lieutenant

Legation — a diplomatic post below the level of an embassy, reserved for nations without a traditional hereditary monarchy

La Marseillaise — a French Revolutionary War song and later French

Louis d'Or — a French gold coin and monetary unit before the Franc
national anthem

Prince Vladimir Vassiliev — Russian Under Minister of the Aulic Council Secret Committee

Mechanic — steamer plying the Ohio River

Minister Plenipotentiary — diplomatic rank of representatives to non-monarchies equivalent to an ambassador

Monroe Doctrine — President James Monroe's letter to Congress declaring American opposition to foreign interference in the New World, North, and South America

Natchez — steamer taken by Lafayette from Mobile, Alabama, to New Orleans

Northern Society — one of two branches of a secret organization of reform-minded Russian officers that in 1825 became known as the Decembrists

The Ogre/Corsican Ogre — one of the derogatory nicknames for Napoleon Bonaparte

The New York Patriot — a daily tabloid

Packet ship — sailing craft designed for speed and used to carry correspondence

Palladian-style — architecture is famous for its stately symmetry, classical elements, and grand appearance

Percussion cap — weapons using a percussion primer, introduced in the early 1820s, is a type of single-use percussion ignition device for muzzleloader firearm locks, enabling them to fire reliably in any weather condition

Penny news sheet — inexpensive daily newspapers common in early 19th century America

Pernod — Anise-based French liqueur

Pianissimo — Italian term, singing softly

Republican — another name for the Democratic-Republican party founded by Thomas Jefferson to oppose the Federalists led by Alexander Hamilton

Richmond Light Infantry Blues — company of voluntary militia established in 1789

The Richmond Bank — major financial establishment at the time of Lafayette's visit

Romanov — hereditary ruling house of the Russian Empire

Royal Dragoons — British heavy cavalry regiment

Sabretache — a flat bag or pouch worn suspended from the belt of a cavalry soldier together with the saber

Sanktion — German term for sanction or an official approval

Siciliana — somber music set within a more extensive work such as an opera or symphony

Special Bureau — Czarist Russia's military intelligence branch

Tammany Society — powerful and corrupt political organization associated with Nativism and the Democratic-Republican (later Democratic) Party that later accepted Irish immigrants who dominated it and often called after their meeting place, Tammany Hall

The Teutonic Knights — Germanic religious order of warrior monks

Tugendbund — organization of Prussian nationalist officers formed during the Napoleonic Wars

Uhlans — horse cavalry armed with lances that formed part of the Polish, German, Austrian, and Russian armies

Union Brigade — British heavy cavalry unit at Waterloo consisting of the 6th Inniskilling, the Royal Dragoons, and the 2nd Royal North British Dragoons (the Scots Greys)

Union of Prosperity — masonic-like Russian secret society aimed at reform that spun off into two "societies" that became the Decembrists

Venus and Adonis — one of England's first two operas (c. 1683) by John Blow

Court of Versailles — the grand palace outside Paris where Louis XIV and his successors presided over dandified courtiers and beautiful ladies

Vicomte (Viscount) — hereditary French title Vice-Count, a deputy to the *comte* or count, equivalent to an English earl

Voltigeur — elite light infantry chosen for speed and marksmanship

2nd War against England — The War of 1812

Whist — classic English trick-taking card game popular in the 18th and 19th centuries, and at which Napoleon was known for cheating

Yankee Doodle — unofficial anthem of the American Revolution, possibly derived from an old Irish tune of the 17th or early 18th century

Yellow Oval Room — room on the south side of the second floor of the White House, used as a drawing room under President Adams and later used as a library, office, and family parlor, called "Yellow" from First Lady Dolly Madison's use of yellow damask drapes

Gazetteer

Alexandria, Virginia — port town on the Potomac River

Battery Park — public park in lower Manhattan, formerly sight of defense works

Blodgett Hotel — former hotel and US Customs Office on 7th and F Streets in Washington and replaced by today's Hotel Monaco

Brandywine — river valley and site of the American Revolutionary War battlefield in southeastern Pennsylvania

The Cabildo — magnificent government building in New Orleans and home to Lafayette during his visit (today a museum)

Cairo — port city at the confluence of Mississippi and Ohio Rivers

Cap de la Heve' — peninsula protecting the entrance to the port of Le Havre

Capitol Square — Richmond, Virginia's public mall consisting of state government buildings

Castle Garden — Built as Fort Clinton during the War of 1812 but reopened in 1824 as Castle Garden, a cultural center and theatre near The Battery in lower Manhattan

Chalmette — site of Battle of New Orleans

Champs de Mars — parade field on the western edge of Paris and site of a massacre in 1791

Charleston, South Carolina — major port city on the Atlantic coast

Château de la Grange-Bléneau — Lafayette's castle and final home in the Seine-et-Marne département of France

Eagle Hotel — Richmond, Virginia inn where Lafayette overnighted in October 1824

Fells Point — a harbor town established around 1763 along the north shore of the Baltimore Harbor and the Northwest Branch of the Patapsco River

Fort Lafayette — coastal fortification on a small island called Hendrick's Reef in the Narrows of New York Harbor, renamed Fort Lafayette from Fort Diamond to commemorate the marquis's visit

Georgetown — village nestled between the northwest section of Washington, the Potomac River, and Maryland

Gran Columbia — the lands of Spain's northern South American possessions, including present-day Colombia, mainland Ecuador, Panama, and Venezuela, along with parts of northern Peru and northwestern Brazil.

Grinzing — wine region in the suburbs of Vienna, Austria

Hamburg — large German port on the Elbe River and a significant point of departure for ocean voyages

Hendrick's Reef — small island in the narrows between Brooklyn and Staten Island

The Hermitage — Andrew Jackson's estate outside Nashville, Tennessee

Hohensalzburg Fortress, Salzburg — fort serving as a garrison of the Austrian Army, military administrative headquarters, and prison

Hotel Maison de Ville — oldest hotel in New Orleans

Hotel le Richelieu — hotel on *Rue de Paris* in *Le Havre, France*

Le Havre — French port on the English Channel and Lafayette departure point

Independence Hall — Philadelphia building where the Continental Congress convened

Louisiana — large territory of Spanish North America reaching from the Mississippi River to the Rocky Mountains and Pacific Northwest

Mansion House Hotel — lodging used by Lafayette in Philadelphia

Milan (*Milano*) —city in northern Italy and capital of the Republic of Lombardy and Veneto

Montmartre — the Bohemian district of Paris

Morrisania — an area in the southwestern quadrant of the Bronx

New Windsor — town on New York's Hudson River and one of the Continental Army Headquarters during the Revolutionary War

New York - major port city in the American state of the same name

Old Stone House — small residence in N. 20th Steet in Richmond visited by Lafayette in 1824

Olmutz — in the 19th century, a town in Austria, Moravia, and the present—day Czech Republic where Lafayette was imprisoned at the large fortress

Palacio Real de Madrid — Royal Palace of Madrid, the official residence of the Spanish royal family in the city of Madrid, Spain

Petersburg — small town in central Virginia

Place d' Armes — Plaza of Arms, later Jackson Square, a large open drill field near the old town of New Orleans

Plymouth — channel port in southern England

Port Centre — inner harbor of Le Havre

211 Q Street — safe house in the conspiracy just off Fourth Street in Southeast Washington (fictional)

Redoubt Nine and Ten — outer defense works protecting the British defense works at Yorktown, Virginia, during the Franco-American siege of October 1781

Hotel le Richelieu — hotel on Rue de Paris in Le Havre, France

Richmond — capital of Virginia, nestled along the James River

Rhein-Pfalz — the Rhineland Palatinate region of Germany along the river of that name

Salzburg — city in the Austrian Alps and fictional headquarters of the fictitious "Secret Committee of the Aulic Council"

Saratoga — town in the farm region north of Albany, New York

La Scala — famous opera house in Milan, Italy, opened in August 1778 as the *Nuovo Regio Ducale Teatro alla Scala.*

Shockoe Hill — large rise of land in Richmond, Virginia running north from downtown and the state capitol complex to a point where the hill drops steeply toward Shockoe Creek

Scudder's American Museum — a privately owned collection of strange artifacts established by John Scudder in March 1810

Tripoli — one of the three "Barbary States" along the North African coast

Vieux Carre — Old Square, the historic old quarter of New Orleans

Washington, DC — capital of the United States, carved out from a strip of land along the Potomac River

Washington Navy Yard — US naval headquarters and base in the southeast District of Columbia

West Point — American army fort and home of its new military academy

Williamsburg, Virginia — original capital of Virginia located between the James and York Rivers

Yorktown — small port near the mouth of Virginia's York River and the base of General Cornwallis's Army

About the Author

S.W. O'Connell holds degrees in History (Fordham University) and International Relations (University of Southern California). He is a retired US Army intelligence officer and Defense Intelligence Senior Executive who worked primarily in the field of counterintelligence. Most of his time was spent overseas in US Army Europe and Allied Command Europe, but he admits to a few Pentagon tours and a stint at the John F. Kennedy Center for Special Warfare at Fort Bragg.

A native New Yorker, S.W. O'Connell settled in northern Virginia when he returned from his last overseas tour. His long-held love of history made it only natural that he would turn to the historical novel when he finally succumbed to a decades-long urge to craft fiction.

He is the author of The Yankee Doodle Spies, a series of novels — set during the American Revolution, and a sci-fi historical time travel novel, *Envoy of the Lord*.

The Lafayette Circle is his sixth novel.